*Also by Frances Howitt*

*Wizards of White Haven*

AMELIE

CLAN GREEN BEAR

# NATALYA

Wizards of White Haven

Book Three

*Frances Howitt*

Copyright © Frances Howitt 2014

The moral right of the author has been asserted.

*All characters and events in this publication, other than those clearly in the public domain, are fictitious and any resemblance to real persons, living or dead, is purely coincidental.*

All rights reserved.
No part of this publication may be reproduced, stored in a retrieval system, or transmitted, in any form or by any means, without the prior permission in writing of the author, nor be otherwise circulated in any form of binding or cover other than that in which it is published.

ISBN 978-1494976057

# *Acknowledgements*

With grateful thanks to my editor Patrick
and to my husband for all your help
patience and support.

# Index

Prologue .................................................................. 1

1. Aftermath .............................................................. 3
2. Lost and Found .................................................... 15
3. Rescue .................................................................. 23
4. White Haven ....................................................... 35
5. On Alert .............................................................. 69
6. The Owl ............................................................... 76
7. Surprise Visit ....................................................... 96
8. A New Place ...................................................... 100
9. Battle of Wills ................................................... 115
10. Revelations ........................................................ 133
11. Wayward Children ............................................ 159
12. Good Ideas ........................................................ 172
13. Close Ties .......................................................... 199
14. An Offer ............................................................ 212
15. Decisions ........................................................... 244
16. A Change of Plan .............................................. 255
17. Magical Testing ................................................. 287
18. Returned ............................................................ 298
19. A Whopping Secret ........................................... 312
20. Portal ................................................................. 324
21. Hopes ................................................................ 340
22. Derek ................................................................. 351
23. Family ................................................................ 361
24. An Important Meeting ...................................... 367
25. Making Contact ................................................ 384
26. Lord Aubrey's Visit ........................................... 390
27. Camouflage ....................................................... 434
28. Féarmathuin Castle ........................................... 470
29. Nathaniel ........................................................... 478
30. Life Does Go On ............................................... 492

# *Prologue*

The White Haven academy for magic is run-down and failing. This is due to its political stance on accepting ALL gifted youngsters including training shifters, whose magic is deemed tainted and the people themselves unworthy of mingling with wizards. Approached by the aged acting head master for help, wizard Jim agrees and eventually decides to stay, taking on the role of headmaster despite his youth. He works to set years of decay to rights and make the school strong once more. Both he and his partner Amelie see it as a way to continue their own education and furthermore make it their home. This interference in the school's future attracts much attention however, both from supporters and detractors.

After thwarting an unexpected and unwelcome approach from the renegade warrior Clan Green Bear, Jim negotiates with them and an alliance is born. He soon becomes fast friends with their leader Commander Drako. He also meets and gains support from Lord Aubrey, in whose territory the school resides.

The local Wizard's Guild is not so welcoming however, fearing a wizard of Jim's growing strength operating outside of their control. As a wizard with the rare ability to leach the power and innate ability from other wizard's, Jim is a resource many would like to control or harness.

Wizard Jared, leader of the Eastern Guild's military arm, knows Jim's leach ability is fed every time he merges with another strong wizard. Parting him from Amelie is one way of attempting to limit his growth. Additionally, with her in their custody, they hope to have a way of blackmailing him into obedience. Jared disguises himself and his team's magical signature as that of a dragon knowing that lure will bring her out alone. Unfortunately for him, Jim is able to foil the kidnap attempt and overpowers the team's subsequent attack, in a terrifying display of raw magical strength that surprises and shocks everyone.

However, having bested a battle squad of twenty wizards, Jim finds himself overwhelmed by power he has no idea of how to handle or indeed offload. He only now realises that taking on excessive power comes at a cost he might not be able to pay.

1

# *Aftermath*

Amelie passed through the main-gates and heard them thud closed behind them, the locking bars rasping decisively into place. She let out a small sigh of relief; now they were safe from further attack. She glanced up at the peepholes in the towers above but suddenly it was too much effort to even search for the identities of those operating the gates. She shivered in the night's chill breeze and drew her baby closer.

She eyed the massive lion Jim had become. It was not entirely surprising that no one had come down off the walls to join them. His lion was scary enough normally, but this new stature was terrifying. She had seen smaller plough-horses! Most worrying however was the barely contained magical energy shimmering around him.

In marked contrast, she felt bruised, battered and weary. She was tempted to ask if he would carry her. The lion's broad furry back looked invitingly comfortable. Then she considered him again and realised he was not remotely in control of himself. The vast power his leach ability had siphoned off, was still coursing through his body and almost overwhelming him. He clearly needed time to figure out how to handle it or offload it. The last thing that either of them needed was for him to accidentally leach further magic from her, or Daisy, through a simple touch. She knew he had to fight that temptation every day, and he was unlikely to have the self-control right now to prevent it. It would not be fair to make him touch either of them. Daisy gurgled at her, not remotely upset with the evening's events. She reached out towards her father and the lion made a soft chuffing sound in response but did not come within reach. Amelie met Jim's golden eyes, amused that Daisy accepted his altered form with no concern. She stroked the softly rounded cheek and slowly resumed walking. It was only a half-mile back up to the school and the sanctuary of their quarters, but her feet dragged. She was relieved Jim did not try to hasten her or show any sign of impatience. He silently matched her pace, his manner protective, concerned and also introspective.

Jim absently wondered what time it was; sometime in the small hours of the morning, certainly. The tree-lined avenue blocked much of the moonlight, making it particularly dark, but his lion form had no difficulty seeing. The branches creaked in the wind, causing the inky shadows to leap and shift. He still could not calm himself and knew he trod a fine line to remain in control. The excess magic was bubbling up out of him, rattling as if a pot left too long on the stove. He had no clue what destruction might ensue if such a quantity of magic escaped in a careless thought or gesture. Although he had successfully foiled Jared's attempt to kidnap Amelie, the fight had definitely left its mark on him. Amelie had returned to human form to carry their baby and her pace was weary and slow. He knew the battle she'd fought before he arrived had sapped her strength. He ground his teeth trying to keep a lid on his anger. She was a new mother; her strength was already limited. Reaching their apartment, he watched over them as they settled down to catch what remained of the night in sleep.

Jim eyed their sleeping forms enviously, but felt far too energised to be able to relax. He knew if he remained in the room, he would only disturb their rest. Still edgy, and with his family now safely home and sleeping, he left their quarters.

Something glowing in the darkness of the unlit corridor he traversed caught his eye. Stopping, he stared in shock at the image in the mirror. He hadn't realised he'd remained in his lion form or that he was now three times his usual size. The other disturbing thing he noticed, was the very visible blue-white shimmer of energy leaking off his body. He'd robbed the magical power from twenty mature wizards. Then, if that hadn't been enough, the energy stored in the perimeter wall had been attracted sufficiently to spark, sending more power to him, even though he hadn't touched it, or sought it. Already wrestling with unaccustomed power, he tried to send it back, but then discovered it was difficult to return without shattering the wall! He supposed he had been trying to offload more power than it had originally stored. In hindsight, he knew the transfer would have worked better if he had had time to send it in a controlled and steady flow. He shrugged; there hadn't been time to spare to craft a suitable spell. The wall spell would need checking sometime, because something had changed for it to seem self-aware and seek him out.

What had been most astonishing about the battle was the way that he had managed to leach the magic from the spells thrown at him, somehow disarming and converting them back to raw power. He'd never heard of any of these things being possible before. The long and the short of it was however, that he really needed to expel this ridiculous strength before he caused accidents. He was almost out of control and everyone would feel it. He turned to get a better look at the changes the battle had wrought in him, shaking his head in rueful astonishment. He had grown enormously; he had to duck his head and breathe-in to pass through a standard door! He truly hoped this was not a permanent change to his alternate form. A lion the size of a plough-horse was going to terrify everyone.

Aware the cooks would soon be surfacing to begin making the day's bread, he hurried past the kitchen door and out into the huge glasshouse. When he first arrived at the school this had been wilderness and the glass smashed open to the elements. He was satisfied to note order had now been restored. Many of the neat raised beds bore the shoots of thriving plants that would yield a variety of food crops in the weeks and months to come. He jumped as a metal watering can rocked as he passed. He hadn't touched it yet it was clearly reacting to him. He tentatively lifted a paw towards a trowel and a small electric shock zapped out of him to it. This was not good! Amongst so much glass, metal and delicate life, he dared not linger. Reaching the double doors, he hesitated; they were metal and so was the handle. Grinding his teeth, he magically opened the door, struggling to control and tamp down the strength of the spell and not rip the door off its hinges. As it was, the whole glasshouse structure creaked ominously.

He hurried outside and away from the house. Only then did he breathe more easily having managed to avoid creating any disasters so far. What could he do to sort this out? He turned up the path leading to the training ground, aware it would be safely deserted at this pre-dawn hour. Bordering the track on one side was a large expanse of thick woodland, which felt quiet and restful. Lost in thought, recalling the astonishing ease with which he'd felled so many wizards earlier, he was surprised to find he'd wandered off the track deep into the woods. Belatedly looking around, he realised his paws were following a barely discernible path and that something seemed to be drawing him on. Curious as to what might be out here; he expanded his senses. Looking with more than ordinary vision, he noticed some weird lights twinkling faintly through the trees ahead of him. Stepping into a small clearing, he discovered the glittering came from a pile of jumbled stone and rubble half hidden by tall weeds. Magic imbued this stone! Some of the stone remained intact as precisely worked blocks, but much had been pulverised. He curiously noted some of the stone showed signs of ornate carving and ancient lettering. Unfortunately, it was impossible to guess what had been here. Someone had made a thorough job of dismantling or smashing the structure and the subsequent growth of tall weeds and mossy overgrowth completed the disguise.

'I wonder what kind of building stood here?' he murmured to himself. The cleared space was small and there did not seem to be enough stone, for it to have been anything but a tiny structure. Having said that, he had no idea how long this ruin had been here. For all he knew, trees could have encroached on the original clearing and grown up since the building had fallen. He had not found any references to a building in this location when he had been looking for the architectural plans for the stables. However, he was well aware there were no formal plans on record for every building on site. He had always wondered why there was such a large gap between the school and training ground buildings. Buried deep in thick woodland, this was a very secluded spot and well away from the student thoroughfares. What was this? Had something been built for an illegal or clandestine purpose? Why had it been so thoroughly demolished?

Whilst the power coursing through his body made him feel invincible, he knew there was considerable danger in casting a spell to rebuild something when he had no clue as to its original scale. Out here however, he was far from anyone, so it was moderately safe to experiment. He certainly had to do something to drain off the excess power surging around him so dangerously. When he used his magic on building projects, it usually drained his power quite quickly; he hoped this would be enough to at least let him regain control if not return him to normal.

He began with a spell to reinstate the foundations of the building. To his surprise, very little stone moved. The only noticeable thing that happened was that the weeds vanished and a smooth stone plinth, only a step above the forest floor, replaced some badly broken and uneven stone slabs. Now he could see that the structure was definitely small, in fact only twelve feet square. Slowly and warily, he called the scattered rubble and stone to resume its original shape and position in the building. Despite his caution, and just when he was about to cancel the spell thinking he had finished, there was a sudden and heavy drain on his power, completely out of proportion to the size of the building. As the dust settled, he found he had rebuilt a graceful double door-sized open archway. Beautiful carving adorned its upper edge. He looked through to thick forest beyond, with no hint of a path or cleared space leading onwards. Puzzled, he looked about him carefully wondering what it was and why it was here. Was it all that remained of the door to a larger building? Were there other ruined structures nearby? He was also puzzled to note that the archway's stone no longer glittered. The magic originally incorporated into it was no longer bleeding out, but properly and silently contained. He suspected his magic had now restored whatever spell had originally been on this structure.

A bird flew through the trees above his head, squawking shrill warning of a predator's presence and he looked up. Watching as many birds took flight from his vicinity, he noticed that something was now glittering faintly about twenty feet in the air directly above the archway. What the hell was that? No answers forthcoming he moved closer to the arch to examine it in the dim dawn light. Noticing that the right-hand pillar of the arch was carved he warily moved closer to look at the writing. Moss clung to the stone, particularly in the indentations of the lettering. Whatever it said, probably related to the twinkling circular display above his head. The style of the arch reminded him of something he had seen before but exactly what escaped him. He stepped off the plinth to get a better angle to see the phenomenon up in the air but as he did so, it winked out.

He stared in shock as recognition surged through him. Was this a portal? Had he accidentally rebuilt the activator for an air portal? He knew proximity to a person with magic activated them. The one in the prison had been disguised by being inset into a wall, but the size and shape was just the same as this. Unfortunately, his lion did not have wings; this would be of limited use to him. However, this was such an important find; he did need to confirm his guess was correct. Where did this one lead? It probably said on this engraved panel. He started brushing off the moss with his paw so he could see what it said. Unfortunately, whilst his paw was excellent for clearing large areas in one go, since he still hadn't shrunk to his usual lion size, it was clumsy and none too precise.

He just had time to curse as a flash almost blinded him. What symbol or activator had he caught? The light came from above him. He gaped, where the pale twinkling outline had been was now a great swirling vortex, flashing blue-white lights. Recovering his scattered wits, he tried to leap back out of the way, but his paw now seemed glued to the pillar. He suddenly realised he was pinned immobile, but of most concern was that his strength was being drawn out of him hard and relentlessly. His power was being stolen for some purpose, and he had no control or say over its use. Would he have enough power to fulfil whatever the spell needed, because if not, this could kill him? What was happening? He gazed up; this was not just unnerving but terrifying. The violently swirling vortex descended towards him like a whirlpool, its maw looming closer and closer as though it wanted to swallow him. There was a weird and unnerving moment of suction, his body feeling light but fortunately not quite floating off the ground. It was like standing on a high mountain precipice feeling you were about to be blown off. He was sure that his paw, glued to the arch, was all that was anchoring him to ground! He shrank down, closing his eyes and waited helplessly for it to devour him. Unexpectedly, there was a small boom, the earth quivered and then everything stilled.

Opening his eyes tentatively he realised the vortex had gone. The archway however was no longer empty. Contained within the glinting archway was a strange dark shadow. The suction vanished from his paw and he collapsed, panting hard and gaping in shock. This was definitely a portal. Had he just inadvertently found the sequence to anchor it to the ground? Were they all air portals unless anchored by these be-spelled arches? He recalled Amelie mentioning, that where they had fallen out of the prison portal onto this continent, there had also been ancient ruins. That portal too, probably just needed to be rebuilt, and then anchored to be useable from the ground this end. Rather a long trek to go back, even though he knew the destination was intact. It would probably be quicker and safer to travel by sea if he ever wanted to return to his home continent. Exiting through a prison would be problematic, to put it mildly. There had been other Portals, but if they had all been smashed, a great deal of power would be required to rebuild. Of course, unless records existed somewhere, it would only become clear where each one went after they had been rebuilt. Locating them would be a challenge in itself too.

He suddenly realised he felt weak and spent; clearly, this anchoring took a huge amount of magical power. He doubted he could do this spell alone again.

Where did this portal come out though? He didn't recognise the Erien name inscribed on the column. The most worrying aspect was that the portal was dark. He clearly remembered seeing sunshine at his destination when he'd come through from the prison portal. It had swung his decision on whether to risk it. This one however was dark. Many portals had been locked away. Was its destination inside a dungeon or vault? What if it came out in a guardhouse and he had to fight his way free? The other issue was the question of whether this one had been bricked up at the other end. Would he step through, only to be slammed against a wall, trapped from returning? He simply didn't know enough about the portals; what was and was not possible. He needed to do some research. Once he knew where this one came out, he could hazard a guess as to what he might find at the other end. He stepped off the plinth and the glittering ceased. He could now see through the archway to the forest beyond; the portal had closed as his magic retreated. Now there wasn't such a tempting open door, he could stand back and think a little more rationally. Amelie would be furious if he went off exploring without saying a word, especially when this could, in all likelihood, be extremely risky.

He looked down at his paw and saw to his relief that he was back to his usual size. He no longer emitted sparks of excess energy either. He felt tired which probably meant he had successfully offloaded the majority of the surplus power. As he returned to the house he realised the rebuilding and then anchoring spells had used up the magic of twenty strong wizards. Perhaps that extraordinary strength requirement was why it had not been repaired before now. It suddenly occurred to him that in these troubled times, it might have been left unrepaired to stop intruders from popping in to the grounds unannounced to cause havoc. Mm, he was going to have to secure it. The last thing anyone needed was for students to come across it, successfully activate it and get themselves into trouble, either.

He returned to the portal and built a be-spelled fence around the archway, preventing access to it from either direction, without his knowledge. The hidden and relatively inaccessible location meant no-one was likely to stumble across it accidentally either. He decided he would keep this discovery to himself until he was ready to handle the inevitable demands for exploration and investigation that would ensue.

Satisfied he'd made it as safe as possible, he returned to the house and his bed knowing he now at last would be able to sleep.

2

# *Lost and Found*

'Sir, we have found someone in the woods. He's badly injured.' Freddie eyed Jim warily. 'Could he be one of the wizards you fought last night?'

'It might be Derek, Jared's second in command,' Jim mused recalling the events of last night. He remembered tossing Derek, the leader of the meld team, aside into the trees. 'I didn't mean to injure him but it's certainly possible,' Jim responded thoughtfully. 'I left Jared beaten but standing at the end of the battle. I assumed he would have searched out all his men and taken them home with him. Anyway, I'd better come and find out,' he added.

'We watched the leader run as soon as you came inside and his legs would hold! You're saying you purposely left another out there? Why?' Freddie asked as they walked together down the drive. He hadn't thought the enormous lion looked remotely in control of his actions, but was fighting on instinct alone. Instinct would normally ensure any threats to his family were eliminated. He'd been surprised there hadn't been a blood-bath. Perhaps rendering the wizards unconscious had been sufficient to pacify Jim's beast.

'Derek showed remorse and was trying to be fair. He did lower the walls of Amelie's trap sufficiently for me to give her clothes and then allowed us to speak.'

'And your lion remembered that, even in the heat of battle?'

'I confess the battle was mostly a blur. I can't entirely recall what happened,' Jim admitted. 'Is that usual?'

'Yes. Once you're in the thick of hard fighting, instinct and training takes over, and that certainly looked to be what happened to your lion. Now I think about it, I do recall you flicking someone aside with a paw. He flew through the air and landed in the forest like a thrown stick.' Freddie eyed Jim for a few minutes as they walked.

'What are you thinking?' Jim asked, aware of his regard but politely not spying on Freddie's mind.

'Well, your lion form altered and you stayed that way even after the battle. Is that a permanent change?'

'No. I'd grown a bit, hadn't I,' he said with a grin and noticed even the usually imperturbable wolf seemed apprehensive. 'I drained off the excess power and returned to my normal size a bit later. Was I scary?'

'Yes,' Freddie admitted.

'Good. Maybe I won't have to do it again.'

'There is that,' Freddie conceded with the ghost of a smile.

'Ah, while I think about it, I've to meet with some of the school's suppliers in Briarton tomorrow morning. Want to come?'

'You'd planned on travelling alone?' Freddie asked in concern.

'Well, for some reason volunteers seem few on the ground this time. I keep telling people I'm still me and that I'm back to normal.' Unexpectedly Freddie snorted at that. 'What?'

'Jim, you don't feel the same, even to me and I'm not a wizard. We all watched you beat twenty battle prepared wizards on your own. You can't blame people for being nervous of such strength.'

'Ok, I can understand that, but I haven't done anything unusual since.' He faltered as Freddie halted and turned to eye him.

'You're lying,' Freddie observed. 'Do I need to know what you actually did to drain off that power?'

'I can never put much past you, can I?' Jim responded with a faint grin, but he respected the wolf man's courage and directness. 'I rebuilt some ruins I found on the grounds. They're deep in the forest between school and training ground. I'd appreciate it if you'd keep this to yourself though and deter your people from approaching the area for the time being.'

'It poses some hazard? What did you do?' Freddie asked quickly and anxiously.

'I found something really exciting. But until I've done some investigation, and checked into its safety, I'd rather keep its existence quiet. I've put a fence around it to stop anyone accidentally getting close enough to get into trouble.'

'That's most reassuring,' Freddie remarked drily. 'Have you told Drako?'

'Not yet. He will want to explore as soon as he knows about it and that could be dangerous. You are the Clan's head of security. It was appropriate to make you aware there was something there.'

'Thank you for that consideration, but you do realise you're making me anxious.'

'Yes, and you'll go and look,' Jim acknowledged. 'Once you do you'll understand the need for secrecy, my caution and why I've placed a barrier around it.'

'Ok,' Freddie responded. Jim was correct that he'd be up there checking it out the moment he was free. His curiosity was alive with questions he knew Jim didn't yet want to answer.

'So, where's he been put?' Jim asked as they turned into the village. He was aware of being stared at; Freddie's nervousness in his presence was clearly not an isolated reaction.

'I stashed him at Dustin's place.'

Jim nodded; it was unwise for Drako to be seen by strangers. Dustin was a very capable wolf, although he too was eyeing Jim a little nervously as they walked up the lane to his cottage. Dustin invited them in to the house and gestured to the corner of his living room where one of the ubiquitous school beds had been put to use. Jim eyed the sleeping man lying there. Splints on both legs gave mute evidence of injuries that the wolves had treated.

'Wizard Derek,' Jim said quietly aware the man had woken at their entry and was now feigning sleep. He also sensed Derek's pain washing over him.

Derek's eyes opened and he nervously turned his head. 'Wizard Jim. I was wondering where I'd been taken,' he added glancing at the two other men present; quickly ascertaining they were animus before returning his full attention to the formidable wizard before him. It was almost a shock to see how young he was to already have such a powerful presence.

'The men found you whilst out hunting I believe,' Jim said approaching closer and reaching out a hand.

'What are you going to do?' Derek quavered, recoiling from the hand. 'Are you going to kill me, like the others?'

'Kill you? No. I didn't kill any of your merge team either. I left them drained but otherwise unharmed. I believe they got up and left the following morning,' he remarked, glancing at Freddie who nodded confirmation. 'I'm sorry, I didn't realise they hadn't taken you with them. I knew you'd become separated but assumed your team would look for you before leaving.'

'They're alive?' Derek asked, relief flooding him. 'What about Jared?' he dared ask. Since Jared had been the primary instigator behind the plot to kidnap Jim's family, if anyone should have borne the brunt of Jim's defensive fury, it was him.

'He too lives. He has Amelie's timely intervention to thank for that,' Jim said tonelessly. 'Do you wish me to relieve your pain?'

'You would do that? For me?' Jim just looked at him, waiting, so Derek simply nodded. Jim grasped both of Derek's ankles and he gulped in relief as the pain blocking spell took effect. Jim removed his hands immediately making Derek aware that he had no intention of invading his mind just now, when he was too weak to have any defences. 'Thank you,' Derek managed in appreciation.

'Right, let's get you to sickbay,' Jim said briskly. 'Thank you Dustin, Freddie,' he added, glancing at the wolf-men with a sincere nod. He then levitated Derek, ensuring he remained perfectly horizontal and his broken legs were supported for the trip up to the school where the trained healers could care for him.

'We have much to talk about,' Jim remarked as he walked along with Derek floating beside him. The villagers were wide-eyed as they watched them pass and equally, Derek was observing the village with great curiosity, or as well as he could from his awkward position. Those intelligent eyes returned to him at that. 'Don't worry; it'll wait until you're fixed-up.'

'Yes, there is much to discuss,' Derek agreed. He and the Guild in general knew very little about this man. Wizard Tobias had reported that Jim was normally a calm and generous character, but that he was very defensive of those under his protection. Any man would be understandably furious with his family under attack. Threatening a wizard, who was known to be a leach with unknown capabilities, was foolhardy in the extreme. Derek had not agreed with Jared's plan, but had been unable to persuade his superior of its obvious flaws. Derek knew that he was completely vulnerable now and at this wizard's mercy. He was grateful that Jim was being so forgiving and reasonable, when he did not have to be. This was someone he wanted to get to know better and quickly. He hoped he'd be allowed to talk to the staff and other residents at the school while he recuperated, to gather a fuller picture. What plans did Jim have now though? Jim had categorically beaten Jared and a battle trained squad of twenty. What else was he capable of? Where did the guild now stand when Jim had categorically proven he didn't need to bow before their authority?

3

# *Rescue*

Natalya anxiously peered around the corner to check the busy street. She cursed under her breath as a pair of uniformed hunters appeared out of a side street ahead of her. A richly dressed man joined them to confer. She noticed his head turning, constantly scanning the crowds; searching. A wizard was with them to hunt her! Grr! His gaze hadn't settled yet; he hadn't pinpointed her location. It was market day and the streets were thronging with people. The crowds had provided good cover to move amongst unnoticed. She ducked behind a crowd of men going in a different direction and silently cursed when they glanced at her speculatively. She was easily as tall as most men and wisps of her long white blond hair escaped her hood and shone in the early morning sun. She naturally stood out from the crowd which wasn't remotely useful when she was being hunted. She'd had to detour so many times to avoid the two teams of hunters she was beginning to panic. She'd been working her way across the small but congested town to a different gate having found the first one too well-guarded and could now see the town walls, but yet again she'd been headed off.

She'd originally planned to cross the wall under cover of darkness the previous night, but security had been unexpectedly tight. She'd been forced to hide in the middle of town instead and wait for morning in the hope she could slip out amongst the crowds. She'd gone to each exit from the town and discovered wizards keeping watch at the two busy main gates. Every gate was guarded by soldiers, but the two wizards kept moving between them. She knew very well that a wizard would easily be able to feel her magic and know she was animus once they got close enough.

Trapped inside the town's walls it was only a matter of time before she was cornered; time for a new strategy. Down a narrow backstreet, she spotted a dark alleyway filled with stinking rubbish and ducked into it. She crouched down behind a pile of broken crates, out of sight of anyone passing. She quickly removed her clothes, stuffing them into her bag. She closed her eyes concentrating and transformed into a domestic tabby cat. She glanced regretfully at her bag with her few meagre possessions and nudged it out of direct sight. She had no option but to leave her things behind. In cat form, she could not possibly carry a bag as big as she was; everyone would know she was not a true cat. She walked out of the alley and immediately noticed a tall young man looking directly and intently at her. He didn't look like a catcher nor was he either of the pesky wizards she'd seen too much of over the last few hours. Whatever he was he exuded a tangible aura of power that was rather mixed in character but unnervingly powerful. He most definitely put the two wizards on her tail in the shade!

'I'm Jim. Don't run little one. We can help you get out of here,' Jim told her quietly, then glanced up the street at a second man. 'Freddie, how's it looking?' he called softly.

The man so addressed jogged over to them quickly. He too was tall but with dark reddish brown hair and warm green eyes. She could immediately tell he was animus and something about him calmed her frayed nerves and allowed her to catch her breath.

'There are two hunters and someone with them that looks like a wizard to me,' he said quickly but his eyes hadn't left the small blue eyed cat watching them both warily. He was surprised she hadn't bolted at Jim's approach. Even he could sense the aura of Jim's powerful magic and to someone running from wizards, he expected her immediate distrust.

'You reassure her,' Jim told him. 'I'd better divert that wizard.'

Natalya blinked, shocked by the calmly delivered statement. The blond man almost seemed to glide away, authority and assurance in his movements.

'He can be a bit overpowering,' Freddie confided cheerfully and the cat's head tilted. 'Jim's a lion,' he added, suspecting little further explanation was necessary and hoping that would help. 'Have you got clothes somewhere? We shouldn't leave anything behind with your scent on; they might be able to use it to track you.'

Natalya glanced again at the blond man keeping watch at the head of the narrow street. Should she trust them? If Freddie had been alone she wouldn't have hesitated, but Jim was distinctly unnerving. Freddie still waited for her decision so she quickly gestured behind her at the alley. He went in and unerringly homed in on her backpack despite the appalling stench of rotting rubbish. If he could find it so easily, then he was right, her pursuers might have been able to as well.

Once clear of the stinking alley Freddie put his nose to the canvas bag to properly take her scent. He heard a growl; she was watching him. She would know he could track her now he was learning her scent. 'Sorry, but this smells so much better than everything else,' he whispered glancing around them at the foul place. He quickly put his arms through the backpack's two straps so his hands were free again.

'Looks like our route's clear. Come on,' Freddie said to her noticing Jim gesture and the tabby came to his side, peered round the corner and trotted beside him across the intersection. He resisted the urge to scoop the cat up into his arms. She didn't trust them yet and her current form, whilst small, was fully equipped to do him serious damage if provoked. They joined Jim and cautiously looked around.

Jim walked casually but briskly into the open and crossed another street. He checked the new lane was safe before nodding to Freddie to follow.

Natalya stayed at Freddie's side, very relieved she was not alone. In cat form she could hide easily and climb well but she also couldn't see over the various obstructions as the men could. They walked swiftly down yet another lane then headed for a storehouse wall where there was a stack of crates. To her surprise Jim suddenly vanished.

'He loves his theatrics,' Freddie told her.

Natalya noticed his amusement and decided he respected, but wasn't daunted by, the lion man. Behind the crates was a metal grille propped open against the wall. Then she noticed the black hole in the street. She could scent that the lion had gone down into this smelly black hole but she was nervous.

'After you,' Freddie said with a rather courtly gesture. 'Don't worry; it's mostly dry and not too much of a drop. Or would you rather I carried you?'

Natalya was surprised by the offer; he seemed genuine. She heard voices approaching and knew he heard them too. She jumped into the black hole, and as he'd promised, didn't fall into foul water. The storm drain tunnel was largely dry and she immediately moved away so Freddie wouldn't land on her.

Freddie followed quickly but used the ancient ladder of metal rungs hammered into the wall so he could grab the conspicuously open heavy grille and close it after him. Stepping into the tunnel he realised that whilst Jim had already gone on ahead, the cat had not and was waiting for him. Her large pale blue eyes glinted in the gloom. He jogged where the tunnel was clear enough, aware the cat ran by his side rather than following him. Despite her small frame she bounded over obstacles easily and kept pace with him.

'This isn't a safe place to be when it's raining,' he told her. 'It fills up fast and water blasts along here faster than most people can run. But at least the force washes the rubbish out so we can get through.'

She glanced at him wondering how he had breath for speech whilst running swiftly along an obstructed and very dark tunnel. The grilled drain holes above were widely spaced and cast only small pools of light. She stumbled, only just managing to avoid a heap of rank smelling garbage. She growled to herself for her lack of attention on where she was putting her feet. They carried on in silence but for the quiet patter of their feet and their quick breathing. Even wearing boots Freddie made little sound and her velvet padded paws were designed for silence. She almost lost track of time and wondered how much of the town they were able to traverse down here. At least this meant they would be far from the wizard closing in on her last position. A loud rushing noise grew ahead of them and in a small pool of light they caught up with Jim.

'We can't go any further in this tunnel,' Jim explained to the cat whilst they caught their breath. 'It drops steeply beyond here into a pool that goes underground. We have horses, but we'll need to hide you to get out the gates. It's best you don't change until we get back. The wizard they had with them will probably be able to feel the surge of magic that always accompanies an animus change; that's how I found you. That other wizard obviously felt it too, which is why we had to move quickly. I'm going to have to beware casting any spells myself,' he added to Freddie. 'I can't risk exposing us. We're just going to have to rely on our wits rather than me,' he warned. 'Quickly, the coast is clear,' Jim added pushing the heavy grille open and climbing out.

Freddie simply reached down and picked up the cat lifting her out of the drain and setting her down in the street. He climbed out and quickly closed the grille. This exit was particularly useful because it was close to the north gate; one of the busiest entrances to the town. They walked casually to the huge livery stables where everyone locally kept their horses, space being at a premium farther into the town.

'How are we going to hide you?' Jim mused, considering the cat. 'I suppose one of us will need to carry you. At least your form is small. You've got a bag there Freddie,' he added brightening.

Natalya carefully wiped her paws on some tufts of clean grass, fastidiously ridding them of wet smelly dirt while assessing both men. She was not going to be shoved in her own backpack, thank-you! She met Freddie's gaze, trotted towards him and leapt up into his arms relying on him to catch her so she wouldn't need to claw his clothes, or skin, for that matter.

Freddie caught the small leaping body before she landed. He lifted her up to eye level and met bright ice blue eyes. She hung limply in his hands and he quickly altered his grasp worried he might be hurting her holding her under her armpits. He brought her against his chest wondering what she'd thought of. She wriggled and he released his grip so she could move. To his surprise she pushed her head between the buttons of his coat for a moment. She looked up at him, her paw patted the button and she chirped questioningly at him. Freddie unbuttoned it and the cat immediately climbed inside his coat, accepting his invitation. He pulled the drawstring about his hips tighter making a ledge for her to rest on without falling out of the bottom of the coat. It was a very strange feeling to have something warm and alive pressed against his stomach.

'Are you alright in there?' Freddie asked, his hand running over the warm shape gently.

Loud purring issued from his coat and he could feel the sound vibrating against him. He glanced at Jim and realised he was laughing.

'You look pregnant or exceedingly fond of pies,' Jim teased him.

'It won't be so obvious when I'm in the saddle,' Freddie responded absently his attention still on the warm softly purring creature curled so trustingly against him. He couldn't resist stroking the warm shape, particularly now Jim had disappeared into the livery to get both of their horses. The cat moved and he suddenly felt a furry foot against his skin rather than through his shirt. The velvety foot stroked him briefly then withdrew from between the buttons of his shirt and he breathed again. He'd abruptly been reminded this was an animus woman he held, not an affectionate kitty. He flushed, a little embarrassed she would have to remind him, but something about her made him feel very protective.

'Need any help mounting?' Jim asked him handing over the reins.

'No. Let's get out of here,' Freddie said mounting carefully so he didn't crush her against the horse. They rode to join the queue waiting to pass out through the checkpoint at the gate. Freddie opened the upper half of his coat so it gaped, distorting the shape of his body and therefore disguising the fold where she lay. It also helped cool them both; their combined body heat was making him overly warm. He noticed one of the guards had a dog that was watching and sniffing at the people passing by. He hoped it wouldn't react to the scent of a cat, although his own scent mingled with hers might confuse it. Generally dogs turned aggressive or were nervous of his wolf scent. However, Jim's lion scent had a tendency to reduce most guard dogs to whimpering in terror if they couldn't run away. Fortunately he noticed this dog veered away, clearly taking the flight option and not wanting to get any closer to them.

One of the guards picked out and detained a tall blond woman ahead of them. A second but much shorter blond woman was also separated out and pulled aside; both were young. He glanced down inside his coat and met her eyes gleaming back at him. 'You don't happen to be young and blond?' he whispered. 'The gate guards have stopped two women with that description. Someone's obviously determined to catch you,' he added quietly. He felt claws flex in alarm pricking his skin for the first time. 'Don't worry, we'll be past soon,' he murmured.

'Move along,' the gate guard ordered in a bored tone. A man on horseback, with a bag of what appeared to be shopping and a beer belly didn't warrant a second look. Animus and wizards were always skinny.

'What's going on?' Jim asked the guard as they came alongside.

'We've to arrest any blond young woman we find trying to leave. We've had word of a trouble maker,' the guard volunteered with a shrug. He didn't notice his colleague glance at him in surprise for so readily answering Jim's question and for being so open about their orders.

'That seems a little extreme,' Jim mentioned mildly, his gaze pinning the guard's eyes. 'Surely they would tell you who the trouble maker was if there was a real crime? Who's pressing the charges?'

'It's some out of town wizard. We've just been told to hold any blond woman until the wizard can come and identify her.'

'Ah, so you're at the beck and call of a foreign wizard? I didn't think a foreigner would have the right to order you about?' Jim asked, again keeping his tone light and casual.

Freddie had passed Jim now, pretending they were not together but he, like a large part of the crowd was silently listening. He hoped Jim's magical prompting wasn't going to draw the enemy wizard.

'You're right. I don't have to take orders from them. They're outside of their jurisdiction,' the guard said in aggrieved tones. Jim clearly had the guard in the palm of his hand. 'I can't have one of my men tied up holding our own people from their work for no good reason. Charlie, release those two and get back to work; we've a backlog stacking up here.' He glanced back round but the blond man had gone.

'What did you hear?' Freddie asked as Jim joined him beyond the gates. Jim gave a tiny shake of his head and Freddie noticed the taller of the blond women was watching them, but so too were several others.

Jim glanced at the scattered people. 'Come closer,' he said, quietly enough that only those with extra sensitive magical hearing would hear him. 'That town's no longer safe while the catchers have inquisitor wizards with them. I run White Haven school twelve miles north of here. You'll see its white walls and a moat. That's a safe haven and you'll all be welcome. Don't touch the walls for any reason, there's a defensive spell on them,' he added. He wheeled his horse and led Freddie away quickly before the guard he'd spoken with saw him and his carefully clouded memory resurfaced.

4

# *White Haven*

They cantered steadily along the road putting distance between them and Briarton and possible detection by the wizard. Jim's own presence could not be completely masked; he exuded far too strong a power signature to hide entirely from another wizard. Instead, he'd amplified his presence, whilst diluting the source so that the whole town seemed to reek of power. That would confuse other wizards' senses and their ability to track any weaker animus signals. It should also put them on warning that there was someone of power nearby best not to tangle with. Getting rapidly away from town was the best solution so that Jim's spell would simply fade, hopefully before the wizards could get a fix on the source. When they had passed the last of the small villages along their route and felt safer, they slowed to a walk.

'It's about time we found out why they were going to such trouble to catch your little friend. Why do they want someone that hides behind a stranger like a mouse,' Jim added bluntly.

They both heard her growl at his insult.

'Jim,' Freddie reproved and wrapped his arm around the warm little shape snuggled against him.

'Why are you protecting her? You don't even know her name,' Jim added.

Freddie looked down, 'did I hear you right? Your name is Natalya?'

She purred and rubbed her head on his taut belly liking the way he said her name. Reluctantly she climbed out of the warm refuge of his coat and perched on the front of the saddle to look around them. Freddie's large hand steadied her.

'This is White Haven School?' Natalya asked seeing big defensive gates ahead with flanking white towers and gleaming flawless glossy white walls. Something about the walls drew her attention but she remembered Jim warning the others not to touch. With the warning in mind she guessed it was a magical compulsion she sensed.

'Yes, we're one of the few places left that teaches animus as well as wizard students. So given the current levels of intolerance to animus people, it seemed prudent to improve the fortifications,' Jim told her.

'Now it not only feels secure but the changes mean we no longer look like a soft target. It was tricky deciding on what to do; too much would have looked as conspicuous as not enough.'

As they got closer she realised there was a wide moat defending the walls. She was relieved to note this meant that no innocent could touch the walls by accident. Someone considering climbing or breaching the wall would first have to swim the moat. This moat was unexpectedly aesthetically pleasing and was a far cry from the usual stagnant ring of smelly sludgy water surrounding most fortifications. Ducks paddled on the water and there were reeds and water lilies thriving at the edges as though the moat had been here for years. They crossed an elegantly arched bridge and she peered over the side. The water unexpectedly rippled with a current like a river too and fish were visible in the clear water. Glancing up she noticed movement; people were watching them from the pair of square towers flanking the gate which clanked and opened as they approached. They passed through a short gatehouse tunnel and the gates closed behind them. She noticed a man standing at the foot of the tower nod to Freddie and look at her curiously.

'White Haven School,' Jim announced, gesturing at the huge country house visible about half a mile away up the tree lined drive. A tall and impenetrably thick hedge bordered the drive on their left and she could hear sounds of life on the other side. A small open gateway pierced the hedge and Jim turned his horse onto the lane that passed through the gateway. 'White Haven Village.'

Natalya gazed with interest at the large and prosperous looking village they were entering. She could just see the perimeter wall between the large buildings on her left and realised the wide central street ran parallel to it. Whilst on the left of the street the land was fairly level, the terrain on the right hand side had several undulations and even a small hill. The buildings varied in style reflecting the differing businesses taking place there and each sat in an ample plot. She could hear industry taking place everywhere and scented all manner of things, from the timber yard, to a bakery, to a forge. She also noticed that whilst the school was made of the same white stone as the perimeter wall, the village houses were more varied. Some were built of timber; others were of a mellow tan brick or were a combination of stone with curved tan roof tiles. There was a welcoming and homely feel to the village.

'This is a beautiful place,' she offered, her attention now on the people going about their business. 'Where are we going?'

'To introduce you to the village head man,' Jim told her.

'That's not you then?'

'No. I'm the school's headmaster and am ultimately responsible for everyone inside these walls. Drako reports to me but looks after this animus village.'

'Everyone living here is animus?' Natalya asked in shock. She'd never have guessed there were so many left free. She looked again at the people in sight; yes all were tall and athletic.

'Predominantly, yes. The school is for both wizards and animus students, so it's useful that I am both,' Jim told her. 'We mix freely here, everyone contributing to our welfare or safety. Without experienced animus warriors like Freddie I wouldn't be able to protect my animus students. I understand I no longer sound completely wizard in nature. The inquisitors would come for me just as surely as anyone else and as they tried to come for my lady.'

Natalya noticed Jim's expression of anger and felt Freddie's hand flex also in mention of this woman. But neither said any more and she was left wondering. They reached a broad open square with a simple central fountain, evidently used for drinking. It was peaceful and invitingly shaded by a large oak tree. On a pair of benches some women sat together chatting whilst their hands continued with the mundane chores of weaving baskets or knitting. Whilst the women acknowledged Freddie warmly, they were a little more reticent when they saw Jim and indeed her. A lane opened up on their right and they turned up it heading for a beautiful house at the top of a small hill.

'That's my house,' Freddie remarked pointing to a smaller and less remarkable house on their left nearest the top.

Natalya nodded, eyeing the attractive and private home wistfully. She wondered if there was a Mrs Freddie in there but didn't feel she could ask. Another man nodded to Freddie from a house opposite and she felt the weight of his gaze. Hardly surprising; she was a stranger and in these difficult times they would be suspicious. She caught movement out of the corner of her eyes; a tall handsome man was rising to his feet from a swing seat on the veranda of the house they were approaching. There was strength and power of personality here too, yet he had a calm serene demeanour. Jim halted at a hitching rail at the side of the house and dismounted. Freddie guided his horse there too. She leaped down as soon as the horse stopped so Freddie could dismount, but waited for him rather than follow Jim round to the front.

'Come inside and change,' Freddie said to her with a glance of permission to Drako. He'd noticed she'd waited for him again and that she seemed nervous and very small. He led her to the cloakroom just off the entrance hall and placed her bag inside. 'I'll be just outside,' he murmured and closed the door giving her privacy.

Natalya was glad of the chance to be alone and use the facilities to wash her hands and feet properly. There were definite negatives to running in dirty places without boots. She could hear voices in the other room but none sounded aggressive or angry and she relaxed a little. She dragged her fingers through the hair that had escaped her long braid noticing how wild and knotted it all was in the mirror. Seeing her reflection she washed her face too. She glanced wistfully at the small tiled bath in the corner, but they were waiting for her. She straightened her shoulders resolutely and opened the door.

'I'm happy to meet you properly Freddie,' she said, suddenly feeling rather shy under his gaze. He seemed quite different viewed with human eyes. She could see the warrior in him now and appreciate his height and the breadth of his shoulders. 'Thank you for helping me escape,' she said and took his hand to emphasise her words. 'What's wrong?' she added when he remained silent.

'Freddie, how long do you intend to keep her out there all to yourself?' Jim called and appeared in the doorway. 'Ah, like that is it?' he commented in amusement. 'It's not like you to be tongue tied,' he teased. 'But I see why.'

'Come and meet everyone,' Freddie suggested keeping hold of her hand and stopping Jim from taking over. 'This is Commander Drako of Clan Green Bear and headman of White Haven village,' Freddie introduced. 'This is Natalya.'

'Pleased to meet you,' Drako said shaking her hand. 'Welcome,' he added. 'You've obviously met Freddie, my second in command,' Drako said not commenting on the fact Freddie's scent was all over her. That was a possessive wolf trait to mark a female. Perhaps she didn't realise and his scent on her was accidental, but Freddie was acting very attentively towards her. Then again, she was a particularly attractive, if a little daunting, looking woman. 'This is

Cassaria, my wife,' Drako said bringing Cassy forward. 'She is a wizard student here.'

Natalya took the other woman's hands in greeting, liking her on sight. She'd been wondering why the one woman in the room was so small. Animus people were always considered tall by ordinaries, but wizards could be any height.

'Call me Cassy. I hope you don't mind my saying, but you've got a very powerful talent. Can you be more than one animal?' Cassy felt Natalya's sudden alarm and nervousness and squeezed her hand reassuringly. The men on the other hand were now paying close and eager attention on the answer. 'Jim's girlfriend is a multi shape shifter and can be any animal she wants. I've seen her as a panther, an eagle, a horse and even a dragon. She's rather disconcertingly powerful but a lovely person.'

This multi shifter was Jim's lady? But a woman who could become a dragon was probably a good match for a lion.

'I cannot take bird form and I find herbivores difficult,' Natalya admitted. 'I like four legged carnivores.'

'What is your true alternate form?' Jim asked, striding closer to her suddenly and deliberately scaring her.

'I don't know,' Natalya said nervously but she stood her ground and stared back at him warily. His blue eyes suddenly changed colour to a rich gold that was very alarming. She felt a buzzing and his clothes removed themselves from his skin in a split second. He knelt, shimmered and a huge powerful lion stood before her and way too close for comfort.

'Change little kitty,' Jim the lion growled. She continued to glare at him refusing to be intimidated. He gestured with his paw deliberately. She squealed in dismay as her clothes unfastened and floated off her body despite her best efforts to keep hold of them. She knelt and shimmered as he had. Jim chuckled in delight now. He was muzzle to muzzle with a massive tiger. The tigress growled at him, revealing huge fangs. She was almost as big as his lion and certainly a far cry from the domestic tabby she'd arrived as. Now he understood why she hadn't seemed overly frightened of his lion.

'Superbly realised tiger,' Jim said prowling around her and noting even the intricate stripes were perfect. She had clearly spent time in this form and was comfortable with it. 'But this isn't your true form. Have you tried a lion?' he asked slightly wistfully.

'No and that's not a shape I'd try here.'

'Why? Amelie can easily be a lioness but she does it only rarely. She prefers the panther; I don't know why.'

'Don't you know anything about being a lion?' Natalya snorted and shook her head. Unless a woman liked being submissive to her man she would chafe as a lioness in a lion's presence. A lion always dominated his pride females even though the females were the hunters and a woman capable of being such a powerful cat would probably choose a more independent type of cat with a male around. She shimmered and became her medium cat the lynx. Her tiger was too similar and related to a lion. Lions liked prides; he might be on the lookout for another female and she had no wish to fall into that trap.

'No, that's not you either,' Jim told her. 'You're not a cat at all, are you,' he commented, objectively considering how he'd seen her instinctively acting up to now. Cats did not run with others, they ran alone. 'You have dog traits,' he suggested.

'I've never been a dog,' Natalya objected, but knew what she had been. She closed her eyes shimmering again. She heard a strange half choked sound from Freddie behind her but met the lion's gaze questioningly and he nodded.

'She'll make a fine addition,' Jim told Drako. 'I know how much you like your wolves.' He paused with his head up. 'I think I hear the ones we saw in town arriving. I'd best go down and check them over. Coming Drako?'

'More are arriving?' Drako asked absently, far more interested in watching as Freddie shimmered into his reddish grey wolf. Freddie's head was held high and his posture taut as he touched noses with Natalya's beautiful black white and grey patterned wolf. Then his tail began wagging. Her ice blue eyes fitted this form perfectly.

'She's exhausted and hungry Freddie,' Cassy reminded, aware of just how eagerly focussed he was on her. 'When did you eat last Natalya?'

'I don't remember,' Natalya responded tearing her eyes from the stunning red wolf before her.

'Let me remedy that,' Freddie suggested and her feathery tail waved again. He headed for the door, glancing at Drako for permission to leave and suddenly noticing just how interested they all were in his interaction with her. As she had been doing all morning, she followed his every move, remaining exactly by his side as they left the house and started down the hill. But now it all made sense and he knew why it had felt right. His scent on her coat was doubly intoxicating now he was in wolf form. Abruptly he had an irresistible urge to howl. He stopped and let it flow out of him. The notes might sound mournful to the human ear but they were anything but.

Natalya cocked her head at him in surprise. Another howl close by answered him then two more. He howled again and she joined him, her voice blending around his. There was a silence and then the answers had changed in tone to ones of eager query. Three males came into sight. All were large wolves like Freddie and they trotted up the slope, their ears pricked and tails wagging. One was almost black but the other two were the more usual marled grey.

Freddie stood with his head high and tail curved out in the alpha male pose. It was a posture the others knew but had never seen him hold so determinedly. The new blue eyed female with the strikingly marked coat and already bearing his scent was the reason.

'I am Natalya,' she said to the males generally. 'Pleased to meet you all,' she added. Freddie still stood rather rigidly, clearly on guard in case one of the others made a move on her. She nudged his shoulder amused by his posture and that he kept so still. She then licked his muzzle and his pose melted. 'I'm hungry,' she reminded.

'The school has the best food,' Freddie said and began trotting. He constantly made sure she was there by his side, still disbelieving of his luck. The warriors or rather his pack followed. There was a group of people at the gates when they left the village. Several were watching but Freddie didn't care; running wild in his animal form was exhilarating and one of the best things of being animus. He was surprised, but then gratified, that Johnny and Rupert began playing with each other, nipping and bowling the other over as they ran together. They were undoubtedly showing off. The addition of this one female had instantly turned them into a real pack.

Natalya bounded by his side across the grass feeling a great sense of belonging and camaraderie. She didn't even know these other male's names yet either. It was enough that Freddie was the alpha and that they were all welcoming her to join them.

Freddie led her away from the clusters of students sitting in the grass or lounging near the front doors enjoying the warm sunshine. Round the back of the house she admired a huge glasshouse integrated into a courtyard. Several small outbuildings were clustered here along with a walled vegetable garden handy for the kitchens. But most importantly, as far as she was concerned, the wafts of cooking smells assailing her nose originated here.

'We forgot our clothes,' Freddie suddenly remarked ruefully.

'You haven't stashed any up here for this kind of need?' Natalya asked in surprise.

'No. Perhaps we should,' Freddie acknowledged. 'Hang on, maybe there's something we can use in the wash house.'

'Don't you run in wolf fur very often?' Natalya asked whilst following him inside one of the outbuildings.

'Not up to the house. In the village and grounds yes, there's plenty of space. But you have to understand that our village is less than a year old. Drako negotiated with Jim for a place of refuge within school walls for our clan. It was winter and there were a lot of us driven from our homes and lands. Jim organised the students and the wizards built houses for us. Many of the previously scattered members of our clan have since joined us, and every day other animus people find their way here. We've kind of spilled out of what was originally granted us and our population has more than doubled. Drako has told us to tread lightly. We don't want the wizards to become irritated by our increasing numbers and resent us.'

'So why remain here? What is it about this place that draws you if you're only here on sufferance?'

'Drako and Jim. They are a very powerful combination, especially now Cassy has joined us. Jim is a powerful wizard and I've seen him do astonishing things, but as he keeps telling us, he is only one man. To defend youngsters and a place as large and complex as this he needs experienced warriors. That is where Clan Green Bear comes in. Of course no ordinary is going to match an animus warrior; our senses and strength far surpass them. It's the wizards we worry about. But here, Jim can pull together the older students to help power big defensive spells if necessary, but it's hard on them. Most are still teenagers and he would have to choose spells that will not turn their stomachs or more importantly frighten them into running home. He needs the wizard parents on side to thwart or undermine any plans to attack or destroy the school. He doesn't need the students to know just how often there are attempts to breach our defences; they'd panic needlessly. But essentially we have a mutually beneficial arrangement worked out here. So what brought you here?'

'You brought me precisely here,' she told him whilst rummaging in a basket of dirty clothes. She pulled out a dress wincing a little at its odour but it was the only one likely to fit. Then she noticed a disgusting stain down the front and threw it back. She rummaged in a basket of male clothing next and pulled out two pairs of trousers and two shirts that were less obviously stained.

'Will these fit you?' she asked pushing the items towards him with her nose. Freddie shimmered and grew into his human body yet retained his wolf fur. She stared at him, astonished by his feat. 'How did you do that?' she asked observing that he could now dress without revealing his bare skin inappropriately. She admired his thick fur trying not to linger in any of the areas she was most curious about.

'There's a knack to it but anyone can learn,' he said. 'Keep the image of your fur in your mind whilst you relax into your human form,' he advised. 'Are you sure you've the strength just now?' he asked quickly, well aware of how many forms she'd changed into and thus strength she'd expended today. And that was since he'd found her running for her life.

Natalya closed her eyes and her bare skin was only visible for a moment before her wolf fur reinstated itself.

'Well done,' Freddie said warmly. 'Feels a little strange doesn't it?'

'Yes. Useful though,' she added grinning at him and aware his eyes were straying. She quickly pulled on shirt and trousers, fastening both before letting her fur vanish. They were too baggy on her but the trouser length was only just long enough. She tied the shirt tails in a knot at her waist so the male clothing looked less shapeless. 'Do I look acceptable?'

'You smell of another male,' Freddie couldn't help complaining.

'So do you,' she told him.

He noticed her raised brows and hastily changed fully to human form aware suddenly of how possessive he'd sounded. As a wolf, actively pursuing and claiming a new female for his own was acceptable, as a man it was not. He'd only just met her and he needed to keep in mind she would have her own wishes and plans that were unlikely to include him. 'Let's see what goodies the cooks have left over from lunch,' he suggested.

'Why did you come up here for lunch if you're trying to remain inconspicuous?'

'I lived up here longer than most and the cooks know I fill the larder for them. They don't mind me,' he grinned at her engagingly and she laughed.

Natalya noticed the wolves Freddie had called to hadn't gone but sat in the grass nearby, watching and waiting. 'Don't they have anywhere they should be?

'They want to meet you,' Freddie told her simply. He led her quickly out of their sight however down a corridor and into the dining hall. He took her to an empty table by the windows and sat her down. 'You sit and rest. I'll go and speak with the cooks.'

She watched him thread his way between the tables of this huge room and disappear into a doorway at the other end. The big oak tables were freshly scrubbed clean, the flagstone floor swept and even the chairs were tucked neatly under the tables. She suspected the kitchen would be just as organised and clean. She idly watched the students moving about outside on the lawn. Several separate groups were seated in the grass, perhaps they were having their lessons outside? The day was unusually warm and sunny, one of the first this spring. It wasn't surprising everyone wanted to be outside enjoying it. It was a restful calm scene and exceedingly different from her increasingly desperate search for sanctuary that had been her life for the last three weeks.

She glanced up as Freddie returned. She'd been so lost in her thoughts that she hadn't noticed him come across. 'Are they having lessons out there?'

'Looks like it. Might as well make the most of the sunshine; it's been a long winter.'

'True enough,' she agreed. 'It just seems weird to see them so happy, safe and occupied in learning magic after the frantic few weeks I've just had. People have been trying to kill me because of my magic.' She shook her head and watched him settle down opposite her.

'Here you can be just as safe as them,' he said softly and took her hands across the table in tactile emphasis.

She noticed whilst they talked he alertly kept an eye on everything around them; he'd obviously spent a long time hunting and being hunted. 'Why did you howl when we left that house?'

'Why did you join me?' he countered his gaze abruptly intent on her.

'I've no idea what I was saying or why I felt I had to,' she admitted. 'I've never howled before, but it felt good.'

'You didn't know I was a wolf?'

'No. You were obviously animus and something predatory, but I wasn't scared of you.' Instead she'd been drawn to the man with the laughing green eyes. Not that she was going to admit that to him.

'But you were scared of Jim?

'Yes, even when he was trying to be charming.'

'Why did you tell him you wouldn't be a lion?'

'Because he is one. Lion males instinctively surround themselves with a number of females, particularly if they're in their prime. Even my tiger tempted him.'

Freddie considered her words whilst tucking in to the hot meal one of the cooks had just placed before them both. He'd never met a lion animus prior to Jim, so didn't know their usual traits well enough to refute her observation. Whilst Cassy had also been wary of Jim, he'd never witnessed him actually doing anything to warrant both women's uneasy reactions.

'What is Drako?' Natalya asked.

'A black bear and so is his sister Ebony. That's her outside with the long black hair.'

'She looks a lot like Drako,' Natalya commented eyeing the stunning woman. Then she noticed Ebony reach down and tug a seated man to his feet. He rose, wrapped his arms about her and kissed her. It was a brief kiss but revealed the passion between them. He turned to quell the whistles and laughter of those students around him, but wore a broad grin.

'That's Max. He's the deputy head here and the animus teacher,' Freddie told her aware of the direction of her gaze and trying to calm his sudden and unexpected jealousy that she was looking at another man.

'He's animus. What is he?'

'An owl.'

'A bear and an owl? That's weird,' Natalya mused. 'It doesn't seem to be a problem for them. What of Cassy? How does a bear cope with a wizard?'

'Very well actually. They are devoted to each other. She has taught him how to link their minds so they can share their thoughts. She is remarkable, but then her spirit takes the form of a white wolf.'

'Ah, so you would approve,' Natalya laughed. 'Is that why you like me?' she asked suddenly and before she lost her nerve. 'Because you felt the wolf in me?'

'It's possible,' he conceded. 'Although your kitty was very cute and affectionate,' he added with a grin.

She flushed knowing he was referring to her snuggling against his body and hiding inside his coat. But she'd sensed his honest intention was to protect her. She'd desperately needed some respite from being hunted and she'd relaxed, feeling safely hidden and protected, for the first time in weeks. His gentle touch had helped settle her overwrought nerves and been strangely calming. She wished she could pretend to be a helpless and defenceless little cat again and let him take over, but he'd seen her tiger and she had some shreds of pride remaining. She glanced around them again feeling rather exposed here in this big airy room. She tried to quell her cowardly wish to hide behind Freddie, realising she was already relying on him to guide and protect her in this new place full of wizards. She knew she was being foolish to put her complete trust in her saviour on such short acquaintance and also to think she could commandeer his help exclusively. He was the alpha wolf of a pack of strong warriors; he would have commitments.

Someone came into the room and glanced her way curiously. She strove not to jump up and nervously push herself into Freddie's arms for protection. She knew there was a real attraction between them. She couldn't go to him now and expect him to consider any physical contact purely casual and insignificant despite her need for simple tactile comfort. She gritted her teeth, trying hard to get a grip. She didn't want him to think she was neurotic and unstable; he'd run a mile! She didn't dare ask what he'd thought of her wolf. She glanced at him again; he was quiet but watchful. Then he smiled at her and she felt her tangled emotions calm a little. She turned her attention to finishing the wonderfully filling roast dinner. She was aware he had a small smile on his face but he said nothing and pretended to concentrate on eating too.

'Well that hit the spot, thank you,' she said putting down her fork and sitting back replete. His plate was already empty; he'd also clearly been hungry.

A woman came out of the kitchen to take their plates. 'Anything more for you dears?' she asked.

Freddie glanced at Natalya questioningly and she shook her head. 'No, that was plenty, thank you,' he responded to the cook and she shuffled away with their plates.

'What are they doing now?' Natalya asked noticing a pair of men coming out of the kitchen carrying a heavy urn which they set on a table. They set out a second on the other side of the room.

'They're putting out the tea for the student's afternoon break. This is where they have it. Do you want some to wash down lunch? It's good.'

'Please,' she agreed, noticing stacks of mugs and plates of biscuits had also been put out. She followed him and accepted the hot mug he poured and handed her. This time he sat on one of the large window seats on the side wall. She joined him there, leaning back against the upholstery in a patch of sunshine and sipping her tea. It all felt surreal, too relaxed and safe. Three tall men came in, glanced Freddie's way and headed for the tea urn.

'Guess they got bored waiting outside to meet you,' Freddie told her.

'They are your wolves?' Natalya asked eyeing the athletically muscular young men. All were dark haired, tall and lean. They also kept glancing curiously her way.

'Yes; looks like they've brought their own clothes, though.'

'Sensible, given what we had to rummage through,' she told him with a grimace of distaste.

'True,' Freddie acknowledged and wondering if he stank offensively to her. The clothes they wore had been put into the laundry for a reason.

Natalya rose to her feet and took the hand of the first wolf man, learning his name was Rupert. Rupert quickly sat down, allowing Johnny and Dustin to come forward to shake her hand and introduce themselves. She liked what she saw of these men and smiled in response to their various words of welcome. Strangely, they made her feel protected and at ease. Then she noticed the deputy head enter the room and she hastily sat down nervously sliding right up against Freddie. But the owl had seen her and was coming over.

'Welcome to White Haven. I'm Max the deputy head here,' Max said.

'Pleased to meet you, Deputy Max. I am Natalya,' she responded politely but didn't get up. Instead, she pressed closer to Freddie, and Dustin the beta, sat closely on her other side, the males closing ranks around her. Were her nerves so obvious? She certainly wasn't going to get up and shake his hand. He seemed to get the hint and moved off to get his own tea. She finished her mug quickly and set it down.

'I can't meet any more people. Please excuse me,' she added and almost ran from the room, escaping out the back. She hurried into the laundry room, closing the door behind her. Alone at last, she stood with her eyes closed, fighting tears. The door opened and she scented Freddie.

'What just happened?' Freddie asked, and turned her around to face him.

She wrapped her arms about him and pressed her face against his warm neck. 'I'm sorry, but I have to leave. My presence here puts you all in danger. I am being hunted.'

'We've all been hunted. Here you can be safe.'

'You don't understand,' she said miserably. 'The wizards in town were there specifically to capture me. Because of me all the animus hiding in town were driven out and exposed to danger. You have such a rare and wonderful place here. I must draw them away from you.'

'But we got you clean away,' he objected. 'You didn't leave any tracks or scent on the ground leading here. Stay,' he urged.

'I'd never forgive myself if you got hurt or captured because of me,' she whispered into his neck. She felt his arms tighten around her hugging her close. It felt wonderfully comforting. She backed off from him, suddenly wondering why someone she'd only met that day had become so important to her. 'I'm sorry. I seem to be clinging to you today. It's most unlike me.'

'I'm happy to hear it,' Freddie told her with a quick grin.

'But I don't understand it. I don't even know you,' she said.

'Your wolf recognises mine. Wolves need other wolves; they don't like being alone. That's probably what you're feeling. It's natural to seek help and it's also natural for us to extend it to those in our pack.'

'I'm not a member of your pack. I'm a stranger.'

'We have unanimously accepted you into our pack,' he told her gently.

'You have? When? I mean, I don't remember asking to join.'

'You howled with us,' he said simply, although her attitude towards him personally and vice versa was what had swung it so decisively and quickly. He couldn't tell her his wolf had chosen her as his mate at first sight of her wolf. Jim said that was her true alternate form and he believed it.

'Freddie, you know I didn't know what I was doing. I'm not going to hold you to that. It's not safe for me to stay in one place. I'll draw trouble to everyone here.'

'You instinctively knew you could seek my protection today and also to howl with me. You are more in tune with your wolf instincts than you know. Come, let's get out of these stinky clothes and run in the sunshine.' He shrugged out of the shirt throwing it back in the laundry basket. He knew she was looking at him and was pleased. He let his fur bristle over his human body reminding her of this magic before ridding himself of the cumbersome trousers.

Natalya copied him, grinning at managing to cover her bare skin with fur. The clothes returned to the baskets, she changed fully to wolf form and followed him out into the sunshine.

As they passed the dining room windows, she glanced in and growled quietly to see both the lion man and the owl man standing together watching her.

'Why don't you like Max?' Freddie asked. She ran silently for a few moments before answering.

'I am being hunted by an owl man under the wizard's orders. I know this Max is someone else, but I can't help being nervous,' she admitted. 'It's not easy to escape a bird, especially when he has wizard backup on the ground able to flush me out of hiding. It was difficult to hunt too; he deliberately messed up so many hunts I got weak. I was starving by the time I got to town, but there at least I could give them the slip for a time and eat.'

'I can see why you dislike owls,' Freddie said. 'He never approached you on the ground?'

'No. I was travelling in tiger form; he didn't dare. That's a good form when you're alone.'

'I suppose it would be. Your wolf would have been faster though. Where is this owl now?' he asked sharply.

'I lost him two days ago when I entered Briarton. I think he directed the wizard to my location but then left it to him. Or maybe he left because the catchers joined the wizard there. Actually, I don't think he'd have been able to track me so easily amongst so many people, and an owl would be conspicuously out of place in a town. Since I managed to hide in your coat on the way here I hope he hasn't any clue where I am. But my main worry is the people Jim invited back here. The guards arrested two blond women. He may have heard about that and assumed one to be me. They came here rather directly I should think.'

'You have a point. Was it just one animus traitor tracking you?' Freddie asked his tone hardening.

'I only know of one owl. The wizards might have someone else under their control though,' she added anxiously.

'We need to warn the others,' Freddie said decisively and glanced back towards the house where Jim was. 'We'll see Drako first,' he said knowing she didn't really want to see Jim, particularly with Max present.

They trotted quickly across the grass and the rest of their pack rose from the grass to join them. The other three male wolves bounded together nipping at each other playfully and preening before the new young female in their midst.

Natalya watched them and her mood lightened before their playful high spirits. She stayed close by Freddie's side but watched the others too. The knowledge they wanted her to join them, to run like this every day was very tempting. Suddenly Freddie bowled her over. She stared up at him in surprise. His paw held her down lightly on her back then he licked her face. She could see the playful interest on his face; he was testing her. She suspected he didn't really like her watching the other males. Something touched her back foot and she flinched; one of the others had brushed her. She drew her foot away but Freddie was suddenly growling; his gaze fixed on the other male warningly. She rose between them and prodded Freddie with a paw diverting his attention. His lips slowly covered his fangs but he kept glaring at the other male. She licked his muzzle once, quelling his overreaction, and trotted off forcing them to hurry after her.

She could see two people sitting on the swing seat on the leader's house's veranda. The bear man and the wizard sat together so peacefully and looked so romantic that she faltered. Freddie came alongside.

'Are you sure we should disturb them?' she asked.

'They will want to know. Besides, it's not as though they're otherwise occupied. We could ask Cassy to tell Jim for us,' he suggested.

'You must think me such a coward,' she whispered unhappily.

'No, but something has scared you. Let me help,' he coaxed gently, but said nothing more. He'd travelled with and been the protector for hunted families. He knew people did not always act predictably or sanely under unrelenting stress. She looked into his eyes and again licked his muzzle. He was very tempted to return to human form and kiss her but that was not her intention; she was merely thanking him in wolf fashion. 'I could get used to that,' he said softly and she ducked away. He trotted on again, Natalya automatically matching his pace. The rest of their pack followed closely behind not wishing to be left out.

The pack sat back beside Natalya at the foot of the steps while Freddie went up to speak with Drako. She listened to Freddie, aware the pack was also listening to her story, with intent interest. She slowly climbed the stairs and moved up behind Freddie miserably, her head hanging.

'Freddie, I will leave tonight,' she told him. She glanced round at the chorus of "no's", not only from Freddie but his pack and their leader Drako too. 'But I endanger everyone. I must lead them away,' she told them.

'Come inside Natalya,' Cassy said, rising to her feet. 'You've told the men what they face; let them worry about it.' She calmly led the wolf inside the house, closing the door behind them.

Natalya was momentarily surprised she should so readily obey and follow the little woman away from Freddie's side, but she sensed no animosity from Cassy. She noticed her bag left abandoned here earlier and now she had her own clothes changed back into human form. Cassy waved her into an armchair and sat opposite.

'I'm so sorry to be causing so much trouble and worry. If I'd known where Freddie was taking me I might not have agreed to come,' Natalya said miserably wringing her hands.

'Why did you trust him so quickly?' Cassy asked curiously.

'I don't know. I was desperate I suppose and he seemed to genuinely wish to help. The other man I wasn't so sure of. But there was something about Freddie I responded to. He thinks it's because we are both wolves and instinctively recognised one another despite me being in cat form. Does that make sense?'

'Actually it does. I've certainly called on Freddie's help too,' Cassy admitted. 'He seems so calm and assured on the outside but he has a sparkling active mind. He is a deeply caring and compassionate person too,' Cassy added.

'You mean he's protecting me because I've been looking helpless?'

'A hunted cornered woman would trigger that in him yes,' Cassy admitted easily. 'But from what I've seen, he is very keen on you. He isn't married and there appears to be real attraction between you. Am I wrong?'

'No, you're not wrong. But it seems to have happened astonishingly fast. I don't know him and shouldn't let myself be distracted by a gorgeous man, no matter how tempting his wolf is. Besides, he doesn't know me either. How can he know I'm not a spy or working for one of the catchers?'

'Because Jim would have looked into your mind just enough to answer exactly those questions,' Cassy told her. 'Jim was hunted by an animus wolf man and he's had a few scares since he came here. He checks everyone. That's one of the reasons we trust you and know you'll be safer here. Bear in mind we have good old fashioned walls to keep the un-friendly out. We have wizards who can defend us against other wizards and strength in numbers. Don't try and go it alone. Too many animus people have been picked off one by one because they were alone and had no one to aid them. You're here now and the pack clearly wants you to stay.'

'I would be a burden and have no place here. I didn't see any inn; not that I have any money left,' she added despondently.

'Don't worry about any of that. Freddie will make a place for you and ensure you are taken care of. Most of them have been homeless and dependent on other people's hospitality. We understand your situation and no one is going to look down on you,' she added gently. She was aware Freddie was at the door, awaiting permission to come in. She sent Drako this further part of her conversation on their private link, knowing he was telling Freddie of Natalya's main concerns.

'Come in Freddie,' Cassy called raising her voice and the wolf entered. 'Natalya's exhausted and could use some sleep. You've got a spare room at your place haven't you?'

'Of course,' Freddie acknowledged quickly, rather surprised Cassy should suggest it. But if she thought

Natalya wouldn't object, or anyone else for that matter, he would gladly take her guidance on how to proceed.

'Is that alright by you?' Freddie asked Natalya, making sure she had a chance to speak up. She was watching him rather directly and he found himself digging his claws into the rug and shuffling a foot nervously.

'Sounds good to me, but are you certain I would not be inconveniencing you?' Natalya asked.

'Not at all; I live alone. But you haven't seen the place yet. Come on over and see for yourself if you'd like to stay,' Freddie suggested. 'It isn't a big house like this; well I don't need much inside space.'

Natalya found she was amused that he was rambling nervously at the thought of her staying in his home. She rose from her chair unsteadily and went to the door. 'Are you going to show me anytime soon?' she couldn't resist asking, seeing his wolf frozen. He trotted quickly over and she opened the door for him. 'Thank you Cassy,' she said and followed the red wolf outside.

'Come on, you're too tired to talk further,' he said gently, aware she'd wilted and urged her down the steps.

She knew he was right, so she simply nodded to Drako rather than stopping to speak with him. She followed Freddie slowly, her energy suddenly almost nonexistent. She found she had difficulty putting one foot before the other. The wolf shimmered into a fur coated man and Freddie wrapped an arm about her waist supporting her. She let him. 'Sorry. I don't know why I'm so weak all of a sudden,' she apologised.

'That's what happens when you've pushed yourself too hard for too long,' he told her, leading her up the steps to his house. He let her stand for a moment in the living area while he closed the door behind them, then he swept her up into his arms and carried her up the stairs.

'What are you doing?' she squeaked in alarm.

He set her down on his bed gently. 'You need to sleep and I doubt you'd have managed the stairs.'

'This is your bed,' she whispered aware of his scent on it and that they were quite alone. 'You don't have a second bed then?'

'Not yet. Don't worry about that. Just sleep, I will go downstairs so you can relax.'

'I will smell of you,' she commented, watching him closely.

'You already do,' he said and grinned, happy she should know and appreciate what that meant between male and female wolves. Everyone already thought of her as his.

She suddenly realised that in lying inside his coat she'd been wrapped completely in things that scented of him. She hadn't thought of that at the time, only of feeling safe and secure.

'You seem very pleased your rescue has rubbed off on me. We have just met remember. I hope you're not helping me just because I smell of you and it's simply an instinctive wolf thing?' He looked hurt by that suggestion and she dropped her gaze.

'I am not just a wolf. If I were I would have already claimed you,' he told her and noticed her eyes widen in surprise. 'Sleep, Natalya. You are safe.'

'Am I safe from you?' she murmured as he began to leave. He turned back and she saw a man's hunger in the gaze he swept over her, here, lying in his own bed. He was right, he wasn't only a wolf; he was clearly a passionate man, too. His beautiful thick red white and grey marbled fur covered a lean, athletically muscled body, but it was his honest, intelligent and expressive eyes that drew her most. She thought him very attractive. He smiled at her reassuringly then closed the door firmly behind him. She listened to him go back downstairs and relaxed. She tugged the covers up to her chin, snug and warm and surrounded by his scent. Before she knew it, she was asleep.

5

# On Alert

Freddie was mortified that he'd told her he wanted to claim her! What was he thinking admitting that to her face! He hoped he hadn't scared her off being so forward, but carrying her in his arms and tucking her into his own bed had added a very possessive element to his attraction.

He returned to wolf form and curled up in a patch of sunshine outside his open front door where he could both keep watch and be close enough to hear her should she call. He rested his chin on his front paws aware the pack had settled at the foot of his stairs. They were keeping each other company but he also felt they were standing guard. He was surprised they didn't come up and join him on the wide veranda as they normally would, but with Natalya just upstairs, things had changed. They were respecting his territory as though she was already his mate. He remembered

Cassy complaining that Drako had moved too fast when they first started seeing each other. This was even faster he ruefully knew. But he couldn't help how strongly he felt already.

Freddie glanced up the hill; Drako and Cassy sat together on their swing seat. Everything seemed peaceful and serene yet he couldn't relax. His mind seethed with images and thoughts of her. The last thing he wanted was for her to stay in someone else's house, but he'd just admitted to her he only had one bed. She would be wondering if he was going to insist she share his bed with him tonight. Oh, how he wished it, but that would be unacceptable. As Cassy had said, he did have an empty second bedroom; he just needed to locate a bed. That would help take the pressure off.

'Do any of you still have the school bed or a spare mattress down here?' he asked his pack.

'I do,' Dustin said. 'You wish her to sleep apart from you?' he asked.

'She's sleeping in my bed right now but I don't think she's ready for me to be in it with her. We did just meet today,' Freddie reminded them.

'We'll go fetch it for you,' Dustin volunteered and they all rose and trotted over to Dustin's house. The bed was already partially disassembled and his house on the same lane to Freddie's, so they were back within ten minutes. Freddie allowed them to help him get the unwieldy metal poles and pieces up the stairs and into the second bedroom. They assembled it quietly, not wishing to disturb Natalya's sleep. None were surprised Freddie ushered them back outside as soon as they were done.

Freddie got up and prowled round the house, even going back upstairs to listen at the bedroom door to her breathing. He went out on the upper balcony, looked around carefully, and then jumped up onto his roof. Whilst his reddish mottled coat toned with the terracotta roof tiles, he was careful to stay off the ridge where his outline would be conspicuous. Because his house was partway up the hillock he could see over the village rooftops to the perimeter wall, but only from this rather precarious vantage point. In wolf form particularly, he had excellent senses of sight, hearing and smell. He sat still and scanned the breeze coming to him from the forest. That was where enemies tended to hide whilst waiting for nightfall. Not detecting anything untoward, he next turned his attention to the main gates. There were many faint scents confusing the breeze in that direction however. It was difficult to know if it was gate guards, visitors or even scents carried from the nearest human village a few miles beyond the walls.

*'Freddie, what are you up to?'*

It took him a moment to recognise Cassy's voice speaking quietly in his mind. He turned and saw her watching him.

*'Just checking all is well,'* he spoke the words in his mind knowing Cassy could pick them up. *'The enemy*

wizard and Catchers were hot on Natalya's trail this morning. I doubt they've gone home,' he told her and even heard the echo as she spoke mind to mind with Drako.

'Do you sense anything?' she asked.

'Not in the forest, but I can't tell if there's anything untoward by the gates, the scent is too mixed. I think we should do some patrolling of the grounds.'

'Drako agrees, but you should stay with Natalya. She'll panic if she wakes alone. Send your pack, they can trot round discreetly. Drako and I will go to the gates and check that area out,' she told him, already walking hand in hand with Drako down the steps from her house. 'How's Natalya?' she asked and received such a flood of emotion from him she nearly didn't hear the calmly delivered response.

'She's sleeping,' Freddie told her simply.

'Perhaps you should stay up there away from her,' Cassy remarked.

'Why?'

'So you can cool down and concentrate on keeping watch for danger. You're already besotted with her,' Cassy added gleefully.

He groaned mentally that Cassy was witnessing just what a mess his emotions were at the moment. He had an almost overwhelming desire to sit by Natalya's side and gaze at her as she slept.

*'I'll stay here then. Now get out of my head,'* Freddie told her a little sharply, feeling acutely embarrassed. He was left with an impression of her laughter, but what Cassy knew so too would Drako. From the roof he watched Drako speaking with the pack still gathered around his house below him. The pack soon trotted off, saving him from having to come all the way down just to speak with them. Drako and Cassy ambled into the village hand in hand and disappeared amongst the buildings but quite quickly they came back into sight out the other side. They left the village and turned right onto the main school drive heading for the main gates. Freddie kept an eye on them; it was ingrained in him to watch over and defend Drako. He was not only their leader but their clan lord's son. Drako had also been his friend since childhood. They knew each other well. Drako was an experienced and accomplished warrior. Cassy would be able to sense any animus, or wizards for that matter, beyond the gates once the village itself wasn't in the way, confusing the scent. Cassy had told him that such a concentration of animus people actually helped disguise the individual magical signatures emanating from White Haven Village, particularly with wizards close enough to mingle the signature. A wizard would sense a great deal of magical power combined here, but unless they were very strong or very sensitive they wouldn't be able to determine what proportion of the magic was animus and what wizard.

Freddie sat back and kept watch. He could see his pack in the distance, trotting the boundaries and also Cassy and Drako moving about in the watchtower by the front gates. Everyone's lack of alarm slowly reassured him no threat was imminent. He waited until his pack had completed their sweep before coming down from the roof and going back down to his veranda to meet them.

'Any of you detect anything out of place?' Freddie asked once they'd gathered by his door to report.

'I smelt something odd up near the training ground wall but it was very faint and went quickly,' Dustin reported.

'Was it near that copse of trees?' Freddie asked and Dustin nodded. 'There used to be a hole in the wall there. It's where Louis first entered the grounds before we met wizard Jim. As soon as Jim took over, he sealed that hole in the wall, as well as all the others, but I understand there had been a gap for months previously. It stands to reason anyone spying on the school would know of such a handy secret breach in the defences and may be checking to see if it is still there. Or maybe it's simply a local moving about in the forest? Who knows, but we should keep watch on the perimeter. The wizard hunting Natalya was using an animus owl to track her from the air too. I doubt the wizard can get in unnoticed but an owl can bypass all our defences. That's what I'm most concerned with at the moment. We'll do another sweep at dusk in about an hour,' he added so they wouldn't rush off anywhere in the meantime, using up their energy when they might need it all later.

'Freddie,' Natalya called softly and the wolves all turned to look up at her in the upstairs bedroom window.

'I didn't think you'd be awake yet; you haven't slept long,' he chided.

'You didn't really think I was going to did you? Anyway, would you mind if I had a bath? You seem to have a nice tub,' Natalya asked shyly.

'Please go ahead,' he said, only just managing to avoid the temptation of inviting her to make herself at home. 'Take your time,' he added.

'Thank you for standing guard. I'll be ready for your patrol in an hour's time,' she told him and left the window.

'Natalya?' Freddie instantly called her back into sight. 'There's really no need, we can do that. You're worn out. Let us help.'

'Like you, I will only relax once the threat is over and not before,' she told him and closed the window.

'She's determined isn't she?' Dustin commented with a broad grin. Freddie would have his work cut out with this indomitable female.

6

# *The Owl*

Exactly an hour later the blue eyed wolf came downstairs. Freddie stood by the open doorway his ears pricked towards her and his tail waving a silent greeting. He turned and stepped outside and she followed. He nudged his front door closed and noted his pack stood attentively waiting and alertly watching them both. She came to stand side by side with him and suddenly he felt strangely bereft that she no longer scented of him. She now felt like a beautiful stranger rather than already being his. He knew she deserved to be courted properly; but he didn't have to like it! He also had no intention of letting anyone else muscle in. Losing her was unthinkable.

He quickly instructed which areas he'd like the three males to cover. 'Natalya and I will go up to the training ground and check out that copse.' Abruptly she licked his muzzle. 'What was that for?' he asked in surprise and aware his whole train of thought had just slipped from his mind.

'For not trying to leave me behind,' she told him happily.

Freddie stared at her until he realised the others were laughing at him and she was watching and waiting for him. Turning his mind to business, he trotted down the steps and down the lane, Natalya by his side. He was glad for some action after sitting around fretting all afternoon. The others flanked them until their paths diverted.

They trotted up the drive, their steps in unison. He realised she was nearly as big as him; she was a tall and powerful wolf, unusually so for a female. They moved onto the grass trotting silently, their mottled coats blending into the evening twilight. They kept their keen senses fully alert. The main problem was the distraction of each other's presence. He would far rather gaze at her than hunt.

They thoroughly searched the whole area up this end of the grounds, combing the dark copse of trees and the training ground buildings themselves too. Finding nothing untoward she led him away from the buildings to a wide open stretch of grass where she sat down.

'What are you doing?' Freddie asked.

'I'm turning myself into a tempting target. If that owl's about he'll come to us. He never can resist waking and harassing helpless creatures,' she said with calm disgust.

Freddie sat with her but angled to face her so they could both see anything trying to creep up behind them. 'Has that owl seen you in wolf form?'

'No. He's only seen me as a tiger. I had no choice but to change from my kitty. He's a very big owl and could have easily grabbed me in that form. My tiger isn't helpless, easy prey. He didn't dare come too close.'

'Tell me about yourself,' Freddie invited eagerly. 'Where do you come from?'

'Braytree island originally. My parents were both very gifted, mother a wizard and father animus. They were teachers and when I was young they accepted work on the mainland. I don't really remember too much of that time, but I know father was attacked just for being animus and had to leave us. Mother was arrested when I was ten, I don't know on what charge and we were separated. I was taken to a lord's manor. I never saw either of my parents again and never learned what became of them. I can only assume they were murdered,' she said bleakly. 'Not long after my arrival, the lord pressed me to reveal my animus form. I'd heard from one of the servants that the guards were wary of me because they knew I had ability but not what form I was able to take. They worried I might be something fearsome. I'm not sure why they thought that, I was just a ten year old girl.'

'You don't have a weak body or character; that's what they would see. I imagine that was just as clear when you were a child. Our personality is what dictates our animal form. They were right to be concerned.'

She nodded; that made sense. 'They feared me so I searched for a creature that couldn't be misused and was considered harmless. So I tried a cat, the little tabby, copying a stray I saw. No-one knew I could be something else; well I didn't either at that point. Fortunately, by the time I did realise, I'd also learned it wasn't safe for anyone at the manor to know.'

'I thought you'd been in wolf form?'

'I saw a real wolf about two years later. I'd slipped over the wall and was walking alone in the woods one evening when I was meant to be in bed. He seemed curious about me and came close. I suppose it appealed to me that he was so wild and free as well as being so gentle. He was also beautifully coloured. I copied his form and colour and ran with him for a few hours. But I was a child and tired quickly. When I returned home he followed me but the guards saw him and drove him off. They never saw me; I was always careful that they never knew I'd been out. My cat was very useful for that. I believe he lingered nearby for a few days before leaving. I was dreadfully lonely, as was he, but knew that if I met him again he'd be encouraged to stay nearby and someone would kill him. I never let anyone see my wolf form, or any other shape I practiced in secret. It was better to become a pet cat rather than something he could misuse.'

'So what happened?' Freddie asked.

'A wizard used to visit the lord regularly and often brought his son. Nathaniel was a few years older than me and training to be a wizard. I became their source of entertainment. One day the son turned up alone. I was summoned before our lord, and told to be in human form. One of my friends from the stables heard the order and warned me that I shouldn't go, that they had plans for me. But before I could turn about and flee I was grabbed and taken before them.'

'What plans? What happened?' Freddie asked seeing stormy emotions on her face.

'My lord had decided to marry me off to Nathaniel. He would then have a tame wizard to call on in his holdings. Any child of mine was likely to be talented and become his to groom into something more useful than I obviously was to him.'

'So the wizard we saw in town today; that was your suitor?'

'No! That was one of the catcher team leaders. Suitor indeed! Nathaniel wanted the salary the lord was offering, the comfy apartment and me. He's a thug. He knew no one would criticise him for beating and brutalising a useless animus woman. They actually held me down so he could rape me. They knew once I was pregnant I wouldn't be able to change into my cat, I'd become slow and easy to manipulate. I got free enough to change; he couldn't rape my cat. I scratched and bit like a demon before escaping out the window.

I've been running from him for three weeks now. He knows he's been close many times. I suppose my escape has caused considerable embarrassment and probably lost him a cushy career. The lord must have been under some obligation to keep me at his holdings and not running loose. I know he had offers from others wanting to take me off his hands, but he always declined. Nathaniel's deal with him specified that I continue to live there, so having lost me, he must have been ordered to retrieve me. Having said that, now he's called in the catchers, he must have decided to cut his losses and see me dead.'

'That's awful. The way you've been used makes my blood boil,' Freddie growled angrily.

She licked his face gently, trying to calm and distract his anger. 'I'm no longer hungry, tired and alone,' she told him, remembering his words to her.

'So what happens if this owl does come?' Freddie asked glancing around them again carefully now darkness had fallen properly and an owl would be in his element. 'I assume you have a plan?' he added noticing just how relaxed she appeared.

'I've been thinking about it yes. He'll probably dive at us; try to take us by surprise, especially sitting out here in the open. If he recognises me he may try and grab me but he's never seen me in this form. Obviously with two of us the odds are better to turn the tables. But those buildings are handy for shelter if we need it,' she added.

Freddie nodded, they couldn't do much planning. An owl in flight was out of reach, but for him to grab Natalya he would have to either land or attempt to capture her in a low pass. Owls had ferociously long sharp talons designed to grab and impale their prey. He didn't like to imagine what those things would do to either of them.

Their wolves had speed agility and excellent senses, but their only weapon was their teeth. He looked round sharply, hearing the little creatures in the wood suddenly fall silent.

Natalya heard the warning lack of sound too and was searching the cloudy dark sky. 'There,' she whispered hearing the faint but distinctive sound of soft wings that she'd become adept at listening for in the last weeks.

Freddie yelped; a man sized owl was plunging towards them at frightening speed, talons outstretched and only moments from striking. They leapt aside and began running in separate directions.

The owl swerved and went after the nearest wolf; the one that had yelped. Natalya turned and tried to run up behind the low flying owl following Freddie but Freddie was running too fast. He was running flat out to avoid the talons of the owl; she simply could not catch up, nor would she be able to leap on to the owl's back. She turned and ran back to the buildings instead.

'Freddie, get inside!' she called to him.

He couldn't see her but the building was where her voice was coming from. The owl wheeled with him and tried to block him but he leaped at the creature teeth bared. The owl squawked and veered away sharply. Freddie's teeth snapped on empty air but he could now run unimpeded for the safety of the building hearing the creature turning to follow. He ran inside and pushed the door shut in the owl's face. He searched the dark interior but Natalya wasn't there. If she was still outside she was in danger. He stepped back outside cautiously and searched for the owl; he couldn't see it. Freddie raised his nose and howled warning to his pack. The owl squawked in anger and dived at him, silencing him mid howl. Freddie was blocked from running back inside so he ran around the building, the owl hot on his heels. How had Natalya evaded such a vicious and fast hunter? Where was she? But if the owl was still flying after him it could not have found her.

He got back inside and stood, trying to catch his breath, watching the owl sweep on past the open door. He suddenly heard the roof above his head creak and the thuds of bounding feet. He dashed back to the door following the route of the steps. A piercing shriek rent the air and he gaped in amazement. The owl was plunging helplessly earthward with a huge tiger clamped to his back! The owl's wings could do little more than slow their rapid descent. His body cushioned her fall but they fell apart on impact.

The tiger was up and had pounced on the human sized owl again before he could do more than hop. The tiger smashed the owl flat on his face, her claws pinning him. He wildly tried to throw her off, thrashing his wings dangerously. The tiger snarled, responding by digging in her claws deeper. The owl snapped and bit with his wickedly sharp beak trying to maim or drive off the heavy legs with their dagger tipped paws that were impaling his body and holding him down. He made contact, forcing one paw to let go for a moment. His big powerful wings thrashed as he tried to lever himself up beneath the tiger's weight but also aiming to smash them into the tiger's face. The owl squawked; one of his wings had been grabbed painfully and was being restrained.

Freddie locked on to the flapping wing with his wolf teeth and stretched it out flat. Now only one wing thrashed dangerously, but that too was grabbed; the pack had arrived. While Dustin latched on to the other wing copying Freddie, the other two males came and actually sat on the powerful wings immobilising them.

'Wait,' an authoritative voice commanded.

Natalya spared a glance and realised the lion was trotting swiftly towards her with a huge black bear. It was Jim that had spoken; maybe he'd realised she'd just been about to snap this vile creature's neck.

Jim muttered something and the owl shrieked, his body unexpectedly converting into his human form. It meant the claws digging deeply into his sides dragged and tore as his limbs reconfigured themselves.

Freddie found he was now holding a man's hand in his teeth and that blood was filling his mouth. He released the hand and spat out the blood. Johnny and Rupert sitting on the man's arms were now sufficient to aid Natalya. The stranger still lay pinned on his belly beneath Natalya's heavy tiger form. Blood oozed around each of her paws and her sides heaved.

Natalya glanced round and knew with satisfaction that each of these hunters would help her should this owl man break free. They stared intently at him, many with teeth instinctively bared. The lion approached and she felt the owl flinch.

'Is he linked to the wizard?' Natalya asked quickly.

'He's reaching for him, now you've reminded him,' Jim said slightly absently, his focus on the owl man.

'Get out of his head,' Natalya ordered and, warning delivered, she bit the man's neck. Her tiger's teeth punctured deeply but she let him bleed to death. She could have dealt an instantly fatal blow, but ripping the jugular gave Jim a few moments to leave the dying man's consciousness. She jumped away avoiding the spurting blood pooling around her enemy's head.

'What did you do that for?' the lion hissed at her angrily.

'To save our lives,' Natalya growled back nose to nose with the lion. 'In a few moments more that wizard was going to be able to see all our faces through that owl's eyes. I couldn't have held him if the wizard had been able to take control of his body.'

'I could have stopped him,' the lion growled.

'Then he would have learned something else about the people here,' Natalya snapped glancing around. 'Now all he really knows is that his vicious servant is dead.' The lion didn't reply, acknowledging by his silence that she was correct. She glanced aside at Freddie, feeling him come to her side silently backing her up. She shimmered once more into wolf form, yelping once as her injured leg complained at the change of form. Jim stepped forward but she backed away from him turned and trotted away.

'Let me see your leg,' Freddie urged once they'd gone part of the way back to the village and her anxious pace had slowed. She was limping badly but didn't seem to acknowledge the pain. He wondered how often she had forced her body to continue to flee even through injury; to ignore pain.

She stopped and glanced round relieved the rest of the pack was with them. She sat down, her belly to the soft grass; glad to rest her back leg. 'Freddie, what am I to do?' she asked anxiously.

'Well first, you can take a nice hot bath and get some sleep,' Freddie told her.

'I meant about that wizard. I should leave now, tonight and draw him away.'

'No,' Freddie immediately objected. 'You're safe here, especially now that traitorous owl has been dealt with. Congratulations by the way,' he added.

'Congratulations? What, for killing a man?' she said bleakly. She covered her bloody face with both paws, hiding from the beautiful wolf.

'You are not a killer,' Freddie told her. 'What he did was inexcusable. If he'd just been following orders he would not have attacked me without provocation as he did. I would have snapped his neck without hesitation just for that, never mind what he's done to you. Don't feel a moment's remorse. I know it's never easy to end a life, but sometimes it has to be done. You should be proud you managed to see it through. Any one of us would have done it for you if you'd asked or needed us to. But he was your enemy. It was better for you to finish it.'

Natalya stared into his sincere face and heard the rest of the pack adding their assurances and agreement to his words. It felt good to let his words soak in, to be accepted. She glanced round; the lion and bear were approaching. Where the owl's corpse had been was now a swirling eddy of rapidly dispersing dust.

Freddie nudged her, making her return her attention to him instead rather than consider fleeing. He moved closer and began very gently licking the blood from her injured leg. Not all the blood was hers, but until it was cleaned away the actual injury was obscured. He was fully aware that she was now more concerned with the pain of his ministrations than the approach of their leaders. He met Drako's eyes whilst continuing to treat her injury. Drako nodded and merely said he'd speak to them in the morning.

Natalya observed the silent exchange of glances between Freddie and the bear and that the bear then nudged the faltering lion to carry on past.

'What just happened?' Natalya asked also hoping he'd talk rather than painfully wash her wound.

'Did you want them to stop and talk just now?'

'No, but how did you tell the bear, I mean Drako?'

'We've known each other since childhood,' Freddie said and resumed his attentions.

She yelped and moved away from him. 'Freddie! Enough. It hurts.'

'I'm sorry. I just wanted to be sure it was clean,' he said and began licking the blood from her face instead, not wanting her to have any visual reminders of death on her face.

Natalya watched him, knowing what he was doing and enjoying both his attention and thoughtfulness. He was wordlessly proving to her that he had no reservations about her despite the fact she'd killed a man in front of them all. She suddenly noticed his licks had become slower and rather sensual around her muzzle; he was no longer simply washing her face. She pulled away, not ready to answer his seductive ploys. She got up and each wolf followed suit. She looked around them carefully; but the huge parkland meadow was empty as far as she could see in the moonlight. She felt safe and secure knowing a wall surrounded them; that nothing could simply walk in. As Freddie had said, she'd dealt with the one threat able to fly in over these defences. The wizard couldn't fly.

'Come home,' Freddie said nudging her gently. 'You'll feel better for a good night's sleep.'

'But what of the wizard?'

'Jim knows about him. Let him worry about keeping him out. Our walls have rebuffed wizards easily enough before,' he added.

She sighed anxiously, but there was little point in sitting worrying about whether he would get in. As Freddie kept trying to tell her, she was no longer alone. The duty of keeping watch was now divided. She let him nudge her towards the village and the comfy little house he called home. She couldn't deny her need to put her head down and sleep. Freddie walked by her side and the others followed. None of them seemed to chafe at her slow limping progress. Instead, she felt they were guarding her, or maybe they always felt safer together. She remained on guard, an eye constantly roving her surroundings as she limped painfully.

'I could carry you,' Freddie offered.

'You've carried me so many times already today. It's embarrassing to be so weak,' she admitted. He simply stood silently before her and she gratefully nodded. She didn't have the strength to change into her kitty but shrinking her wolf into a cub took less effort.

The males exclaimed and gathered round her, tails wagging and instinctively even more protective of the little wolf cub in their midst.

Freddie was shocked by her all over again. He watched the others fawning over the cub noticing that she seemed overwhelmed. Her eyes locked on his and she hopped the few paces between them. She touched noses with him and he sat down flat on his belly. Her little tail wagged and her tongue swiped his muzzle gently then she was moving round and clambering on to his back. He felt the odd sensation of a warm living presence on his back, and was aware of her legs dangling down his sides. He climbed to his feet carefully, keeping his back as level as possible, trying not to tip her off. Knowing a trot would jar her, he kept to a walk. He was tired too; it'd been a very long and fraught day. She was also not as light as a real cub of that size, although considerably less than her adult wolf.

'Where are we going?' Natalya asked, clinging tightly as he climbed up the stairs in his house and walked past his bedroom along a short corridor.

Freddie nudged open a door and walked over to a single bed. 'I thought you might be more comfortable having a room of your own,' he told her and sat down.

'You made a place for me?' she asked sliding from his warm back. 'Thank you so much.' She felt overwhelmed again by his thoughtfulness and generosity. Without making any fuss he'd taken the pressure off by giving her some private space where she could relax alone.

'Have your bath. I'll get some dinner together in a bit,' Freddie offered and her tail wagged happily.

Natalya had another bath, properly ridding her skin of the owl's blood. This time she felt she could take her time soaking her aches. She unravelled her hair from its customary braid, finger combing bits of twig and briar from it that had probably been in there for weeks. She'd certainly not felt safe enough or had the proper washing facilities for long enough to bother with more than dunking her head in water. Thick hair that fell nearly to her waist was far too much bother out of its plait. Now she would wash it properly and get rid of the tangled snarls.

She caught her gashed leg climbing out of the bath and hissed. She limped back to her room and found a clean white strip of cloth draped on the bed that would serve nicely as a bandage. She wrapped her shin carefully before looking at the other item laid out on the bed. It was a pale bleached cotton dress. Cassy's scent was on it but only lightly; so she'd handled it but not worn it. Cassy must have selected it for her.

Natalya gladly shed her stained and dirty shirt and trousers and pulled on the dress. It was sleeveless and simply wrapped around so she could adjust it to fit. She threaded the thin belt through a hole at the waist and through a loop on her other hip to wrap around her and secure the flap. Just like that she was dressed in something clean and nice for a change. A wide toothed comb also sat on the bed and she almost pounced on it. She sat and slowly worked on freeing the dreadful tangles from her hair. She scented delicious cooking smells and her stomach growled. She abandoned her hair and went downstairs. She stood for a moment in the living area watching a very domesticated looking Freddie moving about purposefully in the kitchen. He went still, sensing her and turned his head. His brows raised and he turned properly. His gaze swept over her in a thorough survey and he came quickly to her side.

'That dress looks great on you,' he said softly. This change of attire into something feminine, coupled with her long hair being wet, but loose and wild, transformed her into a stunning beauty. She smiled shyly at him and he swallowed nervously. He reached out and took the comb still in her hand. He pulled a heavy lock of pale hair forward from its hiding place behind her back unable to resist touching. 'How are you feeling? I thought you'd be sleeping.'

'I'm too hungry to sleep. Can I help with anything?' she asked trying to divert his intent stare.

'Thank you but no. I'd rather you rested that leg. Where would you like to sit, here or outside?' he asked giving her back the comb.

She went to the door; the wide veranda had only one chair but the evening was unseasonably warm and inviting. From the looks of that chair he spent a lot of time out here. She sat in his chair and smiled at him. He ducked back inside and brought another chair out, placing it near her.

'It'd be nice to eat out here,' she suggested. 'We just need a table.'

'That's a good idea.' He idly wondered why he'd never thought of doing so. He hefted the small but heavy kitchen table outside and suddenly the veranda felt transformed into a comfortable relaxing living area. They ate in peaceful silence, soaking up the tranquil evening and watching each other over a flickering candle.

'You never said why you and Jim were in town today so fortuitously,' she said, once she'd finished eating. 'Were you expecting me?'

'Not at all. When Jim goes into town to order supplies for the school, someone usually goes with him. He needs someone to watch his back while he's dealing with the merchants. It's my good fortune that he happened to ask me along. Anyway, he sensed an animus pass by and we saw soldiers rushing in the same direction. We followed in case we could help.'

'Thank you for looking after me today,' Natalya said. 'I'm not sure I'd have got through it without you,' she added softly.

'Of course you would. You're strong and resourceful,' he told her trying to bolster her spirits. She was innately strong enough to be both wolf and tiger. To have become this timid appalled him; it spoke of years of physical or mental abuse.

'I was alone and cornered, but I would not have gone with the lion man. It was only you I felt I could trust,' she said collecting up their plates and hiding her face from him. She evaded his hands and hurried inside to dump the dishes in the sink. She had given herself to a stranger and she still had no idea why.

'I'm glad you did,' Freddie said having followed her.

'I can't believe I climbed into your coat,' she commented gazing at his shirt or rather the skin she could see through the open neckline.

'You surprised me too. A good surprise though; you felt very nice,' he added grinning at her.

She snorted softly then laughed.

'You should get an early night. You need to sleep.' She nodded rueful acceptance so he put an arm around her, helping her limp back up the stairs to her room.

'Thank you Freddie. Good night,' she murmured.

'Sleep well. Call if you need anything,' he added and closed her door before he gave way to the temptation to kiss her.

Natalya listened to him tidying up downstairs and then barring the door. Barely ten minutes later, he came up and went to bed. Clearly he was tired too. She fell asleep quickly, more at peace than she'd been in months.

7

# *Surprise Visit*

Amelie awoke abruptly. She lay still wondering what could have woken her so abruptly.

*'My queen. Where are you?'*

*'Stripe?'* Amelie responded in surprise. *'Is that really you?'*

*'Who else would I be?'* the dragon responded.

'Jim, wake up.'

'What?' he responded drowsily.

'I think I'm hearing Stripe. He sounds really close,' Amelie added, hastily dressing. After Jared's trick in mimicking a dragon to entice her out, she didn't plan on going outside alone, especially without Jim's knowledge.

'Damn,' Jim exclaimed and Amelie joined him at the window. Just outside on the lawn was the vast green dragon that now turned his head and looked at them directly. 'Wonder what he wants this time.'

'Only one way to find out,' Amelie responded, and hastily put warm clothes on Daisy.

'Hello Stripe,' Amelie greeted walking up to the dragon.

*'My queen. That is your youngling?'*

'Yes. This is Daisy,' Amelie responded and was surprised that Stripe reached down and gently nuzzled her baby. Daisy giggled and grabbed the dragon's sensitive nose in her fist making her parents wince in horror. 'Sorry,' Amelie said quickly as Stripe pulled free with surprising gentleness.

*'She will be a fine bold queen,'* Stripe remarked.

'What brings you here?' Amelie asked.

*'I find I am in need of your assistance once again,'* Stripe admitted. *'Tania has become obsessed with watching humans. I think she seeks to become like you, my queen. She has found a way to alter her form to one like yours. She has become human.'*

'Tania has transformed into a human?' Jim exclaimed. 'How is that possible?'

*'I do not know,'* Stripe admitted. *'She is now amongst humans where I cannot reach her without being seen. She ignores my call for her to return.'*

'Why would she do such a thing?' Amelie asked.

*'She has become rebellious. She might still be a child but queens do not have to listen to males. She would only obey a queen or her mother. She would listen to you, she always has,'* he added. *'Will you come? Now? I waited for the darkness so that humans would not see me. I can carry you.'*

'Jim, I need to go. The sooner we retrieve her, the better. Goodness knows how she thinks she ought to be acting and what people will make of her.'

'Yes. Do you want me to come with you?' Jim asked.

'No. You had an enemy attack tonight on one of the new animus people, and saw an Inquisitor squad in town only an hour away. You need to be here.'

'I suppose you're right. Just promise me you'll be careful. Are you planning on riding on his back?'

'Well, like he says, its dark and no-one will see us. I can't say as I fancy being held amongst his claws.'

'I'll fashion you a saddle then,' he offered and immediately cast a spell to tailor something to fit between the spines on the dragon's back. He also created a carry pouch so Amelie could hold Daisy securely across her chest where she could keep her in sight.

Stripe huffed a little at the odd feel of the saddle suddenly appearing on his back, but then watched closely as Jim helped Amelie and Daisy up into it, settling her securely. As soon as Jim stepped back Stripe rose to his feet, warning the little human to step back further. Then with no more ado he sprang into the air.

8

# A New Place

Natalya woke early next morning feeling surprisingly refreshed. She sat out on the veranda with a cup of tea working the remaining knots out of her hair and watching the activity on the main village street. She put the kettle back on the stove and made a fresh cup for Freddie when she heard him begin moving about upstairs. She heard him trotting down the stairs and decided he looked even better this morning, rested and relaxed, especially when he smiled his surprised thanks for the tea she placed in his hands.

'It's a beautiful day,' she commented returning outside to her seat. 'Summer feels on its way today.'

'Yes. Did you sleep well?' he asked coming to sit beside her in the early morning sunshine.

'Very well. It's so peaceful and calm here.' She watched him stretch out his legs, crossing them at the ankle. Accustomed as she was to towering over most men, she stared, fascinated by his long bare feet. Hers actually looked delicate and dainty in comparison.

'Something amiss?' Freddie asked.

'You've got even bigger feet than me!'

He burst out laughing at the absurd random comment. 'I am a man and taller,' he couldn't help pointing out.

'I said that out loud? Sorry,' she said flushing at his laughter. He shifted his chair so it was directly alongside hers then stretched out his legs again, meeting her gaze with a challenging raised brow. She copied his posture, her legs beside his. His legs were certainly longer too but she mostly noticed the warmth emanating from his leg resting against hers.

'Are you warm enough?' Freddie asked.

'Just about,' she shrugged. This dress was going to be perfect for warm days, but the early morning chill was seeping into her bare arms and feet especially. She curled her legs sideways tucking her feet under the dress on the chair seat, which helped.

Freddie abruptly sat forward and unbuttoned his shirt. He pulled it off and proffered it to her. 'Here, it's clean,' he added when she hesitated.

Natalya took the shirt and put it on quickly. It was odd to feel residual warmth in it from his body. 'Thank you. I hope you've another,' she added eyeing his bare skin. 'You're getting cold.'

He shrugged, more interested in watching her reaction to sight of his upper half. He decided she was attracted to him and it wasn't just because he'd rescued her. Her gaze kept returning to him, surveying him covertly. He happily went inside to get another shirt, his question answered.

They had breakfast out on the veranda waving at people passing. They watched Cassy come out and walk briskly down the lane towards them.

'Well you two look a picture,' Cassy remarked with a broad grin.

'Thank you so much for the dress,' Natalya said quickly.

'Let's see it,' Cassy said coming up the steps to join them. 'I wasn't sure it would fit.'

Natalya rose and pulled off Freddie's shirt so Cassy could see. She twirled making the full skirt whirl around her for a moment. She couldn't do anymore; her leg was complaining. But acting girly was fun occasionally. She stood, balancing her weight on the table top and pushed her wayward hair back.

'That looks good on you, don't you agree Freddie?' Cassy asked aware he was transfixed. He was clearly smitten.

Natalya noticed Cassy was teasing Freddie; he dropped his head, his cheeks a little red.

'Is it you I have to thank for the comb too?' Natalya asked fishing it out of her pocket.

'I didn't know if you had one and by the looks of Freddie's mop he probably doesn't.'

'Thanks!' Freddie complained. 'Cassy, while you're here could you have a quick look at Natalya's leg? She was injured last night.'

'Didn't Jim heal you?' Cassy asked with a frown. She immediately waved Natalya back into the chair and knelt down beside the bandage wrapped leg.

'No, but then we didn't really stop to chat afterwards,' Natalya admitted whilst Cassy unwound the bandage. 'Hang on; you said he could have healed me?'

'Yes, he's got quite a bit of experience with magical healing. I've only done it once on Drako.' Cassy met Freddie's gaze and thought her question, *'why didn't he heal her?'*

*'She wouldn't want him so close. She doesn't fully trust him and they did have a battle of wills last night. Jim was in*

*lion form and annoyed yet she stood her ground and made him back down,'* Freddie told her.

Cassy absorbed that, along with a rerun of the scene. It suited Freddie perfectly for Natalya to remain out of Jim's clutches; he was definitely protective of her. He was also proud of and in awe of her.

'Let's see what I can do to ease this for you,' Cassy remarked leaving Freddie's mind and putting her hands either side of the injury. She avoided being distracted by Natalya's thoughts, although only surface thoughts were visible, which in itself was puzzling. Natalya clearly had a shielded mind, unusual for an animus. Cassy frowned at her own inattention and concentrated on the painful and jagged deep gash. The lessons Amelie had imparted to her came to the fore and she let her consciousness leave her body and enter Natalya's leg by way of her hands. She searched the wound expelling small particles of infectious dirt first. Once it was clean she bathed the area in magic encouraging Natalya's own magic to grab hold and use the extra strength to heal more quickly than it would otherwise have done on its own. Just a few minutes later the leg felt right; the gash sealed smoothly.

Cassy sat back limp and breathing heavily. That kind of focussed concentration was hard work, especially when it necessitated shouldering someone's pain. She simply wasn't used to handling that kind pain or working through it.

'Thank you Cassy,' Freddie said sincerely and pulled her to her feet. 'Take my strength; you've got your lessons yet to go to.'

'I'll be ok,' Cassy objected.

'Once you've replenished yourself,' Freddie told her and took her hands. 'Drako will give me an earful for not looking out for you,' Freddie added prompting her smile. Suddenly he felt her taking his strength. He'd never get used to the weirdness of doing this.

'Thank you Freddie,' Cassy said monitoring him closely so she didn't overly sap his strength. But the temptation to fully recharge herself to the detriment of the host was always a danger a wizard had to guard against. It was so easy for a wizard to misuse their power. Draining the strength from others could be fatal to the donor.

'What just happened? Why's Freddie gone white?' Natalya asked in alarm.

'I used my strength healing you,' Cassy explained. 'Freddie gave me some of his. He just needs to rest and he'll be fine.'

'You put your strength into me didn't you? Can you put some of mine into Freddie to help him?' Natalya asked.

'Probably,' Cassy said eyeing Natalya in surprise.

'I'll be fine in a little while,' Freddie tried to reassure her. But he was secretly very pleased she was concerned for his health.

'Freddie, I've almost lost count of the times you've expended yourself for me. Cassy please do it. I don't like seeing him so pale and wan.'

Cassy nodded, understanding the need to even such a debt where possible. She took Freddie's hand and Natalya's and began transferring until both were evenly tired before releasing them.

'Thank you Cassy. That was very weird but he looks better and that's all that matters.'

'That's all that matters?' Freddie asked in surprise.

'Yes, but don't let it go to your head. Now I'm feeling better I need you to be able to keep up with me,' Natalya told him and then noticed one of the men from their pack come out of one of the adjacent houses. 'If you couldn't then I'm sure one of the pack would be happy to volunteer.'

Freddie followed her gaze to Dustin and he growled. 'That will not be necessary. I am fully able.' He heard Cassy giggle and saw her exchange a bright smile with Natalya. 'You two are going to be the death of me,' he grumbled realising he was being teased again.

Natalya followed Cassy down the steps. 'Thank you again Cassy. If there's ever anything I can do for you please ask.'

Cassy inclined her head in acknowledgement. She waved to Drako feeling him outside; he was on their veranda watching her. She took her leave hurrying up to the school before she was late for her first class.

Natalya returned to her chair finished her tea and again wrestled with the remaining knots in her hair. 'Do you have any scissors?'

'Not if you're thinking of cutting your hair,' Freddie said.

She growled at him and slapped the comb down on the table in disgust. Freddie took the comb, 'may I try?'

'It's not worth the hassle. I only keep it because mother told me once that an animus woman never cuts her hair.'

'She was right,' he said and moved his chair behind her. He patiently worked loose the birds-nest at the back then went over the rest of her hair smoothing the very long strands. He glanced up, suddenly aware they were not alone. Drako was leaning against his railings and the rest of the pack had gathered too.

'Hi Drako, didn't see you there,' Freddie admitted and put down the comb. He felt Natalya jump; she'd been all but asleep under his caressing ministrations.

'Noticed that,' Drako said with a wry grin. It was most unlike Freddie for anyone to be able to sneak up on him. But Drako knew only too well the havoc a woman could play on a man's mind if he fell in love.

'Won't you come up?' Natalya invited Drako, rising hastily to her feet. 'We can bring another chair.' Abruptly she stopped talking, looking back at Freddie. 'Sorry, this is your home,' she whispered to him.

'No, don't rush about, I've ample space at mine for everyone,' Drako said amiably. He'd noticed that none of Freddie's pack had set foot on the veranda since Natalya's arrival. Once only had they come in and that was bearing a school bed and chaperoned. He'd noticed Freddie look a little tense at the thought of so many men coming into his territory. Freddie's wolf was very much in charge emotionally, Drako suspected. Natalya swung her head again between Drako and Freddie and her hair floated round in a cloud of white.

'Freddie can't you find me some scissors? A knife would do,' she huffed, trying to part her hair so she could see.

'No. Just stand still. I'll sort it,' he told her. He swiftly plaited the top so it would be contained out of her eyes and was less likely to knot. But he rather liked seeing some of it loose. 'Is that better?'

'Scissors would have been better,' she muttered and, her back to these other men, she met his eyes. He seemed rather uncertain of how serious she was. As she'd done in wolf form she sought to reassure him. She gave him a swift kiss on his lips, whirled and trotted down the steps.

Freddie ignored Drako's broad grin, his attention on Natalya. She turned to look up at him and he hastily joined her. She was looking only at him and waiting for him. Reassured, he walked by her side, Drako beside him and the pack following.

Drako ushered them into his home but rather than go into the office he led them into his lounge. These men were the ones he knew best and had spent most of his time with, many since childhood. There was no point standing on ceremony with them; they knew each other too well, warts and all.

Natalya sat in one of the armchairs so Drako sat in the one opposite. The pack settled onto the sofa made for three, leaving Freddie without a chair. 'You could bring over one of the dining chairs,' Drako suggested to him.

'I'm ok here,' Freddie said sitting on the floor, his back against Natalya's chair beside her feet. He knew it was his wolf urging him to position himself between other males and his female. But going with his instinct meant he could relax rather than trying to fight it.

'Here Freddie,' Natalya murmured passing him a cushion off her chair.

Freddie accepted the cushion, grateful he was off the stone flag floor. She hadn't insisted he act in any other way or chided him for feeling protective. Instead she was letting him do as he pleased whilst thinking of his well being and comfort. These reactions gladdened his heart and also spoke volumes to the pack.

Drako asked about what exactly had happened the previous night leading up to the owl's death. Freddie related the story. The pack had witnessed Natalya's leap off the roof onto the flying owl's back, but Drako hadn't. Nor had any of them witnessed the owl chasing Freddie so vindictively. Freddie then went on to briefly explain why a wizard was after Natalya. None of those listening had any doubts that the traitorous owl deserved his fate. It was only right that she, as the victim, should have been the one to administer the justice. They were now anxious about what the wizard might do next. How much did he know? Had he seen any of their faces through the owl before he died? None of them knew whether the owl had just been lucky finding his quarry at the school or whether he'd known to come here. Had he come under the wizard's orders? Did the wizard know where the owl had been when he died, for instance? This uncertainty in the face of a wizard of unknown strength or character was unsettling.

Natalya suddenly flinched and growled. 'Get out of my head,' she said angrily. 'How dare you try and snoop. No, I won't calm down. If you want to speak to me I'll come up and see you. But get out of my head this instant. If you poke your furry little nose in again

I'll bloody it for you,' she added snarling. She fell back limp, the presence gone.

'What just happened?' Freddie asked then he too jerked.

Natalya grabbed Freddie's head between her hands and looked into his eyes. 'Get out of Freddie's head too,' she snapped.

Freddie blinked, breathing again, and Natalya released him.

'Well, what did just happen?' Drako demanded.

'Jim,' Freddie said simply. 'You shocked him,' Freddie added, considering the impression he'd gleaned from the powerful presence.

'Good. Another bloody interfering wizard is the last thing I need.' She glanced round; they were all watching her intently and the silence seemed to drag. 'Why won't they leave me alone?' she wailed curling on the seat and hiding her face from them. She felt hands turning and lifting her but they were Freddie's. She let him take her into his arms, felt him sit in her chair so he could cradle her against him. She wrapped her arms about his neck and hid her face in the hollow of his throat. He was warm, strong and protective; just what she needed. She listened to the men talking; Drako had a particularly soothing voice. It wasn't surprising he was a leader. Abruptly she raised her head towards the front door.

'What's the matter?' Freddie asked feeling her tension return and that she was burrowing into his shirt.

'The damn lion is coming,' she told him and searched his face. She knew no-one else had a problem with the lion man; it was doubtless just her being overly sensitive to him.

Drako got up and went to the window. Sure enough Jim was walking quickly up the lane. He wondered how she'd known, but went to open the door.

'You knew I was coming?' Jim asked noting the door open as he approached.

'I didn't; but she did. What's going on? You've scared her,' Drako said unhappily.

Jim didn't answer but moved straight inside. He stared at the woman in Freddie's arms. Her vivid sky blue eyes stared back at him directly but her mind was closed and he could see she held onto Freddie tightly.

'I'm sorry I shouted at you,' Natalya capitulated. 'I just don't like anyone in my head.'

'I got that message,' Jim replied with the hint of a smile.

'You needn't have run down here, I said I'd come see you later,' she said.

'I know.'

'So why are you here?'

'To find out how an animus woman can knock me on my backside from half a mile away,' Jim said.

'You mean me? I didn't do any such thing, it's not possible,' Natalya responded nervously.

'But you did. You knocked me out of Freddie's mind too. Again, I've never heard of that being possible.' He silently assessed her, glanced absently for a chair and realised there was no more comfortable seating. He gestured at the log pile and an armchair built itself, matching the existing pair. Jim sat down; the quick use of magic had helped take the edge off his mixed feelings of excitement and trepidation. 'You are a puzzle. But one thing is clear, you have more power and ability than we first thought. What is it you are trying to hide from me? Why is your mind so barricaded even I cannot see in?'

'Have you never thought to respect other people's privacy?' she demanded in a calm but coldly controlled voice. 'No-one wants someone else poking about in their mind without consent.'

'Granted, but you are forcing my hand. You are making me suspicious hiding so much. You blithely come here to hide, knowing exactly who the wizard on your tail is, but refusing to tell us about him. You expect me to fend off a wizard without any background knowledge that might help me?'

'I don't expect anything from you,' she contradicted. 'Like the owl, I will deal with him by myself. That had been my intention. I certainly don't expect anyone to fight my battles for me and I have not asked anyone to do so. I know when I'm not welcome,' she added springing to her feet and escaping out the door before anyone could guess her intention and try to stop her.

9

# *Battle of Wills*

Natalya ran behind Drako's house and into the woodland where she was quickly out of their sight. She ran as fast as she could, varying her course to throw them off, but heading for the wall. She checked the direction of the wind and changed into her kitty. Her dress she wrapped in Freddie's darker shirt and hid them beneath a bush before springing up the trunk of a tree. Only moments later Freddie and the pack came into view; their noses to the ground. Following were a big black bear and lion arguing.

Freddie quartered the ground near the wall. The other wolves joined him in the other areas adjacent, all searching for the lost scent.

'Found something,' Dustin called and he wasn't surprised Freddie dashed over.

'My shirt and her dress,' Freddie said clutching both to him. 'She's changed; she could be anywhere now,' he whispered.

'She hasn't crossed the wall,' Jim told him categorically. 'She hasn't had time to be far away.'

'It's your fault she ran,' Freddie snarled angrily and advancing on the much larger lion aggressively. 'You had to keep pushing and prodding her even when you could see she was already backed into a corner. What option did you leave her?'

'She's hiding something. I couldn't take any chances,' Jim said unrepentantly. The wolf rushed him snarling ferociously. The lion just managed to swipe away the attack before the wolf's teeth latched on to him and did serious damage.

Wolf and lion were very unevenly matched but Freddie was not deterred. He was furious. His hopes of love, after so many years alone, cruelly snatched. The lion swiped at him lifting him bodily into the air. Freddie was up and snarling quickly but blood flowed from his shoulder.

Dustin began howling, Rupert and Johnny joined him calling for their lost one to return.

Freddie spared them a glance, the need to join them overcoming his blind fury and fighting instinct. Something made him glance back to see the lion charging him and already way too close to evade. Bracing himself for impact he heard a strange thud.

The lion seemed to have hit a transparent wall and fell. Blood streamed from Jim's nose but he was up quickly, shaking his head then looking around carefully.

'What just happened?' Drako demanded.

'Someone put up a shield around him,' Jim said and finally he sensed the presence he was looking for. 'Come down little kitty,' Jim ordered. The unblinking blue eyes up in the tree stared at him balefully, her anger palpable. She hissed baring her little fangs at him. Jim could see Freddie's attention was completely focussed on her now. He rushed the few paces between them and flattened the wolf, pinning him down. He ignored Freddie's yelp, the wolves and Drako's protests, to stare challengingly up at her. He flexed his claws forcing a whimper from Freddie. A magical blast of force suddenly hit him. It knocked him backwards and off his feet. The tabby cat jumped to the ground and grew into a tiger.

'Don't try and hurt Freddie again,' she growled standing between the two males.

'So he is your weakness as you are his,' Jim commented now understanding why Vako had once said that about him and Amelie.

'Why do you say that?' Natalya asked irritably. 'We are not weak.'

'That wizard knows you are not simply animus then?'

'I don't know what you mean. I am a wolf; you agreed that was what I was.'

Jim simply shook his head. 'Come. We need to talk this through. I apologise for scaring you, I didn't mean to. Now I have a better idea of what you are I shouldn't feel inclined to be scaring you.'

'Good. Then I'll have no need to bloody your nose again,' she said sweetly.

'So what is she?' Drako asked realising she and Jim had reached some kind of understanding.

'Not here,' Natalya said quickly. 'Anyone could be listening,' she added quietly. The males glanced round suddenly alert and moving quickly away from the wall. She met Freddie's eyes nervously but saw no recrimination there. 'Lean on me,' she told him gently. He was a big wolf, she doubted she could carry him any distance but her tiger had a large sturdy frame and he was in need.

Freddie limped but kept pace. He was surprised that simply leaning helped take the weight off his injured leg. No one offered to assist the lion who also limped. But all he really cared about was that she was here with him. She had defended him and stopped Jim's lion in his tracks.

They returned to Drako's house in a tense silence. Freddie stood in the hall while Natalya went into the cloakroom to change and dress. When she came out the men had already done likewise and returned to their previous seats.

'Freddie you're hurt; you take the chair,' Natalya urged him.

'No, I'll get blood on it. I'll be perfectly fine down here,' Freddie responded sliding down to the cushion on the floor.

She rather reluctantly sat down to face Jim, Drako and the other three wolves.

'So what is she?' Drako asked again.

'An animus wizard powerful enough to rival Amelie I suspect,' Jim said.

'She's like Amelie?' Freddie asked.

'Not exactly. Amelie is more animus biased, so she can be any animal she chooses. Natalya has said she has form limitations but the magic side appears to be very strong.'

'I don't have a magic side. I thought that was impossible for an animus?' Natalya protested.

'For an animus it is, but I don't think that's all you are. You have demonstrated to me a number of spells. Most designed to throw me backwards and flatten me,' Jim added absently rubbing a bruise on his leg. 'But they were strong spells nevertheless. You also shielded Freddie whilst holding cat form. You weren't actually touching him or even right beside him either. That took power and considerable ability. More so than many of my experienced wizard students are able to muster. Were you taught to use your magic?' Jim asked leaning forward eagerly.

'I don't know how I did those things, although I know I did do them,' Natalya said slowly, puzzlement in her tone. 'I wasn't thinking about it; I just acted.' She glanced round aware they were all watching her intently. 'I don't remember much of my life before I was taken from my mother and went to live at the manor. Father and my little sister had already gone abroad into hiding by then; I don't know if they still survive.'

'Tell me a little about the wizard.'

Natalya dropped her head her hand seeking Freddie's hair. 'I don't like dredging this stuff up,' she told Jim, then met Freddie's steady gaze. That gaze bolstered her confidence enough to lift her head. 'His father was a wizard, a junior type I think. He used to visit my lord and they'd get drunk together. Sometimes he would bring his son. They used to place bets on how quickly the son could hunt and capture me. Like any animus I was considered vermin and only good for being a bit of sport. They enjoyed setting spell traps to paralyse or trap me in a well or force me to take over from the donkey driving the smith's air furnace. He locked me in the old grain cellar once. I was trapped there for a week. Fortunately I was found before I starved to death. And all that was before he became a man and learned other ways to torment a girl. So you see; he is hunting me for the hell of it, like he has considered it his right to do for years. If he has any redeeming features, I don't know of them.'

'Does this sadistic bully have a name?' Jim asked through gritted teeth.

'Nathaniel,' she said. 'Can you heal Freddie now?' she asked deliberately changing the subject.

'I could, but you probably could too,' Jim told her.

'I wouldn't know where to begin,' Natalya said quickly and nervously. 'I might hurt him.'

'Practice on me,' Jim suggested and pushed up his sleeve to reveal a nasty gash.

'Why?'

'I can guide you more easily if I can feel what's going on. Besides, he attacked me because of you. It's only fitting you heal us both.'

Her eyes narrowed, not agreeing with his logic. But if she could learn to heal someone it'd be a very useful skill, especially with Freddie in need.

'What do I have to do?'

'Come here. Put your hands either side of the wound. Ok, now look at it closely. Send your senses into the wound. Does it feel wrong? Compare it to the flesh around it.' Jim hissed, 'careful, you're trying to mend, not make it worse.'

'Sorry, I was seeing how deep it went,' Natalya apologised. She thought about mending the torn flesh and realised it was moving under her gaze, knitting together in their right places.

'Can you see any dirt or infection?' Jim asked quickly.

She stopped and realised there was indeed a dark "wrong" patch under where she'd just healed. She called it out, forcing the flesh to part again to allow it out.

'Stop hissing. You didn't tell me to look for that before I started healing you,' she told him. Moments later the bloody gash was replaced with a small sealed red line. She released his arm immediately unwilling to prolong contact with this wizard especially now he was no longer distracted by pain. She watched him examine the mark, probably more than superficially then flex his arm.

'Is that acceptable?' she asked.

'Yes,' Jim said trying to keep his surprise to himself. She had accomplished this healing with minimal direction. He'd hoped she would drop her guard a little and ask for assistance; but no. She also didn't seem drained doing it. But through their physical contact he'd taken the opportunity to lightly scan her mind. He discovered many oddly disjointed things in her mind. He thoughtfully watched her hurry back to Freddie.

'I need to see where you're hurt Freddie,' Natalya said softly meeting his eyes. 'Or would you rather Jim heal you?'

'No,' Freddie told her and began unbuttoning his shirt one handed.

Natalya stilled his hand with her own and unbuttoned the few he'd fastened. She gently eased the shirt off over his injured shoulder and looked him over. He had three other gashes marring his skin but they weren't as bad as the shoulder. 'I'm sorry,' she whispered ashamed of indirectly causing such pain. She glanced up at Dustin, aware he and the other wolf men had come over to see just how badly Freddie was injured. Dustin met her eyes and quickly urged the others back to their seat out of her way.

Natalya placed her hands on Freddie's shoulder and gasped at the pain he was in. She gritted her teeth against the natural impulse to let go. He was hurt; he needed her. She set to work, meticulously cleaning any trace of dirt or possible infection from the wound. Only then could she help his body to heal, to knit muscles, torn sinew and blood vessels, back into their right places. She was very relieved to feel the reduction in his pain at each step, to know what she was doing was helping and working.

Freddie watched her, awed by her all over again. Soon his shoulder felt not only healed but as if it had never been injured. But her hands remained on him, her concentration still focussed remotely so he didn't move. Then he realised he had other pains that had been covered by the excruciating shoulder injury. One by one his injuries healed and his pain eased.

Natalya sent her senses all over his body searching for pain or injury. 'You've broken a lot of bones,' she commented. She found a hard knot of scar tissue on his thigh that must have been a nasty wound and assessed it closely. The muscle hadn't knit in quite the right places and the result was a weakness in his strength and a ridge of scarring. 'What happened here?' she asked feeling the scar through his trousers.

'Someone shot me with an arrow. Wasn't easy to get the damn thing out,' Freddie told her.

'Natalya have you just assessed his whole body?' Jim asked.

'Of course. I had to know he wasn't hurt anywhere else. I don't think I can mend that old scar just now though,' she admitted. 'Sorry,' she said and now looked properly at how her mending of his body had turned out.

Freddie got to his feet and moved about assessing his body. He felt tired but fitter than he had in a long time. The injuries Jim's lion had inflicted were completely gone. 'My back doesn't hurt, nor my foot,' he exclaimed.

'I found many injuries. The only one I can't mend so easily is your leg. It's knitted together out of alignment. To sort it properly it'll have to be opened up and re-healed. That's not something I fancy trying and I'm sure it'd hurt.'

Freddie pulled her up off the floor and hugged her. She felt rather limp in his hands and he quickly sat her down in the chair. 'That took a lot out of you didn't it.' Freddie turned to Jim, 'have you any more questions just now?'

'Lots, but they can wait,' Jim said. 'She needs to rest. Natalya, will you please talk to us before you decide to run off again? We are all prepared to help you with that wizard. You know you do have the ability to never be a helpless victim again. But I rather think you could use some training. This is a school remember and you have definite wizard ability. Think about it.' With that Jim left, returning quickly up to the school.

Natalya watched Jim depart thoughtfully. She wondered if she'd ever get a handle on his personality or know whether she could trust him. In lion form he was direct and forbidding but she understood him. In human form he seemed to fluctuate between gentle and welcoming and then distrustful and defensive.

She glanced back and realised all five men were watching her.

'Do you need to sleep Natalya?' Freddie asked solicitously.

'Probably, but I've so many questions going round in my head.'

'Questions for him?' Freddie asked.

'Some, but I'm more interested in your answers,' she told him. 'Jim does not bring out the best in me,' she admitted wryly.

'Were you truly going to leave?' Freddie asked.

'I don't know. I just had to get away from him and be alone.' She fell silent feeling a wave of nausea. 'He's done something to me. I feel different.'

'Different?' Freddie asked hunkering down beside her knees. 'In what way?' She sounded lost and alone.

Natalya put a hand to her head suddenly dizzy and had to close her eyes. 'I've regained lost memories of my childhood. Knowledge and different perceptions are rushing at me and I don't know why.'

'Shall I call Jim back?' Drako asked already reaching for Cassy.

'No. I can't face him so soon,' Natalya told him.

'Cassy then?' Drako asked. 'This sounds like something you need to speak to a wizard about.'

'She's busy with her studies and she's helped me enough. I don't want to interrupt her again.'

'I've passed on your question,' Drako spoke, his voice distracted as he continued to converse with Cassy. 'She's going to ask Jim for you. She's just met him coming in and they're going to his office. Right, here we go. She says Jim thinks someone has put blocks in your mind, hiding your true abilities and memories of them. It may have been done to protect your identity and hide your ability from being found and used as a child. He thinks he may have inadvertently cleared one of the blocks.'

'Does that mean he thinks there are others?'

'Yes, bound to be,' Drako responded quickly having thought of that and asked. 'At this point he says you are likely to feel overwhelmed and unbalanced. But he thinks it unwise to release any more until you've got to grips with this first lot. Once they're all released everything should come into focus. You need to appreciate it won't make sense yet, but there's no point releasing everything; years of memories will be far too much to handle all at once. You should eat something; you're looking grey, and then get some sleep. That will recharge you, which will in turn help settle your mind.'

Natalya eyed Drako hearing his tone warm and change on that last bit. She suspected that had come from Cassy alone. 'Can you thank her for me Drako? That's been most helpful. Now I know why he ran; talk about meddling after I expressly told him to stay out of my head!'

She got up nodded to Drako and left, Freddie as always by her side. Once outside and clear of Drako's house she stopped to breathe deeply and centre herself. It wasn't easy; her mind was whirling with snatches of people and places from her childhood.

'How are you doing?' Freddie asked gently. 'What do you see?'

'I have memories of people that my gut tells me I know and love. But I don't know their names or who they are. I think one is a sister but I can't be sure. It's all so fuzzy. My senses have changed too. I come out here and I see everything differently. I feel your magic pulsing like a heartbeat. The village is a loud jumble of pulses, then I look over at the school and feel them there too, yet they have a different, higher tone. It's like many people each playing drums, at the same time, deliberately and in a way that ought to make sense, but I don't understand the melody. It's so loud and I can't shut them out,' she wailed.

Freddie wrapped his arms around her and felt her rest her head trustingly on his shoulder. 'You hear me; concentrate on me alone. That should help your focus,' he suggested. 'No one with animus hearing can take in conversations near and far at the same time. You already know how to focus and turn down the volume for that. Maybe this new sense can be handled in a similar way?' He felt her go still and tense in his arms. He held her guessing it was best not to interrupt. He needed to give her time to try and figure it out. He rested his face in her hair, breathing in her scent and enjoying the simple feeling of holding her in his arms.

Natalya felt his head lift; he was obviously looking round them, but he didn't release hold. Nor did he comment in any way that she was clinging to him wordlessly in the street. They must look very strange; at least this was a quiet side street. She kissed his cheek. 'Thank you Freddie. That helped,' she told him and noticed a rush of feeling emanating from him as a result of her kiss. She kept hold of his hand and they returned to his house and inside away from prying eyes.

'Tea?' she asked.

'Wouldn't say no', he smiled glad of something simple and mundane to think about. He stoked up the fire in the stove while she rinsed and dried their cups. Next he rummaged in his cupboard and presented a small tightly lidded wooden box with a little flourish. Inside were a stack of oat cookies.

'These are good,' Natalya exclaimed munching a softly chewy honey rich cookie. 'Did you make them?'

'No! I can cook well enough not to starve but baking's beyond me. We have our own bakery in the village. Most of it goes up to the school, but if we've something to trade then we can have some of the good stuff. Otherwise they pass out the excess or the dodgy batches to anyone appearing at an opportune time. First come first served.'

'What did you trade for these?' she asked, appreciating anew that everyone worked. She would have to find a way to contribute.

'A pot of honey. Being a bear's right hand has its benefits. Drako can't resist tracking down and collecting honey. He has a very good nose, especially for that.'

Natalya laughed with him. 'I can't imagine Drako covered in honey. He seems like a neat person.'

'Only in human form.'

'Ah. Freddie, I thought everyone had to work here. Am I keeping you from doing something?'

'Normally I'd be out hunting. But they can manage without me and I'd rather be here today,' he said, his gaze out the window returned to her. The pack, Drako and Jim too, understood his time was best spent here with their newest arrival.

Natalya followed his gaze out the window and spotted the three men of their pack dressed in dark clothing already in the distance jogging across the parkland grass beyond the village. They soon disappeared from sight. Closer to hand she watched a man hurry past and up to Drako's house. He was carrying what looked to be a heavy book and many packages bulged in his satchel.

'That's the school's steward. Let's stay out of Drako's way; he'll be in a foul mood shortly.'

'That little man is trouble?'

'No, he's just odiously nit picking and precise about his numbers,' Freddie explained. 'How can we know we will find three bags of nuts tomorrow? Or that we will be successful today on a hunt specifically for boar?'

'You don't have a storehouse?'

'The school does, but they only tend to take finished or processed things now. That little man will be asking Drako to account for every bag of grain supplied to our bakery, to prove how many loaves we've made for the school, all the fruit we've turned into jars of jam or pickle.'

'That would be annoying to someone whose word is his honour,' Natalya mused.

'You see the problem. Drako is trying to overcome his intolerance, or so he told me,' Freddie snorted.

'He does this alone?'

'Yes. We all have other work to do and he is our leader. He has always taken responsibility for us.'

'I have some small experience at that kind of work. Well, I've assisted; I could help,' Natalya suggested, but reluctantly.

'Much as I'm sure he'd love to pass the job over, it's too much too soon. We cannot ask that of you.

You need to recover, grow strong and learn to handle your new abilities. You also need to learn more about us, and the set up here, before you start volunteering. You may find there are many other equally useful jobs you'd far prefer to do.'

'You're right as usual. I just don't want to be a burden. You've all been so kind to me.'

'I noticed we were all so kind you ran away in tears.'

'There's always someone you don't see eye to eye with and end up butting heads with,' she said with a shrug. 'The rest of you and you in particular have been wonderful.'

'I'm glad we managed to do something right. Now, Cassy said you were to eat and sleep. Were those cookies enough for the moment? I need to go down to the bakery and get some more supplies and you need some sleep. It's still too early for lunch at the school so you could get your sleep now. It's your choice whether we shop and eat here later, or eat up at the school.'

'Let me have ten minutes and then I'll come with you. I'd like to see where they make such delicious things.' He smiled, made a rather courtly bow, which had her giggling, and then he was helping her out of the chair and upstairs to her room.

10

# *Revelations*

Natalya felt considerably better for her sleep, although she ruefully knew her balance wasn't quite right. Her mind was simply crammed far too full. She felt like she was juggling awkward shaped packages, trying not to let go of any one of them and have it vanish forever. Memories she didn't know she'd ever had popped in and out of her mind. Many were just fragments, parts of a scene but not enough to make sense of what was going on. The knowledge someone had gone through her memories hiding parts of them, so the sense was gone, was deeply disturbing. Who had done so, why, and what else was still hidden, was as yet unanswerable.

Freddie was outside chopping wood. She abruptly realised she knew this before looking out the window. How did she know? Someone else in the village could have been making the chopping sounds, but she'd known it was him. She stood at the window watching him. She closed her eyes, breathed slowly and deeply, relaxing herself. Impressions came to her but they were from him. She felt the hot sun burning the back of his neck, the roughness of the split in the axe handle. But these minor irritations didn't dent his happiness. She curiously explored that impression and learned how happy he was that she was here in his home. She heard his thought that she was where she belonged. It was surprisingly good to be wanted like this and she savoured the feeling. She waited until he'd finished a log before trying to reach for his mind.

*'Freddie, can you hear me?'*

The axe fell out of his hand and he turned towards the house. *'Natalya? You're talking to me in my mind?'* Freddie asked, or rather formed the question and let it sit prominently in his mind for her to see.

*'So it would seem. You've done this before then?'* she asked, trying to be casual.

*'Jim and Cassy have both spoken to me mentally,'* Freddie acknowledged, although he tried not to dwell on the shaft of jealousy he'd just felt from her. Once she wasn't sharing his mind he would think on that, savour it. *'I bet you could link us. Cassy was able to link Drako so he can talk to her and reach for her at will.'*

*'I don't know how,'* Natalya told him picking up his eager wistfulness. She also felt the memory he had of Cassy sending him her thanks once with both a

physical and mental touch. It had been intoxicating if only for a moment and very intimate. He greatly hoped to experience the intimacy of shared feeling again, but with Natalya.

*'You should fix that axe handle before it cuts you or breaks completely,'* Natalya told him and broke contact. She re-braided her hair before coming downstairs.

'How did you know about the axe?' Freddie demanded, when she finally appeared. He was more than a little unnerved.

She took his hands and inspected his palms and the red swelling of the blisters forming on them. 'Your hands were sore and so is your neck,' she admitted and had a look there too, seeking proof her senses had been accurate.

'I know they're uncomfortable, but how did you?' Freddie asked. 'You feel my pain then? Have you always been able to hear my thoughts as well?'

'No, and I can't hear your thoughts now. I'm sorry if I've offended you. You did say I should try focussing on you to learn control.'

Freddie heard the slightly defensive and hurt tone. He took her hands and led her back to the big armchair inside, settling her into it. 'I know and I meant it. You just took me by surprise. Normally whenever a wizard contacts me it's almost like receiving a blow, their presence is so loud I am always aware of them. But you didn't cause that sort of pain. They always just contact me to pass on a message. No-one's ever seemed to know or comment on how I feel physically, only mentally.'

'Maybe I'm breaking some taboo of behaviour, encroaching on your privacy.'

He shrugged ignorance of wizard rules. 'Or maybe no-one else was interested in how I feel,' he suggested. His heart lifted to see her expression clear as she nodded and smiled at him. 'Don't you like the thought of others reading my mind?'

'It's not that,' she contradicted embarrassed he could tell she'd been jealous. 'It's that no-one seems to have cared for you. I know you spend a lot of time with your pack, but why have none of you got wives or even girlfriends?'

'Maybe I was waiting for you,' he said softly.

'I'm serious; I've seen three times as many men as women so far and hardly any children.'

'There's your answer as to why we're single. We've been hunted and had to live on the run for too many years. It's hard on a woman. It's hard on the men too, trying to guard and protect a pregnant wife or small children. It's no life for them. We separated and many of the women went into hiding. Unfortunately not enough evaded subsequent capture. We live in hope some did escape and will eventually find their way to us. But we know the women were actively targeted for capture. I was lucky I suppose that I never married; I've never experienced that particular heartache. But most animus strangers we find are male. I think you were actively sought by the inquisitors because you are female, not just because the wizard needed to hire help.'

'They're determined to stamp out animus people aren't they,' she growled. 'Come on, let's go get those supplies. I don't want to sit here dwelling on such gloomy thoughts.'

Freddie was relieved and helped her up. She was clearly still tired and fairly weak. He collected his basket and they went into the village.

'What have you got to trade?' Natalya asked seeing something already in the basket.

'Another little pot of honey and some rabbit skins.'

'Glad we're not empty handed. What do we need?' she asked.

Freddie happily made note of the "we" she referred to, while answering her question. He showed her where everything was to be found, taking her on a tour of the village. He made a point of introducing her to those who either hailed him or that they visited. She seemed interested in everything, asking many questions and expressing her praise for people's individual skill and ingenuity. She laughed and joked often but kept to Freddie's side. As long as he was there, and she could keep touching him for reassurance, she was content to be amongst so many strangers. She didn't seem to notice the smiles she'd created and that followed her.

She slept for a couple of hours after an early lunch feeling far more relaxed with her surroundings. Her full stomach helped to recharge her strength.

'You're looking better,' Freddie greeted her when she finally came down.

'I feel it. You have a very relaxing home,' she said glancing about her in approval and sinking into the one comfortable chair. 'Oh, you don't have two of these do you. Were you sitting?'

'Relax, I was working on a hide outside when I heard you moving about.' He took the boiling kettle off the stove, poured the water into a pot to steep and set out cups. He took their tea outside to the table on the veranda. Whilst he bade her sit, he returned to stretching and working the hide pegged out on a frame.

Natalya watched him closely and decided this softening process was hard work. She drank her tea quickly then got up. 'Let me take a turn while you drink your tea. I take it this is better if it's not stopped part way through?'

'Yes, but are you sure? You don't need to,' Freddie said quickly.

Natalya took the pot of stuff he was working into the leather and the tool from his hand. 'Freddie, your shoulders and back are aching from this. Sit and take a break.'

Freddie dropped into the closest chair and watched, guiding her on technique. 'I don't often have a chance to actually cure or tan the hides I get but they're worth more to trade if this work has already been done. As you can see, it's slow, hard work. Thank you for giving me a hand,' he added. She simply smiled at him and carried on. He sat and watched her, completely unused to having someone to share work like this with. The other men might help out if one of them was injured, but otherwise what each did with his kills was up to them. She shifted position and he saw the section she'd just been working on. 'Have you done this before? You're making a good job of it.'

'Not this particular job. I didn't often have to work at the tannery, but I learned some of the things you needed to do.'

'I've finished, I can take over now.'

'No need, this'll be done in a few minutes anyway.' She noticed his surprise and acceptance of her help. He didn't sit back idly though while she worked, instead, he collected a bundle of sticks stacked against the wall that was separate from the firewood. With a sharp knife he began stripping the bark and twigs off them.

'What are you making?'

'Arrows; you can never have too many when you're out hunting every day. I've already straightened these sticks and they've dried reasonably well. I try and reuse the points as long as possible,' he explained noting her frown at the small basket of metal points; many were the worse for wear, some even going rusty. Another job was going to be cleaning off the rust and sharpening them again. He only managed to finish two arrows in the time it took her to finish the skin.

'I'll strip the bark, wax the shaft and nock the end, if you do the cutting to size and fitting of the points and feathers,' she offered, even while he continued twirling and gluing thread around to fix feathers in place.

'Sounds good to me,' he said cheerfully and handed over the knife and pot of wax to seal the bare wood. He watched her prepare the leafy twig into an arrow shaft; she was deft, followed his guidance and turned out a very acceptable shaft. They worked in companionable unison for the rest of the afternoon until they'd used up all the spare points and had made an ample supply.

Natalya stretched cramping fingers and shoulders, watching Freddie pack the arrows into three quivers. The afternoon was nearly over, the light dimming over the wide open meadow. She wistfully gazed at the meadow and secret forest so close by. She went inside shimmered and became her wolf. She stepped out of her clothes nudging them onto a chair. She glanced up as Freddie came in and noticed just how quickly he dumped what he was carrying. He stepped behind the big armchair, removed his clothes swiftly and changed into his wolf too. They touched noses then were off, bypassing Drako's house to veer into the woods behind.

The wolves ran side by side enjoying the freedom and space to run, particularly when they could share it. In this form their human consciousness receded, freeing the wolf to fully use its eyes, nose and ears to soak up their surroundings. The wolf instincts, playfulness and character dominated the human; an animus usually loved this freedom and simplicity of living.

The meadow was somewhere to run but also to roll about in the sweetly scented spring grass. A fallen log was a prop to leap up and pounce from. Trees were for playing hide and seek and darting away behind. Their spirits were high and they played like puppies.

Freddie returned his consciousness to the fore feeling new and very intensely pleasurable sensations. He was shocked to discover their wolves were mating. Whilst this was a perfectly natural thing, since she was in season, they were not truly wolves. He had no idea if she actually wanted this and all its potential repercussions. He searched his wolf's memory of what had triggered this. He needed to know he hadn't forced her in any way. He didn't realise his angst had stilled his body's movement. He also didn't realise that his lack of motion had pulled Natalya back to the fore of her wolf's mind too.

Natalya too was shocked. She reached for his mind and felt how aghast yet excited and exhilarated he felt physically. He certainly hadn't planned this. He was remembering her wolf's body language turn coy and inviting. His wolf had immediately responded; eager to claim his mate. She had encouraged his wolf to come closer and finally mount. Damn.

'Leave your wolf alone,' Natalya said quietly. 'I know we didn't plan this, but don't ruin such a beautiful moment.' As far as she was concerned, they had gone too far to stop. She felt his relief and that he tried to push his worry into the background. He let his wolf take over again and the shift in his mind was quite marked. Then he began moving again and she gasped. She relinquished her own mind up to her wolf, letting her come forth to fully appreciate her mate's beauty and relish their joining. The knowledge came to her that her wolf was satisfied she'd finally found a mate worthy of siring cubs! To a wolf, life was that simple, to a human it was not necessarily. She wasn't sure she was ready for a child; she'd not given it any thought whatsoever.

When the male parted from his mate Freddie regained control. He felt deliciously sated and his wolf was delighted to have claimed such a fine female. But Freddie the man was anxious about her reaction. He sat down in a patch of soft grass without saying a word. He really had no clue what to say. She followed him, sat down leaning against his warm side and fell asleep. Freddie was rather relieved and sat keeping watch over her.

Natalya woke slowly. Her body felt a little tired and sore; well she'd been working hard this afternoon on unaccustomed tasks helping Freddie with his chores. Freddie sat beside her and she laughed at herself for immediately associating that with safety. She rubbed her face against his shoulder affectionately, but her wolf's sudden smug satisfaction startled her. Her wolf imparted the knowledge that they hadn't come together casually in a fit of animus passion. Her wolf had chosen her mate from the first instant they'd met as wolves and howled together. Now she had claimed him and what's more, he had accepted her claim.

'Have we missed dinner?' Natalya asked, glancing about at how dark it now was.

'Not if we're going up to the school, that's in half an hour,' Freddie responded watching her.

'We'd best hurry then,' she said and quickly trotted off.

'We should talk,' he suggested keeping pace by her side. Her steps faltered then she carried on but faster. She bounded up the steps and into his living room.

'Please don't run from me. I'm so sorry,' he added painfully.

She could feel conflicting emotions pouring out of him as he fought with his wolf. Freddie the man might be appalled he hadn't asked and be ultimately terrified that she would reject him. But his wolf rejoiced, didn't comprehend thoughts of wrongdoing and indeed rejected the concept. The female had been inviting and could have walked away. She hadn't rejected him then, why would she now?

'I'm not running from you, but your thoughts have become very loud,' she warned him.

'You can hear what I'm thinking?' he asked appalled.

'Some.'

'It's my wolf confusing me,' Freddie growled in realisation.

She nodded, realising it was clouding her ability to think too. They both changed back into their human forms. They stared at each other mutely trying to comprehend the enormity of what their wolves had just done to their relationship.

The way she was staring at him pulled him to her side.

'Clothes,' Natalya told him weakly. He felt more predatory now as a man than he had as a wolf! Her gaze travelled over his bare skin again; he was unbearably attractive. Unfortunately he seemed to know she felt that way.

'Are you sure you want clothes?' he asked softly, taking the dress she held up before her like a shield.

Her wide eyed innocent stare and breathlessness called to him. He wrapped his arms around her pulling her against his body. She felt exceedingly good skin to skin and he closed his eyes for a moment to savour the feeling. Her head was tilted back to watch him and he couldn't resist kissing her. Her body melted against him as eager to match itself to his as his was to explore hers.

'Freddie, no more. Please stop,' she whispered breathlessly and pressed a hand to his chest parting them.

'Why? I would feel better for you in this form,' he whispered.

'I know,' she couldn't help admitting. She closed her eyes to his raw need and desire. 'But it would be too much too soon,' she told him particularly since she now knew from her wolf that she was in season and already running a high risk of pregnancy. She resolutely picked up her dress from the chair and dragged it on. She could see his disappointment and reluctance, but he was slowly following suit and dressing. He clearly had no intention of forcing her to do anything against her will and her estimation of him rose even further. She escaped upstairs into the bathroom, away from him and temptation.

'Are you ready to go?' Freddie called up the stairs a few minutes later, having calmed down somewhat. 'We need to leave now to be there in time to get a seat.'

She opened her door and trotted down. His gaze swept her and she was glad she'd had a quick wash and dressed properly. It almost felt like a shield against his tempting sexuality. She'd put on his shirt under the dress knowing it would be cool this evening and letting the long sleeves and collar show only. Thus the man's shirt was disguised under the feminine dress enough not to look too peculiar.

They jogged quickly across the grass taking a short cut. They were wolves; even in human form, they could run swiftly without effort.

Freddie guided her through the crowds that were milling to chat with friends before taking their seats. She was aware of being stared at, but she expected that, she was a stranger here. Freddie took her to a table near the back wall, far from the head table. Glancing at the head table, she met the deputy's eyes. Max smiled a welcome to her so she relaxed enough to sit.

'Hello Freddie, haven't seen you up here for a while. Who's your friend?'

'Kathy meet Natalya,' Freddie introduced. 'You're both wolves.'

'Pleased to meet you,' Natalya said rising to take the other young woman's hand. She'd thought there weren't any female wolves here.

'Was that you howling the other day?' Kathy asked her, immediately sitting opposite.

'Well, he started it and then the others joined in and I couldn't resist,' Natalya admitted glancing sidelong at Freddie. So much had happened since then.

'It was wonderful to hear,' Kathy said warmly. 'This is Laurence,' she added as a young man approached, dragged out a seat and sat beside her.

'Welcome,' Laurence said. 'Is it true you are like Amelie?'

'I haven't met Amelie, but I've been told we have some similarities,' Natalya admitted with a shrug.

'We went scouting the forest with Amelie once,' Laurence said. 'She was in panther form and damned scary.'

'And that was before you saw her change into a dragon,' Kathy teased. They shared a laugh and both eyed Natalya speculatively. 'So you can be any animal?'

'No, my ability is different. I stick to four legged carnivores.'

'Freddie said you were a wolf, how do you know that, if you can be anything?'

'Jim told me that was what I was. He had me change into a number of animals and said my character was wolf.'

'Unless you're feeling defensive, in which case your tiger comes out,' Freddie commented.

'So your power animal is a tiger,' Laurence mused, 'interesting.'

Natalya looked round, feeling a heavy presence; Jim was entering the room. She put her head down and brought a shield up.

Jim paused in the doorway feeling the massed wizard presences and the occasional animus people. An odd space humming with power caught his attention. Curious he turned, weaving through the tables to the source of the odd feeling. He noticed Freddie first, which considering Natalya was a tall striking woman with cascades of white blonde hair, that was unexpected. She was the source, as he'd suspected. She was seated with her back to him, but turned to face him, clearly fully aware of his approach before he had a chance to speak.

'Interesting shield, Natalya,' he commented. 'Come see me after dinner,' he asked, saw her nod in acknowledgement and moved off to the head table.

Natalya sourly watched him go. 'We should have stayed at yours,' she told Freddie.

'If he has something to say he'll seek you out wherever you are,' Freddie responded. 'Besides, I could do with a good cooked meal and you're skin and bones.'

'Thanks!' Natalya responded drolly. Then their attention was fully diverted by the platters arriving on the tables before them.

While their first course was taken away, the young man on Natalya's other side turned to her.

'Hello, I'm Jasper,' he introduced himself. 'I'm sorry but I couldn't help hearing Wizard Jim mention you were shielding yourself. What kind of shield?' he asked curiously. He'd shaken her hand so it clearly wasn't a physical boundary.

Natalya considered him for a moment; he was harmless looking and shy, but a wizard. 'A mental shield. He knows I don't like people snooping. I'm still learning to control my magic. I thought it better to lock people out rather than risk hurting them by throwing them out.'

'You threw Jim out of your mind?' Jasper asked in astonishment.

'So he told me,' she admitted with a shrug. 'He was being annoying. I thought after the run-in's we've had so far he'd get the message and avoid me,' she added to Freddie quietly.

'He hasn't managed to best you and bring you to heel,' Freddie told her.

'That's an odd thing to say,' Kathy commented. 'Why do you think that?'

'Because he keeps provoking her to anger. It's quite deliberate. I've never seen him act that way,' Freddie explained.

'He'll be testing and pushing you to reveal your character and limits,' Jasper suggested. 'He does that to a certain degree with everyone.'

'I'm fed up with being poked and prodded,' Natalya complained. 'I'm tired.'

'I know,' Freddie pacified gently.

'You must have a lot of power for him to take such an interest,' Jasper suggested. 'Unless,' he mused, his gaze drifting over a very attractive young woman with piercing eyes.

'Unless what?' Natalya asked.

'You are like him, an animus wizard. You're also an attractive woman,' Jasper observed. 'Of course he would show interest,' Jasper noticed Freddie's sharp glance and clenched jaw and tried to hide his smile.

'Whatever his reasons, I daresay I'll deal with them as they arise,' she said with a shrug of disinterest. But she took Freddie's clenched fist and stroked it. His unease vanished and no one was in any doubt their feelings were mutual. She continued her meal as though Jasper's observation was of no relevance to her and Freddie took his cue from her.

Everyone else within earshot did too, guessing this was a touchy subject, best dropped in her presence. The talk quickly turned to innocuous gossip instead. One of the new women had turned out to be troublesome, taunting one of the men into fighting with someone else over her.

Natalya was very glad the fight between Jim and Freddie had been kept secret. That would certainly be food for avid gossip. Jim was the headmaster; he couldn't be seen to be fighting. That a wolf animus would even attempt to fight a lion animus was foolhardy, but knowing that lion had wizard abilities to call on too would be considered desperately one sided.

'Do you want to stay here while I go talk to Jim?' Natalya asked Freddie softly under cover of the students dragging their chairs out and departing.

'Why?'

'I don't want you two scrapping again.'

'Don't try to protect me,' Freddie told her, annoyed now that she thought him a liability. He was an Alpha wolf, damn it! 'I need to know he's not mistreating you.'

'I know. I was only giving you the option. You know how irritating he can be and some of it was directly aimed at you. He's jealous of you,' she told him with a small smile. They rose and together went over to the head table.

'Hello deputy Max,' Natalya said and put out her hand.

Max rose and took the offered hand rather surprised she was choosing to touch him.

'I apologise if I was a little rude at our first meeting,' she continued. 'It was not intentional.'

'I understand you had reservations learning I was an owl. Well founded distrust given the nature of the one hunting you. I hope you don't hold my form against me?'

'Not at all,' she assured although she had. She released his strong hand hastily. His gaze was direct and assessing but friendly. He felt like someone you could count on. She found she wasn't surprised Jim had chosen him as a deputy for a place as big as this.

'This is Bruno, he teaches physical combat,' Max introduced the man beside him.

'Pleased to meet you,' Natalya said assessing the burly man and easily accepting his hand.

'And this is Vako, also a teacher,' Jim said, smoothly coming in to the conversation. They all noted she regarded Vako for a moment but did not take his proffered hand.

'Will you be joining our classes?' Vako asked her smiling at her reticence.

'I haven't decided,' Natalya responded unnerved by the old man's sharp gaze; he was obviously another wizard.

'You probably should. It's difficult to tell how your magic manifests itself most strongly though when you are so shielded. But the impenetrable nature and strength of your shield is an indication you have plenty of magic. You should learn how to use it before it gets out of control and hurts someone.'

'You've been trying to get past my shield?' she asked angrily.

'No!' Jim assured her hastily. 'You would feel it if anyone tried that, you know you would. What he means is that we can see your shield like a wall. We don't have to try and breach it to know it's there. And just like an actual wall we can see yours is tall, seamless and strong. Normally a wizard would only construct and hold such a shield under concerted attack. You must be exhausted.' He glanced at Freddie, hearing his mix of concern at her health and anger that she should feel so threatened.

'Why do you feel so threatened here?' Vako asked proving he'd also heard Freddie's angst.

Natalya glanced round at Freddie for a moment. 'You're snooping on Freddie now,' she complained drawing him protectively behind her. 'You wonder why I don't trust you wizards when I can see you using everyone around you without their permission or knowledge.'

'We weren't snooping,' Jim denied. 'He was broadcasting, very loudly. We couldn't help hearing him, just like you did.'

Natalya scowled, knowing that was correct but not hearing any denial of her claim they were using those around them.

'Natalya we don't use people like you're suggesting,' Jim hastily added, noticing her expression. 'This is a school with a whole range of gifted people. To teach effectively we need to find out what each pupil is capable of. This is not only to tailor our teaching but also so we are aware of anyone with potentially dangerous abilities or indeed inclinations. We are obligated to safeguard all our pupils, even from each other. Freddie has never been a pupil. He hasn't been taught how to contain strong emotions and not broadcast them. Since he is generally a calm responsible character we've never thought it necessary to teach him. You on the other hand make us all very nervous. We know you've been hunted by a wizard with not only inquisitor assistance but also by a particularly savage and twisted owl animus. How you evaded them we still don't know. You can multi shape shift but only into very capable predators. That inclination would not normally be a problem but does not help calm us when you are so secretive. When I tried to contact you mentally your first reaction was to treat it as an attack. You knew it was me yet you retaliated in a most unexpected way. Not only did you throw me out of your mind, but somehow you were able to physically throw my body back too. I still don't know how you did that and from half a mile away. You healed me and then Freddie whilst holding on to that shield. I don't know how that's possible, yet you've done it. Really Natalya, I don't think you have anything to fear from us. You are very strong and resourceful. I doubt anyone could force you to anything against your will. Please, we promise we will not attempt to snoop, but we need you to drop that shield so we can see your aura and discover what you are. We cannot help you if you refuse to trust us to such a degree.'

Natalya turned to Freddie, evidently to his surprise. But he was still her anchor and the only one she actually trusted. She waited for Freddie's advice; he knew these people. Freddie nodded but took her hand squeezing it gently for reassurance.

Natalya watched Jim closely as she lowered her shield. He flinched and breathed deeply. Vako more obviously reacted by sitting bolt upright in his chair, his eyes wide.

'I see why you needed to develop such a strong shield while you were on the run,' Jim told her. 'Your power signature glows. You must have had some kind of shield up the entire time you've been here? I'd have felt such a presence from miles away.' He glanced at Vako helplessly.

'She is a true warrior wizard,' Vako announced.

'She's not an animus warrior wizard then?' Jim asked a little confused.

'No, that's what Amelie is. Natalya's animus ability is rooted from her survival instinct which also governs her warrior. But her gift is wizard. Amelie is biased on the opposite side being animus first and wizard second. Both of you are astonishingly strong and equally rare.'

Natalya felt Jim's emotions were raw with longing hearing Amelie's name. But for the first time Natalya saw a few images of the woman before Jim got control of himself and closed off. It had been enough of an eye opener though. Natalya abruptly slid to the floor as her mind once again was swamped in images. More fragments linked up and short scenes floated past. She was vaguely aware Freddie was lifting her into his arms and settling her across his lap instead of leaving her on the cold stone floor. She could feel his concern and rush of anger, wondering if one of them had caused her collapse.

'Jim, I think I may have seen your lady before. Show her to me,' Natalya asked holding out her hand.

Jim was deeply concerned at the way she'd collapsed into herself so suddenly. She'd also never sought to touch him before. Obviously she was aware it was easier to share minds doing that. He took her hand, keeping his shield up but letting many memories of Amelie surface into his more public upper thoughts. Suddenly images began to be passed his way in return. Natalya was showing him memories of two little girls playing on a beach. One was blonde, the other girl dark haired, but both with vivid blue eyes. Their parents called and he saw a blonde father and black haired mother. He focussed more intently on the dark little girl; Amelie!

'Amelie is your sister,' Jim exclaimed. 'No wonder there are so many similarities between you. You're the older one?'

'I think so. Why would my mother hide these memories from me?' Natalya whispered, suddenly knowing that was who had done it.

'Perhaps so you wouldn't give her away if you were questioned. Or maybe it was to keep your magic from surfacing fully and revealing itself unwisely. I suspect such power as yours could not be hidden entirely. The duress you suffered as a child brought your survival instincts to the fore but appeared to everyone as animus ability only. That's what would have been of most use to you. You have changed though in the last few days. When I found you in that town I didn't feel such power in you. You were obviously a strong animus but that was all I sensed at the time. Normally I'm pretty sensitive to things like that. I think that as your memories have begun to surface, so too has the ability to use your magic, together with the magic itself. I think your mother has done a remarkably successful job of hiding your ability from notice.'

Natalya considered that. Yes, her mother would have tried to protect her.

'Mother was the wizard and father animus. I know that yet I still can't remember their names,' she cried in frustration.

'I cannot release another block just yet,' Jim told her gently. 'It's too soon and will be more than you'll be able to deal with in one go. You've already had a huge breakthrough. You need time to sleep on it and learn to handle it. You're exhausted. I suggest you call it a night and turn in now.' Jim said in dismissal and watched Freddie take her hand and lead her out.

'She is Amelie's older sister? Well that explains a great many things. Her power rather puts you in the shade,' Vako added to Jim.

'I know. I just hope she doesn't realise too quickly. I'd rather get her on side first,' Jim admitted. 'You might remember I told you I knew that I wasn't especially strong. Well, not unless I'm borrowing strength from other people. It stands to reason we'd come across stronger talents running a school as we do.' He then dismissed everyone and returned to his doubly empty quarters having been reminded his family were off somewhere without him.

11

# Wayward Children

Amelie looked back but Jim was very quickly lost to view in the darkness. The school's lights faded from sight and then they were flying over the perimeter wall and passing over forest. Stripe's huge wings carried them with effortless speed and she marvelled at being on his back. She was riding a dragon! How many people could ever say they had done that? She tucked Daisy, in her carry sack, properly inside her coat to better protect her from the wind and was glad that her daughter was quickly asleep.

She eyed Stripe's huge but graceful form. She had loved being in dragon form. Whilst she enjoyed learning to use her magic and having friends, after spending years alone in a dungeon she valued her freedom and seeing open sky too. Life was simpler as a dragon, with no worries over what others thought, obeying new rules or fitting in. Tania would have much to learn if she wished to pass as a human from time to time. The main question was whether a dragon either could, or was even prepared to, learn human ways. They were undoubtedly intelligent, but could be arrogant, believing in their superiority. Humility and accepting orders was not one of their natural traits! The dragonets had been endlessly entertaining and she had missed watching them grow and develop. On the few occasions Stripe had called on her for aid, she'd been astonished each time at how much they had all changed. Clearly dragons developed into independent individuals at a far younger age than humans. She had not been there when they learned to fly either, which was a major milestone for a dragon.

*'Are you alright, love?'*

*'Jim! Yes, we're perfectly fine. He's looking after us. Look through my eyes. Flying like this is wonderful.'* She shared her view of the moonlit forest rushing past beneath her, the peaceful silence around them and Stripe's powerful wings driving them forward.

*'Rather you than me,'* Jim admitted. He didn't like heights much and just watching the treetops slip past made him queasy. However being able to so closely watch a real dragon flying was an experience in itself once he could step back from his own discomfort and view it objectively. He was quite happy to experience it second-hand. *'I'm glad to hear you're both ok.'*

*'Yes, Daisy's asleep even. I'm glad you thought of this saddle though; I feel a lot safer having something to hold on to,'* she added, feeling him still there with her and

sharing this experience. She knew it reassured him greatly to know for sure she was not in danger and that Stripe was taking care of them.

*'Let me know how it goes; if you can. You know, it's already getting harder to share detail; you must have travelled a hell of a distance already,'* he remarked a little uneasily. *'I thought you'd be there by now.'*

*'I did too. Distances feel different when you can fly them. Don't worry, we'll be fine. I'll let you know if I can't get back tonight,'* she promised and sent him a quick burst of affection that he reciprocated before disconnecting contact. She absently patted Stripe's neck and the great head tilted, an eye looking back at her.

*'Your mate worries?'* Stripe asked.

*'Of course. Could you hear us speaking?'* it suddenly occurred to her to wonder.

*'Certainly. I know your voice and your body touches mine.'*

*'Ah, proximity. Is it much farther yet to travel?'* She'd forgotten that since dragons naturally spoke to one another mentally, that sense was particularly developed. Close proximity helped the clarity of the connection and actual touch meant a private conversation was possible. She heard the slightly flirtatious tone to his words and knew he had also noticed her enjoyment of flying with him. Since they

touched she wondered what else he might have picked up from her mind.

*'No. We should arrive close to dawn.'*

*'In just a few minutes then? Good, I'm getting cold,'* she responded. The sky was no longer as dark and the still night had given way to a cold wind, which also signalled the turn of night to day.

*'She is there, my queen,'* Stripe said and projected his vision of the village, so far below them, for her.

The dragon's rapid flight made the gusty wind whistle past and caused Amelie's eyes to tear. She blinked and looked again in astonishment. She could just make out the shape of a tiny village on a hillside way below them, marked by a thin plume of smoke. Stripe could see far better than that and in astonishing detail. He could identify the shapes of penned animals and a few people moving about, even at this distance. *'It's best they don't see you. Land on the far side of the hill. We'll walk closer,'* she suggested. *'Those trees will provide cover for us.'*

Stripe found a clear enough spot to land and she slid from his back. *'You need to rest, my queen,'* he suggested curling around her where she stood partially beneath the wide canopy of a mature oak.

*'You don't want me to go straight to Tania?'*

*'She yet sleeps. There is time for you to refresh yourself.'*

*'Well in that case, I shall sit down for a few minutes,'* she responded gratefully and dared lean against Stripe's side. His body provided both windbreak and exuded delicious warmth that her chilled body appreciated. Before she realised it she'd relaxed and fallen asleep, having missed much of the night's rest.

Amelie peered through the bushes down the slope to the bustling village below. It was a very small village with only five houses gathered around a well in the muddy central square. Its inhabitants were obviously poor, yet moved about purposefully, some tending geese and pigs in their pens while others were busy digging over and planting crops in walled vegetable plots.

She noticed a skinny teenager staggering out of a shed on the far side with a heavy burden in his arms. He placed it on top of the neat stack already there against the shed wall and she heard a metallic clang. Ah, so this was why the village was here; there must be a mine nearby. She now realised the smoke and hot acrid smells were from smelting. Those must be ingots of whatever metal they mined here. On the other side of the shed, stood a squat building, its waterwheel turning slowly in the small but swiftly flowing stream. Perhaps they used the waterwheel to power the bellows for the forge or other smelting equipment. She was curious about what they did here exactly and could see why the villager's constant outdoors activity had attracted the inquisitive Tania.

Stripe lay on his belly beside her, his head partially pushed through the dense vegetation that concealed his huge form. It helped that he was naturally a dark green and so blended with the trees and foliage he sat amongst. She pushed her hair back yet again somewhat irritably. He always insisted on being physically close and his breathing in her ear was blowing her hair around and into her eyes. On the upside, his proximity was helping to warm her. The flight had sent a chill right through her and then she had fallen asleep outside and before she had warmed up properly. She still shivered. Spring was not a good time of year to be sitting outside on a damp windy hillside.

His glinting emerald eyes seemed intently focussed on the village, but she realised he was also watching her and Daisy. The weak sunshine gave his scales a silky sheen. She idly wondered whether polishing would turn them shiny and bring out the colour. Then she ruefully shook her head; no, she was not going to volunteer! There was a great expanse of scales covering this dragon. His head alone was as long as she was tall! Having said that, maybe she could bespell a yard brush to scrub him? The errant image of a broom chasing after this dignified and serious dragon would definitely be fun to watch!

*'Thank you for agreeing to come. I wasn't sure you would wish to help.'*

'I watched your children hatch and take their first steps in the world, Stripe. I might not be their mother but I cared for them at their most vulnerable. I still feel a connection,' she admitted. 'I'd never have guessed this shape-shifting you say Tania has done was at all possible.' She considered him, now able to appreciate that the magic he possessed was comparable to a strong animus or indeed a wizard. She had always assumed that, like an animus, a dragon's magic was structured for specific tasks and therefore of limited alternate use. If they could change form that rather begged the question of what else they might be capable of. 'Goodness knows what kind of mischief she's got up to already amongst humans. You were right to call me.'

Stripe very gently nuzzled her cheek with his soft nose, expressing his thanks and appreciation, before returning his attention to the humans moving in and out of sight amongst the buildings below them.

She'd been sitting in the grass watching for quite some minutes before the right child finally came into view.

'Tania,' Amelie exclaimed under her breath.

*'How do you know that is her?'* Stripe asked. *'I sense she is close, but her form thwarts my perceptions somehow.'*

'Do you see any other children with blue hair?' Amelie responded. 'That might be a natural colour for a dragon, but it is not for a human. She will be drawing a lot of attention and it could become hostile.'

*'Hostile? They would not harm a child, a female child, surely?'*

'Humans are plentiful and unpredictable; they are not always kind to one another, particularly to someone they consider unusual.'

*'They are territorial?'*

'Yes, especially in lean times. However, most people will tolerate a child trespassing because they understand a child does not understand or always recognise boundaries. However, they will expect the child's parents to come for her without delay.'

*'What aren't you telling me?'* Stripe demanded. *'There is some danger I'm not aware of, isn't there?'*

'Human males are generally stronger than the females. It is their role to protect their family,' she said and Stripe nodded. 'However, they do differ from dragons in that they do not automatically revere or obey their own or any other female. Some males have been known to covet and even attack an undefended female. They are not all like that of course, but few men would allow their mate to place herself in the reach of unknown males, especially with such a young baby.'

Stripe growled in disgust. *'Your mate knows these risks yet he did not accompany you here.'*

'Jim knows how protective you are. He trusts you and expects you to keep me from harm,' Amelie explained and Stripe stopped growling.

*'Yet you had planned to go down there without me and without even hinting there might be some danger to yourself.'*

'I am not entirely helpless. Besides, what could you do? It'd be nice if you could walk down there with me, but only Tania has worked out how to do that.' She stood up and headed for the village, aware of Stripe's frustration and feelings of inadequacy. Both emotions were foreign to his nature.

Stripe watched his bold little queen stride down the hill, her long black hair blowing in the wind. She was so small, yet her courage was undeniable. When Tania noticed her, she ran to wrap her arms about her. Their affection for one another was clear. However, before they could take more than one step back towards him, other humans intervened and he could only watch as his females were led away and into a den where he could no longer see them.

*'What is happening? Why are you not returning?'* Stripe demanded.

*'The people who have been looking after her wish to meet me and Tania seems to have a need to show me everything. She is asking me questions about everything she sees,'* Amelie added.

*'She knows I am here waiting?'*

*'Yes. Unfortunately, now we're both here, she feels safe enough to linger. We are being watched too closely to speak freely and she is not thinking of guarding her words. If we*

*argue she is bound to forget herself entirely and reveal something we don't need these people to know.'*

*'Please be careful,'* Stripe urged.

*'Hopefully her curiosity will be assuaged soon and we can leave without fuss.'*

Stripe wasn't so sanguine and settled down where he could continue to watch the village, prepared for a lengthy wait. Tania always questioned everything and demanded answers before she would even consider moving on. She was not alone in this, her brothers and sisters were equally curious, but she differed from them in her fascination for anything human. He almost jumped up when at last they came into view. However, they did not leave the village, although Amelie looked up towards him. Resignation and weariness was in her body language and Stripe growled. Tania was going to have a lot to answer for.

*'Come Tania, you've dallied long enough,'* he ordered. A small growl was his only answer.

As the afternoon wore on the sky darkened early with heavy clouds. He scented not just the approach of rain but a substantial storm. He growled; they needed to leave. He recalled Tania's taunt that she could do something he could not and that he was too scared to even try. Yet it was Amelie's disappointment that he couldn't accompany her, which filled him. Unfortunately, he had no idea what Tania had done to accomplish her transformation. If he knew how he would do it. He ground his teeth in frustration that he could not simply walk down there to retrieve them.

*'My queen, a storm approaches. We must leave.'*

*'A brief storm?'*

*'I feel dense pressure building. Come quickly.'*

*'She is ignoring me in favour of eating and it's not a pretty sight. Where can we go?'*

*'We will rejoin the others of course.'*

*'Ok. What of her siblings? I assume they don't yet know about this?'*

*'I thought it unwise to mention it.'*

*'Are you prepared for the effects seeing her changed form will have on them?'*

*'What do you mean? Once we have her back she will stop this silliness, revert and all will be well.'*

*'I'm not sure if she knows how to revert back to her dragon form. If you take her back like this you won't have just one confused child, but several. Surely it's better to wait until she is back in her normal form before you return her to the others. It rather looks like she is going to need help with that.'*

Stripe watched her step outside the door and look skywards just as the first of the rain began to fall. Other faces appeared at the door and windows and Amelie hastily returned inside. The rain quickly grew heavier and then turned into hail.

*'I cannot take Daisy out in this.'* She gave a small sigh of frustration listening to the pounding on the roof. *'Stripe, it's probably best you return to look after the others and leave Tania to me for the time being.'*

*'Are you certain? You will not be defended if I leave,'* Stripe reminded uneasily.

*'I am not a weakling and so far the people seem hospitable. However, the rest of your family is entirely undefended at the moment is it not?'*

*'True, but none are as prone to trouble-making as Tania. They will be just where I left them.'*

*'Go to them. They need you too. I know you've taken shelter under a tree, but you'll soon be leaving tracks in the mud that these villagers will find and be worried about later.'*

*'Very well. I will go to them. Once this stops I'll bring them closer so I can come to you quickly if you have need,'* Stripe declared.

*'Thank you,'* Amelie said seriously and only because she knew where he was and had particularly keen vision did she see him take off and leave in the pelting hailstorm.

Now she was in sole charge of a young baby whilst keeping control of an opinionated dragon that looked like a ten year old girl, but had blue hair, no social skills, no table manners and was agog at things that should be commonplace to a human of that age! Fabulous! Jim was not going to be happy either.

12

# *Good Ideas*

It took Natalya the best part of a week to sort out and learn to handle her new memories and most importantly her magic. She had had an odd encounter once or twice up at the school and now avoided it and its wizards. Cassy explained that she was "loud" and inadvertently giving off something like a static charge to anyone sensitive to magic. To a wizard it proved she was not fully in control of her magic. Such raw power in inexperienced hands made people uneasy in her presence. Fortunately, as far as Natalya was concerned, animus people didn't seem bothered by it. Many could feel it but weren't affected by it. Even so, upsetting people bothered her.

Cassy came and spent some time each evening helping her figure out how to gain control of her magic. Jim might have taught her more quickly but she preferred Cassy's slower and less critical approach.

Cassy helped her find a way that worked for her rather than try to impose a rigid set of rules. Progress was slowly made until Cassy announced she was no longer broadcasting dangerous vibes. Only once she had basic control over her magic could she realistically join classes. Lessons were complicated and dangerous enough when even wording a spell incorrectly could be disastrous. A warrior wizard had far more power than everyone else and so it was critical she kept control or the possibility of serious accidents was amplified.

***

'Can I come with you hunting today?' Natalya asked Freddie a little tentatively. She'd been sending him out daily, refusing to let him hang around the house unproductively just because she had to. Everyone needed all the hunters to be actively gathering food. She had been contributing by skinning the animals he brought home and cleaning the hides, but otherwise she felt rather useless. She made sure he had food to take with him each day and cooked each evening. She also gathered suitable sticks to season ready to make into arrows. She fully understood his preference to make his own ammunition and take care of his weapons. His life depended on them not failing at a crucial moment. She least of all wanted something to fail him through her own shoddy or inept workmanship when it could cost him his life. Few of the creatures they hunted were without defences. Boars and stags might be herbivores but they would charge and kill a predator threatening them if they could. What allowed her to sleep when he went out day after day was the knowledge that whilst he hunted in human form, he could always become a wolf. He was not without resources to fall back on.

She had been spacing her chores needing to rebuild her strength. But time sitting still was not idle. She needed quiet time to reflect and try to make sense of the memory fragments crowding her mind. The lessons Cassy was attempting to teach her required thought too.

'Can you use a bow?' Freddie asked.

'Not yet. I was hoping you would teach me.'

'How did you hunt before?'

'My tiger is pretty useful.'

'Yes, I suppose it would be. Trying to sell meat or hides with big teeth marks isn't going to be easy though. Nobody wants to eat something that looks like it's already been gnawed!'

Natalya laughed at his dry tone, but understood what he was saying. She knew he was assessing her seriousness; what they did was dangerous. However, if that was really her wish, he wanted to be the one to teach her the skills of the hunt. Between him and the rest of the pack, she would learn from the best.

'We've some time before the others arrive,' Freddie said, coming to a decision. 'Let me give you the basics and see your aim.' He was definitely curious to see what she might be capable of. He picked up his spare bow and second quiver and led her outside and into the field. He showed her how to stand and watched to see if she could draw this bow. It was designed for him, not a woman, but she was tall and strong.

'I think you'd do better with a less powerful bow. That one is too big for you really, but I suppose it'll suffice until we can make you one. Ok, see that old rotten log? We'll use that to target on. That's it, hold it up and keep it steady. Draw it back level with your mouth so you can sight along the arrow. Release when you're ready.'

'Now I know why you've got such powerful muscles,' she said eyeing his shoulders, arms and chest, appreciatively. She'd only pulled this bow a few times but already her shoulders ached. It was an unfamiliar exercise but she persevered until she could hit the log consistently. She glanced round feeling other presences; the pack was watching. Damn.

'Does anyone have a smaller bow?' Freddie asked them. 'She's using my spare and it's too big really.'

'I still have my old travelling bow,' Dustin suggested. 'That's a small bow and now I've this one I don't use it anymore. Just a minute,' he added and hurried off.

Natalya went to collect the arrows she'd fired while they waited for Dustin's return. She knew she would then have to try out the new bow and was slightly uncomfortable with an audience of such experienced men. She was rather glad of the chance for a rest; her shoulders were stiff and aching. But by the time Dustin returned she had collected all the arrows.

Freddie watched her, he couldn't help it. He knew the others laughed at him for his preoccupation but they all wished they were in his shoes with such a girlfriend. He took the arrows from her, sliding them back into the quiver on her back. He then put his hands to her shoulders and gave her a quick massage before handing her Dustin's bow.

'Thank you,' she said softly; he had eased her tense muscles surprisingly effectively. 'Oh, this bow is a lot easier,' she exclaimed and let fly. Her accuracy was far better with this bow too. 'This is a nice bow Dustin, thank you for letting me borrow it,' she told him examining the well tended wood. It showed many signs of hard use and age but felt sound. 'What's the verdict Freddie? Would you prefer me to stay here and practice with this? I don't want to be a liability on a hunt.'

'Obviously you need more practice but I doubt you'd be a liability. You've already learned to hunt as a tiger. Shooting at standing targets isn't going to teach you to hunt for real. If you'd still like to come, then by all means, join us.'

She planted a kiss on his cheek happily. 'Just a minute then, I'll fetch our lunch.'

'You've changed,' Freddie commented when she reappeared. He surveyed her rather worn and ripped trousers and shirt. They were the clothes she'd come in. He ruefully realised she had no others and he'd forgotten to show her where she could get replacements. At least they were now clean.

'Well, a white dress and white hair aren't very useful camouflage,' she told him aware he was staring at her headscarf and general scruffiness in dismay. She stepped out onto the veranda and saw the others waiting by the steps.

'Now you've all looked me up and down you can tell me if I've forgotten anything?'

'Your bow,' Dustin suggested mildly, his gaze switching between her and Freddie.

Freddie took the bow from the table and showed her how to detach and then restring it properly. She was then shown how to carry the bow safely in its special carry sleeve. She copied the way the men carried their quivers on their backs and tucked her own dagger in its sheath at her belt. She handed Freddie the small belt pouch with his travel rations. He couldn't help his smug grin at his fellows that she was so obviously taking care of him. Then they were off jogging across the meadow to the small people gate on the far side that led into the forest.

'There's some kind of spell on this gate,' Natalya observed, as Freddie opened the gate.

'Yes, Jim mentioned triggers so he knows when anyone passes through our defences,' Freddie told her. 'Wonder if he's awake yet,' he added for although they were leaving a little later than usual it was still very early.

'You wake him at dawn every morning?' Natalya asked in glee.

Freddie grinned back at her. 'Wait for it,' he smiled in anticipation as the five of them passed through the gate.

Natalya took his hand, 'can I listen?' she asked and he nodded. 'Here he comes,' she warned feeling a searching presence target Freddie.

*'Is that you Freddie?'* Jim's voice was definitely sleepy. *'Who's with you?'* he asked, his tone sharpening. *'Five of you have passed through the gate.'*

*'Good morning Jim,'* Natalya sent back on the link he'd made with Freddie. *'It's too beautiful a morning to lie in bed,'* she told him, now having seen the green dappled trees ahead and feeling the urge to run free in the forest. She felt Jim grab her image, wistfulness to join them apparent.

*'Much as I understand the impulse to run with your lover Natalya, are you sure it's wise? Whilst we haven't heard anything more from your pursuers, they probably haven't forgotten about you.'*

*'Did you sense me?'*

*'No, you must be shielding again?'*

*'Yes, but only lightly. You did say a strong shield was what drew you before. The main thing I needed to know was whether you could sense me. If you can't, then wizards are unlikely to be able to either. In that case I'm in no more danger than anyone else out here.'*

*'Very well,'* Jim acceded heavily. *'Freddie I'm relying on you to keep alert for anything that doesn't smell right. The inquisitors are conspicuous by their absence. I want to be sure you are all on the lookout for traps designed for an animus. Good hunting,'* he added and vanished.

Freddie passed on Jim's warning to the others. Only when Jim felt there might be real cause for concern did he actually say anything. The hunters had been the ones to find and flag many threats. Since they'd settled here permanently they were now a non moving target for their enemies to discover. It was only a matter of time.

'Let's go north into the old forest,' Freddie said. 'We haven't been that way in a while and it should be safer. Rupert you take point,' he added. They strung their bows and with Natalya in their middle began jogging swiftly into the trees following Rupert.

Natalya ran beside Freddie or followed him depending on the terrain. Despite their swift pace they made very little noise. When they came across a small stream Freddie called a halt. Natalya glanced at the men realising it was only for her benefit they'd stopped. None of them said a word as she caught her breath. 'Do you catch fish as well?' she asked seeing some small ones here.

'Not usually. It takes too long sitting in one place. We prefer to grab something as big as possible and get home,' Dustin told her, coming to look at the fish she'd spotted.

'Is there a lake in the grounds?'

'We thought about creating a small one in the second village but mainly settled on a cistern for water. Why?'

'It'd be a useful food source to catch and stock a lake to ward against hard times,' she suggested.

'Those aren't worth eating,' Dustin pointed out.

'True, but there were bigger ones in the moat. Does anyone breed captive animals? Or must you hunt from the wild everything you need to eat?'

'Jim asked us to keep chickens and so the school bought some. He likes eggs for breakfast I believe,' Freddie said. 'The bakers need eggs too and they're useful creatures. The school has a few cows for milk, but that's about as far as we've got. None of us have the coin to buy domestic animals. What had you in mind?'

'If we could capture deer or boar for instance, they could roam the grounds, breed and we'd always have their young to eat and something to trade.'

'But we'd be out of a job.'

'Nonsense, there will always be a need for other meats and supplies. But it might take the pressure off you. Well, once we manage to catch enough to start a big enough herd.'

'I like it,' Freddie admitted. 'I for one would love to be able to spend more time at home when I need to. We also run the risk of not only being caught every time we go out, but also leading our enemies to our door. So, my dear how are we going to capture and get an undamaged wild creature back home with us? They aren't likely to want to co-operate, you know.'

'I'll have to think about it,' she admitted. 'Just find some animals I can practice on.'

'All that sounds like a challenge,' Dustin commented. 'But well worth pursuing I suspect. The last time we had to stay home because of wizards too close for comfort we ran our stores very low. They didn't stop us hunting for many days either. I like the thought of live animals in the park to fall back on or for when it suits us. Are you working on a spell to catch something?'

'Yes.' She glanced up feeling a small heartbeat; a pheasant sat concealed high up in the branches of a tree. '*Sleep,*' she commanded pointing at the presence.

The men felt the small spike of magic and heard a thud. Rupert brought the pheasant over to show them, but it was dead.

'Was the spell too strong?' Dustin asked.

'No,' Freddie said, handling the still warm bird. 'Look, it snapped its neck falling out of the tree.'

'Never mind, this'll be nice for dinner tonight,' Natalya suggested and tied the feet of the bird together so she could drape it over her shoulder.

Freddie brightened considerably at that prospect and they jogged on.

Eventually they did find a herd of deer. They were only fallow deer rather than the larger red deer but they were big enough to be worthwhile.

Natalya came to the fore quietly. She could clearly see the watchful stag so concentrated on him. Using a subtle mental push she urged him to become sleepy. She watched the stag shake his head irritably at first, but then he slowly sat down and went to sleep. This was far less stressful for him and calmed the herd. Seeing her spell was working she widened the area it covered to those closest. Unfortunately only two does were close enough to capture, the others were more spread out. One further doe came to nudge her stag uncertainly and fell under the spell's influence.

Freddie crept forward seeing four were down; the rest of the herd promptly ran off. They lay sleeping apparently peacefully. But a large number of small birds, reptiles and insects littered the ground around the deer. The men picked up a number of small birds gingerly, took them a few paces away and watched as they revived and flew away.

'I'm starting to feel sleepy Natalya,' Freddie told her in alarm having been close beside the deer assessing them whilst the men took care of the other creatures.

'Ooops, sorry. Stand clear and let me figure out how to change this spell without them all waking up and escaping.'

'How are we going to get them back?' Dustin asked Freddie quietly. 'We can't each carry an adult deer all the way back. It's a hell of a distance so laden, especially if they start to wake up.'

'I don't see much alternative,' Freddie said chewing his lip. 'I was thinking of going back for a horse and cart. I'm not sure a cart could get here though. There isn't a trail wide enough. Having said that, maybe all we need to do is get them out of the rough forest to somewhere a cart can take over.'

Natalya heard them and considered the problem. She was floundering, not sure what was or wasn't possible. The thought of each man having to carry a whole deer through a forest for miles was daunting to say the least. It would be easier if she could get them to walk. She moved over to the stag and rested her hand on the warm coat. It was very strange to reach for an animal's mind, it was so different to a human's yet there were enough similarities for recognition.

Under her prompting the stag got to his feet blinking blearily. Keeping contact she was able to urge the animal to walk.

'That's amazing,' Dustin said excitedly. 'Can you get these others to walk as well?'

'Dustin, give her a chance,' Freddie reproved him. 'That might not be possible. It will certainly take a lot of magical strength,' he added in concern. 'We might all have to pull together to carry this off.'

'How do you mean?' Natalya asked in confusion. 'I'm the only wizard, kind of anyway.'

'I've helped Cassy power spells when she needed more strength. Drako has too. We can't initiate them but we can help if you'll let us.'

'It's not that I don't trust you to be able to help, you've already helped me more than you'll ever know. I suppose Jim's right; I need training before I'll have any clue of what I'm doing, or how to use your strength. I'm at a loss.'

'Ok explain to me what you're doing,' Freddie coaxed.

'I went into the stag's mind and asked him to walk and not be scared,' Natalya explained.

'Ok,' Freddie said, 'and these others? You must still be controlling them too because they haven't woken and run off. Is it safe to approach them yet?'

'Yes. I have targeted the does specifically so nothing else should be affected by the sleep command. It's less tiring to narrow the field as it were.'

'You are amazing,' Freddie couldn't help exclaiming. 'Ok, so you've already reached and have command of the does and without touching them. Can you ask them to walk?'

'Possibly, but I can't guide them all,' she added anxiously.

'Will they follow us? We can take one each. We thought that's what we'd have to be doing anyway. But if we don't have to carry them I'm all for it,' Freddie added, kissed her cheek and motioned for the men to take position beside each animal.

The deer walked, the men at their shoulder leaning or tugging to direct their steps.

Natalya directed the stag having finally thought to implant the suggestion in the does to follow him. That way they were less inclined to want to veer off in random directions. They still required assistance to avoid natural hazards and that fully occupied the men.

Freddie went ahead checking the way was safe and finding the clearest route. But he was concerned at their slow pace and the inevitable drain on Natalya, having to hold a difficult spell for such a prolonged length of time.

'Can they go any faster?' Freddie asked once they'd come out of the old densely forested wood and the way was less congested.

Natalya frowned in concentration and her stag began to trot. The others were more ragged in reacting to the change of pace. Some rushed forward overly fast, threatening to overtake the stag, whilst others lagged at the walk and only reluctantly increased their pace once prodded. There was mayhem with each reacting differently and too blind to know and avoid running in to each other.

To Freddie it proved just how tired Natalya already was. He watched her scowl at each beast in turn, forcing it to her will. 'I think it might be wise to call for some assistance before you exhaust yourself completely,' Freddie suggested now running by her side.

'You mean call Jim?'

'Yes. I know you're not happy dealing with him but he can and would aid us,' Freddie told her, deliberately reminding her she was not alone in what she was trying to do. 'I'm also worried that wizard might be able to feel this spell and come for us if we linger.'

Natalya knew he was right but she didn't have to like it. 'You expect me to keep all these beasts running, watch my own feet, as well as try and reach for Jim? I've never done that before you know. I'd rather be still and able to concentrate.'

'I know, but try it. You saw what happened when you changed the spell last time. Take my strength,' he offered.

'I don't even know how to do that. I'm completely useless.'

'No you're not,' Freddie told her and came close enough to take her hand. 'Can you feel my magic? Can you take some?'

'I feel it but I can't figure out something like that whilst doing all this. It's too much.'

'Call Jim then, right now,' Freddie ordered. 'If you won't then I'll shoot these deer. Your health and safety is far more important to me than theirs.'

'Bully,' she muttered. 'If I'm to do this you'll need to take over guiding us. I can't do everything you know.'

'Yes you can,' he told her but came close enough to hold the deer and overlap her grip on it. 'Ok, now call him.'

'I tried but I don't think I can do it,' Natalya told him miserably. She stumbled then as a presence latched on to her mind.

*'Natalya, was that you whispering in my ear?'* Jim asked.

*'Yes. I didn't think I'd managed to reach you,'* Natalya told him. *'Freddie says we need some help.'*

*'What the hell are you doing? You're a shadow of your usual self.'* Jim absorbed the startling images she sent him and realised that even as they conversed she ran merged with a stag. *'Let Freddie take over powering the spell on that stag. The others can do the same for their animals.'*

*'How? I didn't think an animus could do spells.'*

*'They can't initiate but their magic is real and when they're in human form they're not using it. Right, where's Freddie?'*

*'I must warn him,'* Natalya objected instantly, her gaze turning to him.

*'Attached to you as usual,'* Jim muttered. *'Well that makes things simpler.'* Whilst she hastily told Freddie that Jim had plans for using his magic, Jim explored her spell. He transferred the power from her to Freddie then cut her out of it entirely.

Freddie gasped at the very strange and essentially physical blow that landed on him, courtesy of Jim. Both he and the stag stumbled, feeling the lurch.

*'Is he coping?'* Jim asked her.

*'I think so, just.'*

*'Good, go to the next man and link with him so I can detach you from that one,'* Jim told her.

Natalya hastily told Dustin what was about to befall him. The link with Jim buzzed at her. She was aware that Jim was mentally calling someone to ask for his horse to be saddled, while he waited for her to get into position with Dustin. Dustin then became responsible for his doe. She knew Jim had already hurried out of the house and down to the stables. He only paused to link each hunter to his doe.

'Jim's just come through the people gate and is on his way to us,' Natalya announced. The men had slowed the pace, definitely feeling the strain. At least knowing Jim was on his way was reassuring. Natalya's strength was almost gone, but she guided Jim to them. She also helped the men as they flagged, or if they let their spell slip and she had to act quickly to reinstate it before the animal woke. Certainly the animals weren't as far under as before and were thus more troublesome. But the men were able largely to keep hold and control their charge's wayward steps.

Jim crested a small hill and stopped. Approaching was a most startling sight, even though he'd been prepared for it. Four men each had their arms around the neck of a large wild deer, one of them a magnificent stag, and were walking with them as though the deer were tame. Few horses would walk as tamely without a bridle. Natalya walked on the other side of the stag to Freddie. She looked like it was only her arm around the animal that was keeping her upright. Jim hastened to meet them and instantly pushed each animal into sleep.

'Thanks for coming Jim,' Natalya said looking up at him. Her legs had folded along with the stag's.

'I thought you'd gone out today with the hunters to hunt something? You're meant to kill these things rather than have them kill you,' Jim chided. 'Can I ask why?'

'To start our own breeding herd,' Freddie responded. 'They can live wild in the grounds and be a reserve for times of need. We thought it a good idea, but were a little too successful in the numbers we captured.'

'I see. You were planning to bring them all back alive?'

'If it was possible. We thought it'd be easier to have them walk, rather than carry them the whole way,' Natalya told him.

'Yes, you have a point; they do look heavy,' Jim conceded. He watched her dig in a pouch at her belt and bring out a sandwich. Her hands shook but she ate unaided. Freddie followed her lead, eating a very similar looking sandwich. The other men ate if they'd remembered to bring something. They all began to look better for the food and rest. But whilst they rested

Jim held the animals under the spell alone. He couldn't give them the full time they needed.

Jim helped Natalya to her feet. 'Are you ready to get going again?'

'No, but we need to,' she conceded. 'How are we going to do this? You can't run the whole spell all the way back.'

'You take the horse Natalya. Freddie you go ahead and check the way is clear. Fortunately this spell isn't a loud one, but if a wizard is nearby he could sense it. Using animus magic to help power it has helped dilute the wizard signature and help spread the load. Men get into position with your deer,' Jim instructed. He took Natalya's hand, merged them and let her know how he'd done that. He then set to work with their combined strength setting each man to power the spell on his own deer. Jim took control of the stag, broke physical contact with Natalya and urged her onto his horse. Now both he and Natalya were beside the men they could help power those spells reducing the load.

Natalya grimly held on, providing her strength where necessary. She was glad she didn't have to walk; guiding the horse in her weakened state was taxing enough. She glanced back at Jim and realised he was having more difficulty with the stag than she had.

'Why do you think that is?' Jim asked her, aware of her observation.

'Your eyes have gone yellow as they do when your lion is close to the surface. The stag probably senses your lion and that would of course make him uneasy.'

'He might feel my lion even when I'm in human form?'

'Why not? You're touching his mind. He will feel the predator in you,' she explained. She felt Jim make an effort to suppress his lion character. It was difficult, because his lion always came to the fore under duress and these spells were taking a great deal of strength. It surprised her he was so willing to accept her advice, although the stag did become calmer after that.

It seemed to take forever to reach the walls and finally enter through the People Gate. Freddie closed and bolted the gate behind them. 'All secure. You can release them now.'

Jim cancelled the spell with a sweep of his hand. The men stepped back from their deer just as the creatures showed signs of waking. They watched in silence as the tiny herd bolted away across the grass, clearly none the worse for their unusual experience.

The men however collapsed in the grass. Natalya slipped off the horse to join them. Jim sat with them, sapped of his usual great strength.

'We'd better spread the word that these are not for hunting,' Freddie said. 'It'll be most annoying, after this effort, to find someone's gone and shot them.'

'Too true. I'll tell the school if you can spread the word in the village,' Jim said glancing at each of the men so they would all take responsibility. Natalya had curled in the grass and fallen asleep. He wasn't surprised she slept only that she had just here and out in the open.

'Thank you for aiding us,' Freddie said formally.

'Calling me wasn't her idea, was it?' Jim asked. 'She certainly implied that from the outset.'

'It doesn't matter who the idea came from; she knew I was right that we needed assistance.'

'So she really didn't want to call me?' Jim sighed. 'I'd hoped her call meant she was starting to trust me. Clearly I was wrong.'

'Actually I think you're right,' Freddie contradicted. 'She has spent a lot of time with Cassy. She could have called her instead.'

'Cassy would have struggled with this spell. It was hard enough for me,' Jim admitted. 'Your Natalya is very strong, but these hair-brained schemes are going to be her undoing if she's not more careful. All wizards have their limits and until she learns the boundaries and what is and isn't possible she may be a danger, not only to herself, but those around her.'

'You mean she needs training?' Freddie clarified.

'Yes. She's like a child that's been given a razor edged sword to play with and is only supervised by other children. Accidents are inevitable and unfortunately you wouldn't necessarily be able to tell when she was heading for one.'

'I understand,' Freddie said shortly. 'I'll speak with her.'

Jim nodded, knowing when a subject was closed. 'Do you have a link with her?'

'No. Why do you ask?'

'You're no longer broadcasting. In fact you appear to be shielded,' Jim told him and noted Freddie's surprise and quick glance to the sleeping woman beside him.

'She's done that then? She's not powering a spell on me is she?' he asked, suddenly worried.

'She's created it for you but you're powering it. Don't worry; it's only a very small shield, similar to what we wizards use for mental privacy. That's very unlikely to sap your strength.'

'That's a relief to know. So you can't read my mind?'

'I could but only by breaking your shield. You would certainly know if anyone tried to do that. This kind of shield prevents accidental or casual snooping, as she puts it. Finding one tends to remind a wizard they are trespassing.' Jim glanced at Dustin and noticed he was watching Freddie idly stroking Natalya's hair. 'You're shielded too!' Jim exclaimed, then looked more closely at the others. 'All of you have mental shields. She has been busy! I see what she thinks is a priority. Any idea why she's done this?'

'On a few occasions wizards have told me my thoughts are sufficiently loud that they don't need to be searching my mind to hear what I'm thinking,' Freddie said slowly, whilst thinking it through. 'She seems to want to protect me,' he added cheerfully. 'I suppose that while that wizard is out there and inquisitors as well, giving all of us shields will stop them reading our minds without us knowing. She's given us a small defence against them.'

'That does sound like her,' Jim conceded. 'Anyway I'd better get back to work.'

They watched him catch his straying horse and canter back up to the school's stables.

'How is she?' Dustin asked once Jim had gone.

'Exhausted, but I'm sure she'll be fine after some decent rest and food,' he added, glancing at the dead pheasant wistfully. 'Guess I'm cooking tonight.'

'She's been cooking for you too?' Dustin asked with shock. 'You have a warrior wizard beauty stuck indoors slaving over a hot stove for you? No wonder she wanted to come hunting instead. Don't you remember she's not only a big capable wolf, she's a terrifying tiger and a wizard as well?'

'I know. I suppose she makes it easy for me to forget that bit. She's so considerate and is always doing things for me. It's hard not to enjoy being looked after. My problem is that she doesn't want us to think she's a burden. She wants to help pay her way and earn her share. She fears we'll think she's too much trouble and force her to leave.'

'For pity's sake Freddie, marry her. You can't let her slip through your fingers.'

'I've no intention of letting that happen, as you well know. But it would be wrong of me to demand such a decision and commitment from her yet. She's barely been here a fortnight. That's too soon for any relationship.'

'Are you having doubts then?' Dustin asked in surprise.

'No. I fell for her from the first moment I met her in human form. I didn't even know she was a wolf at that point and then our wolves howled together.' He sighed heavily. 'She's a powerful warrior wizard. Any day now she's going to start her training to be a real wizard. I cannot do spells nor understand wizard magic. She will leave me behind.'

'Freddie?' Natalya said drowsily. 'What's wrong? What's upset you?' She was wrapped in his arms, his face buried in her hair. She could feel echoes of strong emotions coming through his shield.

'Nothing's wrong,' he assured her, disgusted with himself for waking her. 'I'm sorry to have disturbed you.'

Natalya looked around them, wondering what had distressed him. The pack sat peacefully in the grass beside them, all present and unharmed. No-one else was nearby. She got to her feet slowly and took his hand. 'Are you going to tell me?'

'It's nothing,' he said evasively.

'It didn't feel like nothing. It felt like you were in pain.'

'I was being silly and scaring myself,' he admitted, 'over something that might never happen. I'm just letting my fatigue get the better of me. Can you walk? You'll rest more comfortably at home and if we're going to enjoy this pheasant any time soon I need to get it prepared for roasting.'

She let him drop the subject, not having the energy to pursue it. Freddie had said enough however, for her to know he worried about the future. What aspect she didn't know but she would find out. Right now all she could think of was making it home. The knowledge a soft comfortable bed awaited her and the promise of roasted pheasant later spurred her on.

The men followed, all exceedingly tired. But they had succeeded in bringing home the core of a new breeding herd and that was a considerable achievement.

13

# Close Ties

Cassy walked up the lane and saw Natalya on her veranda working on something. 'Hi Natalya, where's Freddie?'

'Hunting; I didn't think I ought to inflict my presence on them two days running. I heard they were complaining up at the school that we'd failed to bring home a kill. They didn't consider those deer a success, just because we decided not to kill them. They were moaning too that Jim said no-one else could shoot them. Someone told Freddie he should have found something else to put in the meat locker if we were going to do something weird like this!'

'Yes, I heard that. Some people are so blinkered. They fail to see the need to plan for the future,' Cassy remarked, falling into the chair beside Natalya. 'Congratulations on them by the way. I think it's an excellent plan to farm deer. We have the perfect place here for it.'

'I thought so,' Natalya added glancing across the wide meadow where any number of herbivores would thrive. 'So, are you finished for the day? It's early isn't it?'

'I've just got a free lesson. The others are learning something Jim already taught me. It's nice to have a couple of hours added to the lunch break.'

'What of Drako? Are you meeting him?' Natalya asked casually but observed Cassy's gaze turn unseeing, and a small smile cross her face before she returned to the present. 'You've just spoken to him?'

'Yes. He's grouching now at having to work when I've got time off,' Cassy laughed. 'How does Freddie feel about you putting your feet up today?'

'I don't know,' Natalya shrugged. 'He never says anything.'

'I know he's short of words sometimes but surely you know how he's feeling?'

'No, not unless he says or does something to tell me; I don't pry,' Natalya added a little defensively.

'I know that, I just thought that since you two seem inseparable and you're actually living in his house, you'd have established a link with him. You haven't then?'

'No,' Natalya responded, rather shocked by Cassy's surprise that she hadn't yet done so.

'Doesn't he want one?' Cassy asked, fairly sure he would.

'He did mention it, but it was pretty well the first day we met! It wasn't remotely appropriate to be thinking of,' Natalya said. She guiltily recalled she'd shut him off at that point, not at all liking the thought a stranger could view her mind at will. Doubtless he remembered her reaction and hadn't wanted to risk upsetting her again.

'I remember when Jim first mentioned the possibility of linking with someone,' Cassy said. 'He likened it to making love. You either trust that one person enough to share your body or you don't. It's the same, if not even more important, with your mind. A link is private; no-one else can listen in, if that's your worry.'

'Freddie and I aren't lovers. I've had some bad experiences. He might not want to be linked with me.'

'You don't honestly think Freddie is the kind of man to run because you've had a difficult life. He isn't likely to be so easily put off. It's clear to all of us that he has strong feelings for you.'

'So what made you decide with Drako?' Natalya asked hastily, diverting Cassy's train of thought.

'I didn't plan it. We'd only just met properly that afternoon. I'd been in love with Drako for weeks but only dared approach him the first day I saw him in bear form. His bear is cuddly, warm and approachable. He knew I'd designed his house; well the interior anyway, so he was keen to talk to me. But then we got caught in the side effects of Jim changing into a lion for the first time. He was broadcasting raw power and it affected every woman nearby. I just couldn't stop myself cuddling up to the bear, touching his beautiful soft coat. But worse, I ended up talking to him mentally, telling him the kinds of things you don't put into words; things that are reserved for lovers. Needless to say it was awkward meeting him in human form later that night after the spell had worn off. He didn't know whether what I'd told him was simply spell induced. I shared his mind to find the truth of his feelings, then hearing his fear of rejection I bade him follow my presence in his mind and his link to me was made. Once we'd done that so early in our acquaintanceship he became exceedingly keen on me. He pursued me, or he would say he courted me, rather single-mindedly.'

'You resisted his advances? Why?'

'He's an animus leader of a hunted people and an experienced warrior. I'm just a junior and insignificant wizard. There were many reasons to go slowly from then on.'

'Something prompted you to make the link that first night. What was it?'

'He kissed me, seriously kissed me and urged me to look into his mind to prove the sincerity of his feelings. I also saw how scared of rejection he was and how nervous he was that I might not truly feel the same way. Without thinking I lowered my guard and suddenly he was reading me as though he was a wizard. That's all it took to create our link.'

'So you didn't plan it; but you did love him,' Natalya mused. 'Have you ever regretted letting someone see your deepest thoughts like that?'

'No, I trust him. We understand each other and our relationship is wonderful as a result. Yes, it took a little adjusting to, initially. He was essentially a complete stranger to me at the time and we certainly didn't live together in advance like you and Freddie. Don't you ever want to know how Freddie's feeling? Or know if he's hurting?'

'Yes, the temptation's always there. I reached for him once when he was chopping wood. Luckily I thought to wait until he was between logs because he dropped the axe. He was immediately aware of me. But it seemed to freak him out that I could tell he was getting sunburn on his neck and blisters on his hands from a split in the axe handle. I haven't really tried again.'

'That's the kind of detail you get, but it's only one half of a link,' Cassy told her, a little shocked by the level of detail Natalya had been able to gather of Freddie's physical state when they weren't properly linked or even touching. But then again Natalya was strong in her magic. 'All you need to do is just do that again and ask him to follow your presence in his mind.'

'I need to discuss it with him first of course,' Natalya said. 'He's animus, he may not be comfortable with or want something like that.'

'So ask him,' Cassy challenged, knowing Natalya feared letting down her guard mentally and that such distrust was unhealthy.

'Now?' Natalya gulped, knowing Cassy was watching her closely and hating to feel cowardly. *'Freddie, can you talk?'* Natalya called mentally, but quietly, trying not to startle him.

*'Natalya? Is everything ok?'* Freddie responded instantly, letting his words sit clearly for her to see.

She felt him halt, explaining in a quick aside to his men why he'd stopped. *'I'm interrupting your hunting,'* she apologised quickly. *'We can talk tonight.'*

*'I'm listening, tell me now.'*

*'Cassy's here. She said I should ask you if you wanted to link with me,'* Natalya said in an embarrassed rush.

'Didn't you tell her you know I do?' Freddie responded.

'You mentioned it once when we first met but haven't suggested it since. You're animus; it's not a usual thing. You seemed upset when I touched you that time you were chopping wood.'

'Natalya, you took me by surprise, but you know how I feel. Unfortunately I am animus, if I could have forged this link I would have tried to already. You keep so much from me. I assumed you hadn't done it because you didn't trust me.'

'I do trust you.'

'Then tell me how it's done,' he urged.

'Are you sure you want to try this?' she asked uncertainly.

'Yes. Tell me.'

'You're supposed to reach for my presence in your mind. That's all I know.' She felt him immediately act and a warm presence blossomed in her mind for a moment then was gone.

'I'm coming back,' he told her. He told his men Natalya needed him and with no further explanation he began running.

'He's coming home,' Natalya told Cassy. 'He's growling yet running.'

'Did he make contact?' Cassy asked, hearing Natalya's confusion.

'Only for a moment. He's never growled at me before.'

'Did you put up your shield to block him?'

'I don't know,' Natalya responded uneasily, that thought not having occurred to her. She looked inwardly and groaned miserably; that's exactly what she'd done to him. She'd heard his message by picking it up from his mind as she usually did. He hadn't been able to speak directly into her mind. She nodded miserably to Cassy.

'He's on his way back?'

'Yes. I told him he didn't need to but he ignored me. He's running, fast,' she added anxiously wondering how she was going to face him.

'You're not trying to tell me he would consider hunting in any way more important to him than this?' Cassy laughed at such folly.

'Might I have hurt him shutting him out?' Natalya asked anxiously.

'His feelings, certainly. Physically, I don't know. I hear when you threw Jim out of your mind you actually threw him across the room. You should check on him. Unless you'd rather wait until he limps home?'

Natalya winced at the thought of Freddie limping home alone and she reached for him. *'Freddie I'm sorry. I wasn't thinking,'* she whispered to him. He didn't respond, his simmering silence enough of a chiding answer. She searched for pain but aside from knowing he was running at great speed, his body was working with the efficient endurance of the wolf. She heard him growl tersely, in answer to Jim's query, as he passed through the gate, and that, although curious, Jim left his mind. Then she could see him running across the grass.

Cassy noticed Natalya's intent stare and could now see a man running at astonishing speed across the grass in the distance. Natalya's hands were shaking. She got up nervously and went inside to return with a glass of water. They both watched the figure until he disappeared from sight as he entered the village. When he reappeared at the foot of the lane he was jogging at a more sedate pace.

'I'd better leave you some privacy,' Cassy said. 'Unless you want me to stay?'

'No, but thank you,' Natalya managed to say sincerely. Her attention was focussed on Freddie. She barely noticed Cassy leave. The man walking up the steps to meet her felt almost a stranger. He was staring at her intently. He was breathing quickly and his eyes were bright but otherwise he showed no sign of his sprint. He came closer and she hastily thrust the glass of water towards him. His warm hands closed over hers to take the glass.

'Thank you, but you're doing it again,' he chided.

'What?'

'Looking in my mind for what I need. How far did you look?' he asked with a small smile.

'Only enough to know you were thirsty,' she admitted.

'Pity,' he responded and drank.

Natalya watched him, wondering what he was referring to. His manner was very sexy. She could see his throat working as he swallowed, tipping his head back to finish all the water. How could that be erotic to see? She had no idea, but it was.

'Did it never occur to you I might like to know what you want?' He put the glass down absently. 'I don't even know how you really feel about me. I'm getting the impression you only like me because of my wolf.' He picked up the glass again and went inside to put it in the kitchen. She silently followed him inside, as he'd hoped she would. Now they were finally in private.

'I didn't know you felt like that. I thought you liked having me stay here in your home,' she began unhappily. 'Do you want me to leave?'

'No of course I don't want you to leave,' he said in exasperation. 'Natalya I'm in love with you. I want us to be together always. I'd hoped you would learn to love me as much as you do my wolf,' he added in a small voice.

Natalya stared at him and then reached for his mind, needing to know he meant what he said. She was shocked he thought she only valued his wolf and her heart twisted. She bypassed the more public upper mind and explored how he was really feeling. His mind was whirling with hope she might accept him, mixed with sharp pain at the thought she might be about to reject him. She assessed that and discovered he harboured a deep fear of being put aside in favour of someone more worthy. Another wizard would be able to truly share the wizard world. Jim's interest in her had sparked this. Freddie was painfully aware Jim had easily beaten him physically; he had no way of fighting off someone as powerful as Jim and it scared him.

Without thinking about it she soothed him mentally. *'Don't you know by now I'm not interested in wizards? Now I've found you I'm not looking at other men anymore. No one else compares in the slightest.'*

Freddie gladly soaked up the reassurance she was sending him; her words lifted his heart. Her mind might still be shielded but her physical body was right here. He took her into his arms and kissed her. It was his only way to express himself to her. Drako had confided that physically getting close and kissing had been the way he'd reached Cassy. Freddie hoped that pointer would work equally for him. In the meantime he relished the opportunity to hold her, kiss her and try his best to tempt her. She gave every indication of enjoying kissing him as much as he did her. Minutes passed and her shield slipped then fell away entirely. He didn't immediately pounce, waiting to see if she'd put it back up again. He tentatively followed her presence in his mind back to her.

Freddie found himself in an astonishing new place swirling with trepidation, desire and hot passion. He discovered the very odd sensation of feeling how she experienced his kiss. He learned what she preferred and that she liked being held in his arms very much. The feel of his strength and hot body pressed against hers was intoxicating her!

*'You've found your way into my head then?'*

*'Please don't throw me out,'* he urged quickly. *'This is wonderful,'* he enthused, feeling they were actually sharing. Being able to send her his words was only half of it; he could also feel her emotions and exceptionally enlightening they were. He glimpsed some childhood memories as well as other more recent and painful memories of her rape and torture at the hands of the wizard. The wizard now had a face, as well as a name. Nathaniel was a blandly featured, heavy set and rather ugly individual. Freddie growled to himself, aware Natalya was silently watching and waiting to see what he would do in the way of riffling through her

memories. She was expecting disgust and aversion to set in once he discovered some of the darkly offensive things that she felt had tainted her. He shook his head in dismay and skipped on quickly, hoping his curiosity was not abusing her trust. *'Sorry love.'* Sharing her mind, he felt her reaction to his words. She felt she didn't deserve him? She thought him beautiful, courageous and strong? He noticed her amusement that she'd caught him preening at that. Well, it wasn't every day you learned the one you loved felt that way.

'I love you; the whole you,' she whispered in his ear, aware of that question still nagging at him. But it was something that had been hard to admit to herself, let alone him.

'You do?' he whispered and held her tight. His nature was wolf; when he gave his love, he entrusted his whole heart. He'd been terrified she might run from such commitment or not return the sentiment, ripping him asunder and leaving him a hollow shell.

'Come and show me what you mean by love,' she invited, leading him towards the stairs. His kisses, desire and love, had awakened an urgent need to claim this man. She felt his immediate rush of eagerness having heard her intention and laughed out loud in delight.

He grinned back at her and towed her upstairs where he could prove his love in comfort, privacy and at leisure.

14

# *An Offer*

Natalya woke next morning, stretched and snuggled back against Freddie. He wrapped his arms around her and pulled her on top of him where he could kiss her more easily. They were soon so involved with each other that the outside world was completely forgotten. The ability to experience what the other was feeling, to know exactly what they needed, was heady. She might have been slightly shocked at some of his erotic thoughts, but there was no denying fulfilling some of them had been exceptionally rewarding. Their passion for each other seemed to know no bounds.

Freddie jumped, swearing, hearing someone knocking on his front door. He went to the window and realised the pack were down there.

'Are you coming with us today?' Dustin asked, having heard the window creak. He grinned to see

Freddie looking very tousled and that he glanced behind him before answering. Clearly he was not alone in his bedroom.

'Go my love,' Natalya urged him; aware he didn't want to get out of bed. 'It's high time I found a teacher and began learning to be useful.'

'Are you sure you wouldn't rather I came with you for that?'

'Of course I'd rather not face those wizards alone, but it's time I did. I'm acting cowardly and it grates.'

Freddie understood she needed to face her childhood fears and overcome them herself. It was not something he could do for her and she was right that it was something she needed to just get on and do. He swiftly dressed and tied back his hair. Natalya pulled her dress on swiftly and followed him downstairs.

'I hope you'll be wearing more than that when you go up to the school,' he couldn't help chiding aware she wore nothing under that dress.

'Of course, but I shall take a bath before I go. It's one thing for your men to know what we've been up to, but it's disrespectful to sit indoors unwashed.'

'I think you smell wonderful,' he told her.

'That's your possessive wolf talking,' she laughed. Whilst Freddie was gathering his weapons and putting on his boots Natalya opened the front door.

'Good morning,' she called cheerfully. 'He won't be long.' She went back in and quickly started pulling food out of the cold room. 'Freddie hang on, you need to eat.'

'They're waiting.'

'We forgot to eat last night and haven't had anything yet this morning,' she told him, knowing her words would be perfectly audible to the men just outside the open door.

Freddie noticed her glance outside and realised the pack all wore broad grins. She tugged him to his chair by the table outside but he resisted sitting down.

'Do you want to flake out later?' she asked. 'I can assure you that won't impress me.'

He heard not quite muffled sniggers now and realised she was playing to the men as much as him. He relented with as good a grace as he could manage and sat down at the table. She pressed a small kiss to his brow before disappearing back inside. Very quickly she had put bread and cheese before him, hot tea and was then busy wrapping a small bundle which was carefully packed in his belt pouch.

'Does everyone have snacks for later?' she asked the patiently waiting men.

'Don't worry about us, my lady,' Dustin responded. 'We are all perfectly capable of taking care of ourselves,' he added rather pointedly to Freddie.

'I am well aware you are all fit capable men Dustin. However, as the only female member of our pack, it is my responsibility to think of the wellbeing of all of you.'

Dustin bowed, 'I apologise. What you say is true. I did not know your wolf instincts were so pure and clear. We know you are not simply wolf; there are many sides to you. You are indeed our alpha female.'

'Thank you Dustin,' she said softly.

Freddie came up behind her and wrapped his arms about her. He knew just how honoured and warm she felt at their acceptance of her, despite being different, into the pack's close knit family. 'So now you've bested a pack of wolves this morning are you ready to face the wizards?'

'No, but I shall speak with Jim in a while,' she told him straightening her shoulders resolutely. 'Anyway, we've dallied long enough this morning,' she began for his ears alone.

'No we haven't,' Freddie contradicted with a cheeky grin. 'But I take your point.' He kissed her more than casually and only reluctantly set her back on her feet. He noticed she had to put an unsteady hand on the table top for support. 'See you later,' he called already striding down the steps.

'*I love you,*' she whispered, brushing his mind with warmth and tenderness.

His steps faltered and he glanced back at her wide eyed; well that was better than a simple farewell! Now he really wished he wasn't going anywhere! Dustin teased him for his so obvious daydreaming and he resolutely turned his attention to business.

Natalya watched them jogging swiftly away and kept a light contact with Freddie. She heard the curious questions the men asked him and his evasive answers. She also heard their congratulations. Then Freddie began to sing, or rather hum a few lines here and there as he ran. That gave the men more cause for laughter and exchanges of bawdy comments at Freddie's exceptionally good mood. They quietened down passing through the gate, shivering as they were each scanned by Jim.

'*You're in a good mood this morning,*' even Jim remarked conversationally to Freddie. '*Is it later than normal?*'

'*Thought you might appreciate a lie-in today,*' Freddie said airily. He could feel Jim's curiosity but also knew his shield was thwarting any prying. That simple instance of being able to retain his privacy before a wizard felt good.

'*That was considerate of you,*' Jim said drily. '*Good hunting,*' he added, feeling the hunters were through and the gate re-secured behind them.

Natalya disconnected from Freddie and hastened to eat and bathe. Once she felt calm and ready she reached for Jim.

'*Can I speak with you?*' she asked politely.

'*Certainly,*' Jim responded. '*Now, or in person?*'

'*You're eating so I'll not intrude. I just wanted to discuss your offer to let me get some schooling. There are clearly things I need to know.*'

Jim hadn't felt her attempt to go into his mind, yet she'd known he was eating. It was clear she had some unusually sensitive perceptions.

'*Come on up to the school, we can talk it over. Breakfast's nearly over so you could come straight away if you wish,*' he invited.

'*Will do,*' she acknowledged and disconnected from him. She checked on Freddie and felt his happiness that she was thinking about him. But reassured all was well, she left the house to walk up to the school. It felt surprisingly good to be hailed and greeted cheerfully by people in the village. They'd been strangers only a fortnight ago but seemed to have accepted her amongst them. She already felt more at home here than she ever had in the years she'd spent at the lord's manor.

Stepping into the dining hall she was struck by the noise. The village bustled but was inhabited by animus people who naturally abhorred too much noise because their hearing was so acute. That natural tendency had been honed by years of living in hiding where to make noise equalled risk of being found. The din of the wizard students was therefore shocking.

Everyone was still seated in the dining hall so she stood just inside the door to wait. She now realised part of the excessive noise was that the students on every table were passing their dirty plates down to one end to be stacked. It was thus quicker and easier for the cleaning staff to take away. She watched, noticing that as soon as a table was cleared the students were evidently then allowed to leave. The hall emptied rapidly and then Jim was standing before her.

She followed him down the corridor and into his office. He waved her into a chair and took one opposite. His office was lined with age darkened oak panelling and bookcases, obviously a historical legacy. Jim looked too young and athletic for this room; it seemed better suited to someone of advanced years as most headmasters usually were. Yet there were many signs of a more vibrant personality; the old and the new did seem to rest quite comfortably together. She guiltily returned her attention to him and realised he was silently watching her. It was odd to hear he was her little sister's partner and that they had a child.

'So, can I join classes?' Natalya asked.

'Of course. What you'd get out of them is less certain however. You've obviously had some training because you know how to shield, not only yourself, but also project the spells necessary to physically shield someone else. You've also been at work giving the hunters mental shields. You don't seem to have a problem communicating mentally. You can heal others without effort. You're a wizard, yet have mastered several animus forms with perfect accuracy,' Jim commented ticking off the points on his fingers. 'So, what areas are you interested in?'

'Defending myself and using my magic properly. I don't know what you think I ought to already know.'

'Do you have skill with any particular weapon?'

'None, well Freddie's just started teaching me the long bow. I was never allowed near real weapons.'

'How about physical contact defence, you know, without a weapon?' Jim asked having made some notes.

'I was always the prey; no-one taught me that kind of thing. That's one of the reasons I developed my tiger.'

'First things first, let's try you on the training ground circuit; it'll be fairly quiet at the moment.' She rose and he considered her attire; a white dress wasn't appropriate nor would it survive sword fighting or wrestling or any of the other weapons practice sessions. Now he thought about it, that garment was the only one he'd seen her wearing, aside from the torn trousers she'd arrived in. He guessed it was all she possessed.

'A quick trip to stores first though. Let's get you something practical to wear.'

'That'd be useful,' she conceded and followed him as he briskly strode from the room, down numerous corridors, before meeting up with a matronly woman he introduced as Mrs White.

'She needs a sturdy trouser outfit for the training yards,' Jim instructed Mrs White. 'I'll be back in a few minutes,' he added and left them to it.

Natalya was glad he'd gone; she now felt freer to relax and try on this and that handed to her by the friendly Mrs White. Eventually they found a pair of leather trousers, meant for a man, but which were the only ones long enough and in her size. They fitted well enough that the overlarge men's shirt could be tucked in and didn't swamp her, certainly with a nice belt to finish it off. Unfortunately, because she was very tall, only men's clothing was long enough in the sleeve or leg. Mrs White handed her a leather waistcoat with a little flourish. Natalya slipped it on and realised it was tailored for a woman. She drew the laces closed and suddenly the whole outfit of male clothing looked tailored for her instead. Socks and boots later she stepped out of the changing area feeling far better equipped and clothed than she had for a long time.

Jim had returned, having also changed and sat perched on the windowsill in the outer room. His gaze swept her and she flushed slightly; clearly he approved.

'Good, you can leave your other stuff in my office,' he offered, again striding through the corridors.

'Why start me with physical lessons rather than magic?' Natalya asked, as they walked up the track to the training ground. 'I thought it was my magic you were most concerned with?'

'You need to learn both the mental and physical ways of defending yourself. I'm doing it this way round because I need to discover what comes naturally to you under duress. I already know you have a lot of magical strength and that you work successfully when acting on your instincts. Obviously that can only take you so far. With some guidance we can explore what areas we need to work on to actually build a successful defence and eventually offense.'

'You plan to teach me yourself?' Natalya asked in surprise. 'I thought you had far too much work to do and had teachers you'd pass me over to?'

'I do, but we need to assess you, and may have to tailor a program to you. I'll need to do most of that assessment. You're also too strong and untrained in the basics to be let loose in a school room with lots of other students. You may need one to one teaching initially.' He glanced at her, aware of her dismay, but how Vako would cope with such a wild cat he couldn't imagine. One of Vako's favourite ploys was to provoke a student, to push them past their fear of letting loose their magic. It was a way of forcing them to expand their abilities. He dreaded to think what might be loosed if he tried that with an already distrustful and exceedingly gifted Natalya.

'You approve of my outfit then? Natalya asked pointedly.

Jim flushed suddenly realising he'd been caught staring. But her leather trousers and waistcoat were very fitted and revealed she had a great figure. 'What man wouldn't approve?' he confided, but refrained from commenting further or looking so obviously.

At the training ground Natalya followed Jim inside, looking around her curiously. They walked down an aisle between tall tiers of seats to the fenced off sandy arena. Inside the ring were three pairs of students practicing different forms of combat. They stood and watched for a few minutes before Bruno spotted them and hurried over.

'Are you here for a workout sir?' Bruno asked noticing the scuffed and battered clothes Jim wore. 'I'm not sure who I've got up here at the moment who could partner you,' he added.

'No, I'm here to give Natalya a workout,' Jim said cheerfully.

'Ah. I thought she was a novice?' Bruno said a little anxiously. 'Wouldn't it be better to pair her with one of the students?' Bruno asked aware of the dangerous glint in Jim's eyes and Natalya's trepidation.

'Don't worry,' Jim said clapping Bruno on the shoulder as he climbed through the fence, 'she's knocked me on my backside twice already. I'm sure she'll survive.'

'Good luck,' Bruno told her, aware of her frown and not blaming her in the slightest. Jim was not an easy opponent at the best of times. He had plenty of physical strength as well as speed. Only the other animus warriors could match his reflexes.

'Come on little kitty,' Jim taunted and threw one of the wooden practice swords to her. 'Let's see what you're made of. Ever handle a sword?'

'No,' Natalya said simply. She had watched soldiers practising but had never been allowed near any weapons. She flinched as Jim abruptly strode up to her. He took her hands and positioned them correctly on the sword. He then bade her copy his stance and a particular motion until she accurately reproduced it.

'Ok, parry me,' he ordered tapping at her hastily raised sword. He did the motion slowly twice, letting her adjust to the feel of an opponent, then he abruptly increased the pace. She matched him, her gaze fixed on his eyes just like Amelie did. He upped the tempo again and again until their arms were flying at each other yet he got very little past her.

'Ok, move your feet,' he instructed even while continuing to parry her sword. He advanced on her forcing her backwards. He grinned, aware she would shortly be up against the fence but she surprised him by sidestepping beforehand and without looking round. He drove her on backwards. She sidestepped several times and without warning, forcing him to overreach and have to readjust quickly. 'New move,' he announced, batting her sword aside and thwacking her shoulder. She growled at him for that and came at him with her attempt at the move. Her sudden offense surprised him and made him hesitate. That hesitation earned her a strike against him. He growled then and attacked with another new move which succeeded in felling her. But instead of falling and submitting or scrambling away from him, she attacked. She kicked out and swept his legs out from under him. He measured his length in the hard sand. He coughed and rolled over quickly to meet her eyes, only to find she was sitting smiling at him.

'Did you see that Bruno?' Jim asked, glancing at the man standing close by, just the other side of the fence. 'She knocked me off my feet yet again.'

'Yes, I noticed that,' Bruno agreed.

'What are we going to do with her?' Jim asked him.

'You did, for the third time, deserve to be knocked on your backside,' she pointed out. She glanced at Bruno then grinned pointedly at Jim.

'Bruno could you stop agreeing with her quite so loudly,' Jim complained a little peevishly, despite the fact the poor man hadn't uttered a word. His thoughts though were loud enough for a wizard to hear. Jim glanced round and realised the others who'd shared the ring when they'd started were all standing at the railings watching. He suspected they'd all stopped immediately to watch his and Natalya's session.

'So what did you learn from this?' Natalya asked.

'You'll make a good sword fighter once you've had some training. Bruno can put together a programme for you,' he added.

'Just sword play?' Bruno asked.

'Not necessarily. I'll leave it to you to find out what will suit her,' Jim conceded. 'Is this a good time of day to train her?'

'How much time can she spend here?' Bruno asked.

'You think she warrants extra sessions?'

'She's welcome to join my warrior class,' Bruno suggested eagerly. 'I know they are all far more advanced but that's where she should be.'

'You don't think she should start in one of the lower classes first?'

'No, she wouldn't thrive there. She obviously learns quickly and is physically strong. She'll soon be able to hold her own.'

'How does that sound to you Natalya? The warrior class meets here after breakfast every day. In fact many are here now,' Jim added, realising more were present now than had been when he first arrived. 'Sorry, are we holding up another class?'

'No. Word has evidently spread that you're here training,' Bruno commented.

Jim suspected from the way Natalya was being ogled that it wasn't him they'd gathered to watch and Bruno's sidelong glance at her confirmed it.

'How long is your class if they come every day?' Natalya asked Bruno.

'All morning,' Bruno said. 'There are many disciplines to cover, from hand to hand combat to all the forms of weaponry through to handling and training a war horse. Can you ride?'

'Yes, but I don't know anything about war horse commands,' she admitted.

'That's for you to learn,' Bruno told her. He was eager now to get started testing her and training her properly. From what he'd just seen she had a great deal of raw potential and such candidates were rare. If Jim hadn't become headmaster Bruno would have suggested he join the class too. With more training Jim could be very good too. As it was, the range of manoeuvres that Drako had taught him sufficed for most circumstances. Jim was, after all, a wizard. He didn't have to rely on physically pounding someone, he could cast any number of spells to either protect himself or indeed disable an opponent from a distance.

'How's your arm?' Jim asked her aware he ached from the blows she'd managed to land on him.

'Sore I suppose,' she admitted and pushed up her sleeve to look. A large purple bruise was just starting to cover her shoulder and upper arm.

'Sorry, let me mend that,' Jim offered coming to her side.

'There's really no need,' she objected, but weakly; it did hurt.

'I'm not having Freddie come and growl at me again. I never thought he could be quite so disconcerting, but where you're concerned he's exceedingly protective.'

'I'm surprised you find that unexpected,' she told him as they slipped between the rails and sat in the stands so students could use the arena again. 'He's the alpha leader of a pack of strong wolves. He didn't become alpha by letting others push him around,' she commented, then fell silent to turn her feelings inward to observe what exactly he was doing to ease her bruises. 'That feels a lot better thank you. Shall I do yours? Assuming I landed any,' she added ruefully.

'You did, I can assure you,' he said with wry chagrin. 'It's just my hip that hurts badly though. I think I landed on it awkwardly.' He watched her place her hands lightly on his waist and thigh over his trousers. 'Can you tell what I've done to it?'

'Just bruised I think,' she told him and immediately copied what he'd done to reduce her bruises. 'Better?' she asked taking her hands off him quickly when he nodded. He smiled at her then rose and went to speak to someone. She picked up a handful of sand and rubbed it between her palms for a moment feeling the need to scrub his scent from her skin. It was very odd to feel like that; it wasn't as though she'd remotely done anything wrong. She absently watched Jim talking to someone and rubbed more sand through her hands. She glanced up, aware of a presence and found a rangy young man had come closer and was watching her curiously. Under his unruly thatch of dark hair she noticed his soft brown eyes shone with intelligence. He seemed to know what she was doing with the sand and she flushed with embarrassment and let the sand fall.

'Hello, I'm Natalya,' she greeted. 'You're animus aren't you?'

'Yes. I'm Jason,' he told her, amused she seemed to accept him just because he was animus. Well that was certainly a refreshing attitude. 'You're Freddie's girl aren't you?'

'Is that how I'm known?' She snorted softly. 'Yes, I suppose I am.'

'What does he think to you fighting the wizard?' Jason asked.

'He knows I'm at the school today to find my place. I need training and they offered to teach me. What they have in mind I've no idea, but Bruno seemed to think he could teach me. Are you in his warrior class?'

'Yes. They asked you to join this class?' Jason asked in surprise.

'Yes. Bruno thought I could do it. I don't know,' she added a little doubtfully. 'I've never even been allowed near a practise ground let alone weapons before. Maybe they expect me to fall flat on my face,' she grumbled then shrugged. 'At least I'll learn something useful. See you,' she added by way of a farewell, seeing Jim glance at her, obviously now ready to go. When she glanced back she noticed Jason was watching her but was now surrounded by others. She supposed that knowing the person she was speaking to was animus she'd automatically lowered her voice. Few of the others would have been able to overhear what they'd spoken about so briefly.

'So, what now?' she asked Jim.

'Morning tea break is about to start. Want to speed run?'

'Speed run?' she queried, but followed him into a jog.

'Feel what I'm doing, but start slowly or you'll trip,' he warned. He felt her reluctantly touch his mind to discover what he was doing, or rather to see the mechanics of how he'd just sped away from her without effort. He heard a giddy laugh and she was abruptly alongside.

'Come on then,' he challenged and increased his pace. They blasted along the track towards the house at about a horse's gallop pace. 'This is even better when you're on horseback. Doubling your own running pace is good but doubling a horse's gallop is astonishing. You have to be careful not to go anywhere they're likely to trip over anything though. It's almost impossible to judge how to jump an obstacle at this kind of pace. If you see one you just slow up to normal pace to tackle it before speeding up again. It's funny, but no-one else seems to have grasped this spell. You constantly surprise me Natalya. You're so like Amelie in that regard. She loves going fast. She likes her horse's gallop, but even better is her eagle or dragon, they truly know real speed.'

'That's more tiring than ordinary running isn't it,' Natalya commented, puffing as she walked up the steps and into the school moments later.

'A little, but mainly it's deceptive. If you'd sprinted that distance you'd understand why you felt breathless. But because you've covered the distance twice as fast, your mind tries to tell you that you haven't gone very far. That's the main reason you feel odd. Yes you add to your weariness by having used some of your magic but it's only like any other spell. I just thought this one might appeal to you in its usefulness.'

'It certainly does. There were many occasions when using that spell would have been very useful.'

'I would point out that it has a major downside in that it's a loud spell. Any wizard or even a sensitive animus would feel it from miles away and be able to track your direction. I haven't found a way to counter that signature yet. Well, to be honest, I haven't given it much thought. Maybe you can come up with a way of making it quiet.'

'Me? Why do you think I might be able to figure out something like that? I wouldn't know where to start,' she said little aghast.

'You are good at shielding. That might be the way to do it.' He shrugged then turned his attention to pouring them both mugs of tea then juggling a handful of biscuits as well and taking them to the nearest vacant chair. Natalya sat near him, glancing around curiously at the people surrounding them and listening to snatches of conversations. But she rather single-mindedly concentrated on her tea and biscuits. She had expended a great deal of energy and effort already this morning and clearly needed the food boost. She turned towards the window and whilst continuing to sip her tea, her mind seemed elsewhere. A faint hum of power surrounded her and Jim noticed she was smiling.

'Who are you talking to?' Jim asked.

'Freddie,' she said simply and continued sharing her experiences of this morning with her love.

'So, does he approve of your joining the warrior class?' Jim asked her and gleefully suspected from her frown and inward looking pause that she hadn't told him that bit. Freddie was a warrior and would know exactly what such training would involve. Whether he would wish his lady to train to fight and voluntarily put herself in harm's way, was likely to be the sticking point. No man really wished that.

'He'll come around,' she told Jim airily. 'I make my own decisions and besides he's already started teaching me to use the long bow.'

Jim noticed her wince and he grinned; clearly Freddie was having plenty to say on the matter.

'So what's next?' she asked Jim and was glad Freddie quietened to listen.

'Well the warrior class usually does alternate afternoons with Vako, for magical combat training and Terry for tactics and logistics. I think Vako has a junior class starting after break. I'll just see if he minds us sitting in on it today.'

'Don't you need to be somewhere? Surely if I'm just sitting in I'll be ok?' Natalya asked.

'Vako's classes usually involve every person present. He will want to see what you're capable of at the earliest opportunity,' Jim warned her.

'Ok,' she acknowledged and idly watched him go to speak with Vako. Vako turned to look at her and a small smile played across his face. She suspected this old man was looking forward to testing her. It suddenly occurred to her that if she was to join the warrior class she'd also have to be in the senior classes in the other subjects. How could she possibly cope with lessons she had no background knowledge of? It was going to be impossible to understand. She followed Jim into a classroom and took one of the little individual desks at the back of the room. The seats filled with young wizards, all much younger than her. She was aware of their dour expressions as they entered the class only lightening on spotting Jim and her in the room.

Natalya's eyes soon began to glaze and she was not alone. Vako's monologue was so dull and used so many incomprehensible terms and language that she stopped listening.

'Natalya, perhaps you'd like to go first,' Vako announced.

Natalya jerked guiltily noticing every eye was on her. Clearly her inattention had not gone unnoticed. Without looking at him she felt for Jim's mental signature and skimmed his mind. In an instant she grasped both what was required and also how it was done before he was aware of her presence and blocked her. She also gathered a perception that even Jim was struggling to stay awake.

'Creating fire was it?' Natalya asked. Vako frowned but nodded. She concentrated and lit a flame on the end of her finger.

'Good,' Vako was forced to concede. 'Can you make it bigger?' He watched blue flames fly over two feet above her hand. 'Notice everyone that Natalya's flames are blue. Can anyone tell me why?'

'Because that isn't real fire. It's just light,' one of the boys spoke up.

'Correct. So why, when I asked for fire, did you produce light?' Vako pounced on her verbally.

'Would you have preferred me to set fire to my desk or yours?' she enquired, unperturbed by him. 'I understood real fire requires real fuel to sustain, does it not?'

Vako threw a pencil sized stick at her without warning. But she easily caught the awkwardly aimed missile. This time yellow flames flowed over the wood in her hands. Smoke plumed and the pale wood visibly blackened. There was no doubt this time. She extinguished it and put it down, more interested to watch as Vako passed sticks round to everyone else and bade them have a go. Not all were successful, but Vako did manage to help those in their understanding. Natalya was more impressed by that real assistance than she had been of the rest of the lesson.

'Thank you Vako, we'll leave you now. That was most informative,' Jim said, rising suddenly.

Natalya glanced at him, the lesson was only partway through, but Jim gestured and she rose hastily to accompany him out of the room.

Jim closed the door behind them and strode to his office. 'You should not have done that,' he chided.

'What?'

'Gone to sleep and then fished the answer out of my head.'

'I know and I'm sorry, but I couldn't take in whatever it was he was trying to say. I learned in a moment from you what he failed to teach me in an hour,' Natalya told him.

'I noticed that,' Jim said and pulled absently at his lip. 'I believe the advanced classes are more interesting, but I'm not sure you have enough of the basics to even begin to participate.'

'That crossed my mind when you were discussing putting me in that class. What can we do? I'll never learn anything like that.'

'When Cassy went away once with Drako she missed three weeks of lessons. I went to her classes, compressed those lessons and then transferred them to her mind for her. She didn't fail her exams. Now, you don't actually need some of that but I could share it with you. It'd help in many areas of your understanding, particularly with technical terms. Knowing how many spells are crafted will also help you figure out how to tailor them for other uses. What do you say?'

'Sounds useful. You said it was three week's worth of lessons?'

'Yes, none of them physical workouts either, it's all magical theory and practical applications.'

'How long will it take to teach me this?' Natalya asked a little anxiously. It sounded a great idea but she could tell Jim had some sort of reservation to doing it.

'That depends on you, well both of us, not melting from the strain,' he admitted. 'It gave me dreadful headaches with Cassy. Hopefully it'll be easier a second time round.

'This will cause you pain?' Natalya queried unhappily.

'I'll have to teach you how to block my pain, and then we'll be fine,' he suggested wryly. 'Ready?'

'You want to start now?'

'Might as well. We've just over an hour before lunch. I believe your class is with tactics this afternoon so you could join that. Alternatively you could stay here and see how much we can cover in that time?'

'I don't know what's best,' she admitted, feeling well out of her depth.

'Let's see how we get on now and then decide, ok?' he suggested and she nodded. 'Are you linked to Freddie?'

'Not at the moment, why?'

'Lock him out or tell him not to try to disturb you. Drako proved himself a nuisance when he insisted on monitoring Cassy when I did this for her. It made it doubly difficult for all of us. Have you told him?'

'No, I've just shielded. He'll worry otherwise and besides, he's busy.'

Jim was relieved she was taking his advice and ensuring Freddie wasn't an issue. Now he didn't have to worry about bleed over of the spell to a vulnerable animus mind. He moved his chair alongside hers and reached out his hand to her. 'You still don't trust me do you,' he couldn't help complaining, observing her hesitation before she took his hand.

'It's not because I don't trust you,' she felt obliged to explain. He seemed hurt she avoided him so obviously. 'You're not my man and you are a wizard. I will always avoid touching you. I truly do appreciate the time and effort you've expended helping me.'

'But I'm not your man,' he finished for her with a small smile. Now he understood he felt better. Being constantly rebuffed by someone he both wanted and needed to help was upsetting. 'I consider you family,' he told her gently. 'You are aunt to my daughter Daisy,' he added and suddenly realised she'd not considered that. But then it was probably a little odd when Amelie wasn't here. The sisters hadn't seen each other in years and Natalya had never met Daisy.

'No one will truly talk to me about Amelie. I don't even know why she isn't here. Did you two have a fight or has she actually left you?' Natalya asked.

'This is another reason you don't trust me, isn't it,' Jim perceived her doubts. 'We will talk, but later. In short your sister and I are very happy, but she was called away to help a troubled youngster. I have no idea when she'll be able to return, but it wasn't meant to take as long as it already has,' he added unhappily. 'Anyway, we must make a start on this session.'

'Ok, I'm ready when you are,' Natalya told him feeling his angst and knowing he wasn't lying.

Jim carefully cleared his mind of extraneous thoughts and concentrated on bringing to mind the lessons he'd compiled for Cassy so many months ago. Then he sorted them, trying to remember in what order they needed to be. He started transmitting each lesson in quick bursts. He paused briefly between each segment, firstly so she had a chance to deal with the information and secondly because he needed to organise his own thoughts into coherence before sending the next lot.

Suddenly the bell sounded outside his door, making them both jump. He had time to finish that lesson before second bell, but was surprised at how quickly the hour had passed.

Natalya felt him decide where to stop and his approval for how much they'd managed to cover in a very short time.

'Thank you Jim. You've given me a great deal to think on,' Natalya told him. 'Do you have a headache?'

Jim laughed, 'no thankfully. How about you? It's meant to be me checking on you.'

'My head feels very full but it doesn't hurt.'

'Excellent,' he said getting up and putting his chair back in its customary spot. 'Freddie seems to have a habit of waking me at dawn and it's a long time before I really need to be up for breakfast. Perhaps we should arrange to meet for an hour before breakfast so we can cover these sessions. I imagine you're awake at that hour too, or does he let you sleep on?'

'No, I'm up when he is, well not ready to leave the house, but I get his breakfast and lunch organised.'

'Lucky man,' Jim commented. 'Ok, if we both get up when he leaves we'll have plenty of time to get these lessons organised as well as answer any questions you'll have as we go along. How does that sound?'

'Like a plan,' she approved and with that agreed she followed him to the dining hall for lunch.

She was surprised to hear someone call her name. Jason patted an empty chair beside him at an otherwise full table. There were no females at that table but she recognised several faces from the training ground this morning. These then were probably the warriors and her new class mates. Someone else hailed her and she waved at Kathy but there was no room at Kathy's table so she walked quickly to the seat she suspected Jason had kept for her. She was one of the last to arrive, but fortunately because Jim had to walk right to the front, she managed to sit before he did.

'Thanks Jason,' she said. 'Seems crowded over here,' she commented glancing at the adjacent tables which were all fully occupied.

'This is the warrior section, it's usually crowded,' Jason told her.

'But not with women I notice,' she said, feeling a little conspicuous.

'Is it true you're joining our class?' the man opposite her asked.

'So I've been told,' she shrugged. 'I'm Natalya,' she said pointedly.

'We know. You're Amelie's sister?'

'Yes.'

'I'm Marko,' he added, abruptly recalling he hadn't said. 'You did well against Jim this morning. He's fast and strong. So how long have you been fighting?'

'You saw my first lesson this morning!' Natalya laughed sourly.

'That was your first sword fight?' Marko asked.

'Didn't you see him have to show me how to hold that damn stick?'

'Well yes, but...' Marko glanced at Jason helplessly.

'What he means is that we're surprised you should be joining our class when you're a beginner,' Jason explained.

'Surprises me too, but Bruno seemed to think I'd learn the basics quickly.' She glanced from one to the other of the two men actually talking to her. The others were silently listening but she felt they disapproved of her being put into their class. Perhaps she needed to prove her worthiness before they'd accept her? She shrugged; what they thought of her was immaterial as long as they did not prevent her learning. Food arrived then and she was very glad attention was diverted to that instead. The men had all had a busy and physically active morning. They all ate heartily so her own large appetite went unremarked.

'Is it tactics you go to next?' she asked Jason at the end of the meal when people were starting to leave.

'Yes, well, after break. We have another hour yet. You're joining us for that?'

'Yes. Could you do me a favour? Jim's pressed so much knowledge in my head that I need a nap. Could you call me when it's time?'

'Certainly,' Jason agreed following her outside into the bright sunshine. He watched her loosen her clothes and shimmer into a huge tiger. The tiger's bright orange eyes assessed him and the other men who'd also come outside. Then she turned and walked into the shade of a nearby tree and lay down. She was almost completely hidden from sight in the long grass.

'Shit, did you see that?' Marko exclaimed. 'I thought she was an animus wolf?'

'She's Amelie's sister remember, who knows what she truly is,' someone else said nervously.

'She is not animus. She is a true warrior wizard,' Jason told them quietly and noticed an ear was turned towards them. 'Didn't you hear that last week she pounced on an enemy owl animus in flight and killed him? She was in tiger form then,' Jason told the others quietly. 'Don't underestimate her or get on her wrong side.'

'Is that why you were so friendly from the start?' Marko asked.

'Partly. It was only good manners of course, but she's well worth looking at,' he added, knowing that was what the others thought and would most readily believe.

'You've your eye on her then?'

'No; despite her current form she's wolf and has Freddie. She won't take kindly to advances from anyone. Freddie won't appreciate anyone making a move on her and I wouldn't want to cross him either. Just remember, she might look alone but she isn't. She has a pack of wolves ready to be at her back,' Jason warned. The men wandered off then to do their own thing, but Jason remained nearby, keeping an eye on her resting place while she slept. Her tiger form would naturally deter most childish pranks but not necessarily all. He loosened his clothing as she'd done and shimmered into his wild dog. He approached her and orange eyes opened. He sat down nearby where he was just in the shade of her tree.

'Keeping an eye on me Jason?' she asked.

'No wolf likes being alone,' he said. 'Besides, you seem to have the right idea.'

'Thanks,' she murmured and closed her eyes again.

15

# *Decisions*

Natalya found the tactics class fascinating. She'd never appreciated just how many things a commander had to consider before deploying troops in strategic positions or going into battle. She didn't know why some of the class seemed bored; she thought Terry an engaging and interesting teacher. She hung back a little on the exercises, nervous of revealing the true extent of her ignorance. Students were grouped in teams around landscaped sand tables where enemy formations were already laid out. They were asked to position their own troops in response and show the tactics they'd use to overcome the enemy or gain the advantage. Terry explained that there was often no right or wrong way and the way each team's tactics differed proved the point. Each group's plan was examined and the positive points highlighted as were any flaws. He proved to them that it was usually the plan that had had several minds assessing it that had least flaws. No one person could see every angle and discover every flaw, although it was usually the vision of just one individual that prevailed. This class also helped her distinguish the leaders from the followers amongst her fellow students and also those with calculating minds.

After lessons she walked back to Freddie's home slowly, glad to be alone for a few minutes to make sense of a very full day. She was tired but excited. Freddie wasn't home yet when she got in so she sat on the veranda with her feet up, mulling over whether to call on Cassy.

'*Cassy?*' she called mentally. '*Are you home?*'

'*Natalya, is that you?*' Cassy responded, and went to the window. Natalya waved to her from her house just down the lane.

'*I could do with talking with you whenever you've got a few minutes,*' Natalya asked.

'*Come now if you'd like,*' Cassy invited curiously. She finished changing and went downstairs and out onto the veranda. 'Natalya's coming up,' she said to Drako already out on the swing seat.

'So I see,' he said and patted the seat beside him. Cassy joined him, enjoying a quick cuddle whilst Natalya walked up.

'Shall I leave you two ladies for a private chat?' Drako asked as Natalya came up the steps.

'No need,' Natalya said quickly. 'You look far too comfortable just there. Besides you'd probably be the best one to advise me on another subject.'

'Please sit down,' Drako invited now alertly curious.

'You probably know Jim extended an invitation for me to get some training. Well I talked it over with Freddie and we agreed I should just do it. You all know I'm fairly useless with just the bits and pieces I do know. So anyway I went to Jim this morning. He took me straight up to the training ground, handed me one of those sword sticks and gave me a bit of a lesson. Anyway, after I knocked him on his backside, Bruno asked if I would join the warrior class. He didn't seem worried I've had no training and would be far behind all his other students. Drako, am I being foolish accepting this offer? I asked Freddie earlier but couldn't seem to get him past being annoyed Jim had fought and flattened me. He wasn't making a lot of sense so I had to leave him to calm down.'

'Would you allow me to see this fight? I might then be in a better position to advise you,' Drako asked. He noticed Natalya glanced at Cassy first for permission, before she came over and placed a hand on his shoulder. Images flowed to him clear and bright as though he'd been there. He watched the whole fight from her point of view from entering the ring and having Jim throw a sword at her. He too shared Bruno's view that Jim deserved the unceremonious tripping she'd inflicted on him.

Natalya released her touch and Drako blinked back to the present.

'I see he's remembered the moves I taught him. I do believe he used his entire repertoire on you this morning. I daresay that's why he stopped, not just because you didn't leave him a leg to stand on,' he chuckled then became serious. 'That was quite a brutal initiation. I understand completely why Freddie would be upset to witness that. I assume he linked with you?'

'Yes, he likes his new ability,' she said drily.

'I don't doubt that,' Drako chuckled again, remembering when that intimacy was new for him with Cassy. 'But it does of course make it doubly hard to witness our partner in pain or under attack.'

'I suppose it does,' she considered that and realised Freddie's anger had probably stemmed from protective fear for her, rather than anger at her, and frustration that he was too far away to aid her.

'I take it that Jim's test hasn't put you off learning sword fighting?' Drako asked.

'Not at all. It just proved to me that it was something I ought to be able to learn, given the chance. I'm not happy being unable to defend myself. People have taken advantage of me because of that all my life. They've sought to keep me ignorant and vulnerable.'

'I understand that drive. I don't know if you realise it but Freddie could teach you. Or I, if it's something you wanted. You could then learn other skills at the school. Cassy does many different subjects.'

'I know; that's what I wanted to talk to her about. Well, Jim told me I was going to struggle in the warrior class when it came to the magical side. I've had so little in the way of tuition. So before lunch he put some of your lessons in my head. He said he'd put them together when you went away with Drako.'

'He did what?' Cassy and Drako said in unison.

'He called them your condensed lessons. He said they would help me learn.'

'Are you ok? They were painful,' Cassy said in dismay. 'I can't believe he talked you into that. Does Freddie know?'

'No, Jim told me not to link with him during the session.'

'What don't I know about?' Freddie asked coming round the side of the house where he'd been listening on his approach downwind. 'What else are you keeping from me?' There was a wealth of hurt in his tone.

'I'm not planning on keeping anything from you,' Natalya said gently. 'I just wanted to be sure I wasn't distracting you on the hunt and cause an accident.'

She held out her hand to him and he immediately came to take it.

Freddie pulled her to her feet and looked her over making sure she was physically unharmed. He quickly sat down in her chair and pulled her onto his lap where with that amount of physical contact they could converse privately without effort.

Cassy and Drako silently waited, well aware that reiterating the conversation they'd just been having would only take moments, mind to mind, on a link. They watched Freddie pull her closer, cradling her against his body protectively. There was no need for words to know how he felt about her news. She wrapped her arms about his neck and leaned her cheek against his and his grip on her eased.

Natalya straightened up and turned to see Cassy and Drako were snuggled together too.

'Cassy, how much use did you find the information Jim passed to you? I mean, I know he sent me lots of stuff but I don't feel I know anything more than I did before. It's strange.'

'Well you won't have covered a great deal in your first session and in only an hour,' Cassy said. 'Has he scheduled more sessions?'

'Yes. He said that since Freddie wakes us both at dawn every day we may as well meet before breakfast. That way it's not intruding on lessons or the normal working day.'

'Ok, but dawn? Why do you get up so early Freddie?' Cassy asked in dismay.

'It's the best time of day for hunting,' he responded. 'It's when the animals are moving about and going to water. We're also less likely to run into other people at that time.'

'Makes sense. I'd still rather be asleep,' Cassy admitted and guessed by the sounds of it Jim did too. 'Who wants a beer?' Cassy asked brightly. 'The brewers assure me this latest batch is the best yet. Natalya, want to give me a hand?' Cassy went inside and closed the door behind them. 'That's better, now we can leave the boys to talk,' Cassy remarked, knowing Drako had some suggestions to give Freddie. She quickly filled four mugs, pressed Natalya into a seat in the lounge with a mug before taking the men theirs. Cassy then flopped into a chair opposite Natalya and sipped her beer. 'They were right, this is actually quite good,' she said absently. 'So, you've met your new classmates? The warrior classes don't mix a great deal and I don't remember seeing any women amongst them. How were they with you?'

'I've only spoken with two of them; Jason and Marko so far. Jason's animus and seemed to want to look out for me. I'm not sure why or whether I can trust him. You know how it is with overly friendly men!'

'I know what you mean,' Cassy grimaced. 'And the last thing you want to do is let Freddie think he's got reason to be worried or jealous. I'll ask Drako. Ah,

I thought so, Jason is clan. Drako thinks he'll respect your relationship with Freddie, assuming he knows about it,' Cassy added.

'The first thing Jason said to me was "you're Freddie's girl aren't you?"' Natalya laughed.

'They don't miss much do they? So how did you answer that one?'

'I agreed. It felt weird for a complete stranger to call me that. I suppose if he lives in the village he'd have heard someone say something, or maybe seen me out with Freddie,' she shrugged, it was no secret.

'So you also met Marko. Did you know he broke Jim's shoulder, ribs and fingers the first time they fought? I know he was given an enchanted sword to inflict serious damage on Jim and Jim forgave him, but watch your step. He's one of the most skilled with a sword I believe and I've always found him pleasant enough, but he will blindly follow orders.'

'A necessary trait to instil in a soldier; but thanks for the warning. Anyone else I should know about?'

'Sorry, I don't know anyone else in that class. As I said, they don't mix much. I'm sure you'll soon figure them out. Anyway, you were asking about the use of the lessons with Jim. For me they were very useful indeed. Like you say you don't feel you know any more than when you started. But you will find answers come to you when you need them that you never knew you knew. You know what I mean? That's what happened for me anyway. He's probably right that they'll help you get to grips with a whole bunch of different types of spells. You should be able to use most of it.'

'Thank you Cassy, as usual you've helped put my mind at ease. I've just got to see if Freddie agrees to my doing warrior classes. He didn't seem very happy at the thought earlier and I'd rather not go against his wishes. But what's the point of everyone calling me a warrior wizard if I haven't learned how to actually be one?'

'I hadn't thought of it like that. Certainly you can always switch to something else if you do discover you don't like it,' Cassy said walking her to the door.

Natalya noticed Freddie and Drako were in deep conversation.

'They complain women like to chat,' Cassy said mischievously. 'Men gossip worse than a flock of starlings given the chance.'

Natalya laughed agreement and went to Freddie. 'Stay and finish your conversation. I'll see you at home,' she suggested.

'No, I'm coming,' Freddie said quickly and stood. 'Thanks Drako,' he added, and they took their leave.

'So how do you really feel about me joining this class?' Natalya asked anxiously, as soon as they got inside.

'I'm not thrilled at the prospect of you getting hurt. With such training accidents are likely. But more importantly, I'm not keen on you ever going to war and voluntarily putting yourself in harm's way. However, all that said, I do think it's sensible for you to learn self defence and how to better use your magic. You can rely on me to help you as much as I'm able,' he told her seriously. 'Does that answer your questions?'

'Yes,' she said knowing he was being honest but that there was more on his mind on this subject than he was prepared to voice just now. She didn't press the issue however in case he changed his mind.

'Good. I'm hungry,' he said deliberately changing the subject. He headed for the kitchen hopefully and swallowed his disappointment at the lack of any cooking. She'd only just got home too and would have had a substantial cooked lunch, compared to his sandwiches. 'I knew dinner waiting for me when I got home was too good to last. You've made me soft in just a few short weeks,' he laughed wryly. 'Oh well, I'm sure we can rustle something up between us quickly.'

'There's the smoked ham in the larder,' she suggested and he immediately went to get it. It was rather nice to work together preparing their meal. It eased her guilt that she'd failed to cater for him. But if she was going to get home from a full day of lessons so late in the afternoon, then gathering supplies and preparing meals would need some figuring out and require adjustments from both of them.

She gladly curled beside him after dinner, content with his physical closeness. She didn't object that he wasn't linking with her; she didn't need to know what he was thinking all of the time. She respected his need for the privacy of his own thoughts.

16

# A Change of Plan

Freddie woke at his usual predawn time, awakening with the bird's first greeting of the new day. He cuddled Natalya before getting out of bed.

'Is it time to get up already?' Natalya asked him, sleepily aware his warmth had just gone.

'I'm afraid so. The birds are singing,' he told her.

'I don't like it when you're not in here with me,' she complained.

'I'm happy to hear it,' he responded and leaned over to kiss her. She wrapped her arms about him and purposely overbalanced him onto the bed. 'What are you up to my little temptress?'

'Starting the day properly,' she told him kissing him soundly and letting her hands rove over his exceedingly tempting bare skin.

He laughed helplessly not remotely immune to her ploys. 'We haven't time for this,' he objected weakly.

'Not for what I'd really like,' she agreed flooding his mind with images. 'Are you denying me then?'

'You're incorrigible. I see you need taking in hand,' he told her, decisively getting back into bed. 'It's a good job I'm coming with you to your lessons today.'

'You're doing what?'

'Teaching you. It's fortunate I've got just what you need,' he added, taking advantage of their link to flood her mind with sensual images in return to divert her. He'd been wondering last night how to broach the subject Drako had suggested to him. He knew he could genuinely assist her whilst easing his own mind of what and who she would be facing in the ring. It hadn't occurred to him he'd be using his body to convince her.

'You're right, that is a far better way to start the day,' he said not many minutes later. Their union might have been brief but it had been thoroughly satisfying nonetheless.

'I thought you'd agree,' she said hurrying to bathe quickly. 'What about the men? Are you sending them out without you?'

'I'll talk to them, see what they'd prefer,' he told her then trotted down to organise breakfast before they arrived.

When Natalya came down she found Freddie out on the veranda his gaze across the field. The hunters were already in the distance jogging steadily. He watched until they passed out through the gate without incident. 'They wanted to share in your training,' Freddie told her. 'But since there are about three hours until official lessons begin they thought they'd see if they can nab something quickly. I think they just want an excuse for a lazy day,' he confided.

'*Natalya?*' Jim's voice blossomed in her mind suddenly. '*Are you up? Where's Freddie? I don't remember feeling him leave just now.*'

Natalya could feel Jim's sleepiness. '*We're just having breakfast. We'll be with you in about 20 minutes if that's ok with you?*'

'*I'd best get out of bed them,*' Jim groused, but lightly and left her mind.

'He didn't query my coming with you then?' Freddie asked.

'No, but then he didn't really sound properly awake,' she warned. 'So, are you going to tell me what you've been planning?'

'I will be your sparring partner today. I haven't had much call to use a sword recently but I'm reasonably good with one. I can teach you the basic moves that everyone else will already know. I imagine our link will help you quickly grasp new moves as well.'

'My being at a far lower level than everyone else needn't stop the others practicing then. Thank you my love, it's a great idea.'

'Drako thought of it,' Freddie admitted. 'He told me that when he was teaching Jim he had to be very precise in teaching him to do the motion exactly right from the start. Being a wizard he was quite different to teach, mainly because he had perfect recall of a move, so if he learned it wrong then it'd be difficult to re-learn. He warned me you might be the same. He thought from your memory of the fight with Jim that you acted very similarly.'

'I was copying him, remember,' Natalya pointed out. Although, she knew Jim had only to show her a move for her to remember it. However, watching someone else doing a move and then trying to replicate it yourself, but in reverse, was difficult when you couldn't see yourself. You couldn't be sure you were doing it accurately. That was what took the time for her. They cleared up the breakfast things quickly and were on their way up to the school hand in hand.

'It might be better for you to wait outside,' Jim told Freddie as they arrived at his office.

'No, I'll watch,' Freddie said eye to eye with Jim. 'I understood that it was only if I linked with Natalya while you worked that could cause problems.'

'Yes, that's what slows down the process, causes extra work and ultimately pain,' Jim conceded, holding the door wide open for them both to enter. He sat in the chair he'd already repositioned beside another. Freddie picked up one of the other armchairs and took it to the window further away from them. Jim was relieved by that move and his respect for the man increased.

'Ready Natalya?'

Natalya took her eyes off Freddie a little guiltily and took Jim's hand. A flood of odd mutterings, glimpses of spells in action and copious explanations streamed into her mind. She had no idea how Jim was doing this, but if the information made sense to her when she needed it, then it would all be worthwhile.

'Natalya could you please clear your mind,' Jim chided.

'Clear my mind? What do you mean? I thought you were busy filling it.'

'Do you have any idea how difficult it is to concentrate on the technicalities of herbology spells when you're daydreaming of the sex you had this morning?' Jim said drily.

'Sorry,' she said, flushing red with embarrassment. Freddie laughed, his eyes gleaming.

Jim had to laugh, before he studiously cleared his own mind enough to start on the next lot of spells. Freddie sat quietly, glancing out the window at anyone passing or watching them but trying not to be intrusive about it.

'Ok, the bell's about to go. Here,' Jim handed her a large pine cone. 'Turn that into something.'

'Into what?' Natalya asked but Jim remained silent; this then was meant to be a test. She looked it over, fascinated by the intricacy of its natural design. She held it between both hands, closed her eyes and felt it move. She was startled by what she saw.

'Let me see,' Jim asked, holding out his hand. He could tell she was rather reluctant to give it up. He stared at it in surprise. She'd turned it into a wooden cup. The interior was smooth and perfectly rounded whilst the exterior retained the cone's seed segments but now in their closed shape. The cup was beautiful and fitted the palm of her hand perfectly. He had no doubt it would retain water and be practically useful. He handed it to Freddie who'd come closer to see.

'This is amazing,' Freddie enthused warmly.

'You are quite different from Amelie,' Jim remarked. 'Her animus side is more dominant. She would have seen that cone as part of a tree's life cycle. She probably would have made it sprout. She has great difficulty working with wood. Her spells always trigger the wood to grow. You can imagine the fun we had when she made the horse paddock's fence posts start to grow. However, this proves you can access and use the knowledge I'm giving you. Excellent work. Come on, I daresay you skinny pair could eat something, if only for appearances, at breakfast.'

'Always,' Freddie grinned. 'We only had a light snack earlier,' he said and they followed Jim to the dining hall. Breakfast was a far more laid back affair than lunch. Everyone simply grabbed the nearest seat unless they were up early enough or particularly wanted to choose their dining companions.

'Hi Jason,' Natalya said seeing him arrive, looking for a seat nearby. She noticed his hesitation when he saw Freddie, but then he came over.

'Hi Natalya, Freddie. Can I join you?' Jason asked, making it, to Natalya's ears at least, a formal request.

'Of course,' Freddie responded.

'Jason's in the warrior class,' Natalya told Freddie. 'He was about the only one prepared to talk to me yesterday and make me welcome.'

'You have my thanks for that,' Freddie told him quietly.

'We don't see you up here very often, certainly not for breakfast,' Jason commented.

'No, I've normally been hunting for a couple of hours by now. Today however, I thought I'd lend a hand keeping this one out of trouble,' he said of Natalya.

'I see,' Jason said wondering how the others would view him just walking into their class. The others had been eagerly discussing who was going to partner her today. They were going to be sadly disappointed.

Up at the training ground Freddie went directly to speak with Bruno. He smoothly persuaded Bruno that if he took care of providing Natalya with basic tuition then it could only benefit the rest of the class, who then wouldn't be held back. He then invited Bruno to dictate what moves to start with.

'Before we get to that and teaching, I'd be interested to see your style,' Bruno said, eyeing the tall warrior speculatively.

'Certainly,' Freddie responded amiably and selected one of the wooden practice swords laid out. 'Anyone wish to spar with me?' Freddie asked the gathered students directly. Several immediately stepped forward but Jason wasn't one of them. 'You, what's your name?'

'Marko.'

'Are you ready Marko?' Freddie enquired, as he stepped through the barrier into the arena where Marko was already standing.

*'Why did you pick him?'* Natalya asked privately on their link.

*'Because you didn't want me to. You were thinking about him,'* Freddie told her, a hint of jealousy creeping into his voice.

*'He badly injured Jim.'*

*'That is not so difficult,'* Freddie responded. *'Besides, I've been known to badly injure opponents too. Do not worry my love. We are only going to be sparring.'*

*'No, he will be testing you,'* she told him.

*'Of course he will try,'* Freddie told her complacently.

Natalya silently watched as they got started, determined not to divert his attention further with idle chat. She moved back to the seating and allowed his confidence to calm her. Freddie began by giving Marko a small half bow, his eyes never leaving Marko's face and forcing Marko to hastily and rather sloppily follow suit. He stood facing Marko, appearing completely relaxed and unconcerned and letting Marko make the first move.

Freddie parried the first move with such blinding speed that it took everyone by surprise. Marko's sword flew from his grasp to land in the sand several paces away. He'd been disarmed and was completely vulnerable in a split moment.

'Do I have your attention now?' Freddie asked.

'Yes sir, sorry sir,' Marko stammered, more than a little daunted.

'Good, let's start again,' Freddie told him and watched Marko scramble to pick up his sword. He knew he shouldn't have done that, but Marko's bow had lacked respect and furthermore he had been ogling Natalya. This time when Marko engaged him he met and countered each move in a long unbroken exchange that had them moving about the arena. Freddie allowed Marko to dictate the moves and also to push him back, letting Marko think he had the upper hand, although not one blow of Marko's landed. As soon as he became sloppy Freddie took control and began to attack. He increased the speed of his blows forcing Marko to try and match him. 'Enough,' Freddie said abruptly. 'You're tiring.' He didn't mention the fact he'd just been able to land quite a few blows, or that whilst he'd checked the force he'd used, Marko would bear quite a few bruises. If that fight had been for real and using steel Marko would probably be dead. As it was he'd had a good workout and might have learned a few things.

'So, will I suffice to teach Natalya?' Freddie asked Bruno.

'I suppose so. I'd rather have you teaching the seniors though. I didn't know you were so skilled. I thought you were a hunter,' Bruno added.

'I am a warrior first and a hunter when we are not under attack. I have hunted virtually everything that breathes however. We are the clan's primary defensive force, its guardians,' Freddie told him simply. He nodded to his men sitting behind Natalya in the stands. He hadn't noticed them arrive but they looked as though they'd been there a while.

'Are your men similarly skilled?' Bruno asked following his gaze.

'We all have had the same training but have separate areas of expertise,' Freddie said with a shrug.

Bruno nodded, realising that these men were Clan Green Bear's elite warriors. They already held a highly respected place within the Clan hierarchy and had no need to brag of their skills. They simply went out, day after day, bringing back meat for the school, but also defending the school's borders. That was all of more immediate importance and use than asking them to help train students.

'How do you normally train and keep your skills sharp?' Bruno asked.

'If we ever get time off and have the energy we practice. Obviously we are using some of our skills every day but I haven't touched a sword for months.'

'You and your men are all here now. They could practice if they wished. You are all welcome to come and use this facility when it suits you. It does the students good to see what will come with experience and also what a good swordsman looks like.'

'Thank you,' Freddie said sincerely. He was glad Bruno wasn't asking them to take on students; none of them had the energy. Day after day they were chasing after elusive game in the woods whilst always having to be alert for ambush.

'Natalya, come and pick a sword,' Bruno said briskly. 'Don't just grab the nearest. Look at them and feel their weight. You'll notice we have three different styles, but also within those we have ones of varying lengths and weights. This is because people come in different sizes, have varying strength and different preferences on fighting style. So to help our students find what works best for them we have several choices of sword to mimic real blades. The one you've got in your hand is a broad sword which is longer and heavier than this one which is designed for close formation fighting. Some favour this curved scimitar blade while others prefer the skinny rapier which we don't have in wood. Each requires a different method to handle effectively.'

Natalya put back the broadsword she had in her hand in favour of one a little lighter. 'I assume it's better to use the same weapon as your opponent?'

'Not necessarily. It's better to use the one you know best and have the greatest skill with. A broadsword for instance has a lot of power, can cut through light armour and has a long reach. But because it's heavy it's slower to swing than a lighter blade.'

'So an inferior weapon can prevail over a stronger blade if it's in the hands of someone knowledgeable.'

'Or quicker to swing,' Bruno told her. 'Remember, in a real fight it is irrelevant how well armed someone is. If they aren't quick enough to effectively defend themselves then they'll fall.'

She nodded and joined Freddie in the arena. She was glad the other students had paired up and were already practising; she didn't want to be the focus of attention. But if she could learn to move as gracefully as Freddie she would be delighted

Freddie began slowly, showing her how to stand so her weight was balanced, how to grip the sword; too tight was as bad as too loose. Then he worked his way through a number of moves, sometimes standing beside her so she could follow the move without having to think of doing it in reverse as she would if he stood in front of her. But mostly he guided her through their link, showing her what he saw of her moves and also what exactly she was doing wrong. In each exercise he made sure she had the motion correctly mastered at the very slow pace before moving on.

'Ok, you now have enough moves to try parrying me properly,' Freddie told her. He brought up his sword swiftly and met hers with a thwack. They went through the entire sequence, correcting anything as they went along and letting her get a feel for how each move felt and flowed if done correctly. He increased the pace to one approaching normal human battle and smiled that she made very few errors. Their link enabled him to send her his approval or chiding as appropriate so she needn't have any of that audible to her classmates. Once she'd mastered each move he mixed up the order he threw them at her, forcing her to figure out how to react to his motions rather than expect a certain move and thus reaction to come next.

When they paused for a breather, Dustin came to the fence. 'Perhaps a better test would be against someone she's not linked to,' he suggested.

'Are you offering?' Freddie asked.

'Yes.'

'Ok,' Freddie agreed. 'You've probably seen I've just covered the absolute basics so far, so nothing else yet.'

'No problem,' Dustin said taking a fresh sword from the pile. 'Are you ok, or do you need a few minutes?' Dustin asked her, well aware unaccustomed exercises like this were very tiring.

'I could certainly do with a fresh pair of arms,' Natalya admitted. 'But you're here now,' she added and moved into a ready stance.

Dustin's bow seemed more genuine than Freddie's had been to Marko, but then she wasn't a stranger to Dustin. She mirrored his bow keeping eye contact and was surprised that Dustin seemed to change character with this formality. She'd never seen this cool calculating side to him. He was every bit the warrior now and he was more than a little daunting to face. He came at her quickly and she was hard pressed to match him.

'You're right, this is very different with you,' she told him. He grinned at being proved right. She struggled to keep up; he moved with a lazy elegance of motion that was deceptive in its speed.

*'Let his body language help guide you,'* Freddie advised mentally.

*'I hadn't thought of that. Why didn't you tell me that earlier?'* she complained on their link.

*'Sorry, it's so automatic; I didn't realise you wouldn't be considering that.'*

She assessed Dustin afresh. He was animus and understood body language. It was after all, the primary way animals communicated. To change into an animal successfully an animus person had to study their chosen creature and that included the way it communicated to others of its kind. She began to see the way he shifted his weight in readiness to change direction to either evade her or attack from a different side.

'Are you reading my mind?' Dustin asked suspiciously, as she suddenly began to move with him and it became far more difficult to get around her guard.

'No, your body,' she told him aware they weren't meant to be using magic whilst fighting in here.

His expression cleared; that he understood. He'd forgotten how good it felt to spar against a new quick opponent. It wasn't just testing out each other's reflexes and skills physically; it was also a battle of wits and will. Natalya had the raw ability in abundance and when she increased her skill levels she'd be a formidable opponent.

'Good work,' Dustin told her and disengaged. He could see other students beginning to part and guessed they would have a break soon.

'So what's your verdict?' Natalya asked him as they walked back to the side.

'You're learning well. You're also tired and need a break,' he added with a glance to Freddie, aware he was listening.

'Time for break everyone,' Bruno announced at that point and those still fighting broke apart. 'Are you coming with us to the house for break?' Bruno asked Freddie and glanced at his men to include them. 'We have much to discuss.'

'In that case, certainly,' Freddie responded amiably and they left the building. 'Why do you walk all the way back to the school for break?'

'It's better for the students. If we had a quick drink up here they wouldn't truly relax or calm down. Also it's a bit isolated up here. The boys tend to stick together at lunch, but break is more relaxed and they can mix with other students more easily.'

'Ah, flirting time,' Freddie grinned.

'You could put it like that,' Bruno agreed and tried to hide his smile that Dustin hastily tried to smooth his hair and Rupert surreptitiously sniffed his armpit.

Natalya was very glad to grab a mug and sit down. The last two hours had been strenuous, physically as well as mentally, trying to remember what she was meant to be doing. Reacting quickly to an attack, or get thumped was exhausting, not to mention painful. Whilst she knew Freddie had actively tried not to hurt her when they made contact, inevitably each blow that did land ached. Her hands felt bruised too from swords pounding her sword. To her credit none of the blows that landed had forced her to whimper and run away. She'd withstood them without backing down. She knew from her link with Freddie that he regarded her ability to handle the pain as quite remarkable. Usually it took time to learn to handle the inevitable consequences of fighting; the pain. Everyone instinctively tried to veer away from and avoid pain. Learning to continue moving through pain or even injury was something she'd already learned the hard way from the wizard and his son's attacks in her youth. Wailing at them to stop hurting her had only increased their glee and satisfaction. She had quickly learned to grit her teeth and endure in silence if she couldn't get away. Only the old stable man had given her the perspective to learn that what was done to her was wrong and cruel, rather than something she should not only expect but deserve. He had treated her wounds and been a shoulder to cry on. But he didn't allow self pity to creep in to her soul. He taught her to become self reliant and how to survive. He and the stable lads looked out for her and provided a refuge and company when no-one was about. He tried to teach her to be comfortable alone rather than continue being rebuffed by those who actually wanted to be friendly but whom were ordered not to be by their supervisors. It was hard; she needed company. She now knew that was an aspect of her wolf's nature. Under his advice she'd turned to befriending animals; they wouldn't betray her trust or stab her in the back.

She wasn't worried about stepping into the pens housing the massive hunting dogs. They weren't aggressive towards her, but they did serve to put off some of the boys seeking to torment her. The dogs accepted her presence amongst them and would even snarl at any person approaching her, regardless of who they were. She learned a lot from watching the dogs interact with one another. She learned how they displayed their strength to one another to settle disputes or rise in the pecking order and that there was strength in numbers. She was surprised to discover only those at the bottom seemed to fight amongst themselves or bully another. It gave perspective to how she was treated and was proof that what the horse master had tried to explain to her was true. Her wizard tormenters were low in rank amongst their peers. They did not deserve respect or deference. Equally, she knew better than to show defiance; it only sparked greater fervour in their attacks.

'Sorry, did you say something?' Natalya asked dragging her mind back to the present.

'I was only asking how you liked this morning's lessons,' Jim remarked. 'But you seemed miles away. Go anywhere nice?'

'Hardly,' Freddie said, his gaze on her face and still trying to calm his indignant anger. Hearing her memories of things she would be unlikely to ever share normally, had definite drawbacks.

'I've learned a great deal already this morning,' she said to Jim, finding a smile. 'Freddie and Dustin are very good teachers.'

'Glad to hear it,' Jim said and moved away. Whatever had upset Freddie, seemed to have originated with her. The hunters were now watching him with the direct unblinking and unnerving stare belonging to their wolves. Natalya sat at their centre; the men having gathered all around her as they always seemed to.

'So how'd she do?' Jim asked Bruno instead having moved out of earshot.

'About what we hoped she'd be able to do. You never told me about the hunters though,' Bruno complained.

'What do you mean? I know they can take care of themselves but I've not really seen them in action.'

'Freddie is an exceptional swordsman. He ran rings around Marko without effort. Dustin is less polished but nevertheless very accomplished. I haven't yet seen Rupert or Johnny in action; they seemed content to relax and keep watch on Natalya's progress. They're all very protective of her aren't they?' Bruno added, as aware as Jim of their positioning. 'I thought it would just be her boyfriend I'd have to watch.'

'They're wolves and she makes them into a pack with a future,' Jim said recalling what Max had told him. 'She roots them. I dread to think what would happen if she left. I think they'd go with her if they could,' Jim mused. Vako hailed him then so he rose to return to the practical but mundane aspects of being headmaster.

Natalya noticed Rupert glance up quickly and stare. The other men followed suit but less obviously. 'Hi Kathy,' Natalya called and the only other animus female wolf came over. 'Have you met the pack?'

'Mostly,' Kathy responded nervously. Last time she'd seen them together was before Natalya's arrival. They hadn't been a true pack then; but a band of bachelor males.

'You know Freddie,' Natalya said deciding to formally introduce them all. 'This is Dustin, he's been helping Freddie teach me today.' She watched Dustin take immediate advantage by reaching out to shake Kathy's hand. 'This is Johnny,' she went on letting each man shake Kathy's hand, 'and Rupert.' Rupert's hand shake lingered a little longer than the others. There was no question in Natalya's mind that he was attracted to Kathy and also that she was nervous of him. She'd certainly noticed him. Rupert had also repositioned himself when he sat back down making a space beside Natalya that was also close to him.

'Won't you sit down?' Natalya asked her. 'Rupert's made a space.'

Rupert flushed a little, aware of Natalya's amusement, but quickly returned his attention to Kathy.

'Thank you Rupert,' Kathy acknowledged and his smile returned. She quickly sat down before any more embarrassing attention or meaning could be read into the seat placement. 'So how'd it go this morning with the warrior class?'

'Good,' Natalya responded. 'But then Freddie was the one teaching me.'

'How come?'

'I needed to learn the basics before I could join the rest of the class properly. Freddie offered to do that so I wouldn't be holding anyone up. So, do you do combat training classes?'

'Yes, it's part of our animus class. I haven't done much yet though. The teachers are always inundated with the boys demanding tailored tuition; they can't get around to everyone.' She noticed Freddie frown and share a look with his men; clearly they disapproved. But what could they do, they had important jobs, they were not teachers.

'When is your combat class?' Freddie asked.

'Last lesson, after afternoon tea break. Anyway, must go,' Kathy added seeing students beginning to leave for their next class. 'See you,' she said to Natalya and hurried to join her classmates.

'She might be a woman but she is wolf,' Rupert said watching her leave the room. 'She should be well worth teaching, you'd have thought. Can we go and check it out later?'

Freddie eyed him, well aware of his personal interest in her. 'She has her hound Laurence remember.'

'You think I don't know that?' Rupert scowled. 'Besides he wasn't here with her just now.'

'Rupert,' Freddie chided lightly.

Rupert dropped his head before his alpha's disapproving gaze. He silently waited however; aware Freddie hadn't been happy to hear of their lack of teachers, and therefore patchy training, either.

'We'll check it out if Natalya doesn't need us,' Freddie told him.

'We'd better get going,' Natalya said suddenly aware not that many students remained in the hall now. She rose and the tall hunters moved with her.

Outside on the drive up to the training ground they could see her returning classmates were already in the distance.

'We're going to be late! I'm going to have to learn the timings for all these classes or I'll always be late,' she complained anxiously.

Dustin shimmered into his wolf, stepped out of his clothes, shoving them into a small backpack. His wolf seemed to smile at her. She laughed and changed too. Now they ran easily and quickly as a pack of wolves. Her spirits rose watching Rupert and Johnny bouncing around each other playfully, even as they travelled far faster than a human could run comfortably. They caught up with and bypassed the small group of students. Back inside the training ground Bruno saw them and his gaze had them ducking behind the seating for some privacy in which to change and dress swiftly.

'There see, we weren't late,' Dustin told her cheerfully.

She grinned back at him for a moment then noticed Bruno was watching her. She glanced round following his gaze and realised the pack had surrounded her again. The rest of the class had gathered awaiting Bruno's instructions and the pack stood between them and her. They were always protective of her, yet it never seemed oppressive to her; it was simply how they were. She'd spent all her teenage years alone and unloved wishing to be part of a family. Now through Freddie she had her wish. There was no way she would want them to behave in any other way. However, she moved closer to her classmates so she didn't look like she was hiding behind the pack and felt Bruno's approval.

Bruno began giving many of the senior students instructions to set up and begin archery practice outside. Many of the juniors were sent with them too, which thinned the crowd markedly.

'Ok Natalya. Let's pair you with a student this time. Who wants to partner her?' Bruno asked.

Despite Freddie's presence there was a show of hands from most of them. Natalya was rather surprised so many should be willing to volunteer. 'Jason,' she chose, seeing him also volunteering. He was the only one she'd actually spoken to among those remaining. Marko had gone to the archery field, and since Freddie had categorically beaten him earlier, she was glad he'd gone. She hoped he wasn't still smarting from it.

Bruno gestured and she followed Jason's lead in selecting a practice sword.

'Ok Jason, the basics,' Bruno instructed. 'Slowly.'

'No problem. I remember which moves she has and hasn't covered,' he added.

Natalya was aware of Bruno's raised brows at that admission. She wondered about it too, but hastily met Jason's eyes; he was ready to start. He bowed in the clan way then came at her. Facing him and trying to avoid his sword wasn't easy. He was animus; his definition of going slow was far faster than an ordinary human. Fortunately, Freddie and Dustin had the same fast reflexes so his pace didn't shock her. He was a stranger to her though; it wasn't as easy to guess how he might respond. Equally, he wasn't a battle hardened warrior. He hadn't learned the art of reducing his body language to trick an opponent as Dustin had. He rushed through the moves Freddie had taught her bringing them on in an unbroken sequence that was swift and required her complete attention. He moved on to something else and she frowned slightly; Freddie hadn't taught her this, yet her sword knew how to match it. Ah, the moves Jim had shown her. She heard Freddie growling, obviously he was aware these were moves he hadn't taught her and he thought Jason was overstepping her knowledge. She danced away from Jason, whirled to Freddie and planted a quick kiss on his lips. Freddie stopped growling but didn't seem impressed even when she mentally explained.

'You've got him wrapped round your finger then?' Jason teased.

'Not yet, but I'm working on it!' Natalya responded and they re-engaged. Jason flowed on to five more moves before he called a halt.

'Are you hurt Jason?' Natalya asked aware she'd thumped his arm and it now seemed to hang limply.

'It'll be fine,' he said aware of Freddie approaching.

Freddie met Jason's eyes before pushing back Jason's shirt sleeve. A large red swollen and abraded patch marred his upper arm surrounded by deep bruises.

'Did I do that?' she asked aghast.

'No, you just caught it.'

'Let me mend that for you,' Natalya offered contritely. 'It'll only take a moment,' she added, when he shifted uncertainly, his eyes on Freddie. 'Quit being territorial,' she chided the pair of them and placed her hands on Jason's arm either side of his injury.

Jason gasped feeling very strange. His arm went even hotter for a moment before a wash of welcome coolness flooded the area. She removed her hands and the pain was gone. 'Thank you,' he murmured, thoroughly disconcerted. He'd been thinking of her as an animus despite knowing she wasn't. But this was the first time he'd witnessed her doing something only a wizard could do.

'You healed Jim yesterday too?' He suddenly realised that's what he'd witnessed. He'd wondered at the time why she'd touched Jim when she so clearly wanted rid of his scent moments later. He watched her, aware she wasn't rushing to scour his scent off her hands. Perhaps she thought he might be offended if she did so in front of him. But whatever the reason, it pleased him.

'Yes, an exchange of healing was only fair. Jim told me he felt obliged to heal my bruises. He thought Freddie would get all angry and upset with him otherwise.'

'I can understand that,' Jason told her. She might be teasing Freddie lightly but he completely sympathised with Freddie on that one.

'Natalya, don't tell anyone you can heal or what you've just done for me,' Jason whispered urgently.

'Why?'

'You'll be inundated and then be expected to heal everyone every day. You don't need that pressure.'

'Good advice Jason,' Freddie responded approvingly and turned a quelling eye on Natalya. 'He's right. Healing is exhausting magic. Most people don't realise you have to experience their pain in full to heal them. They would only see that it takes a matter of moments to heal the majority of simple wounds.'

'You have to feel the pain to heal it?' Jason whispered horrified.

'She has to shoulder it in full and still concentrate through it enough to repair the injury,' Freddie explained. 'I only know this through our link. Through her I felt your pain. It's weird,' he admitted.

'I'm so sorry,' Jason said in acute embarrassment. 'I'll be sure never to put either of you through that again.'

'Don't be silly Jason,' Natalya told him. 'I like being able to help. I'm only returning the help you've given me. So, you've kept track of the moves I've been taught then?'

'Yes,' Jason admitted embarrassed yet again. 'It wasn't difficult. You had to be shown each move several times for it to stick. I wasn't learning anything new myself at the time.'

'You were injured because you weren't paying complete attention to your opponent?' Freddie surmised.

'Probably,' Jason shrugged indifferently. 'I got him back for thumping me so hard.'

Freddie chuckled at that, before Bruno caught their attention and sent them off to the archery field. Natalya was glad of the chance to walk and let her arms hang; they ached.

Rupert and Johnny came to the fore now when a demonstration was called for. They didn't show off or make a meal of it; they simply came forward and fired with deadly accuracy. The speed with which they could reload and fire with equal accuracy was what really impressed Bruno. He bid his students make note of how Rupert and Johnny did it. It was easy to fire accurately when you had no pressure to hurry and your target was stationary. Obviously in the real world your target was likely to be moving and certain to be taking evasive action once it had seen you. Speed was the key to success.

Natalya was very glad Freddie had at least begun training her. It was embarrassing to be completely inept beside such effortless skill.

'You're not taking long enough to aim,' Bruno chided her.

'I'm aching. I haven't the strength to hold it longer,' she admitted. 'I am a girl you know,' she couldn't help adding, eyeing Bruno's massive biceps.

'As though your gender has much bearing on your strength,' Bruno said dismissively. 'Your sister once picked me clear off the ground and tossed me several feet. Another time she turned into a dragon, picked Jim and I up and managed to fly while carrying us both. Are you trying to convince me you're an ordinary frail girl?'

'I am not my sister. I have no idea how she managed to do that or why it didn't kill her. I seriously doubt I could lift you alone and Jim's no lightweight either. Why am I always being compared to my little sister? We are not alike and it's exceedingly annoying.'

'My apologies,' Bruno conceded.

'So Amelie took this class too?'

'No. She joined the animus class for most things. I believe that's where she felt most comfortable. That class does of course have some combat training but it's not so in depth or serious as this class.'

'So I'm not just following in my sister's footsteps?' Natalya asked brightening.

'Not at all. I would say very little of what she did, you have done. It is simply that you both have unusually strong talents. We don't know the extent of yours yet or what unusual things you are able to do.'

She pondered that, but she had no clue whether she possessed an unusual skill. If she did she hadn't found it yet. She was only as fast as another animus and she had a great deal to learn about using magic.

The wolves remained with the warrior class for lunch and were inundated with questions from the students on a whole variety of topics. The boys had been very impressed by the skills displayed so far and wanted to know what else they excelled in and also how these skills had been attained. The other main questions were ones asking advice on things individual students were struggling with.

After lunch Natalya led Freddie outside to the big tree. She changed into her wolf, her clothes floating off her and folding themselves in the time it took her to kneel and visualise her wolf shape.

'That's a neat trick,' Freddie acknowledged as he changed and shrugged out of his clothes awkwardly. 'Don't you have another class though?'

'Not for another hour. Fortunately for me we get a long lunch break. It's been a tiring morning with our dawn start and I need a nap.'

'So how do you like this class so far? Do you think this is still what you want to do?' Freddie asked her as the wolves settled around them.

'It's been good so far. But I'll reserve judgement until I've got through the magic classes.'

Freddie laughed and urged her to sleep. The wolves sat with them but so too did Jason in his dark spotted dog form. He sat at the fringe of the pack, continuing a conversation with Rupert. They kept their voices low in deference to Natalya already sleeping. Then each curled up and slept too. They'd all had a long tiring morning too and it was rare they had the opportunity to rest in the day.

17

# Magical Testing

It felt odd to watch the wolves trot for home while she returned to human form and followed Jason to class. She was very glad that he had stayed so she wasn't searching for the next classroom alone and also that the pack had accepted Jason. She learned from Freddie that Jason's father had been the alpha leader of another pack, a dog pack. Tosker had made it back to White Haven to tell Drako of the ambush that had killed the rest of his team before he died from his wounds. He had died with honour and dignity but it had left Jason alone. Fortunately he was no longer a child and was already enrolled and secure with a place in the school. His aunt and uncle took him in so he wasn't completely alone and they had admirably helped to ease his grief. Freddie thought he had recovered well in the last few months. Natalya empathised with him; the loss of one's family was never easy. Having understanding people you could talk to was important. The right friends could pull you out of depression and make you feel alive and worthwhile, or drag you down. He'd seemed rather alone and a dog never liked that. She would be alert on his behalf.

She slid into an empty seat next to Jason near the back of the class. Other students were still arriving and chatting amongst themselves. She was aware of several sidelong glances and guessed she was being discussed. Vako swept into the room and the talking ceased. Students hastened to take their seats.

'Today we're going to be working on shielding,' Vako announced.

Natalya heard several people groan and glanced round in surprise.

'Natalya, what is the purpose of a shield?' Vako demanded before he'd even got to his desk.

'To defend yourself,' she responded promptly.

'Correct at its simplest,' Vako confirmed. 'There are an infinite variety of shields because they can be tailored to any specific need and are only limited by the skill, strength and imagination of the wizard. They do however fall into three main categories. The first covers mental shields. Most wizards learn to construct a privacy shield from an early age, but there are also defensive versions. These are critical under attack to stop your thoughts or indeed any sensitive information being easily read by another wizard. The second main category covers physical shields, i.e. to protect your body from attack. The third category covers shielding someone else. Natalya I believe you have done all three of these shields,' Vako said, verbally pouncing on her again, but with a rather sceptical tone. 'Can you show us?'

She gasped feeling his immediate assault on her mind. She instantly threw up her shield and the pain vanished.

'Class can you feel the hum of power around her now? Each of you try her shield,' Vako invited. He didn't stop them joining together creating small melds to try and get past her. It was a good test and measure of her strength. He kept close watch on her mind or rather on the image she was presenting them all with of a seamless brick wall. Not once did anyone succeed in even chipping it. She faltered once only, her attention going to Jason trying to break up those ganging up on her. 'I'm fine Jason, but thanks,' she told him.

'Ok enough everyone. That's an example of a strong defensive mental shield,' Vako conceded. 'But you can also feel the power she is using up to maintain it. This is not something that can be maintained indefinitely. It is best to know how to construct one fast when the need arises. Ok, next is a physical shield. Perhaps you should move over here Natalya,' Vako suggested. 'We don't want anyone getting hurt by a deflection.'

Natalya warily went to stand against the rear wall of the classroom, safely apart from the other students. She watched Vako closely; he was in turn watching her intently, perhaps waiting for her attention to be diverted and thus drop her guard. Suddenly he threw out his hands and a stream of purple paint flew from his hands towards her. It hit her shield and flowed around it making it visible to everyone. He moved his hands, directing the flow, seeking any holes or flaws in her shield, but shortly she was encased in a purple bubble. She was blind now and began to feel nervous. She hadn't thought paint could be used as a weapon but she couldn't see out and her shield was gleaming around her like a beacon. What had he said about shields being of infinite variety? Was it possible to alter her shield?

'See, she can shield but she's going to run out of air soon,' Vako instructed the class. 'She also can't see if anyone is working a new spell against her and is now a highly visible target for other wizards to take over the assault.' At that moment he heard a strange popping sound and noticed the purple bubble had begun rolling towards him. It was only as it rolled that he noticed a big tear in the back. He stepped aside quickly and realised Natalya was no longer inside. Instead, she stood behind the bubble. He aimed his paint at her directly but she raised her hands and the paint veered to splat against the wall. He stepped away again but the purple bubble followed him. He frowned at it uneasily and suddenly it lifted and slammed into him, swallowing him via the tear. He hastily cut off his paint spell, realising he was filling the inside of the bubble, not to mention his shoes, with paint. He pushed at it trying to find the tear but it had sealed behind him. He tried a number of spells attempting to cut his way out but to no avail. He finally dropped his hands in frustrated defeat and the bubble popped and disintegrated, leaving big flakes of dried paint littering the floor and a purple puddle poured from his shoes.

'Tell me how that one worked,' Vako demanded. He'd been in battles with experienced wizards but had rarely been quite so stumped.

'I tuned the shield to you,' Natalya told him, eyeing his red face and that he needed to sit down. 'While you fought you fed it. Once you gave up it ceased to be.'

Vako mulled that over.

'What category of shield does that come under?' Marko daringly asked.

'Warrior wizard,' Vako muttered. 'No actually that was shielding someone else. What she did was an ingenious variation. She turned a defensive personal shield into an offensive barrier targeting her attacker. What would you have done if this had been an attack for real?'

'Made good my escape. You could no longer attack me, nor could you see where I went. I'd also just turned you into the target for your own men to finish off.'

'Mm, unusual strategy but one that would probably work,' Vako conceded, impressed. 'So, how would you defend a less able ally? Say an animus from wizard attack?'

'I'm not sure, I only did it once.'

'Come now, there's no room for doubts or modesty here. I heard you knocked Jim's lion to the floor, stopping his charge dead.' Vako eyed her, aware the others were shocked by this possibility. Most thought Jim was an exceedingly powerful wizard. It was good for them to know others could be stronger, that he wasn't all-powerful. 'Come and volunteer Jason. Let's see if she'll defend you like you were trying to do for her earlier.'

Natalya stared at Jason in dismay, seeing him immediately go rigid with pain. She acted without thinking. She made a chopping motion with her hand dropping a barrier between Vako and Jason. Vako's spell abruptly rebounded back on him but not squarely. Those students standing on Vako's left got blasted with some of the spell too. Vako winced and jumped aside, obviously trying to avoid the rebound as well as get around her shield. Students scattered in panicked chaos, all trying to avoid the constantly altering stream of fallout.

Abruptly Vako clapped his hands, calling a halt to the spell and gesturing everyone back to their seats.

'If anyone was wondering why she joined this class, that ought to answer it,' Vako said to the class at large. 'What she has demonstrated for us today is the reason she is called a warrior wizard. Aside from her unusual strength, a warrior wizard instinctively knows how to react defensively, unlike a regular wizard who has to learn it. Obviously with tuition she will gain experience and real skill. But the core quick reactions and defensive ability are already there.'

'How did my sister react to that test?'

'I was never able to test her that precise way, but I do know she reacts very differently to you.'

'How?'

'She is an animus warrior wizard. She reacts just as quickly and defensively as you. However, she does not instinctively reach for her magic to counter a threat. Her first response is to become whatever animal she thinks would best cope with the situation. If I was attacking you for real Jason, how would you counter me?'

'My first thought was to leap across and rip out your throat.'

'Yes, a typical animus response. Yet you didn't change form and you didn't even move. I thought I'd see some reaction to a surprise attack. Or was it too much of a surprise?'

'Not at all. I knew Natalya would stop you. You had just told us that she stopped Jim in lion form. With all due respect, he is a more powerful wizard.

Besides, you did warn me that it was to test her not me,' Jason reminded him. Natalya gently squeezed his shoulder for a moment as she returned to her seat. But that briefest of touches took away the pounding headache he was suffering as a result of Vako's attack. It was the nicest thanks he could think of.

'So you were happy to rely on the protection of a complete novice and hide behind a pretty girl?' Vako suggested, watching Jason staring at her.

'She is not just a girl,' Jason contradicted sharply. 'She is probably the strongest wizard student at this school. It would be stupid of me to get between two fighting wizards,' he added scornfully.

'Ah. Actually you do have a valid point that everyone should remember, especially those of you who are animus. Only interfere if your wizard wishes it.' He then moved on to explaining some of the other variations wizards had come up with to counter attack. He didn't call on Natalya or Jason for the remainder of the lesson, aware he'd perhaps singled them out a little too much. Jim had specifically told him not to do so, worried that she might lose control and accidentally injure someone. Vako however felt justified, having proved her level of control was far greater than Jim gave her credit for. Vako had reasoned it would have to be so for her to have achieved what she already had done with her spell casting. Even small spells required control and she'd demonstrated them in his presence.

After the lesson ended Jim entered his classroom waiting until the students had departed with their customary alacrity.

'So how did your lesson go?' Jim asked Vako, whilst glancing around a liberally purple splattered classroom. Many of the students he'd passed in the corridor were also purple spotted. He'd noticed Natalya had purple on the soles of her shoes, but was otherwise completely clean. Jason too by her side was unscathed. In marked contrast, Vako's shoes and socks were a vivid purple and even the hems of his trousers were liberally splashed.

'Very well,' Vako responded.

'You know this whole end of the school was vibrating with power?'

'I had Natalya demonstrate three of her shields,' Vako admitted, knowing no one else could have created such a power signature.

'You tested her then?'

'Of course, but no more than I thought she could handle. I really don't think you need worry over her level of control. Yes she's powerful but she naturally only uses the minimum power needed to achieve each spell.'

'She impressed you then?'

'Yes; she's very creative. Obviously she needs a great deal of tuition but she has a thirst for knowledge in its practical applications.'

'Who made the mess then?' Jim asked glancing pointedly at the lurid paint, thickly coating a whole side of the room.

'I did, or rather I used the colour to reveal her shield to the class. Quite effective for everyone to be able to see what she was doing. It was also a good way to demonstrate how a seemingly harmless spell can be turned into a weapon. But she got out of it unaided.'

'You bombarded a green warrior wizard with paint, knowing how strong she is and also that she has a temper?'

'As far as I've heard or seen, she only appears to have directed anger at you,' Vako said, watching Jim closely. He hadn't been privy to whatever had sparked her ire. But he had certainly seen the coolly polite way she had kept her distance when forced into proximity with Jim in her early days. He hadn't seen them together more recently however to know if they'd resolved their differences. He assumed they must have come to some understanding for her to join lessons and equally for Jim to spend so much of his own time giving her personal tuition.

'The boys in her class are falling over themselves to be close to her, although I don't think she's even noticed them. Young Jason seems the only one who's actually been noticed. He's clearly taken it upon himself to be her friend. He's smart too, that one,' Vako said.

'I hear from Bruno he volunteered to be her sparring partner,' Jim said. 'He then admitted he remembered every move I'd taught her and every move Freddie did today too. The fight he then engaged her with took her through every one of those moves without pause or repetition. I hope he's not expecting that she'll drop Freddie for him.'

'I'd actually wondered if that friendship was something her boyfriend instigated, they've certainly been talking together,' Vako suggested.

'I hope so,' Jim said and went on his way, relieved all appeared well. He fully intended to peer into Natalya's memory tomorrow if he could, to see that paint fight. If Vako had won he'd have been crowing about it. The fact he wasn't volunteering details probably meant he'd pushed her more than he thought Jim would have approved of. She had clearly impressed him but may have embarrassed him in front of the class, too.

18

# *Returned*

'Finally, I'm on my way home,' Amelie called to Jim.

'Glad to hear it,' he responded in relief. 'When?'

'In about half an hour. Can you get everyone off the lawn so we have a place to land?'

'You plan to let Stripe land on the front lawn in broad daylight? I don't think that's a very good idea. We'll have wide-scale panic and we certainly won't be able to keep that news from spreading.'

'I suppose you're right. Where then?'

'There ought to be space enough just outside the People Gate for him to land. That's safely out of the student's sight.

*Then no-one need be any the wiser of his presence or your friendship with a real dragon.'*

'Very well, I'll tell him.'

'I'll meet you there.'

Jim eagerly jogged along the narrow path worn into the grass from the school driveway over to the small People Gate. Whilst there was a nice wide-open stretch of meadow on this side of the gate, it was in clear view to anyone up at the training grounds, or indeed the school's eastern windows. Stripe was simply too large to expect him to land unnoticed in an open field, especially when those at the training ground were mostly animus with keen eyes.

From the gatehouse he watched the big dragon land in what now seemed a small space. Once on the ground however, Jim noticed Stripe's dark green colouration and darker stripes meant the dragon blended amazingly well with the shadowed trees behind him. That was useful to know.

Jim stepped out of the gatehouse and passed through the shadowed archway into their sight. He was well aware that Stripe was watching him closely, but his main attention was on Amelie sliding from the dragon's back. A second person carefully passed down a well wrapped bundle; Daisy. He had time to register that the girl sliding down off the dragon had sapphire blue hair before Amelie was in his arms. He hugged his love and their daughter closely, assuring himself that they had taken no harm.

'You look tired, love,' he commented with a frown and noticed she glanced sideways in both explanation and resignation. 'The blue haired one is Tania?'

'Yes.'

'Why hasn't she reverted?' Jim asked, keeping their conversation private on their link.

'I don't know for sure, but she's certainly enjoying thwarting her father. He couldn't come down to the village to get us in dragon form of course and so while she remained there she was outside of his control. She'll try this ploy again I've no doubt when she next feels like escaping him. She was having far too much fun to listen to me, as well. In some respects it was fortunate there was that storm and that it caused so much damage. She got exceedingly bored with sitting inside waiting for it to pass and then days of trudging through thick mud, sweeping debris and helping with the repairs by fetching and carrying. I know the villagers were glad for some extra hands, but we did not belong there.'

'They must have questioned you about her. What did you say?'

'No one there had any magic, fortunately. I told them she was animus and that her real mother died, leaving her running wild in the forest. I hoped that would explain her lack of manners and understanding of civilised ways in general. It was not easy trying to cover for her. She had no idea how peculiar they thought her.'

*'It all sounds like a completely frustrating time was had.'*

*'Yes, and not just for me,'* she responded glancing at Stripe. He was watching her and she abruptly wondered if he could hear their conversation; he had the last time. *'We really don't need Tania's brothers and sisters seeing her like this. Goodness knows how they'd react. Stripe has enough to cope with in raising them alone, as it is.'*

'Ok Tania, it's time you reverted back to your real self,' Jim said briskly realising Stripe was unable to leave until that happened.

'I don't want to.'

'We all have to do things we don't want to do. You've had your fun. Now it's time to get back to normal.'

'I am a queen. I don't have to listen to you!'

'Queen?' Jim snorted at her. 'You're certainly not yet a queen. You are still a child and you are acting incredibly selfishly. Change back into your true form. Your father is waiting.'

Tania merely shrugged, ignoring them all.

'Now you are also being rude,' Jim informed her. He raised his hand and Tania was suddenly lifted off the ground and pushed against a tree trunk. There she dangled many feet above the ground, wide-eyed in shock.

*'Careful, little lion,'* Stripe warned.

'Look over the wall,' Jim told her having lifted her sufficiently. He absently noticed that Stripe had lifted his head high, his gaze flicking between his daughter, Jim and the view on the other side. Jim was relieved; getting Stripe defensively angry was to be avoided at all costs. So far the dragon was making no attempt to interfere.

'Do you see all the people inside this wall? There are some up here training, many in the main building and yet more down at the far end,' he said pointing to each group. 'I am in charge of and responsible for the safety of each and every one of them. Because you ran away and refused to return, your father had to come here and ask Amelie for help. Do you really think he wanted to have to do that? To admit he couldn't control one rebellious child? Earlier that day I had to deal with some enemy wizards and then an attack on one of my people inside the grounds. Amelie's sister was the target and she was forced to kill him.'

'That was Natalya, my sister?'

'Yes. We didn't know who she was to you of course at the time,' Jim reminded Amelie. He then returned his gaze to Tania. 'Because of these threats I was forced to allow my mate to travel to an unknown village where she would be trespassing on other human's lands, cope with an unknown and potentially dangerous human leader, all whilst caring for a young baby and a dragon child who refused to recognise the danger she was putting everyone in. Oh, and let's not forget the impact on your brothers and sisters. While your escapade was wasting your father's time, he could not be watching over and defending your brothers and sisters. If something had attacked them, their deaths would be squarely your fault. Do you understand?'

'Yes,' Tania said in a small voice. She had tried to free herself but could not. She was pinned immobile by the lion man and her father was not intervening.

'Good. Now apologise to your father. He has a hard enough life raising so many children at once without you making it even more difficult.'

'Sorry papa,' she said quietly and the lion man lowered her to the ground and released her.

'Now, follow my lead,' Jim said. His clothes unfastened and floated off his skin and he knelt. 'It is always best to remember your posture when you alter form from two legs to four. You know your dragon, picture your form clearly in your mind and will the change.'

Tania watched the man shimmer and a lion take his place in awe. 'But there is so much to learn about your world. I want to stay here.' She glanced at her father, hearing his growl, but there was little he could do to stop her. The lion shimmered and reverted to his human form once more. There was no mistaking his annoyance however. Unexpectedly, Amelie gasped and they realised she was looking Stripe's way.

Stripe shook his head uneasily and rose to balance on two feet instead of four. He had a human body! He'd never known this was possible. He had heard Amelie's concern that Tania would do this again if he could not stop her and then listened to Jim's instructions without realising he was also acting on them. He'd never thought it would be so easy to accomplish, even though Tania had managed it.

'Papa, you did it!' Tania exclaimed and ran to him. She looked him over closely then wrapped her human arms about warm soft skin. 'Mama, look!' she added, beckoning. 'Doesn't he look wonderful now?'

'Yes,' Amelie had to admit. Stripe was watching her closely. His eyes might be a vivid grass green but they sparkled with wary intelligence. 'That's quite a transformation.'

'Am I human enough?' Stripe asked forming words with his voice rather than using their usual mental communication. He stepped out from behind Tania so his queen had an uninterrupted view. He was inwardly amused and satisfied to note her gaze travelled over him fully and gave every indication of appreciation.

'You're big, I mean taller than anyone I've ever seen. You've got to be over seven feet tall.' He was exceedingly heavily muscled too. Clearly condensing his dragon mass was no easy matter. His skin was a beautiful burnished bronze, as was Tania's. It was an unusually deep shade for this part of the world, but not unnatural. His hair was black rather than green, except for a paler streak at his left temple. 'What happened here? Have you been injured?' she asked tentatively stroking back the white strands. His hair was short and silky soft.

'I have a mark?' he asked in surprise. 'Yes, I do have an old battle scar there,' he admitted, more interested in savouring her touch.

Amelie hastily removed her hands noticing his reaction. 'Wow! Your teeth are not at all human,' she told him, suddenly noticing he had a mouthful of fangs. 'It looks like you have simply shrunk your dragon teeth to fit a smaller mouth.'

'Anything else?'

'Your eyes are an unusual colour,' she told him refraining from admitting they were beautiful. She could hear Jim's unease; he knew she found Stripe attractive. It was best Stripe didn't know that as well however. 'You'll need to remember that humans don't walk about naked. Whilst shifters are used to seeing each other, they do expect someone to cover up as soon as they can.'

Stripe glanced over at her mate, the male he'd copied and found he'd now covered his bare skin. He knew he wouldn't have found it so easy to change form without seeing exactly how a human male was put together. Amelie was female and very different. She was also wearing things that swamped her form and concealed specific details. Tania too was dressed and her immature body was little use as a guide. He realised he was looking down on her mate; she was right that he'd become a large male. Could he win her? For the first time, claiming the one female he'd ever wanted was a viable possibility now he could share her form. However, he suspected fighting her mate would not go down very well just now, or do him any favours in the long run. He still had dependents as did she; there was time. He turned, suddenly detecting others approaching.

Jim noticed Stripe's action, and that he thrust Amelie and then Tania behind him to face away from the walls. He quickly moved up beside Stripe to scan the forest. 'I think I know who it is,' Jim reassured him. Shortly, a couple of figures tentatively came into view, clearly equally aware someone was already here.

'Jim. Everything ok?'

'Yes fine Freddie. Been acquiring more doe's for our captive herd Natalya?'

'Yes,' she affirmed a little absently. The most enormous and daunting looking man she'd ever seen stood before them and entirely naked. Who the hell was he?

'Go ahead and release those deer,' Jim urged Dustin, spotting him with his arms wrapped around the neck of a deer. Johnny and Rupert were behind him and similarly encumbered. The men hastily and gratefully slipped past the strange man, through the gate to release their captives. Only then could they quickly return to warily observe what was going on here.

'Natalya?' Amelie called and realised her sister hadn't noticed her tucked in the shadow of Stripe's overwhelming presence. Hastily, she pulled the thin blanket off Daisy, glanced up to meet Stripe's eyes before she wrapped the cloth about his hips.

'Thank you,' Stripe rumbled, only just remembering not to call her his queen. He watched her go to the other female and the pair wrapped their arms about each other. He noticed the pale haired female kept an eye on him warily and that the male she'd been closest to when they first appeared watched over them defensively.

*'She is your sister? A full-blooded sibling?'* Stripe asked privately.

*'Yes. We have not seen each other in many years,'* Amelie told him.

*'She is a fine queen, like you,'* he commented in approval. *'Her mate is very defensive. I appear to cause all these males anxiety.'*

'It can hardly be surprising; you're a stranger. And you don't look entirely human,' Amelie responded aloud.

'That's because I am not,' he responded. 'Tania, it is time to change. Tania,' he growled warningly, noting her defiant stance, 'you will do as you're told.'

Tania hissed, aware every eye had just switched to her and were waiting. 'I don't know how.'

'Yes you do, he told you, or were you not listening again?'

Suddenly Natalya shimmered, her clothes floating off and folding themselves as a huge tiger took her place. 'Change form, or feel my teeth,' Natalya growled, having heard from Amelie the problems they'd been having with this rebellious creature. She stalked the girl, her eyes fixed on her in a manner she knew very well tended to terrify. The sooner the child obeyed, the sooner the scarily powerful father would leave and they could all relax. She wanted to sit Amelie down and hear all about what had happened since they had parted, what had happened to their parents and of course to properly meet and hold her niece for the first time.

'You wouldn't dare bite me. My father would eat you,' Tania cried.

'He would not interfere with a queen disciplining a child, especially as he has come to us for exactly this purpose,' Natalya told her and cuffed the child. She had sheathed her claws and checked the force of her blow, but Tania squealed in shock. 'It's about time you learned that disobedience has consequences. My sister hasn't her usual strength right now to deal with you as she should. Daisy is her priority and takes her strength. You are old enough to know what you're doing is wrong. You must consider how your actions are, and have affected, all those around you.'

'But I want to stay here,' Tania complained.

'Right now your place is with your father. You are too young yet and have not earned the privilege of studying here,' Natalya told her. 'There is no place in the human world for those who will not obey their seniors or respect the rules governing all our lives.' Natalya cuffed the girl again, aware she wore a mulish expression and was yet again attempting to talk her way out of obeying. Predatory creatures only respected the strong and Tania had been taking advantage of Amelie's reduced strength. All Natalya's protective instincts had welled up to defend her little sister. Amelie had failed to get through to her by talking; clearly a show of strength was the next recourse.

Tania glanced over at her father and realised his annoyance was not aimed at the tiger female, but at her. Amelie too, was not interfering, but seemed sad. A suddenly far harder slap knocked her sideways and she gaped at the tiger female in shock.

'You weren't even listening to me, were you?'

Tania whimpered and lowered her head in submission. Only her grandmother had ever demanded such unquestioning obedience and she now wondered if her own mother would have behaved the same as this too. She knelt as the lion had done and concentrated. She felt her body wrench itself into a different shape and then suddenly she was looking down on the tiger.

'Good,' Amelie said tonelessly. 'When you want to visit humans again, you come here. It simply isn't safe to go anywhere else. But the only way we will agree to take you in for anything more than a few hours is with your father's approval. You will have to convince him that you have learned from your mistakes and are willing to learn and obey our human laws. Do you understand?'

'Yes,' Tania responded with as good a grace as she could muster.

'Thank you, once again,' Stripe said having gone to Amelie. He rubbed his cheek against hers and savoured the soft delicacy of sensation that this form's skin bestowed. He met the other female's gaze and she allowed him to press his face to hers in the same brief manner. 'You are learning my scent little queen?' he asked softly.

'You are doing the same,' Natalya responded and noticed his smile and his gaze drift over her. Damn, he obviously liked a strong willed female. Except where his children were concerned; they seemed to have him wrapped around their fingers, or whatever the equivalent was for a creature that didn't have fingers! She noticed him glance at Freddie behind her and grin again, but that was definitely more a showing of teeth male to male, and impressive fangs he had too! She stepped back, but was a little surprised that Jim advised them to pull right back to the gateway.

'You wish your cloth?' Stripe asked Amelie before she could follow the others. He hid his satisfaction as she approached and again revealed her appreciation for his form. However, once she had untied the knot and bared him, she stopped looking at his body, keeping her eyes on his face alone. Why?

'You're too close to the trees,' Amelie warned him suspecting he hadn't noticed. He glanced round, and did indeed move further into the open. She backed away quickly and knew he waited until she was safely with the others before he knelt and his form blurred, shimmered and grew and grew. Stripe the dragon soon filled the available space. He gave them another long look before he leaped into the air. His massive wings took him aloft swiftly and they watched him go after Tania. Remarkably quickly they both had disappeared into the distance.

19

# A Whopping Secret

*'Drako, I have something to show you, whenever's convenient,'* Jim said, calling mentally. *'It might be useful for your father to come as well.'*

*'What is it?'*

*'Come and see,'* Jim added and disengaged the contact.

'Is something wrong?' Freddie asked noticing Drako jerk in his swing-seat and then sit still, his expression turned inward. Freddie recognised the signs of a wizard making mental contact. Drako was now frowning, as he strode down the steps.

'I hope not,' Drako responded as Freddie joined him and they walked down the lane. 'Jim has something to show me and thinks dad should be involved.'

'Ah. Good.'

'You know what this is about, don't you?' Drako said sharply, turning to eye his friend.

'Probably. I don't want to spoil the surprise though; if it's what I think then it's a whopper.' Freddie was well aware of Drako's scowl. 'Perhaps Ebony and Darius ought to come too,' Freddie added seriously.

'Now you're seriously worrying me,' Drako admitted but Freddie just shrugged and gestured for Drako to precede him. Yes, the sooner they found Darius and Trent down at the Hideaway, the sooner they could reach Jim and find out what was going on. He reached for Cassy in class and asked her to contact Ebony on his behalf, who was doubtless somewhere up at the school. She had essentially moved in with Max and he hardly saw her anymore, but she seemed happy and that was all that really mattered.

'Do come in,' Jim invited and smiled to find Drako had arrived exceedingly quickly and was accompanied by his father who was shifting impatiently from foot to foot. Darius and Ebony followed, with nervous curiosity on their faces. Freddie brought up the rear and it was clear he hadn't said a word to any of his leaders.

'What's this about?' Trent asked as soon as the door closed. He spared a glance for the aged opulence of this Head Master's office and the young wizard taking centre stage behind a large official desk. Setting the scene was he?

'Do sit down,' Jim invited waving at the four armchairs grouped near the empty fireplace. Trent and the three siblings sat, leaving Freddie leaning against the door.

'Thank you all for coming. I'll get straight to the point. I called you here today because I rebuilt some old ruins I found on the grounds and accidentally reactivated something that has relevance to you.'

'Reactivated what?' Trent asked.

Jim noticed all were at the edge of their seats. 'The building has carvings on it that I thought you might recognise,' and he placed a sketch onto the coffee table in front of Trent.

Trent snatched up the sheet and his eyes widened. 'What the hell?'

Darius grabbed the sheet next and a frown crinkled his brow. 'Is that the ancient symbol for Féarmathuin?'

'Yes it is!' Trent said. 'It's on a building you say? Please, show us this place.'

Jim rose and headed for the door without further ado, everyone following swiftly on his heels. Jim strode through the house, passing through the glass house and outside, where he headed in the direction of the training ground. After a short distance he veered into the woods, following an almost invisible trail that must have been the original path and since been kept open by small animals.

'Wait,' he ordered as they stepped into the small glade right on his heels. He let them come abreast so they could see the shimmering opaque wall before them. He gestured quickly and the wall vanished with a pop.

'What was that?' Darius asked nervously.

'A defensive barrier,' Jim said simply and moved forward; silently indicating it was now safe to advance.

'Is that a Portal?' Drako asked breathlessly, glancing at Jim who nodded. 'You were right Freddie; this is one whopper of a secret. How has it remained hidden all this time?'

'It was smashed into unrecognisable rubble like most portals I've seen,' Jim told them. 'Someone expended a great deal of time and effort going around the country making them unusable. I've no idea when that happened and haven't seen any mention of there being a Portal here in any of the records, so it must have been long ago.'

Trent stepped up onto the plinth to better see the engravings on the right-hand pillar. There was a small rumble and a whooshing sound as a blue-white watery vortex with a black centre, suddenly formed within the confines of the arch. Jim leaped forward and grabbed Trent in case he lost his balance or perhaps attempted to step through.

'It works!' Darius cried in astonished glee. 'Our Portal home works!'

'At this end it does,' Jim said and drew Trent off the plinth so the tempting vortex closed. 'Listen. As I was trying to say just now, many portals were deliberately made inoperable. I might have repaired it here, but we don't know what has been done at the other end. You could be killed going through. It could come out in midair, as this one did, or have been bricked up or buried. Now, this one says it comes out in Féarmathuin, which I believe is your homeland?' He noted Trent's nod. 'Do you know where the Portal was located on your lands? Was it in the open or in a building?'

'The reason our Clan has historically had such close ties with this school was because of this Portal. We kept our Portal secure long after the desecrations elsewhere occurred, but we could not keep it safe at this end,' Trent said. 'Our Portal is inside Féarmathuin Castle itself. It's in a locked room adjacent to the dungeons.'

'What happened to your castle?' Jim asked gently. 'Was it taken over, or broken and abandoned?'

'After the walls were breached with magic they tore it apart,' Trent said bleakly. 'They left nothing defensible for us to return to.'

'You were attacked by wizards?'

'Yes. For hundreds of years Féarmathuin Castle's walls stood against a host of different armies, but everything changed when they sent wizards against us,' Trent said and sat down heavily in the grass.

Jim sat with him, eager to hear what Trent would say. The fall of Féarmathuin Castle was an event spoken of in hushed tones even back home, but no one had known the details of what really happened.

'You probably know that Clan Green Bear had become a politically important target as the last major independent animus power.'

Jim nodded. With their downfall, it was argued that the animus people elsewhere would be broken, the reason and will to fight beaten from them.

'Well, in order to be assured of success in defeating an animus held castle, the King knew he needed wizard assistance. So, he approached the High Wizard's conclave for help. The wizard put in charge of the negotiations at the time was a canny bastard by the name of Sir Cyril. In return for aiding the King, he negotiated for signed permissions allowing wizards to setup and self-govern their own guilds. To fulfil their end of the deal and achieve the independence that wizards had been working towards for years, all they need do was destroy Féarmathuin Castle, the Clan Green Bear stronghold.'

'To accomplish that end the conclave entrusted the job to their most decorated Warrior Wizard, who happened to be Sir Cyril. With him they sent a troop of forty wizards as backup. Unfortunately, once Sir Cyril joined the King's army, he and his wizards fell under the King's cruel thumb. Undoubtedly the King changed the terms of the deal and Cyril was subsequently set on every town or city on their route North, quelling, crushing and defeating all opposition to the King's new laws against animus. With the inevitable delays in taking control of the people enroute, it took them several months march to reach Northern Rosh and the Clan Green Bear lands. It did of course give us time to fortify the town and stockpile food and weapons. A large number of the vulnerable were evacuated, including the elderly, the injured or those with small children. Sent deep into the wilds into hiding, they would be safely away from any fighting. Whilst no one really expected the castle to be breached, since it had successfully defended us for generations, we were worried by the reports of those on their way to us and the trail of destruction they were leaving behind them. Ultimately, our walls proved they were not proof against wizards and unnatural forms of attack.'

'A fierce battle raged for three days before we had to retreat from the field. The losses on both sides were appallingly heavy. The subsequent siege of Féarmathuin Castle came to an abrupt end once the wizard warriors could get close enough to use their spells on the castle walls. With the gates smashed open and the exterior walls of the castle itself breached, we realised they planned to bring the whole place down.'

'How did you get away? This Portal must have been smashed long before that,' Jim asked.

'It was. We kept the room locked. If we could have used the Portal and come here, we would have saved a great many lives.'

'You didn't send your bird animus through then?'

'What?' Trent said, staring at Jim with a frown. 'We thought the Portal was broken. Are you saying we could have used it?'

'Only safely by those of you with wings. The Portals seem to come out in midair unless anchored by these arches. If you could fly, you'd have been fine coming out this end. Amelie and I came through a broken Portal to this continent. She had to carry me down which wasn't much fun for either of us! What the arches do is enable someone without wings to travel through at ground level and of course activate them in the first place.'

'I didn't know that. We don't have that many with a flying form, but they could have carried children I suppose. Having said that our people would have been split up.' He shrugged, it was all in the past now and none had known it was a possibility. 'Fortunately, we did at least have a secret escape tunnel beneath the castle that came out on the other side of the hill. We had already begun sending people through before the town walls fell. We had built many traps and blockades within the town itself to slow the enemy's advance, so lost few lives in the evacuation. I remember hearing an almighty crash and rumble, the very earth shaking as the last of us went into the secret passageways. We ran, fearing the roof would collapse any minute under the weight of the rubble and masonry we could hear tumbling down above us. Those tunnels saved hundreds of lives that day.'

He had gathered his remaining people together in the thick woodland by the tunnel exit, reassuring them as best he could. They had made some preparations for this eventuality by stockpiling travelling gear, tents, food and weapons. Unfortunately, their numbers made them conspicuous and their exit was not far from the castle. The enemy army was large and spread out with many trackers, lookouts and those simply out foraging for food. It was difficult to pass undetected. It was only in hindsight, having experienced being actively pursued by wizards, that he realised Sir Cyril had not flagged their escape route to the King. If he had then the King's army would most certainly have run them down and destroyed them. As it was they managed to get away. From the outset they were harassed and driven, but only by common soldiers either tracking or spotting them by physical means. Sir Cyril had secretly granted them the only chance and indeed mercy he could.

So began their nomadic existence as they travelled on, searching for safe places to hide and harried from pillar to post. After over twenty years banishment, it was good to be planning their return.

'So your Portal is most likely buried. I doubt anyone went to the trouble of bricking it up but bringing a castle down on top of it is problematic enough,' Jim mused thoughtfully.

'Let me go through and investigate,' Darius said quickly to his father.

'Jim's right; it's probably buried Darius. It could be a one way trip.'

'I know, but it's worth the risk.'

'Why? What do you hope to gain?' Trent asked his son. 'Our Castle is in ruins. Our lands were taken long ago, gifted to the King's cronies and our people dispersed.'

'Féarmathuin Castle and our lands are my birthright, as your heir. Without them I am nothing. As you keep telling me, this place is Drako's. I need to go and fight for what's mine. I need to do this.'

He hadn't seen Darius so determined in a long time. 'Very well,' Trent said heavily. 'Make sure you take food, a torch and a shovel in case the portal itself is covered. But I want you to simply have a look and come straight back. Understand? We'll wait here for you to gather your supplies,' Trent added and then returned to examining the markings on the arch, prudently without stepping on the plinth. He heard

Darius run off and only once he was sure his son was out of sight did he turn to eye Jim, whilst settling back down in the grass, his mind awhirl.

'How did you repair this?' Drako asked.

'You might recall I incapacitated twenty wizards by sucking the power from them the other day?' Jim said casually.

'Yes, I think I do recall that. Your lion grew a tad too,' Drako responded drily.

'Yes. I was wandering out here afterwards and found a strewn mass of magic imbued stone. I couldn't tell what had been here, only that it was a small building. Since I know building works tend to use a lot of power and I was overflowing with the stuff I just went ahead and rebuilt it. I can tell you it was no easy task. Anyway, since I didn't recognise the engravings I secured the place against anyone coming across it and activating it by accident while I looked up the markings in the library. Once I was certain where it led I knew you should be told.'

'What do you foresee happening here?' Trent asked.

'I don't have any foresight ability so I cannot advise you. What you do is entirely up to you. However, Darius is right that he needs something to fight for. He is never going to be content living quietly in hiding whilst leaving his inheritance in someone else's hands, especially now there is a possible way to secretly return. There will always be some of your people who would prefer action too. Perhaps rebuilding parts of your castle to serve as a base is the way to stealthily reclaim what's yours.' He glanced up sensing an animus presence and Darius rejoined them. Jim knew he'd been listening and that his eyes were shining with determination and excitement.

Darius gave them all a nod and strode up to the Portal with a sack on his back. He stepped on the plinth, the vortex glowed around him and without hesitation he stepped through and disappeared.

20

# *Portal*

'How do we know he's not dead?' Ebony asked anxiously as minutes passed and Darius did not return.

'Because Portals only work when someone with magic is in close proximity,' Jim explained, gesturing at the watery shimmer still glinting within the arch. 'And, yes, you do have to be alive to generate magic.'

'It's stopped!'

'Closed, you mean. He's probably moved off the plinth to have a look around. Hope he remembered to take something to light his torch with,' Jim added quietly. When the portal was activated it glimmered giving off light that would certainly be useful when in an underground room.

Ten minutes later when they were all starting to fret, the portal activated again and Darius returned.

'You were right, there had been a cave-in and the plinth was partially buried in rubble. I had to clear a path to step off the plinth, but the rest of the room seemed intact. I tried the door but it's locked. I'm not sure what we would need to get through the lock; we might have to break down the door itself.'

'I might be able to help with that,' Jim offered and Darius eagerly stepped back towards the Portal. Jim followed, but so too did Drako, Freddie and where Freddie went his wolves were sure to follow. 'Someone needs to stay behind this time in case something goes wrong,' Jim said noticing just how eager everyone was.

'Ok, I'll stay back,' Ebony offered and watched as, with no more discussion, they all stepped through and disappeared from sight. It was exceedingly odd to think they had travelled hundreds of miles in an instant.

Jim conjured a large globe light and looked around him with great interest. Once this room would have been beautiful, with a polished marble floor inlaid in a striking pattern; a high ceiling supported by pillars and with mosaic murals on the walls. Now, however, the ceiling behind the Portal had caved in. The resultant rubble had flowed around the Portal banking up behind and to the right partially blocking the front. He wondered if activating it, as they now had several times before stepping through, had cleared it of any of the loose obstructions since the archway itself was completely clear, fortunately for Darius.

Jim went over to the exit, which was at the top of a flight of stone stairs and eyed the door set into the ceiling. He sent his senses beyond it, making sure that the door itself wasn't buried and thus holding back an avalanche of rubble likely to bury them.

'What's amusing?' Drako asked noticing Jim's small smile as his hand rested on the metal bound door with its many interlocking bracing bars.

'This,' Jim said and turned the handle. The door clunked, the mechanism pivoted and the locking bars retracted. Then the door swung open.

'It was unlocked?'

'Of course not. It was a very complicated mechanism actually and must have done its job at keeping out your attackers. I'm just good with locks,' Jim added, swinging his globe light forward to the open doorway. He warily stepped out into a wide corridor. Rubble right up to the ceiling blocked the one "open" end, but three closed doors drew his attention. 'Do any of these doors lead out?' he asked, turning to Trent.

'No. That one goes down to the dungeons, and these other two were store-rooms. That's the only way out from here,' Trent added gesturing at the cave-in.'

'Ok, the first priority is to shore up the ceiling around the Portal. Until that's done it isn't safe to disturb anything up here. Come back down with me so I can protect you should it be necessary. Rupert, can you go back through to reassure Ebony. This might take some time and I'd prefer to know someone is keeping watch on our exit.'

'Yes sir.'

'Rupert, get her to bring some snacks over,' Drako added, 'we might well need a boost when we get back.' They watched Rupert vanish through the Portal and then the light it bestowed winked out. 'Jim, are you sure you don't need help to do whatever it is you're about to do?'

'Are you volunteering to lend me your strength?'

'If you need it, then yes. You always prefer to have a merge of strength to call on. We might be animus, but you know we can help.' He noticed Jim glance at the strewn rubble and he gestured to his family and the wolves to join hands, then he held out his hand to Jim.

'Thank you Drako; that will lessen the load considerably. Trent, Darius I know you've not done this before so I appreciate your willingness. Clear your mind of anything you don't want me to see. I have no intention of looking at anyone's memories, but if you think about them while we are merged you will effectively be pushing them in my face. Ok?' Gathering nods of readiness from each, he merged them. He felt his power swelling and used his heightened senses to investigate where the rubble had come from and then try to get it to return from whence it had come. Then, with much of the rubble gone, he was able to see more clearly the outlines of the ceiling, the pillar that had given way and reinstate them to their former strength and positions. Only then did he release his team from the merge and they all could examine his repairs. The ceiling was now intact and certainly felt a safer place to be. The thought of letting people come and go through this portal with such an unstable roof would not have let him sleep at night. If they were trapped the other side and unable to return through the Portal then they had a substantial and very risky journey to return overland.

'Ok, let's see if that's helped with the rubble upstairs,' Jim suggested. He knew they were all reeling somewhat from the unexpected drain on their strength, but the resultant success spoke for itself.

The rubble in the corridor was still deep and a substantial barrier, but it had retracted considerably and there was now a small gap at the ceiling level. Freddie was already clambering up to peer through as the rest of them arrived.

'What do you see?' Darius asked.

'More rubble. I think part of the room above has fallen into this corridor. It's lighter up here though. I think we must be close to windows or an outer wall.'

'Be careful Freddie, Natalya will have all our hides if you break so much as a fingernail,' Jim remarked and Freddie grinned. He noticed Freddie glance at Dustin and Johnny and the two men clambered up to help him. Soon, they had cleared sufficient stone for everyone to crawl through.

'The Great Hall!' Trent exclaimed as he climbed through the hole at ceiling height then came out from under the corridor's ceiling. He stood up, clambered over a stretch of rubble and accepted Freddie's hand to pull him up onto the original floor of the room above. The huge double story room was a mess. The hall floor had collapsed in almost a quarter of the room making them clamber up from below the floor like rats. They stood and stared at the devastation. One of the side walls had partially come down, which now let the sun and clearly many winters of weather in. Part of the vaulted roof had collapsed too. It was little wonder there had been cave-ins below.

'Stand still everyone, let me check no-one else is here,' Jim ordered. He dropped a shield over them and could then concentrate on any other living creature. Aside from a whole variety of vermin signatures, they were alone. He released the shield and followed them outside into the sunshine to take a proper look at the scale of the devastation.

As castles went Féarmathuin Castle was not big, nor very complex in design, but it had been heavily fortified. It would not have been easy to take by conventional force. The castle was set on a steep hill with a sheer cliff at its back. It overlooked a rugged, densely forested, landscape of craggy hills with mountains in the distance. The air was brisk but filled with fresh clean pine scents. Jim could easily see the appeal of such a place. He eyed his companions and sensed their wistfulness. This was definitely a place ideally suited to bears and wolves. However, it was broad daylight and they'd spent long enough here for Ebony to worry whilst she waited for them to return.

Jim led a sombre and contemplative party back down to the Portal room. Utilising a fork he'd found buried in the rubble, he fashioned a key for the door and presented it to Darius.

'I suggest you leave the door locked and the key in this room,' Jim said. 'Now we've cleared a path to the Portal from the outside you'll need to find a way to hide this access. We don't need inquisitors finding their way to the school uninvited.'

'Understood,' Darius responded clutching the key. He put the key in the lock, turned it and both saw and heard the bars lock into place. He was almost reluctant to leave it behind, but placed the key on the table near the door. It was a little frustrating to have to leave, but he was tired and could see everyone else was too. Letting the wizard make use of their strength might be a little annoying but he couldn't deny the astonishing efficacy and speed of Jim's subsequent repair. That use of strength had clearly been well worth it. As he stepped though the Portal into the warm glade after the others he knew he would be doing this a lot. He helped himself to his share of the sandwiches Ebony had brought them and soon felt better for it.

Darius kept his smile to himself as he saw that Amelie, Cassy and Natalya were sitting with Ebony awaiting their return. None of them seemed particularly impressed that their men had gone off without telling them. He idly wondered which female had first found out where they'd gone. Max was the only partner missing and that was probably only because he wasn't a wizard and couldn't automatically trace Ebony.

'Ladies, if you wouldn't mind giving me a hand, I'll get a proper fence put up to keep out the unwary.' Jim merged them and quivered in shock immediately realising his mistake. What was he thinking merging with two warrior wizards? It was Natalya's strength in particular that was overwhelming him. He'd merged once with her but that had been after she'd nearly expended all her strength on controlling that herd of deer. Today she was not spent and her power was all wizard magic. He was used to Amelie's strength and since it flowed primarily into animus lines, it was what gave his lion such strength. He ruefully knew the battle with the twenty wizards had changed him; he could take on more power faster than had ever been possible before and that was dangerous.

'Nat, Cassy, drop out,' Amelie said quickly, releasing hold of his hand too. They all eyed Jim warily. He was breathing fast; his eyes had turned gold and were a little glazed. He blinked, gestured and a fence appeared, surrounding them in a blur of motion. That had not used up a fraction of the power he had just soaked up, she realised. 'Darius, I assume there's plenty of repair work to be done on the other side?' Amelie asked and he nodded. Amelie glanced at Cassy and her sister and they stepped through the Portal with the whole party following on behind. They clambered out into the ruined Great Hall on Darius's heels and looked about in shock.

'Jim, mend the side wall,' Amelie instructed, since that was the biggest immediate breach to secure access to the hall. The hall was easily two stories high and its repair was likely to quickly soak up his excess magic. Everyone stood back watching as much of the debris left the floor, inside and out and the wall rebuilt itself all the way up to the roofline.

Jim turned slowly, gesturing carefully and all four walls of the Great Hall lost their scars, cracks and other structural weaknesses. He felt almost back to normal now so accepted Cassy's aid alone in repairing the roof and then its shattered external door. Now the Hall could be locked against any casual intrusion. With the roof repaired and sealed against the weather, it gave anyone coming here a large safe place in which to work out of sight and also to store and assemble building materials.

Rebuilding the walls and roof had used a substantial quantity of the debris filling the corridor below, they were all pleased to find. However, they discovered that part of the ongoing blockage in the corridor, was a toppled stone staircase.

'Do you want to have a go carrying on sorting things out in here?' Jim asked Cassy. She had been in his merge teams from the start when they built Drako's village and so had plenty of experience building things. She would know how to design something that was structurally sound.

'Can do,' Cassy said amiably.

'Just remember to keep the magical signature of your spells as quiet as possible. The stone walls will help mask our presence to a degree but we don't want anyone to hear us here.'

She nodded and watched Jim head off outside with Amelie. She imagined there were plenty of things they would need to repair to improve external security.

Cassy remained inside with Natalya and Drako. Cassy merged them and rebuilt the stairs providing access from Hall to the storeroom and Portal corridor. Now the rubble they'd climbed earlier was gone, stairs were essential. Next she rebuilt the door separating the Hall from these stairs. There was still a large hole in the Hall floor, but it was now possible to skirt it, pass through a lockable door and down actual steps to a largely clear corridor below. It was a huge improvement. Beyond where they'd been working, the corridor was still blocked, but actually that was fine for the moment as that prevented alternate access. The buildings that once had been above that corridor were in ruins and were therefore a potential breach in their new defences.

'Can you fix the floor?' Drako asked aware anyone could fall and injure themselves. The Great Hall was an ideal place to setup as a workshop in the short term and he disliked having hazards so close to workers.

'Not without more wood. What used to be here has rotted away in the years it's been exposed to the elements. Jim had to use some of the good timber to seal the roof too.'

'Yes, that was the priority,' Natalya agreed. 'Having said that, is there enough timber to recover the corridor roof?' She asked looking down. 'Whilst the hole into the store room is dangerous, it doesn't really matter from a security point of view. However, I don't like the fact I can see part of the corridor leading to the Portal room from up here. It's not safe. Someone could break in and secretly watch us moving about. If they can see us they can shoot us.'

'You have a point,' Drako remarked.

'She does doesn't she? Glad you came along. I certainly wouldn't have thought of that,' Cassy admitted and eyed the remaining debris around them critically. 'Yes, I'm sure there are enough bits and pieces for me to sort out that section of floor. The rest of that big hole, no. Mm, it'll need to be braced on the top of the corridor walls so should be sturdy.' Cassy took their hands and concentrated on the only good timber left; the snapped and splintered planks that had previously been buried in various piles of rubble. Soon she had them renew themselves into solid planks and repositioned them to cover that critical section. She smiled in relief that she had succeeded. That work also had the fringe benefit of creating a wider approach to the stairway door, meaning it was safer to skirt the adjacent hole. Weary from their exertions they headed outside to see what the others had been up to. For Cassy and Natalya, it was a chance to have a look for themselves at the fabled Féarmathuin Castle, ancestral home of the Green Bear Clan.

Freddie appeared almost as soon as they left the Hall; he'd obviously been watching out for them. He wrapped an arm about Natalya and led them up some stone steps in the corner so they had a clearer view all around them and could look beyond what was left of the upper castle battlements. The upper castle sat atop a crag and occupied quite a small area. The Great Hall had once been the original defensive tower, but in later years two wings had been added on its flanks to provide living accommodation for the family and space in the other wing for the kitchens, a guest suite and quarters for the support staff. Both wings, and indeed the tower, had suffered extensive damage. The fighting had been fierce everywhere and on every level judging by the state of the buildings, although the damage was patchy. Some buildings had been blasted apart, whilst others adjacent seemed intact. Moving to where they could see the upper gates, they were shocked that even the squat gatehouse towers had been splintered. The road that twisted down the steep slope beyond the gates to the lower level was littered with sufficient debris to greatly impede a cart. There was more space on the lower level of the castle and that was where the stables, livestock and troop housing had once been located. The main gates had also been demolished, although it rather looked like someone had been too exuberant in their spell of destruction, causing so much rubble to fall into the gateway that it actually blocked it, creating a substantial obstacle. A hole in the wall to one side of the gates was doubtless how the enemy had actually entered.

The town was spread out on the gentler hillside below the castle walls and had been protected by a wooden palisade. Unfortunately, the palisade had clearly been burned in sections. It would have slowed up the enemy advance sufficiently however for the town's inhabitants to retreat. The major roads through the town were also littered with rather larger debris and deliberate obstacles. Everywhere you looked it was clear the clan had not gone down without a fight.

Mature trees lining the roads softened the bleak ruins and broke up the grey or blackened stone. Large open green spaces were visible at regular intervals, around which the houses seemed to be set, mutely testifying this town had been designed with animus preferences in mind.

Beyond the palisade there were wide cleared areas which would have been where the crops and livestock to feed the Castle and town were farmed. After so many years of neglect the land was a wilderness that the nearby forest was beginning to reclaim. There would be considerable work involved in setting all these things to rights, but it was all here just waiting for them to return and retake it.

'I guess there's no longer any need to build more houses at White Haven,' Natalya remarked, as the others joined them. 'As soon as you repair the castle perimeter wall, people could move back if they kept their presence quiet. With people on site you'd get the repairs accomplished far quicker.'

'We'd get things sorted out in a few days if we could borrow some wizard assistance,' Darius suggested hopefully.

'Yes, but using magic is traceable,' Jim told him. 'I could feel the spells Cassy and Natalya were doing inside, even though they were masked by stone and they were keeping the duration of the spells short and the power low. We have to be careful using magic until such time as you're ready to announce you're back in residence. Until then, the walls will need to be manually rebuilt.'

'Manually?' Drako frowned, 'that could take months.'

'Not to rebuild the upper Castle's defences,' Natalya pointed out. 'There are enough buildings up here to temporarily house workers until the lower castle walls can be secured. Surely it's better to concentrate on one area at a time and get it defendable so people have somewhere to fall back to. Only then will they feel safe enough to come. If they're spread too thin trying to take on everything at once, then the plan will fail. It's only a matter of time before animus presences are detected here after-all.'

'I will plan for that eventuality,' Darius said quietly. 'Once we are noticed and the need for secrecy is over, can we call on wizard help to put things into place quickly?'

'Of course,' Jim assured. 'With that in mind, assembling the timber building materials, so they are readily to hand, would be the other useful thing to prepare and White Haven village does have a good sawmill.'

Darius nodded agreement, glad to have Jim's consent and approval to monopolise the school's sawmill. Luckily the castle wasn't lacking for stone. They had far more buildings in the town than they were likely to need and which could be thinned out to provide good dressed stone to repair the critical castle areas.

'Talking of exposed positions,' Jim mentioned, 'we are probably making quite a loud signature gathered together here where no-one is meant to be.' He knew his signature was often loud and had been shielding himself, but that merely reduced his signature rather than hid it entirely. Of more concern were the two warrior wizard sisters, Cassy who was also relatively strong and eight animus people, who also had a magical signature. He absently fiddled with the pair of small gold coins he'd found in the rubble. No-one had seen them or that he'd put something in his pocket. Neither would anyone miss them. He had plans for this gold, that made his heart lift, but proper preparation was necessary. Jim looked around carefully once again for any human presences and hastily led them all back inside. He congratulated Cassy on her repairs. It was far safer and more dignified walking down steps than clambering over rubble. They now had three locked doors between any intruder and the portal. They all hoped it was enough.

There was undeniably plenty of work necessary before Féarmathuin Castle could be secured. Retaking it through stealth and without a fight so far, gave them a window of opportunity Darius was unlikely to squander. They returned to White Haven in time for dinner, weary but excited by what had been achieved and all with high hopes for the future.

21

# *Hopes*

Jim woke early, as he usually did, courtesy of Freddie's insistence on leaving the grounds at dawn. Fortunately for him, he could monitor and challenge the people passing through the People gate's locks without leaving his bed. He idly mused that should the traffic increase in using that gateway, he might have to ask someone to physically stand guard daily as they did at the main gates. For the moment, his remote surveillance was sufficient to maintain security.

Amelie lay beside him, still peacefully sleeping. Her long raven dark hair was spread across the pillow, inviting him to run his fingers through its silky softness. His heart swelled with happiness; he still couldn't believe his luck that she was his. Since the moment they'd met they had been confronted with life threatening difficulties. Singly, the adversities they faced would have been overwhelming, but joining forces they'd been able to overcome them all, one way or another. He had earned her trust and friendship on their travels and they had both grown and benefited as a result. Theirs was a true partnership where their differing abilities complemented one another. He felt privileged however that she had then chosen to deepen their bond by opening her mind to his, becoming his lover, and together creating a family. Amelie was a natural mother and Daisy was thriving as a result. His daughter was a complete joy. Being a father gave him a deep sense of happiness and he relished being hands on with her care and watching her personality develop.

He knew all too well that he could have lost her in their early days together. Daniel the wolf man had tried to tempt her and more recently, some of the young men here at the school flirted whenever Jim wasn't around. He'd seen her memories of them, and whilst she was merely amused by them, and showed no sign of returning any of their attentions, their actions did annoy him. Jim respected but felt threatened by Stripe more than any other however. He knew Stripe valued her courage and that she admired the dragon in return. He also knew Stripe wished not only for her help in raising his children, but to become his companion full time once more. Dragons were social creatures and Jim feared the day when the dragonets left home and left Stripe alone. Stripe's discovery of how to shift into a human had clearly piqued his curiosity about what else he might be capable of. To Jim that was a worrying development. An intelligent being like a dragon might also enjoy the company of humans from time to time. Jim didn't want to encourage that however; aware there was a risk that such an innately powerful and predatory being could easily seize control of ordinary people and dictate their lives. Stripe had once threatened to eat him, to do away with his rival. He knew very well that Amelie had chastised Stripe for that threat at the time, making the dragon back down. Jim hadn't forgotten and he doubted Stripe had either. Jim understood why Stripe had threatened him; his lion had an instinctive need to eliminate rivals too. He suspected that it was only to keep Amelie's goodwill and favour that Stripe hadn't already attacked him. Perhaps Stripe was taking the stealthy approach by finding problems that he "needed" her help for, thereby remaining a part of her life.

Jim ruefully knew why they all acted as they did; she was an amazing woman and as yet unmarried. She did not yet have a formal commitment to anyone, including him.

He rose and quietly dressed. Tiptoeing into the other room, he pulled out a loose brick from high up in the living room wall, reached inside and took out the small wooden box his project lived in. Popping it in his pocket he replaced the brick. Next he took up the fire-tongs and stirred the remains of last night's fire. Planning ahead, he'd built up the fire before going to bed and there were still some good coals remaining now. Leaving a good coal in the hearth and feeding it some fresh wood to rekindle and keep it going, he transferred the other hot coals to the metal fire bucket along with some kindling to stop them going out as he disturbed them. He put the fireguard back up to stop any sparks flying out onto the rug and then left the apartment.

Soon he was inside the small workshop housing the school's forge. The hot coal burst into fresh flame within the furnace as he provided new fuel and worked the bellows. He removed the metal from his box and dropped it into the smallest crucible. Whilst it heated he set out the tools he'd need and donned the protective apron and gloves. He had noticed Bruce never began working metal without those basic safeguards. Soon, the small piece of metal had softened enough in the heat to allow him to continue shaping it. He held an image in his mind and whilst his smithing skills were rudimentary at best and he was no skilled artisan, his magic made up for it. Shaping lots of highly detailed individual pieces and then welding them together in an aesthetically pleasing way was beyond his abilities! Magic however, was his greatest tool. His project had gone back into the melting pot to begin afresh more times than he wished to count.

He coaxed the gold to extrude not only into the shape he envisaged but with the fine detail necessary to the design's success. He had to work quickly before it cooled and would no longer be malleable. Reheating just one section tended to affect everywhere else too, sometimes with disastrous effects. This project was taking far more time and experimentation than he had imagined but it was worth it. It was not something he wanted to task someone else with, partly because he wanted to do it, but also because he was imbuing the gold with special qualities.

He was glad he wasn't meeting Natalya for additional coaching before breakfast today; if he was he'd have been late. A few days ago he had come to a natural break, having finished a complete segment of lessons, and had suggested a week off. He had since been coming up here three days running, squeezing in some time to work in secret between dawn and breakfast. Secrets were very difficult to maintain when one's partner could read your mind at will. Working whilst she slept was safest all around until he was ready to tell her.

Allowing it to cool once more, he examined it from all sides. Smiling in relief he drilled two tiny holes through the gold to set small glittering chips of sapphire. Then he magically warmed the metal just enough to flow minutely to overlap the edges of the stones so they would not fall out.

Impatiently he magically held the metal in its new form until it had cooled sufficiently to fully solidify. Once it was safe to handle, he checked his creation carefully. There were many reasons this had to be perfect and finally, after days of experimentation and adjustments, he was satisfied. Placing it carefully back in the box he tidied up the forge and headed back to the house.

As usual, time had run away from him and he had to jog back to the house. As it was he heard the distinctive chimes of second bell as he entered the house and only just managed not to be the last person to enter the dining room.

'Hello love. Where did you disappear to this morning?' Amelie asked as serving plates appeared on the tables and there was the sudden noise of everyone rattling crockery.

'You were sleeping so peacefully I didn't want to disturb you.'

'You smell strange,' she added.

'I've been in one of the workshops,' he admitted. 'They are definitely oily mucky places. They still need more reorganising. I suppose I ought to get them cleaned up, so students actually want to use them.'

'You're probably right. Just promise me you aren't going to be the one cleaning them. You do enough of that around here and really, you do have staff for that.'

'I know,' he responded with a small smile. She was so protective sometimes.

'Surely you have more important things to be spending your time and energy on.'

'I do. Especially my favourite girls,' he added glancing from her to Daisy lying in her special carry chair beside their table.

'Are you sure it's ok for you to take her now?' Amelie asked, rising to her feet to leave as everyone else now was.

'Yes of course. Off you go to class,' he reassured. 'We're going to take a nice bath, aren't we Daisy,' he said lifting her in the carry chair. 'Mummy says I need one too,' he added and Daisy giggled.

Amelie watched them for a moment in amusement. She loved watching them together. However, she had a class to go to that she couldn't afford to miss. Whilst she hadn't had much time off with her pregnancy, she had nevertheless fallen behind the rest of her class in the work. She was not yet doing the physically strenuous or dangerous parts of the combat classes either; although participated where she could. She was quickly rebuilding her strength though and once fully able, she would need to put the lessons she had observed only, into practice. The combat arena was no place for a baby however, so she was very glad Jim's position meant he could look after Daisy part of the time. The clatter of weapons practice and general hubbub would not be restful, especially when it was chilly and damp, essentially being outside. The lessons continued regardless of rain or other inclement weather so how could she take a baby up to the archery field? Other classes taking place in the main school were another matter and whilst the teachers weren't impressed by having a baby in their classroom, because Daisy very rarely cried and generally sat silently either sleeping or watching, they allowed it. The main problem was that she was a distraction, for not only Amelie, but the rest of the class. Amelie had to divide her attention when Daisy was awake, monitoring her constantly to cater for her needs before they became a nuisance. Ok, that meant she often had to slip out of class to feed or change her daughter, but if these things were done before Daisy was upset, then she remained content to be quiet the rest of the time.

Amelie followed her classmates into the dining hall for break and spotted Natalya across the room. She was surprised to see her sister was laughing and joking with the entirely male crowd surrounding her. It was good to see her looking relaxed and happy. Neither of them had had an easy time of it after they'd become separated and ended up alone, but it had been worse not knowing what had happened to the rest of their family. Amelie had witnessed her father's murder. He had died defending her, giving up his life that she could have time to escape. Whilst that loss had been traumatic, those painful emotions had been tempered by her pride in his selfless courage and knowledge of his love. She had not been left wondering if he was suffering torture somewhere; she'd been able to grieve and put his soul to rest in her heart. Natalya hadn't had that. Their reunion had been marred by Amelie having to be bearer of those grim tidings. Neither knew the whereabouts of their mother however, or her fate. They both harboured the hope that if they could find each other, then their mother, a powerful wizard in her own right, would somehow find them too.

'How's my favourite niece?'

'Hi Nat,' Amelie responded. 'Oh, she's fine. Full of beans though.'

'Can I pick her up?' Natalya asked since Daisy had stretched out both arms towards her demandingly.

'Looks like you don't have an option,' Amelie laughed and watched her sister pluck Daisy out of the chair. 'Oh, hang on; let me rescue your hair.'

'Thanks! She does like to grab fistfuls, doesn't she?' Natalya agreed with a wince.

'So, what were you all laughing about just now?' Amelie asked curiously.

'Oh, we've just come from Vako's class. He tried to shoot me with purple paint the other day to test my shield and show it to the rest of the class. We've just discovered that he's left the paint splattered on the floor and walls for everyone else to see. It's one hell of a lurid mess. What's interesting though is that you can clearly see the circular outline my shield left against the wall and floor. That one part is clean!'

'Really? So what happened?'

'Oh, it was so funny; the stream of paint kept ricocheting in all directions! The classroom was covered, and so were Vako's shoes. Everyone had to keep running for cover and not all of them escaped!'

Amelie giggled in appreciation. It was clear the lesson had become a highly entertaining free-for-all. How the staid and boring Vako had coped with that chaos, she could barely imagine. It sounded like he'd more than met his match against Natalya, even though she was a novice. It also sounded like this would be one to go down in the White Haven book of legends.

'You were looking upset about something,' Natalya remarked quietly and sat down beside her sister, Daisy in her lap.

'Seeing you reminds me of family,' Amelie admitted. 'I never heard whether sister Trudy's marriage worked out and whether she's safe. She probably has a family of her own by now.'

Natalya searched her still partially fragmented memories and frowned. 'We left before she was married, so I hope that it actually took place and they didn't change their minds. It would of course be risky having her join the family so I wouldn't blame them for backing out. Our sister was a latent though, as far as I know. She should have passed any inspections or purges. Although if she was reported to the authorities as being of our bloodline things might have been tricky,' Natalya said with an unhappy shrug. They simply didn't know. 'I prefer to think of her as being happily settled with a family of her own.'

'Yes, that's really the only way to picture her,' Amelie agreed. 'I still hope we'll find mum.'

'I do too. Living here, and with your Jim making a name for himself in wizard circles, we stand more likelihood of hearing about her, or her hearing about us. For all we know she's one of the wizards they have patrolling the Edmoston border. She probably has no idea where we are either.'

'You really think so?' Amelie asked hopefully.

'To be honest, I've no clue, but there's no point in worrying. The best thing we can do for her is keep our eyes and ears open for news. Someone must know where she is, even after all these years.'

## 22

# *Derek*

---

There was a knock at the door. Jim eyed the closed door for a moment and sighed softly.

'Come in Derek.'

'Thank you sir,' Derek responded and limped to the chair Jim waved him to, hanging his stick on the arm of the chair.

'How are you doing? I see you're still limping.'

'I'm told that will pass in another few days and it won't be long before I'm fully fit again.' Magical healing could achieve many repairs quickly but the fusing of broken bones was not an instant or strong fix. Whilst magic meant the healing time was reduced by about a third, bones did need time for the body to solidify the repair or the bones in question could simply come apart again.

'Glad to hear it. So, I notice you've been having a good wander around in the last couple of days since you were allowed out of bed,' Jim remarked.

'I am curious about what goes on here,' Derek admitted, not entirely surprised Jim had been keeping track of his movements.

'To see if I'm turning out monsters?'

'Many teenagers have rebellious tendencies all of their own,' Derek said with a small grin. 'However, I see no sign that you are influencing their behaviour in anything other than a positive way.'

'Thank you,' Jim said in surprise.

'I find I am relieved and impressed. Many things have changed since I was last here.'

'Oh?'

'I was a student here. A lot has changed in ten years.'

'You were a student here? Ah, that explains many things,' Jim mused absently. 'So what was different?'

'It was quite divided in those days. The animus students had completely separate lessons, predominantly spent up at the training ground. By contrast the wizard students barely left the classroom; it was all academic tuition. We mixed in the dorms, for meals and in the evenings, but when you've been so segregated, very few ever mixed with people outside their own class group.'

'I don't believe that's healthy. If they learn to mix now, they will tolerate and perhaps befriend one another later in life.'

Derek nodded, understanding how that view would of course worry the traditionalists who believed wizards were the elite and that animus were little more than animals and should accept their place as even being behind ordinary humans.

'You also seem to have attracted some powerful students. The whole end of the building was reverberating with power a few days ago and it wasn't you or your wife. I know you felt it because you went to investigate. Who was that?'

'As you say, we do indeed have a number of strong students here in training.'

'You don't trust me,' Derek remarked, understanding his evasiveness. 'It might interest you to know that I contacted my Guild. Apparently they thought I was dead!'

'That must have been a rather disconcerting conversation.'

'Yes. They said they looked for me but because you had taken all their magic they couldn't use their senses to detect me.'

'Jared's magic was intact. He ought to have known. However, I believe he didn't even wait for your team to wake. He left them unprotected and ran away. Your men were fortunate that my gate guards kept an eye on them overnight while they were unconscious.'

'What! He abandoned them at their most vulnerable?' Derek cried in dismay.

'Unfortunately, my men didn't know you'd been separated. No one wanted to risk going out into the woods foraging until your wizards had left or they'd have found you sooner. I'm sorry. I assumed they had taken you with them so didn't think to scan.'

'Jared has been suspended from office. You can be sure I will be reporting these additional transgressions that the others may not be aware of. I'm not sure whether they have appointed anyone in his place yet. I've asked them to keep me informed, although they let slip that someone else has already taken over my job.'

'What did you do there?' Jim asked curiously.

'I was responsible for warrior training and led one of the defensive teams. The team that you did of course thrash, single-handedly. I suppose it's little wonder they sought to replace me. Who would believe that a team could be overcome by one opponent unless they were led or trained by an incompetent? As you probably know, unless you are innately a warrior wizard, fighting skills don't come naturally and require extensive tuition.'

'Well, I wouldn't mind the odd lesson.' Jim remarked and laughed when Derek paled. 'Come on, you must know I was winging it entirely. Fighting does not come easily to me.'

'Yes, I did notice that,' Derek remarked breathing again. 'Your nature is entirely protective.'

'Well, you could always work here,' Jim suggested, watching him closely. 'We have a severe shortage of wizard teachers. Wizard Vako is alone in that role and as you mentioned earlier, we have some strong students. How would you like to teach a true warrior wizard?'

'I thought Amelie was an animus warrior wizard? They need little magical training.'

'I'm not talking about her,' Jim admitted.

'You have a second warrior wizard student?' Derek asked in amazement.

'Yes. Natalya is her sister and she was the one shaking the house and making Vako quake in his boots.'

'Oh. Now that would definitely hold my attention,' Derek admitted. A school led by a Leach, with two warrior wizard students? How many other schools could claim to have attracted such rare talents? 'Do you realise that this school is already considered the place to go for warrior training?'

'Is it? I suppose our warrior classes are the ones that are overflowing with applicants,' Jim mused. 'I haven't advertised our classes as such though. How do you know that's how it's viewed?'

'I interviewed a number of the parents who've been here and enrolled their children. You might not have said so, but the fact every student is expected to participate in some form of self-defence class, was clearly stated. They could also see that you have a well-maintained training area with ample space for several classes to run simultaneously and dedicated areas for specific disciplines. I haven't been up there yet myself but the images I was receiving were clear, as were the parents' approval. It was also apparent that all those physical activities had plenty of participants; they were not amenities only there for show.'

'Well, I must admit I quite like the thought of becoming a warrior academy. With you on board as a qualified wizard with proven warrior teaching skills, we'll be able to promote ourselves properly. It would enable us to justify taking on a higher calibre of student and improve skills generally. By the way, the warrior class is not limited to wizards; we have several animus students in it too. Teaching them therefore is quite a challenge.'

'What do the animus students do when the lesson is about magic?'

'They listen and actually they can often participate. Animus do have magic and they can make good backup for a wizard, but only if they understand what is and isn't possible. It is not a waste of time for them and pooling differing abilities in a combat situation makes for some interesting lessons.'

'I hadn't thought of that. I shall have to sit in on some of their lessons to fully appreciate what you mean of course, but I must admit to being curious.'

'So, are you interested?'

'I am. When do I start?'

'Excellent. Welcome to White Haven,' Jim exclaimed and clasped his hand for a moment aware that not only would he get a feel for Derek's commitment, but Derek would feel Jim's willingness too. It was very useful reassurance on both sides.

'Next Monday is probably best. That will give you time to recover and sort yourself out. Are you sure your guild won't prevent you from working here?' Jim asked.

'I have dedicated myself to teaching our warriors to better protect our borders and the first real action we are sent on is for very dubious reasons against one of our own. Then they left me for dead. I feel no particular loyalty towards them at present. I shall make the most of the change of leadership to slip between the cracks into obscurity. You asked Jared for a teacher and he refused you, I will not. You were correct that teaching our next generation is far more important than sequestering our best wizards at the Edmoston border for a threat that might not come. I don't know if you're aware but academic scores in the wizard academies have dropped markedly over the last few years and it is wholly down to our best and strongest wizards being prevented from teaching what they know. The embargo on this school is a problem too, but I know who to talk to.'

'The parents I've spoken with have expressed their annoyance for that stance. They have shown their support by switching schools for their children, but there seems little more that they can do. If you are trying to disappear you can't exactly be a loud supporter yourself.'

Derek merely smiled. 'I think, wizard Jim, it is time you approached Lord Aubrey with a view to setting yourself up as an Independent Academy.'

'Independent of the guilds?' Jim asked in surprise.

'Yes. You would be justified, given White Haven has effectively been cut off from guild support for some years now. I imagine you are already self-supporting? The school runs entirely from the tuition fees earned?'

'Yes. We run on a shoe-string budget,' Jim admitted.

'The point is that none of the other academies have managed to do that. The guilds help to pay salaries and in return they keep a tight rein on the management decisions taken within our schools. The guild does not have that kind of leverage over you. In fact they have no leverage whatsoever. You have already proven that you cannot be threatened or indeed forcibly intimidated to bring you to the local guild's heel. You are in a perfect position to demand recognition of your independent status.'

'Ok, but why did you say I should approach Lord Aubrey to do this?'

'You cannot entirely be an island. If you are no longer "protected" by a wizard guild you fall into a grey area as to who is ultimately responsible for protecting the school's interests. Since White Haven is in his county it would be wise to officially cede that to him. He would probably support you and would be a strong voice to have at your back.'

'I understand. He did seem to agree with what I was doing here and want to work with me. Mm, an Independent Academy! It certainly would be nice to put the way we're being treated into a positive light and turn the tables. I think parents are being put off approaching us because of the stigma we've been put under.'

'You're undoubtedly right.'

'I like this idea. Does this mean I can finish my own wizard training?'

'You are untrained? Damn, I thought that was just a malicious rumour.'

'I'm part trained. I just need my final year to gain full accreditation. If I do it at an independent academy I won't have to leave.' He glanced at Derek, glad to have these suggestions. He'd never have thought of this; he was simply too busy and too close to the issues to have any clear perspective. 'Of course, helping White Haven become independent will serve you quite well too, won't it? You won't then have to return to the Half Circle dullards watching over the wall.'

'It's true I have a vested interest, but that does mean you can be sure I will work hard to help it happen.'

'I do believe you will.'

23

# *Family*

---

*'Where are my two favourite girls?'* Jim called.

*'We're down at the village with Natalya. Are you going to join us?'* Amelie asked.

*'Yes. I've got something I want to show you,'* Jim responded. He felt her immediate curiosity but blocked her from discovering his secret. He jogged down to the village and up Hunters Lane to the house Natalya shared with Freddie. He found them all out on the sunny veranda fronting the little house. To his surprise, it was Freddie who held Daisy. Natalya and Amelie sat nearby clearly having a relaxed chat.

'Hello Jim,' Freddie greeted aware of Jim's expression. He supposed he wouldn't be terribly impressed to see another man holding his daughter either, or that she was giggling happily.

'She likes you,' Jim remarked leaning on the railings below and observing his daughter's aura and expressions. Freddie quickly offered Daisy to Jim. 'No, please stay as you are. You both look far too happy to disturb! I just need to steal Amelie away for a few minutes if you wouldn't mind keeping an eye on Daisy?'

'Of course. No problem at all,' Freddie responded easily and watched Amelie rise curiously and follow Jim into the woods behind Drako's house where they disappeared from view.

'Is something wrong? You're still blocking me,' Amelie asked.

Jim silently led her to a small but beautifully sunlit clearing before stopping and turning to face her. He looked around them carefully, checking that no-one was close by, that they were completely alone.

'Sorry to pull you away, but I have a question for you.'

'Ok,' she responded uneasily. He seemed in a very odd mood, his mind blocking hers and his gaze intent on her.

Jim got down on one knee and looked up at her astonished face; he'd succeeded in surprising her. 'Will you marry me?' he asked softly. He opened the little box and held it out to her.

'You made this?' she whispered taking the ring out of the box. A tiny gold dragon wrapped around itself forming a circle with a front foot seeming to hold a back foot and then its long tail making a second loop. Tiny sapphire eyes glittered at her and every detail of scales, knobbly spines and furled wings was perfect. 'It's amazingly life-like and so beautiful.' With difficulty she took her eyes from the tiny dragon that almost seemed alive, to meet his waiting gaze. His eyes had turned gold reflecting intense emotions, yet the dominant lion still waited in a submissive pose on his knees before her.

'I had many months of looking at your dragon form,' he reminded. 'If I managed to make this ring beautiful, it's only because you are.' He fell silent again allowing her a chance to think.

'Yes. I would love to be your wife,' she responded simply and was almost engulfed in his arms as he sprang to his feet and then kissed her soundly.

He took the ring and slipped it on her finger and she gasped feeling it move, adjusting itself to fit her perfectly.

'Change form love,' he asked.

'But I don't want to take it off.'

'Then don't,' he responded.

Amelie noticed his small smile and since the ring had already adjusted once, she left it on. Her clothes now in his arms, she knelt and transformed into her dragon. Her dragon's paw did indeed have short clawed "fingers", fewer than her human hand but digits nonetheless. The tiny gold dragon now seemed to be clutching its tail; it had adjusted to fit and was now one loop rather than two. For all that it was now at its maximum size; it still felt secure. She grabbed him, wrapping her dragon's front legs and sinuous neck around him, nuzzling his cheek happily. She stepped apart and transformed into a lioness next. She barely had time to look at how the ring had adjusted to wrap a feline digit when his lion appeared and demanded notice.

Lion and lioness ran together, playing and expressing their happiness to one another. It wasn't often enough that they had the time and freedom to be alone to play like this.

'We should check on Daisy,' she reminded, regretfully calling a halt to their play.

'I suppose you're right,' he said and returned to his human form watching as Amelie did the same. He watched her smiling at the ring, now curled twice about her slender finger and knew the time and effort he'd expended making it had definitely been worth it.

They walked back arm in arm, smiling at each other as they mentally shared their emotions. They might have been an exclusive couple for some time now, but this was marriage. This was permanency;

expressing their intention and desire to spend the rest of their lives together.

Natalya shared a glance with Freddie as the pair returned glowing with happiness.

'Look!' Amelie said bounding up the stairs to her sister and thrusting out her hand. 'We're engaged!'

'Wow. Congratulations,' Natalya responded and hugged her sister tightly. 'So, when's the wedding?'

'We haven't got that far yet. You will help me plan it?'

'Of course I will,' Natalya assured. 'You can count on me. Oh, this is going to be fun. I'm so happy for you. Now let me see that ring again.'

'Jim made it himself,' Amelie said proudly. 'It changes to fit me whatever form I'm in,' she added.

'Really? That's truly amazing,' Natalya responded and glanced over at Jim sitting silently, with Daisy now in his lap, and taking it all in. The man was full of surprises. She wondered how he had figured out what must have been a complex spell. He kept telling everyone he was not fully trained. Clearly the training he had received was of a particularly high standard and he must have been a very good student. She already knew he had a keen mind and excellent memory. She had found him in the library poring over books more than once and suspected he had been quietly adding to his education that way. Was there a spell book somewhere with instructions on how to do this? Somehow she doubted it. Why would a wizard consider creating a spell designed specifically with animus abilities in mind? This spoke of Jim's odd ingenuity and strength. Placing triggers on an inanimate object like a gold ring were easy enough, but making a solid object change shape and into multiple configurations, was another thing altogether.

She reached for Freddie's hand and he silently moved up behind her to take it. Freddie might be feeling a little insignificant and in awe of Jim all over again, but she was relieved he was not a wizard. She leaned in to Freddie's body, appreciating his strength and silent support. Jim simply unnerved her at times. She supposed that if she could share his mind like she did Freddie, she would understand him better and be less confused by his contradictions. As it was, she was glad Amelie was happy with him, it reassured her about Jim's underlying nature, as nothing else could.

24

# An Important Meeting

'Tobias, it's Jim. How are you?'

*'Jim? This is a surprise. I'm fine, thank you for asking.'*

'Are you currently at Cedar Castle?'

*'Yes.'*

'Excellent,' Jim said not mentioning the fact he could feel Tobias's nervousness bleeding through his shield simply to be speaking with him. He thought they'd parted last on good terms. He supposed he'd done the odd thing that might make the Guild anxious since then. He now wondered what rumours were circulating.

*'What can I do for you?'*

*'I would like to arrange a meeting with Lord Aubrey. Could you ask him when would be convenient?'* He sensed Tobias was a little flustered, nervous and definitely curious about the subject of the meeting.

*'Ah, I'll just go and see if he's free at the moment to ask,'* Tobias said as he walked. *'I assume you mean to come here?'*

*'Yes. I'll probably bring Wizard Derek with me,'* Jim threw in.

*'Wizard Derek? I thought he was dead!'* Tobias exclaimed and then he received a view through Jim's eyes of the very man sitting opposite and looking back with some amusement.

*'As you can see, despite rumours to the contrary, he's alive and well. We thought you might not know and that his subsequent arrival on your doorstep might be a shock.'*

*'Yes indeed. Thank you for the consideration. Clearly, I have not been kept updated,'* Tobias murmured in dismay, wondering which of the other stories currently circulating was equally false. *'I have arrived,'* and he allowed Jim to see his view of Lord Aubrey currently sitting at the head of an empty table, eating. He was alone but for a guard by each of the two doors.

'You're hovering Tobias,' Lord Aubrey said, without noticeably looking up.

'Sorry to disturb you sir. I have wizard novice Jim with me,' he said tapping his head and Lord Aubrey's gaze sharpened alertly and he gestured for him to approach. 'He wishes to meet with you whenever would be convenient.'

'Ah,' Lord Aubrey said straightening in his chair.

'He suggested that Wizard Derek might accompany him,' Tobias added meaningfully.

'To prove he's not dead as we've been told? Or for another purpose?'

*'I'm not about to waste my time, or his, when you have seen and can verify that truth,'* Jim said to Tobias. *'No, I have some questions for him that would be best discussed in person.'* Jim watched as Tobias repeated that and he noticed Lord Aubrey nod.

'I can free up some time tomorrow afternoon,' Aubrey suggested amiably.

*'Thank you, My Lord. We'll see you tomorrow afternoon then,'* Jim confirmed and disengaged from Tobias.

'All set then?' Derek asked, noticing the hum of energy branching off Jim, signalling a spell, abruptly cease and his eyes return to the present.

'Yes. They're expecting us tomorrow afternoon. Are you going to be OK riding that far?' He could suggest they take a wagon, but after his most recent trips where having to keep to the pace of a slow wagon had made them a target, he wasn't keen on the idea.

'Your healers are accomplished,' Derek responded. 'As long as I'm not putting excess stress on my bones by running or carrying heavy stuff I'm sure all that was broken will remain mended. If your stables can provide me with a well-mannered horse, then I'll be fine. Besides, if something did happen I'm certain you could put it right. I've heard you've done a fair amount of healing yourself.'

'True, but I'm no expert.' He eyed Derek's arms and legs from where he sat and was relieved to note Derek seemed correct in his prognosis. 'Tobias thought you were dead too. Someone's been busy spreading that rumour.'

'I thought as much,' Derek responded with a shrug. 'Politically speaking, news of my team's defeat might well work in our favour just at the moment.'

'And if it isn't I'm sure we can correct or even create new rumours to better serve our purpose,' Jim added and Derek grinned. Both then headed off to prepare for a dawn start.


'Aiming to make an impression?' Derek asked in approval as he arrived in the courtyard early next morning. Four matched grey horses awaited them and his three companions were attired in very distinguished and complementary outfits in black with silver trim.

'Of course,' Jim responded. The sun was just peering over the horizon and bathing everything in a fresh clean light. Dustin and Rupert were accompanying them. After the attack by hundreds of bandits last time they'd travelled to Cedar Castle, precautions were sensible. Whilst he would have preferred to take the same men as last time, Freddie now had Natalya to watch over. The men wore the same smart livery as last time, although their trousers and shirts were also new and matching. As they would be entering a Lord's castle where they would be judged by the other warriors, Jim felt their appearance was important. They wore sheathed swords and had a crossbow and quiver holstered on their saddles. Their purpose in the party was completely unambiguous.

The cloak Mrs White had presented him with was also black but didn't have the large silver threaded school emblem across the back. His cloak was refreshingly plain, weather-proof whilst richly made. The silver chain fastening was the only ornate touch and fashioned after the school's unicorn emblem. He had followed the wolves' lead in choosing practical clothing that one could actually ride comfortably in for long hours. His long black leather boots were smartly polished but his clothing was fairly unremarkable otherwise. He'd merely ensured what he wore to be seen by Lord Aubrey was clean and new. It wouldn't do to arrive in threadbare or mended clothes. Derek in contrast wore a white shirt with a frivolous frill at throat and cuffs, which was visible under the dark purple cloak. In addition to the rich purple, black brocade embellished his cloak. Derek's boots were decorated too. He didn't visibly carry any conventional weapons; his attire told everyone he was a wizard. Most observers would initially assume he was the leader of their party. Jim had no problem with that. With rumours doubtless abounding of a rogue wizard, he was content to travel incognito and let Derek occupy other travellers' interest.

Near midday, they finally saw Cedar Castle in the hills above them. They had made good time and hadn't seen any signs of bandits. Jim wondered if Lord Aubrey had managed to clear his land of them or if they naturally dispersed in the spring when there was plenty of paying work to be had on the land.

Dustin abruptly stopped and they halted behind him warily. Moments later a squad of uniformed guardsmen rode out of the trees towards them. It soon became clear they had been awaiting their arrival and the squad fell in to escort them up to the castle.

'Your reputation must precede you,' Derek remarked quietly as he rode beside Jim.

'Are they a guard for us, or against us, though?'

'Ah, hadn't thought of it like that. Expecting trouble?' Derek murmured quietly as their escort clattered over the drawbridge. 'What is it?' he added noticing Jim suddenly frowning as they passed through the solidly constructed gateway.

'More than one wizard is already inside,' Jim told him and glanced at Dustin and Rupert to be sure they had heard the warning too. 'We should stay together.'

'Tobias must have reported to the Guild that you were visiting here today,' Derek said and noted Jim's lips thin but he said nothing. They trotted up the winding streets of the lower ward, passed through a second gateway guarding the upper castle and shortly arrived at the road's destination in a large open courtyard.

Grooms were already waiting and Jim quickly dismounted. He nodded to Dustin who moved forward to aid Derek's dismount, avoiding too much of a jar to his legs. As soon as all were afoot, Jim strode up the long flight of steps from the courtyard towards the main residence, where he'd been before. He gestured their escort ahead and his pace made all his companions move smartly to keep up. He warily scanned around them, aware of being in the open with wizard presences nearby and who might prove to be unfriendly.

'Welcome to Cedar Castle. If you'd like to come this way, sirs,' Lord Aubrey's steward said, awaiting them at the door to the residence.

'Avoiding the other party of wizards are we?' Jim asked him, as the man gestured for them to take an alternate route through the formal gardens to the back of the main residence.

'It seemed prudent. Lord Aubrey will be with you shortly,' he added and left them in a small informal reception room that was furnished with comfortable seating.

'Thank you,' Jim said simply and the steward withdrew. The guard escort remained outside, leaving the four of them to relax. Jim absently eyed the tranquil gardens visible through the glass double doors and suspected this chamber was not usually used for visitors.

'I'm surprised the guild members haven't barged in already. They must have sensed you. Although, thinking about it, I can barely feel you at the moment. You're shielding your power signature somehow?'

'It seemed sensible. I'd rather our meeting took place undisturbed.'

The door opened and Lord Aubrey entered with Tobias. Dustin and Rupert hastily left their seats and took up positions by the door.

'Good afternoon My Lord,' Jim said and sketched a quick but respectful bow as did Derek. 'I hope we are not inconveniencing you?'

'What's life without a little drama to add some spice?' Lord Aubrey remarked. 'You at least did make an appointment. So, to what do I owe the pleasure of your visit?' he said crossing the room and sitting down opposite Jim, gesturing for them to be seated.

'Thank you for seeing us on such short notice. I hope you will forgive my getting straight to the point, but I imagine the wizards down the hall will intrude at some point soon.' Aubrey nodded. 'I would like your permission to formally separate White Haven from the Guild's influence and become an independent academy.'

'Why do you need my permission for that? You will simply be formalising the current state of affairs.'

'I prefer to have your approval. I also thought it would be sensible to seek your sponsorship.'

'Ah. Financial sponsorship?'

'No, we are supporting ourselves,' Jim clarified quickly. 'I'm thinking in terms of having a respected voice in our corner. This decision isn't likely to be popular with the Guilds.'

'Or the other lords,' Aubrey added. 'Yes, it will cause a stir, but I happen to think they only have themselves to blame. So, what type of independent academy are you proposing? I hear you are being inundated with students wishing to enrol.'

'We are, and primarily for warrior training,' Jim acknowledged not surprised he had been keeping tabs on them. 'Wizard Derek believes we are already regarded as leaning in that direction,' Jim added. 'He has agreed to join our staff and will upgrade our ability to teach the warrior art skills.'

'Ah. A specialist warrior academy. Yes, I'm certain you can promote yourselves as such successfully. Rumours already abound of your personal exploits,' Aubrey added and watched Jim shift uncomfortably. 'I must admit I'd like to hear about your latest battle. The fact Wizard Derek is not only alive, but is joining forces with you, rather negates the credibility of the story as it had been reported to me.' He eyed the reluctance on both Jim's and Derek's faces and knew something momentous had happened that they were trying to keep under wraps. 'Were there many witnesses?'

'Most of the school turned out I think,' Jim said and glanced at Dustin for confirmation.

Lord Aubrey followed his gaze. 'You witnessed the whole event?' The tall animus man nodded. 'What's your name?'

'Dustin, my lord.'

'Jim, if it's easier, show me his memory of it. I do need to know what really happened.'

Jim raised a brow at Dustin who mutely nodded permission and came closer.

'May I watch too?' Tobias asked as they were about to begin. Jim nodded slightly reluctantly but allowed a hand to be placed on his shoulder. Tobias sucked in his breath sensing the power coiled in this one wizard. A huge feline roar mentally jolted them into the start of the memory. Dustin had heard the roar from a distance but had only just managed to run to the village entrance in time to see a lion galloping past at a blurring pace. The lion had leapt the perimeter wall and disappeared. Dustin had run fast into one of the gate towers and stared out the window at the scene below and close by. Tobias recognised the team of wizards in the scene but hadn't met their prisoners. As the scene unfolded he heard with shock that the woman and baby were Jim's lady and child and that this had been an attempted kidnap. Well that certainly wasn't part of the official story! He'd not been aware Jim could change form either, but he demonstrated it amply when trying to negotiate with Jared. Tobias watched the whole scene unfold in utter awe and shock as Jim felled twenty wizards alone. He continued watching as the towering lion Jim had become returned to the school with his family. Jared had been left defeated but standing. He'd looked around at his fallen team and walked away, leaving them there! The memory continued and it was clear Dustin had remained on watch until the team awoke sometime after dawn. He'd seen them perform a cursory search for something and then stagger off.

'Well, that was most enlightening,' Lord Aubrey admitted, once the vivid and mind boggling display of magic had ceased. 'The official version has left out quite a number of pertinent details,' he said to Tobias, who nodded unhappily. 'The last bit before they left next morning, were they looking for something?'

'Yes. Me,' Derek said. 'I somehow landed in the trees beyond the river, unconscious and injured. If Jared had stuck around to defend his team when they were unconscious, drained of their magic, and completely vulnerably, he'd have been able to sense me. Jim certainly left him sufficient magic.'

'Knowing they were missing someone they could have used their eyes to search properly,' Dustin interjected quietly, his disgust plain. 'We found you just in the tree line, not deep in the forest. You had been there for hours in considerable pain.'

'Their loss is our gain,' Jim said quietly and Dustin nodded and returned to his post at the door. 'Ah, I think the guild members have finally sensed our presence. Considering they were expecting us, you'd have thought they'd have been listening out for us. Their senses must be poor,' Jim added.

'You're shielding,' Derek reminded.

'I can only reduce my signature, not mask it entirely and you haven't been shielding at all.'

'You wish to see them or go out the back?' Lord Aubrey asked.

'Should I be hiding?' Jim asked.

'I thought from what you've just said about shielding that that's exactly what you were doing.'

'No. I merely delayed the inevitable to give us time to talk undisturbed,' Jim said with a shrug.

'Ah. Then by all means open the door Dustin,' Lord Aubrey said and settled back into his chair with the air of someone looking forward to entertainment. He did however pivot his chair so he could see the door more easily.

Dustin prudently waited until he heard a knock at the door before opening it. The idea of flinging it wide and startling already nervous and defensive wizards into doing something rash was not something he wished to risk.

'Can I help you?' Dustin asked politely. He noticed the leader of the small group was eyeing him warily.

'What the hell is an animus doing here?' one of the other wizards asked, but since the rude question hadn't been aimed at Dustin directly he felt no obligation to answer. 'His mind's shielded too. What the hell?'

Dustin opened the door wide and stepped aside. If these men wished to be discourteous he would let them see that Lord Aubrey was present and listening. Five wizards entered the room, ignoring Dustin entirely to stare at the other occupants.

'So it's true,' one of the wizards exclaimed, his gaze fixed on Derek. 'You are alive.'

'Obviously,' Derek remarked coolly. He had never liked wizard Kyle. The young man was selfish, obnoxiously elitist and a social climber who didn't care who he stepped on. If he had any redeeming features Derek didn't know of them.

'Why didn't you return?'

'I'd been injured and was treated at White Haven.'

'Hah, a likely story,' Kyle sneered. 'If you'd actually been incapacitated we'd have found you. We all know you ran off like a bloody coward.'

'What?' Derek spluttered in shocked outrage. 'I did not run.'

'You're a liar as well as a coward? No wonder you didn't dare show your face at Half Circle.'

'How dare you!' Derek snarled, but before he could say anything else Kyle threw a spell at him which stung painfully. He quickly put up a shield and retaliated in fury. He was aware the other four wizards of his previous class were initially shocked immobile but then Kyle snapped at them, obviously realising he couldn't take on Derek alone and win.

Dustin watched the scene in appalled fascination. Tobias stood before Lord Aubrey to shield him from any fallout and he knew better than to get closer and risk them attacking him too. Jim sat motionless watching everything with a predator's focus. A frown passed over Jim's face as the other wizards joined the fight and Derek became hard pressed to maintain his shield. Derek staggered against the wall and Jim abruptly stood and moved in front of Derek.

'Enough!' Jim snapped as three spells landed on him and he felt power suffuse his body. He breathed deeply controlling his urge to shift. No one needed to try to deal with his lion right now. He felt the small surge in energies as someone conjured a further spell. He threw the culprit, Kyle, backwards, slamming him into the far wall where he writhed, invisibly pinned well off the floor. 'I said, enough!' Jim told him. 'Rupert, go reassure the guardsmen, they're becoming frantic,' Jim added in a calm tone and released the seal on the garden doors so he would be able to open them.

'Are you alright, My Lord?' the Captain asked anxiously as they piled into the room. He looked about the room as his Lord casually righted and then resumed his armchair. Ornaments, books and papers lay scattered and small tables had been overturned. Some items had smashed. It was certainly a mess, but most interesting was the fact the obnoxious young wizard, who had barged in earlier, was suspended off the floor, pinned against the wall like a stuck bug.

'Yes, I'm fine,' Lord Aubrey remarked easily. 'Jim has ably spanked these young wizards yet again. I had a ringside seat this time,' he added in satisfaction. There could be no wizard cover-up this time. He watched Jim eye the chaos then wave a hand slowly around the room and furniture righted itself. A smashed lamp fused back together and settled back onto a side table whose splintered leg straightened and repaired itself in time to support it. Books and ornaments repaired themselves and resumed their original places, and the pile of scattered papers flew up, shuffled itself and settled neatly. It wouldn't surprise him if the papers weren't in their original order too. Aubrey couldn't resist going over and picking up the lamp and examining it. He'd seen it lying on the floor, broken into about a dozen pieces. Now there was no sign of even a scratch. 'Thank you,' he said to Jim. Whilst Tobias could probably do this kind of thing too, he never did. He doubted it would even occur to him.

'Right,' Jim said, having finished restoring the room. 'You sorry lot of wizards owe Derek an apology. Firstly, you didn't bother looking for him last week, but left him behind unconscious and hurt. If you don't believe me you only need scan him to see both legs were broken. Secondly, accusing someone of cowardice is exceedingly rude, especially without checking your facts first. Derek is your superior and was your teacher; he deserves more respect than you have yet shown. Apologise.'

'He is not my superior, for I now have his job and he has nothing,' Kyle said.

'You? You think you're in the same league?' Jim snorted. 'Derek was thrashing you easily one to one. You had to get these others to help even the score.' Jim eyed the obstinate young man and began rotating him, still against the wall until he was fixed head down, but that was too easy, so he set Kyle spinning slowly like the hands on a clock. Jim returned to his armchair and noticed Lord Aubrey's amusement and Derek's satisfaction before he turned his gaze on the remaining four wizards who blanched. Each of them was quick to mumble apologies to Derek under Jim's expectant glare. There was a sudden retching sound as Kyle threw up. Jim halted the spinning and was satisfied that the green faced lad had vomited over himself as he spun, rather than on Lord Aubrey's floor or soft furnishings.

'Are you ready to apologise now?' Jim asked him and when the lad didn't immediately answer added, 'now, what can we have you doing next? Dancing for us? That'd be entertaining,' Jim said with mock cheerfulness. He put the wizard down and made him put his arms out ballroom style as though to hold a partner and saw his eyes widen in horror.

'I apologise!' Kyle exclaimed miserably fully aware he had no control over his body at all. He was Jim's puppet and he had a large audience to this humiliation.

'Good. Now that wasn't so difficult, was it?' Jim said. 'Now off you go, you're stinking up the room.'

Kyle flushed and fled, his team hastily following.

'Now, where were we?' Jim asked brightly.

25

# Making Contact

Jim sat in his office wondering how his family was faring. Had they been told he was dead? He thought of his mother and how upset she'd be at receiving such news. He hated deceiving her so callously. He had so much news to impart. He also missed her and simply needed to hear her voice. She was the sensitive one of the family; she would hear his call if anyone could. He had no idea whether his new strength would enable him to speak to her from here. But then there was no way to answer that question without trying. He rose and went to the large mirror over the cosy hearth. He closed his eyes and concentrated on his mother; her mental signature was so well known to him.

*'Mother, can you hear me?'* he called quietly hoping not to startle her.

'I'm sure I just heard Jim,' he heard his mother say to someone else.

'*You did hear me. I'm calling from a long way away,*' he explained quickly.

'*Jim, is that really you? You feel different somehow, but I knew you weren't dead,*' she said, relief colouring her mental tone. '*Where are you? Come and see me and we can talk. You can't be far away to be speaking to me like this,*' she added, eager to set eyes on her son after such an extended absence.

Jim opened his eyes and checked they were still blue before sending his mother the image in the mirror. '*Mother, I'm across the sea in Edmoston. I can't pop in to see you.*'

'*Whatever are you doing all the way over there?*'

'*You know I was arrested? Well there was a portal at the prison. I escaped through it when there was a riot. It came out in South Rosh. It took me months to walk back to some civilisation.*'

'*So, when are you coming home?*'

'*I don't have any plans to at the moment actually. I've found a good place for myself here in Edmoston, running a school for magic.*' He let her see through his eyes the view of his office with its grand aged oak panelling, book lined walls and huge polished desk.

'You're running a school? Why? You're young for that kind of responsibility surely and you haven't even finished your academy training,' his mother commented in obvious concern.

'They're short of teachers and wizards in general after several wars and asked me to take the headmaster role. Besides, you know I'm good with children and I've been able to continue my studies. Father might like to know we've got quite a nice library here.'

'Did you just call someone whilst linked to us?' his mother asked in shock.

'Yes, I want you to meet my fiancée. Amelie is an animus warrior wizard.'

There was a knock at the door and Amelie entered. She assessed him closely noticing his spell was still in progress, yet he'd called her.

'Hello dear. Whatever are you up to now? You know they're all taking bets on what spell you could possibly be doing that's shaking this end of the house.'

'I'm talking to mother.'

'You don't think that's a bit of a reach even for you, without a merge or me?' she chided.

'You're not merged?' his mother exclaimed. 'Jim, how can you take such a foolish risk and how can you be so strong alone?'

Amelie took his hand and suddenly the connection was far clearer and less of a strain. He was now aware his father was also linked and listening, aiding his mother's strength.

*'I've changed mother. I'm told I'm not a Sensitive; I'm actually a Leach. I have some of Amelie's power now.'* He could feel his parents shock at his announcement, but then happiness on his behalf; he would become strong enough to take care of himself and for others not to wish to mess with. Having a Leach for a son would also give the family great kudos; although they wouldn't be able to do any announcing just yet for his safety. Then they were assessing Amelie through his eyes. He gave them in moments, some background information on her family, the dreadful injustice of her imprisonment and how she had aided his escape. He also added that they'd been together a long time now. *'You are now grandparents. We have a daughter called Daisy,'* he added cheerfully and gladly felt their surprise, eager anticipation and congratulations. Now they urgently wished to meet them and see him in person.

*'Perhaps you could visit us in the summer? I'd love you to be at the wedding,'* Jim suggested. *'But only if you think it's safe to travel. I will contact you again soon,'* he promised. *'But in the meantime I'd rather you said nothing to anyone about hearing from me. I was imprisoned, and from the things I've heard there and since, I'm quite happy to be considered dead.'*

*'That seems harsh, but you may not be wrong to be cautious. We will try and contact Amelie's family, let her*

*sister know she is alive and well,*' his mother offered suddenly and she felt Jim's gratitude for that. But she knew just how distraught she'd been having been told her son was missing, presumed captured by felons or dead. Amelie and Jim had been imprisoned in their local prison. Amelie's sister had also lived in the same city, she shouldn't be too difficult to trace. Trudy would certainly be delighted to see the image she'd seen of Amelie through Jim's eyes. Her health, freedom and happiness had been obvious. Trudy might also be living under the stigma of having animus in the family. Now she could hear that Amelie was not simply an animus, she was a powerful wizard. All of her family ought to be able to hold their heads up, despite the fact they wouldn't be able to publicly refute the crown's slanderous claims. But they would know the truth. They would also be comforted to know Amelie and indeed her other sister Natalya were together; alive and well and properly out of the crown's reach.

***

'Sir, our security team has just monitored a powerful mental contact entering the country from across the sea.'

'Do you know its destination and who it was from?'

'Yes sir. They passed it through the surveillance division and they believe the missing student Jim has just contacted his family. We could not eavesdrop on the actual conversation, he had blocked it somehow, but his mother was the recipient of the call.'

'Good work. Bring her in for questioning. You say the signature feels like it originates from abroad, yet still managed to make contact? That would be quite a feat. He could of course just be offshore aboard a ship and on his way home. In any case, she will be able to tell us more and where he is.'

'Shall I advise his Guild? They asked to be kept informed of any contact.'

'Indeed. It appears this missing student has rather more potential and power than we were led to believe. It is little wonder they were so keen to trace him. I find I am now curious to hear his Guild's explanation for losing such an asset.'

26

# Lord Aubrey's Visit

*'Jim? Can you hear me?'*

*'Tobias? Is that you?'*

*'Yes. I'm glad I was able to reach you. My Lord Aubrey would like to visit the school tomorrow, if that will be convenient?'*

*'He's planning to travel here? Has something happened? Has something gone wrong?'*

*'Not that I know of,'* Tobias reassured. *'Simply speaking, he now has a reason to be more closely involved in the school. He wishes to see its facilities for himself.'*

*'Of course. He is welcome to visit whenever he wishes. My only limitation is suitable accommodation. I believe we only have one guest suite. How many will be coming?'*

*'In that case I will restrict our party to my Lord, his bodyguard and myself. We will have a small contingent of soldiers, but they can lay their pallets out anywhere.'*

*'I look forward to seeing you both tomorrow,'* Jim said and they disengaged. He hoped Tobias was correct in his reassurances that his Lord was coming simply to satisfy his curiosity as to how Jim was running things now. He searched out Mrs White's location and then left his office.

'Lord Aubrey is visiting personally?' Mrs White asked a little wide-eyed.

'Yes. He'll have a bodyguard and wizard Tobias with him. I've never seen the guest suite,' Jim remarked and Mrs White led him there.

'The bodyguard can stay here with him,' Mrs White said and gestured to a long upholstered couch clearly designed to double as an occasional bed in the suite's small reception room. The main bedroom held a wide double sized bed, a linen chest, vanity with mirror and small wardrobe. The only other feature was the suite's small bathroom. She shrugged a little apologetically, since the décor and furnishings were a little primitive and showed the years of use they'd suffered.

'Can you have a look for somewhere we could turn into a single bedroom? I imagine the soldiers could sleep in an empty classroom overnight if necessary. While you do that, I'll refresh things as much as I can in here,' he offered.

'That would ease my mind greatly,' Mrs White admitted. Having a lord stay in a shabby room might be construed as a slight. And as housekeeper, these considerations were foremost in her mind, as they reflected on her competence. 'There are a couple of rooms just off the courtyard that we often use for merchants and the like. I can add a few beds so his escort will be comfortable enough there.'

'Ah, excellent. That's one less thing to have to think about. One of these days I'll have to explore this place fully. There are so many nooks and crannies, but all seem to belong to someone. I never know if I'm ok to look or trespassing in someone's personal space.'

'You are the headmaster; you can go where you wish. If you have a question though, you only need ask.'

'Thank you Mrs White. I'm not sure what I'd do without you.'

'My husband says the same thing!' she joked. She glanced at the dismal guest room and for the first time had hope that it might be renovated. He was the first headmaster who had ever cared or looked into these details personally. With the school subsisting almost hand to mouth, she certainly couldn't justify spending good coin on paint and curtains; items that everyone else would consider fripperies.

Later that evening, when she had a few spare minutes, she revisited the guest suite. The yellowed emulsion now looked a deliberate and uniform shade by virtue of refreshing the previously equally yellowed gloss paint in the room to its original colour. The coving, badly chipped skirting boards and doors were now a crisp white. Stains, watermarks and all the chips had vanished. The stained carpet had gone, exposing old but clean timber floorboards whose rich pine colour seemed to warm the room and tone with the walls. A soft mat lay beside the bed to step out onto, which in truth was sufficient. The suite was still only minimally furnished, but without moth holes in the curtains, chips in all the paintwork and stains on the floor, it felt far more inviting. She nodded happily; now she would not be embarrassed to show any guest to this room.

***

'Lord Aubrey, a warm welcome to you,' Jim said trotting down the steps to meet the party just dismounting. 'Won't you come inside?' he added.

'A good day to you, too, although it's been a chilly one so far,' Aubrey responded. He walked up the steps quickly to the shelter of the porch, glad to get out of the dismal heavy rain. He noticed the prompt arrival of grooms to take the horses away and that a matronly woman, introduced as the housekeeper, took charge of his escort. Everything in order, he followed Jim down a long broad corridor and into a warm office.

'Please sit down,' Jim invited with a gesture to the comfortable chairs set before a roaring fire. 'Tea, or something stronger?'

'Tea will be fine,' Aubrey said, removing his sodden coat and noticing a pot and cups already set out on the small table before them. 'I could use some warmth inside me.'

'I know how that feels,' Jim admitted easily and poured each of them drinks. 'You look soaked through,' Jim remarked, aware Lord Aubrey had his hands clasped around the hot cup for warmth and that his clothes showed damp patches beneath his coat. Tobias on the other hand looked completely dry; undoubtedly he'd shielded himself sufficiently to ward off the rain.

'I am. Nothing stays dry after so many hours of incessant rain,' Aubrey said with a shrug and eyed Tobias' slight form anew, since Jim had frowned when doing so. Now he could see that Tobias was completely dry, including his hair. Yes, typically Tobias had looked after himself alone. Well, nothing new there.

'Perhaps you'd like to freshen up before we begin?' Jim suggested having summoned Mrs White again. 'The students will be sitting down to lunch in about an hour. Would you like to join them in the hall, or do you prefer us to sit down more privately?'

'I take it that's where you usually eat? In that case I've no problem joining the masses. It'll give me a chance to see just how many students you've got here now. In the meantime changing into something dry is certainly a welcome idea.'

'Perhaps his lordship would appreciate a hot bath before he catches a chill,' Jim remarked quietly to Mrs White who had entered and been listening to the dinner arrangement discussion.

'This way, my Lord,' Mrs White said and took his heavy coat with them to hang where it could dry.

Jim watched them leave then turned to eye Tobias sipping his tea. He too looked cold, but with a biscuit, hot tea and a fire, he was quickly recovering.

'Thank you, he does forget to look after himself sometimes,' Tobias remarked once his lord had left the room and he was left alone with Jim. He wondered why Jim seemed to be disapproving; he was not Lord Aubrey's maid.

'So, how is the guild viewing my independence?' Jim asked, deciding to find out while they were alone. He had already noticed that Tobias hesitated before speaking about guild matters in front of Lord Aubrey. Perhaps now he would get some straight answers.

'They're not happy about it,' Tobias admitted. 'In fact I'd go as far as to say they're furious.'

'We could have used their support over the last few years. The school would have welcomed it. But having denied us aid they did leave us no option but to learn to survive alone.'

'I don't think they ever thought the school could survive alone, let alone prosper.'

'They're whinging that we didn't go quietly into the night? Idiots. They only have themselves to blame,' Jim responded.

'Of course, but you alone are the one who has actually turned the school's prospects around. It was limping along on its last legs before your arrival. You are the name to blame or credit, depending on your point of view, for its newfound success.'

'Ok, so why is anyone interested now? The school might have been weak but it did continue to function and was ignored for years. What's really changed for the guild?'

'You are a wizard outside of their control and have declared the school as officially independent from the guilds. Your students, when they graduate, will therefore also have an independent status. Whilst most will remain in the county and work, the customary year of free labour that the guild is accustomed to receiving from each graduate as part of the tuition fees, will be diminished. Some hard questions have been asked as to why we've allowed this to happen.'

'I see. Not much I can do about that. The parents know of this ramification and appear to approve. They believe their children are better off being able to choose where they will work. Of course, they are financially better off too, able to be paid for their work from the outset. A full year's worth of pay is not insignificant.'

'Yes,' Tobias said heavily. 'Money is a big motivator and now wizard students have the option of your system, it's little wonder you are receiving so many application requests.'

'So, is that the only thing your guild has a problem with?'

'It's the major issue.'

'Ok, so what else should I know?'

'We received a complaint that you had warned off some official investigators a few weeks ago,' Tobias mentioned eyeing Jim closely.

'Investigators? I don't recall ever meeting any,' Jim said in puzzlement.

'In Briarton. We know you were there that day.'

'I visit Briarton to order school supplies,' Jim conceded. 'I don't recall ever meeting any strange wizards there.' Whilst he knew precisely what Tobias was talking about, he didn't feel inclined to volunteer the story. Natalya had been hunted like a criminal and how she had been treated was what was truly criminal. He had no intention of revealing the identity of whom the "investigators" had been after if they hadn't already done so. Nor that she was actually a warrior wizard and his fiancée's sister. He silently eyed Tobias and knew he had been fishing for information; tough. The fact Tobias believed they truly were simple investigators, meant the information had been tailored high up. It would be problematic to correct that misconception without providing proof or admitting he had interceded on her behalf. Tobias also seemed unaware that what they had actually been doing was illegally hunting people on Lord Aubrey's territory.

'Well, on the basis they reported "someone had sent out a powerful blast of energy as a warning", it does seem likely that they didn't seek you out to be introduced.' He paused, hoping for some kind of explanation, but Jim remained stonily silent. 'Of course, we were aware you were there that day and thus it was clear to us who it had been. The reason you did so is less clear. Certainly they were most put out that you could not be brought in for questioning or indeed disciplined for interfering in their investigation.'

'I imagine they were. So, how long has your guild been keeping watch on me and why are they doing so?'

'Someone has been keeping an eye on you ever since you arrived on this continent. You can be sure that every time you leave school grounds you are being watched.'

'For what purpose?'

'That depends on what it is you are doing,' Tobias admitted.

'So, your purpose in accompanying Lord Aubrey here today is what, exactly? You told me when we first met that I was being watched. This isn't news.'

'I was asked to remind you that the guild is watching and will take action if necessary. No wizard is above the law or should think the guild will stand by and allow any breaches to go unpunished. You may have beaten one team, but we know what you can do now. You cannot hide.' Jim appeared unimpressed, merely raising a brow. 'You might have found a way to shield your presence temporarily, but we knew you didn't leave the school. We know you did not pass through either of the gates or cross the wall, nor did you return through them.'

Jim puzzled over what he meant for a moment before he realised. Ha! So, they couldn't tell he'd travelled through the portal! It was good to know they couldn't detect that magic. He supposed that with the students performing all manner of spells daily in class, there was far too much interference for anyone to detect anything other than a mass of magic use originating within school grounds. They thought he'd hidden his presence with a spell? Ha; they knew nothing! He truly had left, but if they had any kind of hint of the portal, that it was operational, and furthermore where it came out, then they'd know to scan for him there too. That could be awkward for

Darius's team over there trying to work in secret. As it was, it was a timely reminder that he needed to take more care where he went. He had no wish to put the whole rebuild in jeopardy.

'You think this is amusing?' Tobias asked sharply.

'No,' Jim contradicted with a sudden glower. 'Nothing about being spied on and my every move being reported and scrutinised is amusing. Of course, now I am my own boss as it were, you can be sure I will be completing my training shortly to attain full wizard status. Now we have Derek on board, who is of course a wizard experienced in battle training, I'm sure my offensive skills will improve too. The other factor, that you might want to remind your guild of, is that I fought alone before. If I am unjustly attacked, I have any number of wizards here who would willingly aid me.' He noticed Tobias' eyes widen and knew he'd made his point. If the guild came at him, it had better be for a damn good reason. He watched Tobias almost scuttle out the door, with some small satisfaction. He called Derek to take over guesting and supervising Tobias; he really wasn't in the mood.

***

Jim knocked on the guest suite door. Aubrey's bodyguard opened the door, announced him before allowing him into the reception area of the suite. Lord Aubrey came out of the bedroom area clad only in a towel; it was clear he'd bathed.

'I just came to say lunch will be in ten minutes,' Jim said just as a bell began ringing down the corridor.

'That's the dinner bell?' Aubrey asked and laughed. 'That could wake the dead!'

'I know, but it's what they've always used. I think because it works to roust the lazy from their beds in the morning.'

'Ah. Yes, that would do it.'

'What's your name?' Jim asked the bodyguard when Aubrey had disappeared back into the bedroom to dress. He was glad to note the man had changed into dry clothes too.

'Curtis, sir.'

'Do you have everything you need Curtis? I apologise that isn't a proper bed,' he added gesturing at the couch and noticing Curtis was particularly tall and broad. He wondered if his feet would be hanging off the end.

'Everything is satisfactory, thank you sir,' Curtis responded with sincere politeness. In truth he was relieved by their accommodation. It was simple but had all the basics. His lord had a private bedroom and had already relaxed in a rejuvenating hot bath. The rooms were easy to secure being in an upper storey and with only one external door, against which he could place his bed. He gaped then as the young headmaster rested a hand on the small couch and it moved before his eyes. 'Ah, what just happened?'

'Your feet were going to be hanging over the end, Curtis, so I made it longer and wider,' Jim said with a small shrug. The adjustment had taken mere moments but would make the world of difference to a man's comfort. A bodyguard needed to be alert and for that he needed rest, particularly when he had no-one to alternate shifts with.

'Thank you sir,' Curtis murmured so that his lord wouldn't hear. He realised the wizard thought such fundamental alterations were no big deal! If only he could do such things, then his feet need never be cold again!

Shortly, Lord Aubrey had dressed and they headed down the stairs to the dining hall. Aubrey gazed about the hall curiously as he followed Jim down to the front. The room was remarkably full of teenagers and young adults already sitting at the long oak tables or milling around chatting to friends. He was aware of the curious stares as he passed, but there seemed far more acceptance of strangers amongst them than he would have expected, given the uncertain times they lived in. Perhaps they simply felt safe with Jim around to protect them, or maybe they were used to visitors. Then he noticed a striking dark haired young woman watching them, already seated at the table they were approaching. She seemed vaguely familiar but he couldn't place where he might have seen her before. Then they had arrived at the table.

'Lord Aubrey, I'd like to present my fiancée Amelie and our daughter Daisy.'

'Pleased to meet you,' Aubrey said taking her hand in greeting. Jim's fiancée was rumoured to be a wizard of exceptional strength. He noticed the highly unusual dragon ring on her engagement finger and knew it meant something, although he wasn't sure he wanted to know exactly what. Tobias' guild had come to kidnap this woman and he knew now where he'd seen her before, in Jim's animus guardsman's memory of that attack. He released her hand remembering that as a wizard, she would be able to read his thoughts easily through that kind of contact if she wished. She looked back at him with serenity however, so she couldn't have seen anything bad and he was certainly trying not to recall that she had initially been naked in the battle.

'I'm happy to meet you at last sir,' she said with a genuine smile. 'Jim has said so much about his meetings with you. Do sit down,' she added gesturing for him to choose a seat.

'Thank you my lady,' Aubrey responded and sat down beside her where he could see the students in the hall. Many were still hurrying inside and grabbing a seat. Tobias entered with wizard Derek and both nodded politely to him before finding seats further down the table.

'There's a place set for you here, Curtis,' Jim said quietly, gesturing to a small desk that had been brought in so that the bodyguard could sit with his back against the wall at the end of the aisle. The position allowed an unobstructed view of the hall whilst being near enough to Lord Aubrey, on the head table, to keep watch over him. This way, Curtis could also eat, without separately being catered for or leaving his post.

'Thank you sir,' Curtis responded. He wondered about Jim's background. How did he understand just what a bodyguard needed in order to efficiently do his job? Or was he simply reading his mind? This wizard might look young but he'd already gathered quite a reputation for being powerfully gifted and a warrior. He could not imagine that wizard Jim would allow any threat to enter the hall where his fiancée and daughter were. So, he gladly accepted the serving bowls passed to him, that had already been sampled by others at the head table. He knew it would be safe to eat when the same food had been shared amongst so many others.

'Good, the rain's finally stopped,' Jim remarked to Lord Aubrey as they finished dessert.

'Typical! We ride all morning in a downpour and then as soon as we're undercover it stops! Are you sure that's not your doing?'

'You've got to be kidding!' Jim laughed. 'I can't affect the weather. If I could I'd be out making a fortune with the farmers.'

'That's true. Just checking,' Aubrey added.

'So, what would you like to do this afternoon? Did you want to have a look around?'

'Yes. I'd particularly like to see your training ground that I've heard so much about.'

'Certainly. There won't be any students up there until next lesson in another hour, if you'd prefer to see it unoccupied?'

'Why the gap? Everyone's already finished lunch.'

'This extra long lunch-break was something that one of my predecessors instigated. Actually I think it does the students good to have a little free time now in daylight. It's also better for students not to undertake strenuous physical exercise directly after a large meal and lunch is our main meal of the day. Anyone with magic is refreshed by eating, so meals and tea breaks, at regular intervals, aid concentration and learning.' He noticed Aubrey kept glancing outside through the big windows to the restful green vista of lawn and beyond to the wide expanse of meadow dotted with mature trees. Many students had gone outside, chatting in little groups and enjoying the sunshine now that it had made its first real showing for the day.

'Where is your training ground?' Aubrey asked. 'I don't remember seeing anything like that on the way in.'

'You may have noticed that the drive carries on beyond the school buildings. Our training ground is about half a mile behind us. We have ample time to walk up there, or if you prefer, we have fresh horses you're welcome to use?'

'I've been in the saddle too many hours already today,' Aubrey remarked. 'I think a walk would be good to stretch out the old legs.'

They followed as Jim rose from the table and led their party deeper into the building and then stepped out into a huge airy glasshouse. Beds of a whole variety of plants were growing here. Aubrey breathed deeply of the rich scent of earth and thriving greenery. This was an unexpected oasis of nature, and from a practical standpoint, he now had an explanation for some of their self-sufficiency.

'This looks an odd mix of order and wilderness,' Aubrey observed as they passed through.

'You would be right,' Jim responded and glanced around him with approval. 'When we first arrived here, this glasshouse was broken. Nearly every pane of glass had been shattered. They're still working to put everything right. Without this building, it is difficult to grow sufficient food to sustain us. It was the first repair job we were asked to undertake. It took considerable effort, but as you can see, it was worth it.' He opened the door and headed outside. Glancing back he noticed just how curiously everyone was looking at the glasshouse, probably for different reasons, but all seemed impressed.

He frowned slightly as he looked at the path, noticing that there was now a fork with the beginnings of a path leading to the portal. Anyone could see that others had walked that way. He really didn't need curious students to follow suit and venture there. He'd have to mention it to Darius. He knew Darius was busy assembling building materials and transporting them to the portal. It was inevitable that such traffic would be making a clearer path. He would have to think of a way of deterring students from wandering and finding themselves at a portal they knew nothing about. They would be too excited about the find not to talk and such gossip would spread. It was only a matter of time. He headed briskly for the well-marked right hand path that led directly to the main driveway. Once on that track he slowed up and felt he could relax. Darius's people didn't use the main drive to bring their supplies up, but instead came on a more direct route across the grass. Travelling at dinner time when the students were likely to be inside, or under cover of darkness, was still the safest way for his people to remain unnoticed in their work to rebuild Féarmathuin Castle. Limiting their time wasn't exactly ideal though.

'Is that a herd of deer?' Aubrey asked, gesturing to several shapes far across the meadow.

'It would be, yes. We've decided to farm deer. They're cheaper and rather easier to have around than sheep or cattle and we do have the perfect place for them,' Jim added gesturing at the wide expanse of grass than any herbivore would thrive on.

'That does seem a good idea,' Aubrey responded. 'I like venison. So, what are all these buildings for?' he asked now were close enough to distinguish the fact that there was a row of small sheds near a big circular building with a domed roof.

'We have a few small workshops here. They don't get much use to be honest, except for staff repairing things. The two main ones are the carpentry shop and smithy.'

'And these other sheds? They seem more secure,' Aubrey observed.

'Armoury stores,' Jim explained shortly. 'This one has the student's practice weapons,' he explained, opening it up and letting them see the shelves of protective gear and stacked targets. Then there were racks containing wooden swords in different type order, javelins, quarter-staves and even a few battered steel swords with their edges blunted. In another section were cavalry shields and weaponry.

'You seem to have a good range of weapons for students to practice with,' Aubrey observed with approval, picking up and examining several items curiously. 'Everything's rather patched though.' The protective gear in particular showed many signs of hard use, with stuffing coming out or seams torn. A good many items were overdue for replacement. This was however, the first real sign he'd noticed as a direct result of the school's lack of funding. Good quality equipment was expensive and this was one of the areas where students would be suffering.

'If you're planning to attract warrior students in greater numbers and of a higher calibre, it's essential to provide adequate equipment.'

'I agree. Mm, I'll have to divert some people to making replacements,' Jim remarked riffling through a stack of quilted leather jerkins. He realised he'd been remiss in having a look in here before now, but it had never occurred to him to do so.

'Making replacements?' Aubrey queried in surprise.

'That's what we do around here,' Jim admitted. 'New leather isn't hard to come by with so many people to feed. If we needed replacement items in steel then yes, that is more problematic. But then again, a good blacksmith can repair or salvage many a broken blade or repurpose an unused item.'

'You have a good blacksmith then?' Aubrey asked glancing at the small and clearly rarely used smith shop here.

'We do. The main workshop is down in the village, where the majority of our support businesses are located.'

'I would like to see that later,' Aubrey said.

'Certainly,' Jim responded, although he glanced sidelong at Tobias. He'd really rather not take him where he would probably notice and report everyone he saw was animus. 'This other store has the more dangerous items.'

'There isn't much in here,' Aubrey remarked in surprise. There were racks of the main different types of bow; from longbow, the smaller versions to crossbows and of course its differing ammunition. Otherwise however, there were only a couple of broadswords and a pair of spears.

'With real weapons, serious accidents are more likely. It's dangerous to have more than one bout in the ring at a time using real steel, so what we have is sufficient. Besides, swords are expensive.'

'I suppose so, but what happens if one of these were to break? Presumably the lesson would then be over.'

'Not necessarily. The main armoury is in the school building where dangerous items can be properly secured, supervised and safeguarded. If anyone were to break in to these stores here, their mischief would be of a limited nature.'

'Ah. Yes, that makes more sense. I can see it's convenient to store items here, but it is isolated.'

'Exactly. Do you wish to see the archery field? Students are now on their way up.'

'They are?' Aubrey asked wondering how Jim knew that since he was still in the armoury doorway and couldn't see the drive. Aubrey now stepped around the building and did indeed see figures approaching but in the distance still. 'Certainly.'

Jim halted at a post and rail fence just beyond the arena. There were three long narrow fenced areas with an assortment of targets in each.

'This is what they class the beginner lane,' Jim explained, pointing at three large clear targets placed at differing distances, but all relatively close. The middle lane was clearly designed to be more of a challenge and the third was set out with an assortment of tiny targets and others at considerable distances. Jim then moved further along to a gate accessing a wide mostly empty field.

'As you can see there are horse stalls here beside this field. This is where students learn warhorse commands and cavalry manoeuvres. On the far side near the trees you can see some odd bits of hedge, walls and banks set out. That is a horse obstacle course. Students learn to negotiate and guide their horse over a variety of obstacles whilst travelling at speed. It's a new addition to our facilities and has proved very popular with students, the horses and spectators alike.'

'It sounds dangerous,' Derek remarked.

'It's exhilarating, yes! It's actually quite similar to hunting with hounds, but with the challenge being on a technically difficult ride done at the gallop. Riding onto a battlefield is dangerous. It is usually strewn with obstacles, manmade or natural. We do of course take steps to minimise the danger here, by only letting them go around singly. This is a fun and competitive sport for the students, but it does take skill and courage. It will ultimately aid them in coping with whatever challenges they might face travelling across country, without becoming trapped or falling off.'

'Interesting idea. I can see the merit in what you're saying,' Derek admitted eyeing the course speculatively. 'Learning the skills of riding to hounds is usually restricted to the nobility or wealthy. Recruiting good cavalry riders has always therefore been their preserve. Having a wider pool of recruits can only be a good thing.'

'Do you think any will be going round today?' Aubrey asked hopefully.

'To be honest, I don't know. As I said, it's still very new and is just one skill option for our instructors to work on.'

'Have you had a go?' Derek asked.

'No. I rarely have time to come up and there are always too many waiting to have a go whenever the option is open to them.' Jim didn't mention the fact he was not a bold horseman and that course looked scary. His lion came to the surface whenever he was nervous. His horse would undoubtedly sense the lion and panic, which was not ideal during an already potentially dangerous exercise. It was wisest not to risk embarrassment, or indeed serious injury, from being thrown off. 'I have watched some going round though if you'd like to see?'

'Yes please,' Aubrey said eagerly and stepped within reach as did Derek. Jim didn't bother inviting Tobias, leaving it to him to decide whether he wanted to be included. He knew Tobias was leery of touching him. As if Tobias had any remarkable strength or skills Jim would want to leach! Secrets were a far more likely reason for Tobias' reticence. But to his surprise, Tobias reached for contact just as he was about to show the memory to the other two.

'Now that did look fun,' Aubrey remarked as the scenes ended and Jim broke contact. He glanced out at the field again. The students and horses hurtling round the field, leaping fences and springing up then dropping down off banks, had been quite a sight. He wasn't surprised it was popular with spectators too.

'It did, didn't it,' Derek agreed cheerfully. He would find out when the next lesson was scheduled and come and watch. He doubted he'd be alone. Meanwhile they headed back to the buildings and entered the arena. A group of students were gathered around a burly man who was giving instructions. Their party settled into the tiered seating to watch. Derek was a little surprised to note that the man was an ordinary human and also that the class had a mix of animus and wizard students. He said as much to Jim.

'This is a physical combat lesson, in which no-one is allowed to use magic. Bruno has a lot of experience and is a good teacher. Even though he has no useable magic of his own, he can sense when magic is being used or in this case, when anyone is cheating.'

'Ah, useful ability indeed,' Aubrey remarked and then fell silent to watch as the students paired up with wooden practice swords and began working.

Jim glanced at the members of his party; everyone, including Curtis and the small squad of soldiers were watching with considerable interest. Well, everyone except Tobias, who actually looked bored. Jim ignored him and returned his attention to the students. He could easily tell which of the pairs was animus for they moved remarkably swiftly, both their swords and their feet. In comparison, the few wizards in the class looked slow and cumbersome. Bruno moved around, stopping some to correct them or calling advice or instructions as he assessed each pair.

'Is your warrior wizard in this class?' Derek asked.

'No. She's here every morning with the second year's warrior class. She'll be in tactics at the moment. These are also second year students but not from the specialist warrior class.'

'Ah. For non specialist warriors, they seem remarkably accomplished,' Derek observed with approval. 'Damn, those animus are quick,' he added. He was unused to watching animus at work and their differing ability and in particular, their speed, was quite marked.

'Thank you. I'm sure they appreciate knowing that,' Jim said noticing one of the lads glance their way at that point and suspecting he'd heard.

'When can I meet her?'

'I'll introduce you to Natalya at break. If you wish, you and Tobias could sit in on one of the classes while I take Lord Aubrey down to the village. Your legs are still healing and this is ample exercise for the day. Besides, Tobias is looking exceedingly bored up here.'

'Are you sure you don't need us?' Derek asked having glanced at Tobias in surprise to find he was indeed gazing out the door.

'No. You've been in the village already, there's less of interest there for you both,' Jim assured whilst hoping Derek would take the bait. Having Tobias in amongst all of Clan Green Bear's fugitives was risking exposure. Animus people rarely had shielded minds; it would be easy for a wizard to eavesdrop and hear a snippet of thought that might expose their secret. Derek would be doing everyone a favour by keeping Tobias away and occupied.

'The lesson is nearly over. We could start making our way back now if you've seen enough?'

'That was most enlightening,' Aubrey admitted and gladly left the unforgiving hard wooden bench in the draughty building and headed back outside into the weak sunshine.

Jim led Lord Aubrey back into the dining hall, which was again thronging with students, but this time they were not neatly seated at tables. At his glance a small party of students politely vacated a window seat. He settled his guests there on upholstered seats in the sun while he fetched them refreshments.

'May I assist you, sir?' Curtis asked appearing at Jim's elbow.

'Ah, yes. If you could pour drinks for yourself and your lord and take them over, I'll sort the patrollers,' Jim said, busy pouring five cups of tea and loading them on a tray. Being careful to wait until no one was likely to cross its path, he sent the laden tray over to land on the table, amused that the escort sat watching it come with wide eyes. In the meantime, Derek and Tobias had filled their cups from another urn. Thus, in short order Jim could now return to the table with a plate of biscuits as well as his own drink.

'Your food bills must be huge,' Aubrey remarked as he took a biscuit and noticed the size of the platters of biscuits set out for the students and most especially how depleted they very quickly were.

'Yes. Food is the one thing we can't go short of. Someone with magic eats at least twice what a non-magic user does.'

'You mean the animus?' Aubrey asked.

'No, wizards and animus eat exactly the same amounts because they both have magic, it simply manifests in two different ways.'

'I'm not sure I understand the significance of what you're saying; everyone needs to eat,' Aubrey said.

'Think of it like a fire; the more wood you add the hotter and brighter the flames. A fire can subsist with hardly any fuel but you can't expect to do anything useful with it, like cooking, until it's revived and is properly hot.'

'What an unusual comparison but I think I now understand. Animus and wizards, by the same token I'm assuming, therefore, can only do extraordinary things when well fed?'

'Exactly.'

'What's wrong?' Aubrey asked quietly noticing Jim go still and focussed and then he turned around to watch a particular group of rather boisterous students come in and head directly for the tea urn.

*'Natalya.'*

*'Yes?'*

*'I'd like you to come and meet some people.'*

*'Why?'*

'Lord Aubrey wishes to visit the village and its best that wizard Tobias in particular doesn't come with him and perhaps see too much. He would be far more interested in meeting you and certainly wizard Derek has asked to be introduced.'

'Why do they want to meet me?'

'Wizard Derek felt you shaking the building the other day when you threw that paint around. He is due to join our staff next week once his legs have fully healed. You should know he has much experience in training wizards to become warriors. He will become one of your teachers, in fact the primary one, so be nice.'

'I'm to be a diversion?'

'Yes please. I'm sure they'll be interested in accompanying you to your next class too.'

'Thanks a bundle!'

'Just finish your tea and get over here,' he added and beckoned to cover the fact he'd already mentally summoned her.

'You called sir?' Natalya asked Jim politely.

'My lord, I'd like to introduce my fiancée's sister Natalya. She is a warrior wizard,' Jim said.

Natalya discreetly gave the party the once-over, as Jim introduced her; aware the lord, the two wizards and even the guards were watching her closely.

'Lord Aubrey, I believe?' she said and sketched him a quick but respectful bow. Trust Jim to announce her as a warrior wizard; now there would be no disguising herself or fading into anonymity.

'You are a warrior wizard?' Aubrey asked, rising to greet the tall and charismatic woman. She had a fierce aloof beauty like a raptor and eyed them as if she was choosing her next meal or perhaps considering flight. She smiled, dispelling the predatory effect but he realised she was uncomfortable being the centre of attention.

'So I'm told. I'm pleased to meet you sir.'

'Likewise,' Aubrey said and noticed the two wizards eagerly approaching. He stepped back and assessed the small crowd; most were watching Natalya and the two wizards were almost fawning over her. He noticed Jim watching them with a hint of satisfaction; the timing of this introduction was clearly deliberate. Why?

*'Jim, have you told Drako you're bringing people down?'* Natalya privately asked.

*'Not yet. Why? Is something going on down there today?'*

*'You should take Cassy with you on the tour.'*

'Why?'

'Drako can't be seen, so as head woman it's up to Cassy to stand in his place to defend the Clan's interests. I've just spoken with her and she agrees. She'll have to miss last lesson, but she and Drako agree this is potentially more important. She's headed out now. It will seem less strange for her to meet you there than tag along from here.'

'Thank you Natalya, I wouldn't have thought of any of that.'

'I know and my thanks are the two exceedingly curious wizards you've foisted on me. Incidentally, how open should I be with Tobias? I get the feeling you don't like or trust him overly.'

'He's a good little guild member. Don't tell him anything you're not happy being public knowledge.'

'Understood. This is going to be a fun afternoon.'

\*\*\*

Lord Aubrey followed Jim into the village and looked around him in amazement. The village was solidly constructed of stone, brick or timber and looked as though it had been there for years, when in fact he knew it had not. Everywhere was neatly kept and the roads cleanly cobbled in stone.

'Well this is a surprisingly affluent and pleasing looking place to house your staff,' Aubrey remarked.

'Thank you. Although this village is not designed for staff in the conventional sense because we do not exclusively employ them. We have staff cottages and apartments up at the school for those that we do employ. Essentially, this is an independent village positioned to primarily supply the school with its every day needs. Because the workshops are here on site, we have no problems with unexpected supply delays, or businesses deciding to bow to pressure and stop supply, or changing the style of what they make. There are a lot of benefits in this system. Our orders take priority, but the people's time is their own and they are free to fit other things in.'

'You've obviously done a great deal of planning, work and negotiating to set all this up. I'm impressed. This arrangement is another reason the school is beginning to prosper, I imagine?'

'Yes. We've cut down our supplier bills markedly. We aren't yet self-sufficient in many things, but we're working on those that we could do ourselves. It all helps.' Jim led him down the street, pointing out the various industries as they passed. Cassy ambled down the street keeping comfortably ahead of them although Jim knew she was in listening range.

'I couldn't help noticing that your lumber mill is unusually busy even though the yard is already heavily stocked with worked timber planks and posts,' Lord Aubrey remarked. 'What are you planning next?'

Jim eyed him for a long moment; he could hardly admit that it was destined to secretly rebuild Féarmathuin castle.

*'Tell him we're planning to build an Inn on site to cater for the many visitors we receive and of course for your wedding guests,'* Cassy suggested mentally and heard Jim gratefully grab and voice that explanation.

'Interesting. I suppose that would be a money earner too?' Aubrey enquired slyly and Jim shrugged. 'You plan on a bar too? That might become problematic so close to students.'

'I'm sure we can work out a way to bar the underage from alcohol and also discourage general overindulgence.'

'If you can, then that knowledge would be of use elsewhere,' Aubrey observed. 'I doubt parents will appreciate having drunken brawls occurring within school grounds.'

'Too true. I will give it some thought as and when we are up and running. I'm sure some volunteers will present themselves to practice on,' Jim observed with a small smile and Aubrey gave a short bark of laughter.

He noticed just how much Lord Aubrey was looking about him as they traversed the village street, not just looking at the businesses, but also any of the people in view. His interest and curiosity was apparent.

Since he had already expressed an interest, Jim wasn't surprised Lord Aubrey went into the smithy even though they could hear the clang of hammers from outside. Aubrey eyed the racks of completed tools in evidence as well as the pails of nails, bolts and latches. This workshop was most definitely fully in use.

Bruce now had two apprentices to help with the simpler tasks. He'd been inundated with orders for hammers and axes, picks and shovels. Then the farmers needed scythes, ploughs and spades, whilst the timber yard needed saws, files and planes. Everyone needed a variety of knives, whether for domestic use, hunting or defence. Creating a strong sharp blade took time and skill. Now he also had Darius's workforce to outfit and they needed serious weapons too. Drako had popped in only a few minutes ago to warn them of Aubrey's impending visit, which had necessitated a quick scout round to hide any weapons. One useful side effect of returning to Féarmathuin Castle was that it was strewn with wreckage and war debris. Bruce had asked them to collect and bring back any broken metal item they found so he could melt it down to transform into something useful. Broken weapons and armour, mixed with strewn domestic items, was littered all over Féarmathuin since many homes had been ransacked and the fighting fierce enough for people to grab anything they could to fight or shield themselves. He could find a use for most scrap, especially as purchasing new material from traders was expensive and coin was scarce. Unfortunately, much of the scrap brought in had suffered from years of exposure to the elements; rust had taken its toll.

'Impressive,' Lord Aubrey remarked as they left the noisy and burning hot smithy. He couldn't help noticing that the boy hadn't stopped working the bellows to keep the furnace coals glowing orange, even with strangers in his midst. Two youths also continued working at separate tasks alongside the burly smith, creating a dreadful din as they each hammered the glowing metal on their anvil into particular shapes. The smith, briefly introduced as Bruce, did pause to acknowledge the small crowd entering his shop, but also continued working the long length of glowing metal before him. It was clear they were working to some kind of urgent deadline. Aubrey was well aware that a smith could only work metal when it remained hot and malleable so he didn't engage the smith in conversation but allowed him to continue. He did however notice the smith nod respectfully to the young blonde woman who had come closer and now seemed to be accompanying them on the tour. From the glance passed her way, he surmised she was someone of importance in the village and certainly Jim seemed to accept her presence.

While they were given a tour of the bakery and his guards were distracted by the sight and scents of fresh baking, Lord Aubrey gestured Jim aside.

'Is Drako here at the moment?' he asked quietly and noticed Jim's immediate frown of concern. 'These are his people, are they not?'

'What makes you think that?' Jim asked, keeping his voice low too.

'After your visit last winter, one of my patrols spotted you driving the wagon across the river in the snow,' Aubrey explained. 'I recognized him in the party that had come to meet you.'

'Ah.' Jim glanced at the men briefly, making sure none had moved back into earshot.

'I don't think anyone else recognized him in the background. It has been years since anyone has seen him and you were taking centre stage!' Aubrey noticed Jim's direct gaze and whilst he felt no intrusion, he wondered if this wizard had indeed just read his mind.

'Cassaria,' Jim said, aware he was surprising her with use of her full name. 'Is your husband in right now?'

'Husband?' Aubrey repeated softly and noticed the bakers had glanced up alertly too. Jim was now looking at the blonde woman in the direct way Aubrey was beginning to recognize meant they were mentally conversing. She must therefore be a wizard, but Drako had married her?

'If I may, my lady, I would like to see him while I'm here,' Aubrey said to her directly. She glanced sidelong at his guardsmen and raised a brow at him inquiringly. He nodded understanding to which she inclined her head discreetly.

'This way, my Lord,' Cassy invited, gesturing to the door and he joined her swiftly. *'Get inside Drako,'* she urged mentally, aware he preferred his vantage point of the shady swing-seat where he had a wonderful vista and a partial view of his village.

'Ah, your guard companions,' Aubrey remarked to Jim, recognising the tall men emerging from the cottages flanking this steep little lane. That Jim had been allowed to borrow Drako's personal security force meant they must feel safe here and showed an amazing level of co-operation.

'Indeed.'

Persuading his guardsmen to remain outside the house when they were not allowed to check it first for hidden dangers obviously didn't sit well with his men, but they obeyed, partially because Curtis and Jim were going with him.

Cassaria opened the front door and invited Jim and Aubrey inside, closing it gently but firmly in his men's curious faces.

Aubrey followed her into the house and through into a spacious living room, carefully closing the door behind her. He glanced around a large room, simply furnished but remarkably restful. It felt warm and inviting and the views from the unusual pale yellow tinted windows were panoramic. A tall, broad shouldered figure stepped through from the room at the back and into his sight.

'My Lord,' Drako said quietly and bowed. 'Welcome to my home.'

'It is you!' Aubrey exclaimed, only just remembering to keep his voice down. He hugged the young man who had been his squire, realising as he did so that Drako was a very solidly muscled man now rather than the lanky youth he had once been. 'I'm so very glad to see you.' He stepped back and Drako invited him with a gesture to be seated.

Cassy went through to the kitchen to prepare refreshments and Jim went with her, allowing the two men to talk. She nodded at Dustin, discreetly watching through the dining room window, while Rupert kept an eye on the soldiers at the front. She knew the soldiers recognized Rupert and probably all the pack and that it had not escaped their understanding that their Lord was privately meeting someone of importance here with Jim. She heard a guffaw and recognized Lord Aubrey's voice, and glanced through at them. Drako too was laughing about something, but he was far less audible. She glanced at Dustin and noticed his pose was less anxious; he would have heard that laughter too, and perhaps even what had triggered it. Jim settled on the stool in the kitchen by the back door and smiled at her encouragingly. She put a mug before him, glad he had taken the awkwardness away by giving them a chance to talk privately.

She set a tray out on the small table before them and was relieved to watch Lord Aubrey curl his large fingers around a mug and sit back clasping it, not offended to be served in something as mundane as a pottery mug. The pastries she'd asked for whilst at the bakery were clearly a success too, for moments after their appearance on the table, only crumbs remained.

She was a little apprehensive to sit facing this Lord as though she was his equal. It had felt simpler when she'd merely been a part of the crowd. Now however, she could no longer put off sitting beside Drako and meeting Lord Aubrey's assessing gaze.

'I'd like you to meet my wife, Cassaria,' Drako said formally.

'Honoured to meet you, lady Cassaria,' Aubrey responded rising so she would. He took her hand and kissed it near the wedding ring on her finger. The subtly designed ring gave the impression of age, and had been beautifully crafted. This then was probably an heirloom. In fact, it seemed vaguely familiar. She had to look up to meet his gaze since she was relatively small, but she boldly did so. She was very attractive and, first impressions to the contrary, neither timid nor slow of wit. 'Please forgive me for asking, but do your parents know who you have married?'

'They do indeed. They did of course have initial reservations in my choice, but that was before they met him for real. They have also met his father and everyone seemed to get along,' she added with a small smile to Drako.

'They did?' Aubrey queried in surprise.

'My father is a wizard of some standing. Of course Lord Trent would befriend him,' she explained blandly.

'I imagine he would, yes,' Aubrey chuckled. It was good to hear Trent had not fallen into depression but was still interested in political manoeuvring and planning for a brighter future for his people. Doubtless Drako and his new bride had quite a hand in that positivity, alongside this safe refuge. 'I suppose I'd better get going before my men decide to come in to check on me. It relieves my mind greatly to see you happily settled Drako. May good fortune smile on you,' he added and headed out the door.

\*\*\*

*'Why did Lord Aubrey insist on seeing you?'* Jim asked Drako mentally as he followed Aubrey from the house to return back up to the school.

*'You know I was his squire for a time?'*

*'Yes, you mentioned that and that he later went out of his way to help you escape detection to return to your family,'* Jim said. *'I've never understood what motivated him to do that, aside from believing it the fair thing to do.'*

*'We are distantly related,'* Drako told him.

*'Ah, that explains much. He'd be a bear too, I'd imagine, if he had the ability.'*

*'His branch of the family have never had the active animus ability. Some years before the persecution of our people began; his father and my grandfather had a serious falling out. The families never publicly made up, because by*

*the time we privately did, it suited us all to allow people to forget the link.'*

Lord Aubrey too, was reminiscing as he walked. Seeing Drako had brought back so many memories. He wondered how Trent fared; he hadn't dared ask where he was living now. It was enough to know Trent was still regarded as an important part of the family and the Clan Green Bear people as a whole. Clearly he was still alive and well somewhere and probably nearby. Aubrey was glad for Drako's happiness and relieved that he was finally safe and settled. Hearing that he'd been hounded, attacked and his people hurt had been particularly hard for Aubrey to stomach. He'd had his hands tied, watched too closely to be able to intervene.

Lord Trent was Aubrey's second cousin. He remembered the rift between their families, which had come about from a simple miscommunication that had disastrous consequences. Aubrey's father had failed to hear and therefore come to Clan Green Bear's aid in time to make a difference in the crown's earliest persecution, which led to a serious falling out. That family anger was in part fuelled by frustration as they watched the crown's troops gain footholds in their neighbouring territories, thinning Clan Green Bear's allies one by one. That weakening of support subsequently led to Féarmathuin Castle's destruction. The cousins eventually discovered they had both been duped, fed lies to divide and weaken their relative positions. Trent had hunted down the traitor responsible, and thus they turned their anger where it truly belonged. By that time however, the damage had been done, but the public rift in the family had some unforeseen benefits.

Lord Aubrey's side of the family had originally split off because his great grandfather only had latent animus ability. His bride had no magical ability whatsoever and so the magic in their line dwindled generation after generation as they continued to dilute it with plain humans. In contrast, Clan Green Bear were proud of their animus ability and ensured they married other animus to keep themselves strong. Now, it was barely remembered that Lord Trent and Lord Aubrey were related, however distantly.

When Drako was old enough to be apprenticed, Lord Trent had approached Lord Aubrey, knowing he would train the boy as a squire, incidentally giving him the knowledge of etiquette and society that his father could no longer provide. Drako had flourished under Aubrey's wing and the families had secretly regained closer ties once more. Another reason for that was the tragedy of Aubrey's family. His beloved wife had died in childbirth but had left him a son. Drako shared the same dark hair and eyes as Julian, but there the resemblance ended. Julian was raised by a succession of tutors, who all had one thing in common; their failure to instil respect or obedience into the arrogant boy. One of the many things father and son did not agree on was their animus heritage. Julian thought his blood had been tainted and whilst believing his father had done the right thing in choosing a non-animus bride, he did not like to be reminded of it. Drako's presence had been a particular thorn in his side. Drako had effortlessly befriended many of the warriors and in particular the animus patrollers, despite his comparative youth. Julian knew Drako possessed "unnatural" strength and speed advantages over "pure" humans and thus he never confronted him directly. Julian avoided him as much as possible and seemed to prefer spending most of his time away at school.

When Julian returned for holidays however, he made no secret of his annoyance that Drako would be "lurking" somewhere. He had even smiled on hearing how widespread dislike of animus was becoming and that it was turning to hate. Aubrey now knew Julian had been behind writing to the crown enforcers and getting backing for the directive he'd subsequently received to fire all his animus staff. Julian had also made particular reference to Lord Trent's son's whereabouts. He'd been livid when Drako managed to evade capture. However, his letters had not gone unnoticed and Julian himself was now in demand. Without a backward look he left Cedar Castle and his father, having applied to become a crown enforcer. Unfortunately, his new career was cut short only months later when he underestimated an animus adversary and was killed.

Lord Aubrey was completely alone. His son had been a disappointment, but he'd been his son and only heir. Now however, he had a chance to rekindle contact with Drako who had been more of a son to him than Julian and to get to know his new wife.

'Let me know when your Inn is built. I'm curious as to how you're planning on policing the bar. Besides, I now have people to visit,' Aubrey added quietly.

What he really hoped was to be able to meet up with Trent. They hadn't seen each other for far too long and Aubrey missed having someone of like mind to talk to. Meeting up in a lively bar environment was far more appealing than his silent formal dining hall. Drako had the right idea in the design of his house; it was definitely a welcoming home and of course he had a wife to come home to as well.

27

# Camouflage

Jim stood silently, sending his senses out towards the village, seeking a particular person: hmm not there. He turned and scanned in the opposite direction and finally found the signature of the person he wanted and thereby his location. It was early morning and the school was quiet, with the majority of its populace in their first class of the day. Glancing out the window Jim sighed and pulled on his coat. He nodded to the workers tending the plants in the glasshouse on his way through and then was outside. Low clouds lay heavily overhead from which an annoying drizzle seeped. Thick banks of wet mist obscured visibility and gave every view a sinister feel. Turning his collar up and buttoning his coat, he grumbled to himself about his wayward imagination and walked quickly.

The path that he'd been concerned was becoming too clear was still quite overgrown. Long grass snaking around his ankles quickly soaked his trousers and the bushes he had to brush past seemed to delight in offloading their burden of raindrops on him. He pushed a larger branch aside and what felt like an entire bucket of water dropped on his head and poured inside his collar, drenching him. Damn! People tended to notice when he used magic and could often pinpoint his location; they might notice he wasn't in his office. He doubted anyone would bother to follow him outside in this weather however just to discuss some mundane matter. But, enough was enough! He created the quietest shield he could, in terms of magical signature, and then filled it with a hot breeze to dry himself and his clothes. As he walked on he watched with satisfaction as his shield brushed the foliage and the water pattering down now ran in beads and rivulets over an otherwise transparent shield leaving him warm, dry and unaffected. As he stepped out from behind the last of the bushes and into the Portal clearing the men already there jumped and spun to face him.

'Sorry to make you jump,' Jim said quickly and came forward so they could see him better and thus put away the weapons they'd drawn. 'Darius, can I have a word?'

'Wizard Jim. We didn't hear or smell you coming. How is that possible?' Darius asked in consternation and then noticed the very peculiar way the rain was acting around the wizard.

'As the rain shows, I'm shielded. I got soaked through just a few paces into the trees.'

'Yes, miserable weather. Useful trick that, although you now have me worried that other wizards could sneak up on us using such a shield. Anyway, what can I do for you?' He frowned nervously as the water misted shield seemed to move all by itself from between them to hover just above both of their heads. Darius too was now under shelter. 'Thank you.'

'I'm concerned that students might come exploring the paths that your people are now creating and find the Portal. As you can imagine, stopping them from gossiping about such a find would be nigh on impossible.'

'Yes, the same thought has crossed my mind. What can we do? Walking through the same woodland daily is inevitably going to leave tracks and we really need to start using wagons to carry the timber, which will only make it worse.'

'I think what we need to do is build something to visually camouflage the portal. We also need to have an excuse for why there are people working up here at odd times. I'd also feel better if someone was permanently on site and able to guard it.'

'I agree,' Darius responded thoughtfully. 'You have no problem with us working up here in your space?'

'Only if it causes me a problem,' Jim said frankly. 'The current setup is going to be a problem sooner rather than later. What we all need is for the students to think there is nothing odd going on up here that incites curiosity. Your people also need to be able to come and go openly during the day with carts. Any thoughts?'

'Yes, actually I think I have a solution. Our bulkiest loads are primarily going to be from the sawmill. I've noticed that the village doesn't have a lumber yard or charcoal maker and with the extra work we'll need Bruce to do, he really needs more charcoal than the school can currently supply him for his forge. Our camouflage needn't be a useless building. We have a real need for charcoal and that is an industry often positioned in woodland, has to have someone living on site to supervise the burn, and would explain a large shed full of lumber.'

'I like it,' Jim said in relief. 'Do you have anyone with charcoal making experience?'

'I'll find out. Bruce should remember who made it before for him. Since time is of the essence, how do you want to go about creating this?' Darius asked. He watched Jim look around the small clearing critically.

'I suggest you mark the trees blocking the most direct wagon route to the village and get people felling. It makes sense to use logs in the construction since that is what's most readily to hand. Leave the bark on the trees so the buildings will blend in. The shed will need to be of a reasonable length to accommodate the Portal at the back, store planks to either side inside and then have a screen of rough logs meant for the fire in the front. The cottage and shed could be one building, with the shed as a lean-to. That will give us most scope. I think what we need to achieve though, is something that doesn't look overly large, important or sophisticated. Otherwise people will be curious as to why we expended unnecessary effort in a building few will ever see.'

'It would be useful for additional castle workers to be able to bunk here,' Darius mentioned.

'Yes, that is a worthwhile consideration. Perhaps an extra set of rooms above the shed would work best. I'll have to do some sketches.' He stood beside the Portal, at the rear so it wouldn't activate and made some notes of its measurements on a scrap of paper. Then he paced out the size of the clearing; it was small.

'Do you want us to clear any trees here?'

'Not yet. Until I've got a design I won't know what will need to go. I'll have to think about it. I'll pop back later when I've got something to show you and to see how you're getting on. You never know, it might be possible to do some building this afternoon, but only if we have something to work with. I'll tell Drako, if you like, so he can send some people up.'

'That would be very useful, thank you.'

Darius watched Jim disappear back into the dripping gloom and then laughed. 'Well damn! Guess our day just changed course,' he remarked to his two companions, who simply nodded.

Jim wasn't entirely surprised to see Cassy and Natalya enter the library and approach him at break time.

'Told you he'd be here,' Natalya said, spotting him at a table across the room. There was no surprise on his face to see them however, just a gleam of satisfaction. Uh oh, why?

'Of course you knew; you can sense his location,' Cassy responded rolling her eyes.

'Hello ladies. I take it you've been looking for me?'

'As you knew we would,' Natalya responded.

'Indeed.'

'So what's this plan you're cooking up with Darius?' she added, a little uncomfortable with the speculative glance he was favouring both of them with. 'It's something you're planning to foist off onto us isn't it?'

'Foist? No, you're the ones rushing up to me demanding answers and involvement. Of course I am happy to oblige you,' he smiled. 'This is what we're doing,' he added planting his finger on a library entry in the opened book before him, entitled charcoal making. 'Cassy, you should take a look at these illustrations of the various forms of kiln. Whilst I'm not planning on building that for them we do need to be aware of what space such an object will require when planning the size, position and style of the hut and barn I am planning to build. Obviously a kiln doesn't want to be too close to the house, trees or other flammable things.'

'Should we be discussing this here?' Natalya asked quietly, noticing a pair of students entering the previously empty library and glance across at them curiously.

'Come down to my office,' Jim said, closing the book decisively. Once in the privacy of his office, he opened the book again and while Cassy read, with Natalya looking over her shoulder, he collected a large sheet of paper and spread it out on the table.

'Drako said this work was to do with the Portal,' Cassy said. 'What are we really doing?'

'What we are really doing is building over the portal to camouflage it from student's notice. There are paths to the portal now and as the weather improves, students are going to be more inclined to explore and find it. It also makes sense to disguise the traffic travelling to the castle amongst people working at a legitimate trade.'

'Can you show us what you have in mind?' Natalya asked noticing the paper. Cassy had shown her the plans that she and Jasper had created to design the village buildings, so she recognised what had to happen. She'd never seen how it was done however.

'I can try, but it might surprise you to know I'm not very good at making something up from scratch. That's why you're here, Cassy,' he added. He placed his hand flat on the paper and closed his eyes. Under his hand a log cabin slowly emerged. The portal blinked into detailed existence beside it and then more slowly, a shed grew around it. 'See, that's not good enough to cast a spell with.'

'What's this area?' Cassy asked.

'Darius would like space for his castle workers to sleep. I thought if it's above the shed, then it could be a large hidden area. Feel free to amend this Cassy,' he added and watched curiously as she immediately came to take his place. Under her direction, the plan for the hut came to life. A spacious kitchen with dining area took up the front half of the cottage, which would be able to accommodate large numbers. A dividing wall led to a cosy living area at the back, with a staircase up the middle. A door from the kitchen led out to the shed so that castle workers could enter and exit from the portal without going out the front door and perhaps be seen. Natalya gazed at what turned into a three dimensional model as she looked at it, and had some further suggestions, like enclosing the portal in its own room, so the door could be locked and also serve to mask the portal's glow when it was activated. She also suggested being able to get out of the hidden room through a trapdoor down into the portal room.

'Now you know why I wanted your help,' Jim remarked as he looked at plans he knew he could now work confidently from.

'You didn't ask,' Natalya pointed out. Drako's questions had actually brought them here.

'Ok, but I will need your help to turn this into reality. With Amelie as well, we ought to be able to do most of the work between us. I'm going to show Darius these plans now and see how he's getting on. Tell Drako to meet us there if he wants to have a look too,' he added to Cassy and knew by the small hum of energy around her that she was contacting him. If he knew Drako, he'd already be there!

'Do we have to go back to class?' Natalya asked.

'Yes. Your lessons are most important,' Jim told her. 'You can visit the site after lunch if you wish, but make sure you're not followed.'

'Of course not,' Natalya responded, rolling her eyes.

'This is serious. Every time I see you now you're surrounded by the boys from your class,' he added. 'Just make sure you're alone before you decide to come. We won't be doing anything until all three of you ladies are finished classes for the day anyway, so you won't be missing anything important.'

'Ok, we're going to class,' Cassy responded, tugging a slightly more rebellious Natalya with her. Both were highly curious and their partners even more so, since it affected them too and Jim had not talked to them about what he and Darius were proposing.

'Freddie!' Natalya exclaimed, noticing him leaning against the wall outside of the arena. 'Eww, you're all wet,' she added having wrapped her arms around him. She pulled back slightly, looking him over visually and then with their link. 'You're soaked to the skin,' she observed with a frown.

'That's what happens when it rains continuously for hours,' he said with a shrug. *'Your admirers are waiting,'* he added privately, aware her classmates were watching closely.

Natalya threaded her arm around his waist and they began to walk, joining her classmates on the road back to the school and lunch. She grinned, feeling him jump as her spell instantly dried his clothes, making them go hot and slither against his skin. *'Better?'*

*'I'm sure you can tell that it is,'* he responded although it had felt very weird. *'Thank you.'*

*'Ok, now tell me what's been happening. Are we going to the site right now?'*

*'We can eat first. In fact Jim said you weren't to skip lunch. Why would he think you would?'*

*'It was a thought I had,'* she admitted. *'He must have heard me think it. I do know better, honestly. I'm not going to have enough strength later if I don't eat now.'*

*'Exactly and now I'm not feeling quite so uncomfortable I might be able to stand joining the students in the hall for lunch. They are loud.'*

*'You need your strength too.'*

*'Do I?'*

Natalya laughed softly at his flirtatious raised eyebrow. She glanced round and noticed the guys were watching with considerable curiosity. She realised they knew she and Freddie were privately talking and they felt left out. 'Were you watching us practice?' she asked Freddie aloud. 'I've gone up a grade in my sword play.'

'Have you? Well done,' Freddie responded. 'I only saw the last few minutes, but yes, I'd say you have improved a great deal. So has Jason,' he added honestly, catching Jason's eye. Jason had been her sparring partner today and probably was frequently.

'Thank you sir,' Jason responded. Praise from such an accomplished swordsman meant a lot to him. 'Will you consider coming to spar with us some time?'

'You want to spar with me?' Freddie asked in surprise.

'I'd like to learn from the best. Without a shadow of a doubt, that is you,' he added.

'Not above flattery, Jason?' Freddie asked with amusement.

'Whatever works,' Jason shrugged. He knew how to appeal to an alpha wolf's nature. Wolves were often very generous and protective, but you didn't challenge them or their authority with impunity. Natalya was an alpha and she had responded to his friendly overtures and seemed to welcome his company because he never flirted. He knew Freddie tolerated him close to his lady, but that would change if he crossed the line.

'I'll see what I can do,' Freddie assured him and Natalya hugged him closer in silent thanks. Freddie knew Jason had seen her reaction; the lad didn't miss much. Jason's father had been highly respected and alpha of the dog pack. Jason had all the makings of becoming a leader too; there was no question he was smart and courageous. He'd have made a good wolf.

'Thank you,' Jason replied. 'So, you're joining us for lunch today?'

'Yes. We got back in time.'

'Where are the others?'

'We all got soaked through. I imagine they'll be at home now getting warm and dry,' Freddie remarked.

Jason nodded, aware Freddie had indeed looked dripping wet but was now dry thanks to Natalya's magic. Her happiness at his presence was obvious. It was little wonder Freddie sought her out at every opportunity rather than sit alone at home.

Natalya noticed Jim already sitting at the head table with Amelie. He met her eye and nodded. Reassured they were all taking this break, she settled down to take her share from the platter as it passed her place before the men swiped it all. She was hungry and knew she'd need her strength, although what might actually be required of her she still wasn't sure.

Finally the meal was finished and they were allowed to leave. Freddie took her hand and led her out. She glanced back to make sure they were not being followed and noticed Jason hadn't moved from the table but was sitting watching them leave. She hadn't had to say anything or come up with any excuses; Freddie's presence had wordlessly deterred them.

As they neared the portal clearing Natalya sensed an animus presence. 'Do you have people standing guard on these paths?' she asked Freddie quietly.

'Yes. You sense someone?'

She reached out with her senses for more information and felt a familiar presence. 'Dustin's on this path,' she said, speaking at a normal volume so he would hear them. Moments later Dustin stepped out of cover to meet them. 'Hi Dustin,' she said warmly.

'My lady,' Dustin greeted. He frowned in puzzlement as she reached out to touch his shoulder but didn't move away. Under her touch his clothes unexpectedly turned hot, a tiny cloud of steam came off him and then his garments were suddenly dry. 'Ah, thank you,' he murmured, distinctly unsettled, not only by the strangeness of what she'd done, but that she would expend her energy simply for his comfort. She patted his cheek gently and he suddenly felt her affection come through the contact. He also sensed she felt protective of him; she was a true alpha, concerned for the welfare of each member of the pack.

'Any problems?' Freddie asked amused by Dustin's bemusement.

'None,' Dustin responded straightening. He glanced at Freddie's clothes and wasn't surprised he'd been similarly dried. 'What is it my lady?'

'Jim's coming,' she told them and walked on. She noticed a crowd of people in the clearing already and that all looked up when she appeared, then they glanced to either side of her and she realised both Dustin and Freddie were standing beside her. Most went straight back to work. She frowned at the portal's odd appearance for a moment before realising it had been draped with a large dark tarpaulin. Well, someone clearly had some sense, since that made it completely unrecognisable and with the people working at chopping down trees and other loud tasks, this was the most likely time to be discovered.

On the far side of the clearing was a new open space and she walked over to have a closer look. A wider path was being cut into the dense forest that would accommodate a wagon. In this new space the felled trees had been trimmed of their branches and the resulting logs stacked in readiness. Men were still hard at work further along the path felling trees to clear the route to the meadow and subsequently to the village. Teams of horses dragged the fallen trees out of the way so other men could trim them of branches before taking the new logs nearer the clearing ready for use.

She was surprised to note that one of the lumberjacks was Drako. She didn't distract him while he wielded an axe with powerful blows. She couldn't deny he had the build and musculature to be a very effective axe man. The tree fell and Drako stood back breathing heavily while someone else took his axe and took over the trimming work. Clearly everyone was taking a turn sharing out the labour of an exhausting project.

'Hey. Is it lunch time then?' Drako asked, turning and spotting Freddie, Natalya and Dustin.

'Certainly is,' she responded.

Noticing Natalya's gaze drop he recalled he'd taken off his shirt when the rain had made it stick to him and restrict his movements. He picked it off a branch and wrinkled his nose at the dripping thing. He wearily wrung the cold water out of it, knowing it was going to be unpleasant against his skin.

'Shall I dry that before you put it back on?' Natalya asked, watching him. She noticed his surprise but then he glanced at Freddie.

'That would be most welcome,' Drako admitted and held the shirt out. He noticed she didn't touch him, but only the material. Freddie and even Dustin had been dried top to toe so he hadn't been singled out. Pulling on a warm dry shirt was infinitely preferable to a sopping wet one. At least the rain had stopped, although he suspected it would resume later.

'You've certainly been busy,' Natalya remarked as they walked together back to the portal.

'I know how Jim works,' Drako said. 'He hates waiting once he has plans in his hands to work from. I understand you had a hand in them?'

'I merely had a few minor suggestions,' she admitted. 'You've seen them then?'

'Yes,' Drako said. 'Doing this work will give us a number of benefits. Jim said Darius came up with the idea?'

'Jim approached him with the idea of camouflaging the portal with another building. Darius came up with the charcoal maker guise,' Natalya clarified. 'Where is Darius?'

'He's taken a wagon to fetch some hardcore for the foundations,' Drako said and glanced back the way that they'd come. 'It's still awkward to get a wagon along there, but the tree I brought down was the last major obstacle. Once the branches are cleared out of the way he should be able to get through.'

'Do you two work together?' Natalya asked. She'd heard they were not close and had actually fought over Cassy, although she didn't know any more detail than that.

'We know we work better separately and with our own men. He has his loyal followers and I have mine,' Drako admitted with a small shrug. 'It works because he has always been separate and now he has the castle to concentrate on, while I have White Haven.'

'I see that. You are different characters and attract similarly minded followers,' Natalya mused. Drako's people were peaceful, content to put the past behind them, work and make the best of their new home and circumstances. Darius in contrast was a warrior in spirit and prepared to run risks in trying to retake his birthright, even though it would inevitably have to be fought for. His followers believed in that cause and many harboured deep resentments at being driven from their homes and for the many losses of friends and family they had suffered in the intervening years.

Jim, Amelie and Cassy appeared from behind the portal where they'd been assessing the space available against the plans and they moved to join them.

'Do we have enough timber cut now?' Drako asked Jim gesturing at the logs rather haphazardly stacked behind them.

'Drako's been cutting trees down,' Natalya remarked to Cassy and saw her frown and look at him more closely. His shirt was only partially buttoned; a clear indicator he'd been working hard enough to have removed it. Cassy wrapped an arm about him and Natalya grinned at his startled reaction as his trousers suddenly steamed dry. That was definitely something rather personal she had not been about to do to someone else's husband!

'To be honest, I'm not sure how much we'll need until we get started,' Jim admitted. 'I don't want to make it overly large but I doubt any cut wood will go to waste with all the projects ongoing. Lord Aubrey expects us to build an Inn sometime soon too,' Jim added with a glance at Cassy since it had been her idea.

'An Inn; here?' Drako asked.

'There are many visitors to the school who would appreciate the option of staying overnight if there was somewhere locally available,' she said. 'Mum and Dad mentioned having to travel all the way to Briarton, which is twelve miles from here. If our inn looked independently run from the school, visitors would expect to pay for their bed and board,' Cassy explained. 'Of course, we have animus people turning up all the time too. It would take the pressure off everyone if there was somewhere where people knew they could go.'

'Where are you planning to site it?' Drako asked. 'We don't need lots of strangers wandering about our village at all hours.'

Cassy turned to Jim, 'I thought the best location would be outside the village beside the drive, where it will be clearly visible to visitors and equally be properly separate. The area opposite the village near the gates is unused. There would be space there for stables and perhaps a couple of guest paddocks behind.'

'Draw something up Cassy. Perhaps Jasper would give you a hand if you ask him. An Inn is going to be something that will need to be carefully thought through to avoid problems with different guests in close proximity to each other.'

'Yes sir,' Cassy responded knowing he had a valid point about animus who had perhaps come seeking refuge, forced to share space with strange wizards.

They heard a creaking rattle and turned to see Darius approaching, driving a wagon towed by a pair of strong horses.

'Ah, excellent timing Darius,' Jim remarked looking at the substantial load of gravel in the wagon. 'Can you park the wagon over there out of the way? Well, ladies, we could get the footings in now and then we'll all have a better feel for the size of the site.'

Jim glanced at Natalya and bit his lip, then reached out to Amelie and Cassy alone.

Natalya watched Jim as he linked to her sister and Cassy. His eyes closed and he breathed deeply. She suddenly felt power coiling around him. His eyes opened and they were gold; the lion. He took another deep breath for control and his eyes returned to blue. Then he gestured at the ground to the right of the portal and she felt his spell and that he was sending his augmented senses into the earth scanning for problems. Disturbing the earth around a powerful magical object required great caution.

'I think we'd be better building the house above the forest floor,' Jim remarked thoughtfully. He made a sweeping gesture and all the forest floor debris of leaves, twigs, small plants and rocks was swept aside, leaving a large clear rectangular shape. He watched absently as Amelie lifted and moved the insects left behind, depositing them well out of the building zone. 'Cassy, can you and Natalya go and sort the timber, while I lay some of the gravel? We will need to interlock some strong lengths to make the base.'

'Why is he not merging with me?' Natalya asked Cassy quietly, having walked off to view the logs. 'I know he wants to.'

'You know his particular ability draws power and magical ability from others? His lion is a recent development and I believe it is a direct result of merging often enough with Amelie to take on her animus ability. She isn't as strong in her magic as you are. Your magic is probably calling to him, tempting him. You must have seen how he was after merging with you for mere moments; he had to immediately expel it by rebuilding the hall at the castle.'

'Surely if that is all it takes, then he could do this work alone far more quickly?'

'His ability retains some of the power he takes on each time. Yours is simply more than someone who isn't a natural warrior wizard can handle. Don't tempt him; he's strong enough as he is,' Cassy urged seriously. 'Come on, he's ready for us. Let's send over these ones,' she added and merged them.

Natalya learned a great deal as Cassy used their combined strength to guide the logs into position. She made notches in each log to lock them together, crossing them at right angles to form neat corners. In just a few minutes they had the cottage floor delineated. Jim and Amelie then added more gravel to the interior making a thick base that he magically compressed into a firm even layer that flooring could be laid on top of. She stood back while Cassy went to help Jim work out where the walls to the barn should go. Amelie was now occupied feeding Daisy.

'Natalya, you could carry on building a couple more rows on the walls if you'd like,' Jim remarked. 'Grab some animus to spread the load,' he added.

She glanced around her feeling the magic emanating from the animus around her; yes there was strength here she could use. She smiled warmly as Freddie and Dustin immediately stepped forward to volunteer. She'd learned much since she had first tried to use their magic; she now knew what to do to merge their strength to augment hers.

'Thank you. Let's get to work,' she added and turned to draw new slim logs into position. Freddie had seen log cabins and she drew on his memories of how they should look, layering the corners in alternate bias to aid stability. After two more courses which brought the walls up to waist height, she was glad to stop, for Dustin in particular was reeling from the strain. She looked across at how Jim's team were doing to find they'd laid out the barn floor. The portal remained freestanding with a couple of feet of free space behind it since they'd all noticed the whoosh coming out of the back of the portal each time it was activated.

'Well done,' Jim remarked, coming over to see what she'd managed to do with her animus helpers. 'The next rows will be more awkward because there will need to be gaps left for windows, so the timber cannot be anchored in the same way at the corners. This is the image of what you'll need to do later. Right now, you all need to get back. Classes will be starting in ten minutes. Here's a bit of cheese. It'll help replenish your energy for class,' Jim told her. He sighed watching her immediately break it in half and give some to Dustin.

'Don't look at me like that,' she growled at Jim. 'I've taken too much of his strength. We've had a big cooked lunch; Dustin hasn't had any lunch, yet volunteered his strength after standing in the rain keeping guard. He needs this more than I.'

Dustin looked from one to the other, but on the basis she nodded to him and his hands were starting to shake, he knew he was in no shape to refuse. He ate the small but rich morsel and while it was not enough to replenish his strength, it did stop the shakes and he now knew he could get home to some proper food. She ate the remainder under Jim's gaze and then she and Cassy hastened to return to the school and their next class. With all students due back in class imminently it was now safer for everyone else to head home for lunch. The portal was still draped in the tarpaulin but now it simply looked like part of the new building construction.

Natalya slid into her seat moments before the bell rang signalling the start of class. She breathed a sigh of relief that she wasn't actually late as Vako turned to eye the class and glare at the tardy just rushing in.

'What have you been up to?' Jason whispered when Vako turned away again.

'What do you mean? I've been out with Freddie.'

'Mm, your boots are wet and your clothes are covered in leaves and tree sap.'

'I've been in the woods. What's strange about that?' she asked aware others were listening.

Jason noticed her glance around and realised others were watching and listening with great interest. He winced inwardly that he'd demanded answers that were truly none of his business; she was not his. His nose had already informed him she had not been off having sex despite the inference Freddie had given them. Was she trying to pretend they'd been on a romantic stroll through the woods on a chilly wet day? Not likely.

'Sorry, none of my business,' he murmured.

*'I've been working on Clan business, Jason,'* she sent to him mentally. *'Virtually the whole village is involved. We're going back to carry on working after school's finished.'*

Jason's curiosity came alive, but she said nothing more and since she'd chosen to speak mentally, he surmised there was some secrecy or security aspects involved with whatever she'd been doing, so he shouldn't ask out loud. Because he was watching out for it, he also noticed she seemed tired, which was highly unusual. What had she been asked to do? Fortunately class passed uneventfully; Vako did not single out either of them so her weariness and reduced strength, went unremarked.

She gave him a small smile when he helped field and divert questions at break and he knew she recognised and appreciated what he was doing. Freddie's appearance and chat at lunch had sparked much eager curiosity. Their classmates also wondered if Freddie would accept Jason's invitation to come and spar with them. His sparring with Marko had proved just how much they all had to learn and what they might have to face on the battlefield against an experienced swordsman.

Natalya was very glad when the final bell of the school day sounded. She was both nervous and excited about the work and how it would turn out. She'd used her magic and heavy logs jumped to obey. She had never done anything like it before and was amazed what could be achieved in so short a time. She glanced at Jason, following on her heels into the soggy gloomy forest. She sometimes wondered about his motivation in befriending her in the first place, but she couldn't deny she appreciated his friendship. Since the loss of his parents, his mother some years ago and his father recently, she knew he was alone. As an animus dog he needed company; a trait she shared. But earlier he had also acted with instinctive alpha behaviour; needing to know what she'd been doing that necessitated abandoning him, and then when she answered, becoming protective. She knew he needed to belong, be part of a pack, and realised he viewed her as being his pack. Even when the wolf pack had gathered around her, he had found a way to remain with them. Jim might have said she must come alone, but she wasn't going to abandon Jason for a second time today, and besides, he was clan and already knew about the portal.

'Looks like your people have been busy today,' Natalya remarked to Jason as they stepped into the portal clearing and looked about. Jim nodded to her, but Cassy and Amelie hadn't arrived yet.

'What's going on?' Jason asked. 'What's being built?'

'Camouflage for the portal. Bruce needs better fuel now there's so much more demand on him, so it made sense to build a charcoal maker's hut and wood barn to cover both needs.'

'Ingenious,' Jason said and walked over to the new avenue cut through the trees towards the village.

He could just see the meadow dividing this woodland from the village. There were huge piles of cut branches, stacks of planks and complete logs edging the avenue. Yes, people had clearly been hard at work here today.

'They must have carted the biggest logs to the sawmill,' Natalya remarked noticing their absence. The cottage floor had now been neatly covered with flagstones. The clearing itself had been tidied of felled tree debris, so they could move around freely. Little else had changed since she was there at lunch; Jim had presumably left when she did.

'You could get stuck in, whenever you're ready,' Jim told her. He spread out the plans on a handy tree stump, weighting it down with a few rocks, so she could work from it. 'I recommend you start with the door and window frames. Once they're securely in place it'll be easier to wall around them.'

'Ok. What are you going to be doing?'

'Cassy and Amelie are on their way. We'll concentrate on the barn and the portal room. Keep an eye on where we're at because we'll need to work together to link the house and barn rear wall.'

'Will do.'

'Make sure you have sufficient help.'

'What help did he mean?' Jason asked glancing around them. 'He's the only other wizard here.'

'She used Freddie and Dustin earlier,' a deep voice replied and they turned to see Darius sitting nearby aboard a wagonload of planks. 'I guess you're next in line.'

'Are you offering to help us?' Natalya asked.

'I've got plenty to do here transporting materials,' Darius responded aware the wagon needed to be unloaded and taken back to the village.

'There are many hands who could take over,' Natalya said looking up at the big man. His large powerful frame, thick black hair and dark eyes were very similar to Drako's. He was a less open and welcoming character however and was clearly a little suspicious of her, simply because she was a wizard. He had a useful strength of talent however and they were doing this work with his benefit primarily in mind.

'Perhaps,' Darius conceded, suddenly feeling on the spot, pinned by her very direct and assessing gaze.

'I think the big bad bear is scared,' Natalya remarked to Jason. 'I think he's not game enough to try something new, even though he watched Freddie and Dustin doing it.'

'What are you doing?' Jason asked anxiously.

'What do you think I'm doing? I'm baiting the bear,' Natalya responded cheerfully, but didn't take her eyes off the big man now climbing down off the wagon.

'Don't you know better than to bait a bear, little wolf?' Darius asked her softly.

'Nope, tigers have no reason to be scared of bears,' she responded, standing her ground even though he now stood within touching distance and she had to look up. Even though he was purely animus, his raw presence was intimidating.

'You are a tiger too?' Darius asked and watched her eyes turn orange and feline fangs fill her mouth as she smiled at him in both warning and challenge. 'Impressive.' He glanced at Jason as he fidgeted and knew he was conflicted; being male his instincts would be telling him to step forward and intervene, but he was not her mate and as a dog she outranked him in every way. He met her gaze again and breathed deeply of her scent; she was not afraid. 'A beautiful woman like you only need ask,' he said with a warm smile and held out his hand to her. If he was going to do this it had to be on his terms. He was nervous; she was a wizard and he'd had too many bad experiences with malicious wizards. However she was aiding them and his people were watching. Freddie and Dustin knew her better and evidently trusted her and clearly Jason did too. The wolves had good senses, being the clan's guardians; he had no valid reason not to follow their lead. He was many things but a coward wasn't one of them.

'Thank you Darius,' Natalya said as her hand was almost engulfed in his larger hand. 'Have you eaten well today?'

'I had lunch,' Darius responded. 'Why?'

'Dustin didn't tell me he hadn't eaten before he volunteered his strength earlier. As I'm sure you're aware, shifting makes you very hungry and if you don't eat, you can feel weakened. That is because your magic needs food to replenish itself. This work will have the same tiring effect.'

'Thank you for the warning,' Darius said seriously. 'So what do you need from us?'

'This building work takes strength, either physical labour or magical, which is of course far quicker. To use your magical strength I need physical contact, so don't let go without warning. I will be monitoring you both to be sure I don't take too much from you, but if you feel it's becoming difficult, say so. Is this ok with you Jason?'

'Of course. Whatever you need,' Jason replied, and knew Darius eyed him critically. He reached out and held on to her shoulder so she would still have a hand free.

'Let's get started. Oh, I should mention that I have no intention of riffling through either of your minds, but if you think about something while we're merged I am likely to hear it.'

'Understood,' Darius said, relieved she was making these boundaries plain from the outset. Her honesty was refreshing and eased some of his fears. It was a very odd sensation to suddenly feel a presence blossom in his mind. *'Don't worry Darius, I'm not prying, you would feel that kind of intrusion. This is simply connecting the three of us together so we can combine our strength and work as one.'*

'I'm ok,' he whispered, not wanting anyone to know she was reassuring him. He glanced around and realised Drako was watching, as was Jim and many of the Clan. He hastily cleared his expression and as he felt a jolt, he returned his complete attention to what she was doing with their strength. He stared with rapt attention as planks lifted themselves out of the wagon and formed into an empty doorframe. A second doorframe built itself on the inner wall between cottage and barn. Pausing in their work, she let them have a couple of minute's breather, while she looked at the plans again.

'Ready?' she asked and then resumed by creating window frames on either side of the front door, one in the rear wall and two in the side wall. Those jobs done, she assessed both men. Both were holding up well and she took a moment to tell them so to bolster their spirits. They could see for themselves what they'd achieved already. Next they built the front and both side walls of the cottage up to the top of the window frames.

*'How did you manage to get Darius involved?'* Cassy asked mentally.

*'He was nervous of volunteering, but I got around that quite easily actually. Like Drako, he has a good strong talent. So, how do we tackle that back wall?'*

Natalya released her merge with Darius and Jason, all of them breathing hard as though they'd been running and they sat in a row on a handy log. The walls of both cottage and barn had been completed up to head height. One of the clan women came round with a tray that Cassy had brought with her, feeding both teams cheese sandwiches.

'I understand what you mean now by fatigue,' Darius remarked. 'You weren't kidding that this would be hard work,' he added appreciating for the first time just what it must have taken for the wizards to have built an entire village.

'You'll feel better once you've eaten,' Natalya advised, watching over them both. 'How do you think it looks?'

Darius rose and the three of them went into the partially built cottage and then out the side door into the barn area. In contrast to the tiled floor in the cottage, the barn was floored with timber planks. The new floor was on a level with the portal plinth, so no step up was required, but the different floor made the plinth activation stone obvious.

'Yes, this will work. We'll need a ramp at the barn entry for carts, but it's a small step and will be easy enough,' Darius responded.

'So, how do you want the upstairs laying out?' Jim asked having followed them inside.

Darius pondered that for a few minutes. Now the shell of the building was taking shape, he had a better feel for what space would be available and how it could be configured to best suit his needs.

'Show me what you have in mind,' Jim asked holding out his hand.

'With all due respect, I'd rather hold her hand,' Darius responded, glancing at Natalya.

'I don't doubt it,' Jim replied drily. 'Go on then, show her so we all know what to do next.'

Natalya watched Darius come back to her and take her hand, his dark eyes intent on hers. She reached for his mind and found both his nervousness of letting any wizard in, his budding trust of her and then the plans he was considering. *'That's it Darius, I can see what you mean,'* she assured him, whilst listening to his revolving thoughts on what possible scenarios his people might be faced with that this building could cater for if planned thoroughly.

Darius followed her back outside, as did everyone, and over to the plans still sitting on the tree-stump. He watched in amazement as she stared at the existing drawing, rested her hand on the paper and suddenly the images began shifting and altering. The ground floor plan grew to detail the upper floor too. He stared as a three-dimensional model seemed to sprout from the paper, complete with roof. As he stared at different areas at a time, the view altered until he felt he stood inside the model looking around and able to see details. Natalya had taken his hand while he viewed the model and now, as he thought of alterations, he found she was making them happen for him. Now this was teamwork! He finally stepped back and watched as the other wizards had a look at the plans and discussed modifications. Drako had some suggestions too until finally they all agreed it was as thought-through for secrecy, defence and also usability as a charcoal maker's home, as it was possible to be. He caught a familiar scent and glanced round; Freddie stood watching and probably had been there for quite some time as was his custom.

'How did Freddie get so lucky?' Darius asked Jason quietly, having returned to their log seat out of the way of the wizards gathered about the plans.

'Her nature is alpha wolf,' Jason told him with a shrug, unsurprised Darius would be interested; he was a man and had eyes. He was also single. 'I think he and Jim saved her from an inquisitor squad.'

'Inquisitor squad? She's a wizard.'

'Her memory had been blocked, along with most of her magic,' Jason told him. 'She thought and appeared to everyone, as an animus only.'

'Who could have done that?'

'Her mother, from what I understand. They were arrested and separated years ago when she was a child. She thinks her mother did it to protect her, although from what I have no idea.'

'That's an intriguing question. I assume her mother was on the wrong side then?'

'Probably. I know Natalya's father was animus and the family were punished for it.'

'Yet she has chosen an animus man herself?' Darius mused thoughtfully. 'Clearly not all wizards share the same dislike for our kind.'

'Of course not,' Jason told him. 'Jim is reaching and influencing a new generation of wizards through this school and he has Lord Aubrey's backing for it.'

'I just hope times are truly changing for the better and that this is not a completely isolated island of goodwill that will make us drop our defences.'

'That is always a risk, I suppose,' Jason conceded. 'But there is hope for a brighter and saner future.'

'Yes, one must keep that hope,' Darius admitted. 'Ah, looks like she wants us back. Hello Freddie. Are you joining us?'

'Yes. More help lightens the load for all of us and will speed things along,' Freddie explained.

'Exactly,' Natalya confirmed and took Darius's hand again, placed Jason's hand back on her shoulder leaving Freddie to make contact where he would. Feeling all three men's strength flowing into her she nodded to Cassy and they worked together, meshing the timber to interlock with the sides making a strong uniform rear wall to cottage and barn.

'We'll do the crossbeams and staircase if you can make a start on flooring it over,' Jim instructed Natalya.

'No problem,' Natalya affirmed accepting his image of how to go about the construction. She grinned then as the planks flew out of the wagon under her prompting, aligning themselves neatly to affix to the crossbeams as soon as Jim had each in place. She was aware Jim's team was working quickly to keep ahead of her, but they were in theory the stronger team with three wizards. She slowed to work out where the staircase would come up through the floor and thus where she needed to make an appropriate sized hole which needed to be reinforced around the edges. Then before Jim managed to build to the top of the stairs, she had already created railings to box the hole on three sides. Then she released her team for a few minutes rest to allow the other team to catch up.

'Everyone ok?' Natalya asked her team.

'Were you racing Jim's team?' Darius asked.

'Just proving who has the stronger team,' she admitted grinning mischievously.

He threw back his head and gave a short bark of laughter. He accepted the small sandwich she passed to each of them, his eyes twinkling as he ate, willingly refuelling his strength for her. Soon they were ready to go again to build the next section.

Every increment represented far greater progress than a team would be able to achieve building manually. At last, late on in the afternoon, they stood back and eyed a completed building with a huge amount of satisfaction. The portal was concealed and a lockable door aided security in both directions. Now all they needed to do was move someone in to take the lead role in the charcoal maker's business. They would need to build a kiln, but that was not something that was a security risk if someone witnessed it. The clan could clear the tree stumps properly from the new avenue in a time scale that suited them, all whilst able to come and go openly. Everyone agreed this was a very successful and important build and marked a milestone, in practical terms, towards rebuilding Féarmathuin castle.

28

# *Féarmathuin Castle*

Darius warily stepped through the portal into the dark echoing room. The portal gave off a pool of light reaching to the first few feet into the room, but didn't really illuminate much farther. He held up his lantern high to better light the room and released his breath that they were alone and all seemed undisturbed.

He quickly stepped off the plinth, making space for his team to follow him into the room. His men gathered around behind him, gazing about them in awe. The marble tiled floor remained cracked in places, but its beauty was no longer marred by rubble. The portal seemed to create a breeze, his men's torches flickered wildly, the flames threatening hair or clothing.

'Leave the torches here for the moment,' he instructed gesturing at some brackets meant for the purpose set at points around the walls. Once the last person stepped off the plinth, the shimmering watery look of the portal vanished, which would have plunged them into darkness. With clear torchlight however the huge empty underground room was lit clearly enough for the frescoes crowded on the walls to draw everyone's attention. Scenes of the castle, the town below and various animus animals in relaxed poses in forested scenes, adorned the walls. There were also scenes of battle from the Clan's warrior past, but most reflected the Clan's serenity in the natural beauty of their home. Darius let the men have a good look, taking time to view others he had not had time to look at in his last visit. It did everyone good to have this reminder of what they were working to regain.

'Set everything over there, clear of the portal entry,' he instructed and watched as the men reactivated the portal to fetch wheelbarrows stacked with tools and bring them through, followed by a couple of handcarts heavily laden with timber. 'Ok, let's go and make sure no-one's upstairs.'

Now unencumbered, the men drew their weapons and watched as he unlocked the impressively engineered mechanism. The trapdoor at the top of the steps silently opened. Darius had decided to wait for dusk to revisit. His animus had good night vision, appreciably better than the average wizard. They could move around easily whilst wizards, especially insecure ones, would be revealing their positions by surrounding themselves in light. He was glad he had thought to bring the glass sided lantern however, because it had useful shuttered sides to dim or even cut off the light it shed when necessary. The last thing anyone needed was to flag their presence through a careless splash of light, but they did need something to navigate the underground corridors.

He left the faintly glowing shuttered lantern at the top of the trapdoor so if they had to get back in a hurry it was usefully marked for his people. In complete silence they moved on. The corridor had been full to the ceiling with debris last time; it was amazing what the wizards had accomplished. Their feet crunched a little on a layer of grit, but they were careful to keep sound to a minimum. Each was listening carefully for any signs of life. He had the men check that the two storerooms on this level were empty of life before moving on up the stairs. The main hall too was empty, to everyone's relief.

'Go up and check the coast is clear,' he whispered and watched Paul shimmer into his falcon and fly up through holes in the ceiling and up to a narrow window ledge. As this room was part of the original keep's tower, it would originally have been topped by another two floors giving access to the rooftop battlements. When the roof caved in, it took much of the upper floors with it. Jim had repaired the roof, but not the other floors; there had been insufficient good timber left. He idly wondered if that top floor might be a sensible place to repair. It would give anyone staying here a safe place to sleep, or indeed hide, whilst overlooking any breaches to the hall and their exit to the portal. Humans and wizards rarely looked up and a retractable rope ladder would be a simple and silent way of providing security. Before they could consider risking repairs that would necessitate hammering and sawing, they first needed to make sure no enemies lurked within earshot.

He quietly unbarred the large hall door and slowly opened it onto the room beyond. The original narrow defensive room fronting the hall remained a latticework of gaping holes, which had penetrated right through into the main hall prior to Jim's repairs. Now only the outer skin remained broken. Through the holes, the men peered outside, now able to check with their noses too, for anyone lurking. The tower sat on a steep slope, with buildings flanking this entry to the yard. Behind and adjoining the tower were the main living quarters which had taken sufficient damage to be unreachable from the tower room. They would have to go around to check it all out. Finding no-one they warily stepped outside. Darius examined the tower exterior and realised that the repairs that the wizards had made were not visible. The damage on the outside was good camouflage.

'Spread out,' he whispered, 'I need to know where, and how badly, the upper perimeter wall has been breached. I shall be at the gates.' He gestured instructions to Paul and the falcon hopped up to the highest point of the battlements to keep watch for everyone. Because Féarmathuin Castle sat atop a crag, the tower was actually relatively short at two stories. The living quarters were in two wings flanking the tower near the edge of a sheer cliff inaccessible to anyone unable to fly. The lower section of castle continued the walled two wings, which followed the steep slope down. The wings walled in the upper castle from the cliff face and then linked up with the walls defending the lower castle below. In the lower castle, they served the dual purpose that a double wall was defensively stronger than a single one and the space between them could accommodate stables, barracks, the smithy, granary and all manner of other uses in the long thin space. The wings were separated from the living quarters by rooms reinforced with rubble. These defences remained intact he was pleased to note. In fact, both wings were undamaged. However, what drew the eye was the fact that the gates themselves had suffered major damage. The towers flanking the main gates had been toppled, partially reduced to rubble leaving nothing left to attach new gates to. Given their prominent position it would be impossible to replace them without someone noticing.

He eyed the huge pile of strewn rubble; clambering over would be difficult so he absently turned to pass through a hole nearby to view the damage from the outside; it seemed even worse! As he stood assessing the destruction, he abruptly realised why the wall adjacent to the gates had a big hole. The attackers had made such a thorough job of destroying the gate defences, that they had actually created a serious obstacle for themselves!

He carefully scented the breeze sweeping up the hill from the remains of the small town, but nothing human came to him and he relaxed again. He wasn't entirely surprised that the town itself had fallen. When word came to them of attacks and abductions on innocent animus people, including women and children, everyone was shocked and appalled. No appeals were granted, instead, anyone coming forward to complain just disappeared too, all in the crown's name. Lord Trent gave orders to secure the town immediately and everyone pulled together to do so. They had successfully built a wooden palisade, enclosing the town just in time. Those defences successfully rebuffed many attacks by small bands of zealots trying to take them down to earn favour with the crown. Their walls and fighting men repelled attacks for over six years. However, they could not stop a serious army and they could only watch as inevitably an army raised by the king himself drew closer and closer to their remote county. Palisades could be built and repaired quickly but they always succumbed to fire, especially if the defenders were unable to quench those fires promptly. The town had been enclosed, which slowed down the advance, but could not prevent them coming through. It served its purpose however in disguising the fact that the majority of the townsfolk had fled before they'd even arrived. Scouts had reported the presence of a contingent of wizards in the army led by the high ranking warrior wizard Sir Cyril. With that knowledge, the people were urged to flee in good time. Rumours had preceded the army's advance that wizards in one of the king's other armies had not simply defeated, but gone out of their way to crush another animus strongholds. They had kept captured animus on hand, using them to recharge their magic. Sucking someone's magic did not have to kill the donor. Yet everyone heard of the callous way those wizards had acted, fatally draining the animus captives in the process. Fatal magic theft was illegal, but clearly, those wizards had no respect for how their foes died. They only cared that they could refuel themselves to continue their destructive path, and discarded animus people with as little regard as a food wrapper. At Féarmathuin, everyone was forewarned of that risk and it was why exceedingly few animus were captured. Aside from dying, no-one wanted to aid wizards in destroying their homes.

Once his team had re-joined him, he set the best draughtsman to sketching what remained of the gate towers and also the two holes the others on his team had found. Meanwhile, Darius led the rest of them into the town. Firstly they were checking out the extent of the destruction and secondly, checking for anything dangerous in the way of people, animals or indeed traps. They also piled up any portable pieces of metal or discarded weapons they came across to take back to Bruce for recycling.

The sooner he knew exactly what obstacles they faced, the sooner he could determine the best course of action necessary to regain control. Scouts would need to be sent out to search the surrounding countryside. Once he'd gathered intelligence on how far away and the extent of the nearest threat, he could keep watch on it and take appropriate steps. He liked the idea of rebuilding the castle's defences in secret, with the hope that by the time they were noticed, they could rebuff an attack. Working stealthily and camouflaging their repairs was going to be critical to their success.

There was undoubtedly a great deal of work to do here, but he had been given an opportunity he never expected and he was determined not to squander it. He would not fail.

29

# *Nathaniel*

Several weeks had passed since Natalya had started lessons and she was comfortably in the school routine and settled into her class. She couldn't remember ever being happier. Only those with the will or ability to excel were welcome in the elite warrior class. She had won the respect of her peers and been accepted.

Despite being the only woman in the class, Natalya usually managed to hold her own, even in the physical disciplines. No one was equally good at all the different forms, whether target practice, fighting or cavalry. At the end of each month they were tested and graded in each discipline. Their results were posted on the big pin board in the armoury and were the subject of much competitiveness and crowing.

Natalya was steadily rising in proficiency with sword and archery. Wrestling and axe fighting successfully against a man were beyond her however. She simply didn't have a man's strength; particularly against an animus warrior. Having said that, within the contact fighting disciplines she was making progress on the assassin martial art skills. This was where accuracy, stealth, nimbleness and speed were more important than brute strength.

'You're catching up with me,' Jason commented, as they gathered to watch Bruno allotting new scores against their names with his coloured pins.

'I've gone up a grade in archery?' Natalya whispered in pleased surprise seeing Bruno move her pin over into the next column.

'Yes. Well done,' Jason added, then fell silent as Bruno moved on to his own line on the board. He turned to see if Natalya had noticed his own increased grade and went still.

'Natalya? What is it?' he asked urgently. She stood turned away with her fist against her mouth and her eyes wide.

'Dustin? Oh no. Freddie no,' she cried and dashed out the door.

Jason wasn't the only one to hear and follow her outside. At a dead run her clothes flew off and from one stride to the next she became an enormous tiger.

'What's happened?' Bruno asked Jason, staring after her in confusion.

Jason took his eyes off her for a moment, realising they all looked to him to know. 'I think Dustin and maybe all the hunters are in trouble. If there'd been an accident she'd have gone as a wolf, it's faster. Her tiger is her battle response,' Jason said already shedding his own clothes and turning into his dog. 'She may need help,' he added, unsure if they would let him go.

At that moment they heard a roar from over at the house. Jim in lion form was galloping for the gate too, but Natalya was not waiting for him.

'Go,' Bruno said decisively to Jason. The rest of the animus in the warrior class changed into their animal and followed, whilst the wizard members rushed for one of the cavalry horses already up at the arena for practice. Bruno took a horse but also bow and sword from the armoury. He was neither wizard nor animus; he was at a serious disadvantage unarmed.

As Natalya reached the scene the first thing she heard was savage snarling. Realising Freddie was not in pain physically helped remind her not to rush blindly in to whatever had trapped them. She slipped from cover to cover stealthily approaching directly behind Freddie, Rupert and Johnny standing together in wolf form and facing away from her. They were enclosed by something that burned them if they touched it. Freddie was her priority. Until she knew he was safe she couldn't think of anything else. So remaining in hiding she examined the magical barrier. It was a type of shield designed to hold animus people and was brutally simple and effective. Being as magically stealthy as she knew how she infiltrated the spell, disarmed it and turned it into a defensive shield. The wizard who'd created the original spell would feel it if she stopped his spell altogether. Instead, his magic fed a new spell, a shield he would not be able to penetrate. Only once she was sure Freddie and indeed Rupert and Johnny were well defended did she slip around to the other side of the clearing. What she saw boiled her blood.

Nathaniel, the wizard tormenter of her childhood stood in the clearing. At his feet was a bloody and mangled naked man; Dustin. She was shocked rigid. How could anyone cause another so much pain deliberately? But then again she knew this wizard, knew his depraved black heart more than she ever wished to. Even so, what had Dustin ever done to him?

She felt a presence arrive behind her; Jason in his fleet dog animus form. She felt a sudden shift; Nathaniel was drawing magic for another spell. Natalya could see his attention was on Dustin and she threw a shield over Dustin immediately.

'Do not try and hurt him again,' Natalya warned, furiously stalking out of the bushes.

'Well well little Nat is trying out a tiger form. Should I be impressed?' Nathaniel asked scornfully. 'I know you're nothing more dangerous than a pathetic domestic cat.' He watched her continue to silently approach. 'That's close enough,' he ordered.

'Why? I thought you just said you weren't scared of me?' Natalya told him ignoring his order and continuing to slowly advance.

'I'm not scared of a mongrel slave girl. I know you from the inside out,' he added with a smirk and heard the wolves snarl again.

'Here all alone are you? Big mistake,' Natalya told him. 'What happened to your two inquisitor friends? Were they scared off?'

'They had you trapped in Briarton. Unfortunately they sensed the rogue wizard nearby and were under orders to avoid him,' Nathanial admitted with a shrug. The men had been scared silly, recognising a warning shot to leave, delivered by a wizard with a particularly dense and unusual power signature. Given the proximity to White Haven it didn't take a genius to know who it had been from. Rumours of wizard Jim's power, able to overcome a full battle squad, were well-known. 'We all know he seems to like animus. It was obvious where you were likely to end up.'

'So you sent your owl to check. Do you know what happened to your nasty owl man?' Natalya asked. 'I do. You sent him hunting me. Bad idea. I ripped out his throat. It wasn't pretty.'

Nathaniel backed up unconsciously. He'd felt his man die and her description fitted his end. 'Well, he achieved his purpose in finding you, like this beast here,' he added, glancing at the broken man. Without realising it he'd backed off enough for the tiger to reach the man.

'You're safe now Dustin,' Natalya murmured and rubbed her face against his for a moment.

Dustin gasped at the touch; she'd just taken much of his pain. He gazed up at her in awed relief, only to catch a glimpse of the one who'd done this to him standing free, unharmed and looking on. He knew somehow that she didn't attack because she was easing his pain and defending him.

'I got your boyfriend, did I?' Nathaniel chortled. 'Serves him right. You're my pet and no one else's.'

'I am no one's pet,' Natalya said coldly. 'Actually you're wrong, Dustin is not my boyfriend.' She resisted the constant urge to glance over at Freddie. He was fuming that she wouldn't let him out to sink his teeth in Nathaniel.

'Ah, but you do have one and he's here right now,' Nathaniel stated turning his gaze to the three wolves. The one in the centre was clearly the dominant one and also the one snarling with such fury.

'You're right and he badly wants to sink his teeth into you and start shredding your flesh. I could let him but I don't want him tainted by the likes of you.'

'Bold words, if a little unpleasant. You always did like your dogs. I knew you would come running to defend these unnatural beasts. So predictable, but it served to get you to leave the rogue's grounds.'

'You are more of a beast than these men will ever be. Why torture? Why try to maim him?' Natalya couldn't help asking. She was frustrated to have to divide her attention, partly in assessing Dustin's injuries and attempting to heal those that were threatening his life, all whilst maintaining shields and keeping Nathanial from realising what she was doing.

'I'll put him out of his misery then since you're too soft to,' Nathaniel said but aimed his spell directly at the three wolves instead. He gaped; his spell had bounced off, leaving the wolves snarling but unharmed. He spun about and fired at the prone man, but that spell didn't get through either.

'Kill him,' Dustin managed to whisper. 'Don't worry about me.'

'You've brought a wizard,' Nathaniel accused.

'I am the wizard,' Natalya told him, launching her tiger at the fat wizard. He had a shield up but her tiger's pounce toppled him.

'How dare you set people to track and kill me? You've hurt my friends and attacked my man,' Natalya snarled in a red fury. All four feet clawed and rent the bubble of his shield. The shield compressed closer and closer to his body as Nathaniel's magical strength weakened before her savage concerted assault.

'You are a pitiful excuse for a man. Were you jealous of Dustin? Did you wish you had his looks? You are perverted and disgusting, getting your kicks from hurting others. No one will miss you.'

Nathaniel could only stare in horror as the tiger snapped at him with horrendously long sharp white teeth. He couldn't believe the power she exuded; her magic far exceeded anything he'd ever seen before. How had she hidden this throughout her childhood? He looked aside from the terrifying view and realised the wolves had escaped the trap and had gathered closely. A huge gold lion and even bigger black bear stood beside the prone man watching. None of them made any move to stop her. With so many enemies, his hope of rescue vanished. Not one of those faces was forgiving; instead they looked eager to attack.

'I know where your mother is,' Nathaniel gasped desperately.

'My mother is dead. You told me so.'

'I lied. I was told that was what you were to believe so you wouldn't try to go looking for her. Your mother is a top grade wizard; she would not have been killed.'

'You're only saying this to save your own skin,' she accused. 'You haven't said anything convincing,' she added resuming her attack on his shield.

'I know she was tested. Her magic is powerful. It was hoped that despite your being contaminated by an animus father you would produce gifted wizard children. Your line was pure wizard before your father. She had to be punished but the last I heard, she was alive.'

'Where is she?'

'Oh no, you've got to promise not to hurt me.'

'Do you really think you're in any position to make demands?' Natalya asked coldly ripping the final shreds of his shield aside and pinning flesh for the first time. 'Jim?'

Nathaniel followed her gaze but instead of calling her wolf the huge lion was coming over. His shield was gone. Her huge paws were heavy, claws trapping him motionless and he no longer had any magic to defend himself with.

'What's this? I'm not going to tell and then you'll never know the truth.' She flexed her paws letting her claws pierce his skin adding to his terror.

'I thought we'd reach this little snag. That's why my wizard friend here is the solution. You know of him as the Rogue. He can simply take the information from your mind.'

Nathaniel gaped at the terrifying lion staring at him with intense predatory eyes and acknowledged the aura of power crackling around him at this range. He was what she said and not an animus as he'd initially supposed. He knew he was going to die whether he told them voluntarily or not. Without another thought he grabbed his knife from his belt and drove it into the tiger. She shrieked but instead of flinching and falling away, her jaws opened and swept down. He felt a hideous white hot pain in his throat and the world went dark.

Bedlam ensued. Her sudden shriek and bloody retaliation ripping out the man's throat then tossing his limp body aside like a stick was horrifying.

Freddie changed instantly and was at her side as she fell. He grasped the hilt of the knife and pulled it out of her side. Blood spurted thickly between his fingers and he desperately tried to stop her bleeding to death.

'Don't you dare leave me!' Freddie cried cradling her huge heavy tiger as best he could. She shimmered back into human form which was a very mixed blessing. It meant she didn't have the strength to maintain her tiger and it also revealed the blood gushing over her skin.

'Jim, please! Do something,' Freddie cried desperately. She lay wheezing in his arms, struggling just to breathe. 'It went into her lung, didn't it?'

'Sounds that way,' Jim agreed, having just reverted to human form. He put his hands where Freddie's had been on the wound and concentrated. 'Dammit why's she so weak?'

'She replaced the wizard's trap with a shield of her own to protect me,' Freddie explained whilst Jim worked. 'Then she was shielding Dustin and even began healing him so he didn't die on the spot. You saw the rest.'

'I should have known. Getting through a wizard's shield is no easy matter either when they're putting all they have into it,' Jim added.

'Take my strength,' Jason offered suddenly.

'Yes, good idea. Thank you,' Jim said pushing his weary hand though his hair not realising he was smearing himself in her blood. He'd been trying to do some healing of Dustin's injuries while she battled, but hadn't wanted to exhaust himself in case she'd needed help finishing the wizard off. Unfortunately, to straighten broken bones and then begin repairs on so badly injured a man meant considerable magical strength was needed, both to do the work but also to keep Dustin's mind numb of the awful pain. He watched now as everyone present circled her, wrapped in Freddie's arms, offering him a merge. Jim let their strength infuse and reinvigorate him. Now he could concentrate. It was delicate work to repair and re-inflate a punctured lung and needed to be done quickly to prevent the lung filling with fluid. That could be fatal, especially with her blood loss and general weakness. He had to take meticulous care, which was not best done when already tired. But with the meld he felt revived enough to work out what needed to be done to mend an unfamiliar internal injury he couldn't actually see. He was very relieved, and knew everyone else was too, when at last he heard her begin to breathe without wheezing. Now he could attend to the relatively straightforward process of mending torn and damaged muscle and finally skin. He remained in contact a little longer sweeping her body for other injuries masked by the serious one. He paused and moved his hand to her abdomen feeling the flutter of new life. He met Freddie's eyes and saw his small smile; so he already knew and they were keeping it quiet. He respected that prerogative and remained silent on the subject. He then bestowed some of the meld's strength on her to aid her recovery.

'Thank you and well done everyone. She should make a full recovery. But she'll need to rest for at least a week and not shift,' he told Freddie seriously. 'She looks healed, but magical healing needs to be backed up with the body's own reinforcement, and for that it needs time. Right, if everyone would stay together a bit longer we'll get Dustin's pain eased for him.'

'Here, take this.'

Freddie glanced up; one of the wizards from her class was proffering his shirt. The animus students had left their clothes behind so they had nothing to offer. 'Thank you,' Freddie said sincerely and put her in the man's shirt. It was large enough to cover his lady's exposed skin quite well. While he hadn't given it a thought while she was gravely injured, she might not be happy to know all her class mates were viewing her naked body. He and all the animus men were currently naked because Jim needed their magic. But at least they knew the only woman amongst them was asleep. The shirt would also help warm her.

'Use my horse,' Bruno offered Freddie. 'If you get on I'll lift her up to you,' he added. 'Everyone else is walking back with Dustin's litter. I've been pretty useless up to now, but I can help carry that litter.'

'Thank you,' Freddie said and realised that while he'd clothed Natalya, he was still bare skinned. Bruno hadn't said anything, he didn't have to. Freddie hastily covered himself in his wolf's thick fur and mounted the horse. He watched Bruno struggle a little with Natalya's limp but tall and heavy frame trying not to catch her ribs. But soon enough they got her up in front of Freddie where he could hold her on. Noticing how many were watching, he was very glad she was no longer naked.

A rough litter had been assembled to carry Dustin. Freddie moved over to them noticing Dustin's eyes were open.

'How're you doing, my friend?' Freddie asked him anxiously.

'I don't hurt so much now. How is she?' Dustin asked and reached across with a newly healed arm to touch her bare foot dangling nearest him. It was cool to the touch but not cold and he felt a pulse. She lived!

'He stabbed her and punctured her lung!' Freddie said darkly. 'But she will recover.'

'She saved my life,' Dustin said gratefully. 'Take care of her.'

'You can be sure of that. Come on, let's get both of you home,' Freddie declared and led the way out of the clearing.

He noticed a flash, heard a strange crackle and then smelt something gamey turn burnt in moments. He steadied his horse and looked back. Jim had incinerated the dead man. In a few moments nothing remained but splashes of blood and grey ash that the wind picked up and swirled away. No one passing this way would see the evidence unless they knew where to look and even then it was unlikely they'd ever suspect a man had died here. It could just as easily be the site of a game kill. Given some rain or more wind, all the remains would simply vanish as though they'd never been; a fitting if ignoble end.

30

# *Life Does Go On*

Natalya slept a great deal over the next few days. Freddie rigged up a hammock for her on the porch so she could rest comfortably, close to where he was working. She much preferred being able to watch the world go by and also have his company rather than being stuck all alone in the bedroom. She had not had a shortage of visitors though. Amelie visited daily and during their long talks he'd become quite accustomed to keeping watch over Daisy, who was a surprisingly active crawler. When Jim was about he felt a little presumptuous to be holding his child, Amelie actually encouraged him. She told him he could only benefit from learning how to handle a baby since he was soon to be a father and that his child would be Daisy's cousin.

Jason visited often too, stopping by briefly on his way home. Sometimes he was accompanied by others from her class and once by her teacher Bruno. Their obvious concern was deeply touching and lifted her spirits more than they probably knew.

'Where do you think you're going?' Freddie asked noticing she'd dressed, tidied her hair and was not heading for either her hammock or the chairs set out.

'Tactics class,' she told him. 'It's only physical stuff I shouldn't do, right? I don't want to miss any more classes than I have to. I'm so behind everyone else as it is.'

'You don't think walking all the way up to the school and then sitting through a long lesson counts as physical exercise?'

'I can go slowly. I've time enough, if I leave now anyway.'

'It's only been three days. Maybe it's a bit soon to return, love. Your body still needs rest. You slept all morning.'

'Yes, I've rested enough to last me an afternoon.'

'You're determined aren't you,' he sighed putting down the length of wood he was carving.

'What are you doing?' she asked watching him dust off his trousers and wash his hands.

'Coming with you. It's the only way to be sure you don't overdo anything,' he told her. He expected her to kick up and try to prevent his coming along. He knew very well he was being overprotective but he couldn't help it. She was pregnant and had been gravely injured.

'Sorry to pull you away from your carpentry. I think you'll enjoy the lesson too, assuming Terry's happy for you to stay.' His apprehensive expression cleared and the beautiful sunny smile lit his face that she loved. He offered her his arm and they walked slowly up to the school. She reflected how useful it was to know how he felt and thus what to say to avoid any misunderstandings. They didn't remain in each other's mind for long at a time however. It took effort to maintain sufficient external awareness of one's own body to watch where one was going and not to walk into things. They'd both been ribbed by their peers for seemingly gazing into space. Conversing only was easier; it didn't require the same concentration. She'd found it surprisingly effective to converse and only dip into his mind for clarification.

He did the same, although he didn't find it as easy to do. If she was up at the school for instance she always shielded her mind, allowing conversation only. He therefore had to wait until she either allowed him access or returned home in which case she allowed her shield to relax.

'Natalya, I didn't think we'd be seeing you today,' Terry said seeing her in the doorway supported by a tall man.

'I was bored lying in bed. Can Freddie join us today?'

'By all means. I understand you've already joined the odd class to help out,' he added, turning to the hunter.

'Yes and thank you. She shouldn't really be out of bed but Jason told her of yesterday's class and she couldn't resist the lure of your lessons,' Freddie told him. Terry laughed in delight and waved them inside to take seats.

Natalya sighed happily glancing around her and nodding to her classmates. Her life was no longer shadowed by Nathaniel's threatening presence in the world. She had found a home, friends, her sister and most importantly a wonderful man to share her life with. She took Freddie's hand and he returned her smile. They were starting a family of their own and she knew he too was deeply content at the prospect. She could finally leave her past in the past and look forward to the future. She had promised to help her sister plan her wedding after all and what better reminder of the future was that?

The End

Printed in Great Britain
by Amazon